A Dash In Space

by D.C. Sargent

TRIGGER WARNING:
This book contains elements that may be disturbing to some readers, including violence, insults, profanity, stereotypical dialects, vicious animal attacks, xenophobia, and other sensitive topics. Reader discretion advised.

Cover Art: Ken Koeberlein, Koeber Designs
Consult/Content Editing: Madison Sargent Schuler, Celeste Sargent, Tracy Homan, Joshua & Amber Sargent

Paperback ISBN: 978-1-957071-03-9
10 9 8 7 6 5 4 3 2 1

This book is dedicated to all the aliens who don't believe humans exist and to my brother/co-conspiracy theorist Joshua, who can be rather handy regarding such matters and might even have a few good ideas sometimes … occasionally.

Glossary:

Binary System—[**bi**-nah-ree] a two-star solar system
Blagins—[**blag**-inz] a Borzoikan thug
Borzoik—[bor-**zo**-ik] an alien race, demonic
Deek—[deek] a Zahrá Che alien, pilot
Dorkymodo—[**dor**-kee-**mo**-do] cute, lovable monster; nickname
Fareh-Nombie—[**fār**-eh nom-bee] the Gaki home planet
Fl'drowdo—[fla-**drō**-dō] a planet in the Jakkard Reth solar system
(Full) Battle Rattle—[**bat**-l rat-l] to wear all one's combat gear
Gaki—[**gak**-ee] vicious carnivorous land creature(s)
Gelphii—[**gel**-fi] one of three moons orbiting a planet
Gezhack—[ges-**chak**] a Borzoikan thug
Gimeg (Plateau)—[**gi**-meg] a landmark on planet Zahrá Che
Gleshmog—[**glesh**-mog] a vicious alien creature
Goblasi—[go-**blas**-ee] an alien species, illusionists
ID-one-OT—[eye-dee-**one**-oh-tee] idiot spelled alphanumerically
Jael—[jay-**el**] a Zahrá Che alien, pilot
Jag Mosrog—[jag **moz**-rog] an intergalactic space station
Jakkard Reth—[**jak**-ard reth] a solar system
Janosethi—[jan-o-**set**-tee] an alien species, mind masters
Kinety—[kin-**nét**-tee] as in kinetic energy
Lebrigin—[leb-**ri**-gin] clean, clear
Loquú—[lo-**koo**] universal language
Mogulwoop—[**mo**-gul-woop] a derogatory adjective, insult
M'ran Portak—[mer-an **por**-tak] an insult similar to motherfucker
Neontak—[nee-**on**-tak] a planet connected by portal to Zahrá Che.
Octahedron—[oct-a-**hed**-ron] energy crystals
Ohizigi—[oh-i-**zi**-gee] a Saphiridian City
Oknok—[**ahk**-nok] a reptilian alien
(Prime) Joboba—[jō-**bō**-ba] leader of the Saphiridians
Saphiridian—[saf-i-**rid**-ee-an] an alien species, humanoid
Terran—[**ter**-ran] Earthling, any human from Earth
Tiamat—[**tee**-a-mat] watery planet named after goddess of the sea
Toojidium—[too-**jid**-ee-um] Laboratory created element
Torakonium—[tor-ak-**own**-ee-um] Laboratory created element
Urik—[**yur**-ik] a Zahra Che alien, pilot
Wozzjom—[**woz**-jom] stand down, cancel
Zahrá Che—[za-**rah** chee] an alien species, planet, and language

NOTE: Italicized dialog from the Zahrá Che denotes telepathy.

Chapter 1

Torak calculated the angle of the two spaceships approaching planet Earth and scanned the ground for a potential collection site. The planet appeared to be nearing its autumn season with the temperature registering as mild. The atmosphere was safe to breathe according to his analysis, but the composition was lighter than the air on his own planet. The thinner air made his craft feel sluggish and heavier than normal. It had to work harder here. Gravity was a bit weak here as well but appropriate for such a small planet.

Carefully cloaked in the dark sky, Torak double-checked the trajectory of the approaching ships. They were definitely coming to this location. Why this location? He circled his star-fighter over the treetops, searching for the answer to that question. His automator automatically mapped out numerous potential landing zones, but he ignored the recommendations and scanned the landscape himself, looking for anything that would justify the interstellar space travel. Besides, his gut instinct was stronger than any computer. He wasn't sure yet what he was looking for, but this mission was clandestine and too critical to follow protocol. From here on, instinct alone would guide him.

A pair of lights flashed in the distance.

Torak narrowed his eyes, watching the lights with mild interest as they moved slowly across the ground, preceding a small land vehicle. The machine stopped, and the lights blinked off in unison. Whatever the craft was didn't register on his panel. Of course, he didn't expect it to; he'd never been to this planet before. He was positive he'd found the right one, though. He was about to continue his search when a side hatch opened on the small land craft, lighting the inside. Curious again, he hovered his craft overhead, knocking yellowing leaves from nearby branches as a humanoid life form exited the wheeled machine. The creature, whose initial biometric scan registered as a bipedal female, headed at a sneaky crouch into a wooded hill to his left. She was a humanoid Terran—an Earthling.

Torak thrust his fist into the air. "Yes!"

In interest, he craned his neck, following her heat signature until he lost sight of her in the dark woods. Her direction, however, pointed him to a pale campfire on a hill and he squinted at it. Near the firelight, he spotted a large gathering of Earth dwellers and recognized the uniforms, green and blotchy to match vegetation. Without a doubt, this was the Zahrá Che target. He'd nearly missed it.

"Gotcha!" he celebrated again.

These were definitely soldiers—mostly male, according to his initial scan. They were gathered in a clearing surrounded by a ring of trees, their manner calm and relaxed. Good. On the starscreen in front of him, the first of the two Zahrá Che spacecraft blinked into view, which meant he didn't have long. He needed to get a tracker on those soldiers before the collection ships landed. If the Zahrá Che aliens spotted him, they'd abort the mission … again.

That meant this had to be done by hand … and fast. He already looked like an Earthling, with the exception of his eyes which were white, so blending in would be easy as long as his clothing matched. The darkness would hide his eyes, he decided and pulled a planet-specific garment out of his bag. As quickly as he could, he adjusted the cloth over his compression suit. The ankle-length attire looked silly in his opinion, but would easily blend him in.

Torak was ready. Hovering quietly just below the treeline, he looked around for a place to land. Too close and the natives would feel the rumble of his aircraft; too far away and he'd waste time traveling. Carefully, he eased his star-fighter toward the ground where he'd seen the land vehicle. At this distance, his audio signature should sound like a gust of wind to those untrained to recognize it. He touched down at the outer edge of the treeline near a collection of parked transport pods and grabbed two trackers. With a snap, his star-fighter shrunk in size and liquified into a black metal ring that curled around his finger.

*****

Quiet as a bunny, 23-year-old Kinety Dash crept up the rocky embankment and peered through the brush at the soldiers sitting around a small campfire inside a ring of fragrant pine trees. Not one of them knew she was there. Soldiers, ha! Bunch of boy scouts was more like it, she thought mischievously. To be fair, her approach had been well muffled by the noisy buzz of cicadas, but still.

In utter disgust, she found a small pebble and zeroed in on her older brother Rixton. His back was to her, but she didn't need to see his dorky face to know it was him. His dark brown hair was shorter than it had been this morning, implying a haircut, but she recognized his familiar posture and the way he crossed his combat boots. After all his lectures and training on stealth and situational awareness, he deserved to be humiliated in front of his friends. Wearing a shit-eating grin, Kinety tossed the pebble, hitting him right between the shoulder blades. To her amusement, he flicked at his ear and continued talking.

The big dummy.

Kinety face-palmed and rolled her green eyes to the starry heavens, wondering how in the world they'd managed to have the same parents. He was such a klutz. Okay, bigger rock. Wagging her head in fun, she tapped slender fingers over the moonlit ground for something else to throw. She needed either something with more mass or something with more splat. To her surprise, she found it. Startled, she snatched her hand away from the toe of an occupied boot and spun quickly onto her back with a stifled gasp.

A very large, very dark silhouette stood over her with his arms folded ... as if he'd been there for a while.

Kinety scowled in acute annoyance. Where the hell had this guy come from? Not a broken twig, not a rustle of clothing—the butthead. Her look of alarm, no doubt enhanced by the blast of direct moonlight overhead, melted into the guiltiest of smiles. A tiny finger-wave was added as a bonus, but the no-face silhouette remained unamused and rigid, if posture was any indication. Unmoved by her charm, he stood there ... waiting.

In a bid for survival, Kinety produced an emergency bat of thick lashes, but those also failed to soften his unpermissive stance, which left her with nothing else in her arsenal.

A thick, dark arm separated from the larger shadow, the outline of which ended in a flicker of fingers, instructing her to get up. When she did, he gestured her toward the camp.

It was all very irritating.

Scowling, she marched obediently through the woods beneath a tangled mop of chestnut-colored hair haphazardly decorated with twigs and broken leaves. Captain Biceps, who still managed to walk on silent feet, followed. The firelight revealed a blue-eyed, blond bodybuilder with medium masculine features and a strong chin. His hair was cut in severe military fashion, and his uniform screamed ironing board—the exact opposite of her. She had half the forest in her hair, which hung loose down her back in twiggy tangles.

Any other time, her hair would have looked terrific, but she'd crawled to the camp. Grass stains greened the knees of her form-fitting jeans, and a few small burrs clung to the loose, metallic shirt she wore. No biggie. Laundry would take care of that. The fabric still shimmered beautifully when she moved, even if it was slightly twisted now—a quick fix. On her feet, she wore super comfy, absolutely adorable combat boots with raised block-heels and a handy side-zipper for easy on/off. As always, she was the height of fashion, even looking as if she'd been romping with a rendezvous.

They stepped out of the trees.

Forty men in camouflage fatigues sat in a large circle around a roaring fire, watching ... rather quietly ... as she was escorted into the camp. A blade of grass slid onto her forehead, and she shook it away. In her own defense, she hadn't come expecting to combat-crawl through the sagebrush. She smiled anyway.

3

Nearby, she noticed a black panel van parked beside the opposite treeline. Three civilians were busily setting up odd equipment beside it. They completely ignored her.

Kinety stopped in front of her brother.

Rixton, who was sewing camouflage netting, didn't even look up when she stepped into the campfire light. "What are you doing here, Dorkymodo?" he asked, adding a knot to his thread.

A curly-haired soldier sputtered and pointed. "Wait. *This* is Dorkymodo?"

"It is," Rixton confirmed.

"Actually, my name is Kinety," she corrected.

"Kinety? As in Kinety Dash!"

She curtsied.

A red-haired soldier across from them sat forward in interest. "I've heard of you. You have an unusual name."

Kinety nodded as if used to the comment. "Our dad was a scientist," she explained with a gesture toward her brother. "He named me after kinetic energy, which was his field of study. Rixton was named after his professor. And, yes, my brother was born with his glasses on."

"Thank you, Dorkymodo," Rixton said with a glance.

"Why do you call her that?" asked a man to his left.

"She's a kind-hearted little monster, longs to be loved," Rixton muttered, not necessarily under his breath, "and probably ugly."

"Dude, you look just like her."

Snickers erupted around them.

Rixton gave him a scowl, then turned it on his sister. "You need to work on your stealth."

Kinety's green eyes narrowed on her nearly identical sibling, the cretin. He was acting all mature and sophisticated in front of his friends, but she knew better. Physically, he was three years older than her. Mentally? Many, many years younger. "You didn't know I was there," she accused flippantly.

"We all did."

"No. *Brutus*, here, blew my surprise," she argued, giving her outsized captor a quick glare.

"Are you sure?" wondered Rixton.

She wasn't. An observant glance at her attentive audience indeed failed to suggest even one look of surprise—appreciation, perhaps, but not surprise. "Of course, I'm sure," she lied anyway, "unless you were using thermal imaging."

"Or listening for car doors and a distinctively whiny engine," he said, finally putting his netting aside and pinning his matching green eyes on her. "What are you doing here besides scaring nocturnal animals?"

Kinety smiled, back on topic, and plopped down beside him. "I found your note on the counter," she said and busily swung silky brown hair over her shoulder to remove the twigs, "but it was vague, so I searched your room and found your dogtags, which you are supposed to be wearing while in uniform, so I hacked your computer," she finished sweetly. "You didn't say anything about a camping trip with your friends."

Rixton sighed and draped camouflaged arms over spread knees. "That's because it's classified."

Kinety laughed in disbelief. "You're so dramatic," she teased, completely missing the looks passing back and forth between the men around her. "How long are you going to be out here?"

Rixton didn't answer. "Did you find a job today?" he asked, changing the subject.

She handed him a stack of cash. "A quick calendar shoot today, which paid the mortgage and ... ," her voice dropped to a mutter, "a small underwear gig on Monday."

"You said you were done with the underwear."

"Underwear!" echoed a soldier to his right. "Dorkymodo is an underwear model?"

"Swimsuit," she corrected. "I did the underwear, but only once."

"Retired swimsuit," Rixton re-corrected, "and Monday's underwear will make twice."

"Dude, that's awesome!"

Rixton didn't think so. "No. It's disgusting. Have you ever seen your sister in her underwear?" he snapped and pushed his glasses up. "I did and now my vision is blurry. How'd the interview go?"

Kinety grimaced a bit. "I didn't get the job at the newspaper," she said, tongue in cheek.

"That's because you have absolutely no experience as a journalist."

"So?" she countered indignantly. "How hard could it be? You follow people around, ask questions, and then twist their answers to mean something else."

With a look of patient annoyance, Rixton stood, pulled her to her feet, and tugged the front pocket of her jeans wide. "I didn't tell you where I was going because I didn't want you to follow me," he said, stuffing the money inside.

Kinety gestured around her with a manicured hand. "I like camping," she protested.

"Hell, yeah!" cheesed a man behind her.

"There's plenty of room," agreed another in passionate debate.

Rixton ignored them. "You aren't supposed to be here. If the commander catches you, I'm in trouble."

"Why?" she demanded incredulously. "Y'all are just sitting around —well … except Brutus, who was actually on duty."

"That's Arnie."

Kinety, recognizing the name, motioned politely at the big blond. "Ahh. *You're* Arnie. I wasn't sure you actually existed. Nice to finally meet you."

Arnie cocked an eyebrow … still unmoved.

"I think we need to have a barbecue at the Dash house," said someone else.

A discussion ensued.

Another soldier stood, gaping at her, and snapped his fingers. "You're Miss November!" he declared with an excited point.

Rixton made a face. "Yardley, why are you looking at swimsuit magazines?"

"For the posters!" Yardley shot back as if to a moron, then beamed at Kinety. "I have your poster up. You were wearing snowboots!"

Kinety smiled brightly. "Weren't those cute?"

"Wh—you have a poster of my sister on your wall?" Rixton interrupted over his shoulder.

Yardley lowered his finger. "No, it's on the dresser … beside my bed," he said, giving his ear an awkward scratch. "I didn't know that was your sister. Are you single, by the way?"

Before she could answer, Rixton heaved her off the ground and slung her, shrieking, over his shoulder like a sack of dog food. "Say goodnight to Dorkymodo, boys," he said, ignoring the chorus of protests and dodging puny rescue attempts. "She has a tower to climb and dishes to do."

The men shot to their feet in mock protest.

"She is not an animal!" cried a fan.

"Let her go!"

Kinety raised her head and waved bye-bye to the shrinking faces. Through tears and cries of injustice, the men waved back. Rixton, in a dramatic show of stoicism, marched purposefully to the edge of the clearing and set the put-out Kinety on her feet. "Go home, Dorkymodo," he said, giving her a playful push in the right direction, "before you get caught."

Her eyes went wide. "Caught by whom?" she teased.

"The bad guys."

Kinety surrendered. "Okay, fine. Gimme a kiss," she said, stretching to her toes and puckering her lips.

Rixton made a face. "What? Gross! Get out of here," he laughed, giving her a push.

Smiling, Kinety strolled through the field toward her car, more than satisfied with herself.

Chapter 2

Torak ran for a small patch of trees halfway across the moonlit field, careful not to crunch the ground beneath his boots, and hurried into the shadows. Overhead, an odd bird-like animal hooted, startling him. He ducked. Unsure what it was or how dangerous, he looked up and—Wham!

Torak spun sharply and grabbed ... *her*. He froze, barely catching the deadly toojidium charge stinging his palm, and blinked down at the very female he'd lost in the woods. The girl jolted in fright but held the blood-curdling scream she was about to set free.

Torak knew why. She recognized him—everyone did—even on this remote planet. Instead of crying out, though, she peered at him with large green eyes as if in curiosity. A pulse thumped hard at the base of her neck after her start, but she didn't panic, she didn't faint, and she didn't beg for mercy. He was impressed. Most people did as soon as they recognized him.

This woman was braver than most.

Frozen in fierce eye-lock, he registered an instant attraction to her, a surprise, to say the least. Attraction was the last emotion he expected just then, considering the circumstances, but there it was. Duty, the reaction that should have been front and center, lollygagged somewhere in the background, leaving him wondering what in the hell he was doing here holding this ridiculously attractive human.

Like an idiot, Torak gaped at her. He'd never seen a full-blooded Earthling this close before. He didn't know what he might have expected, but this wasn't it. He detected no threat, though. Her face was quite pleasant and easy to look at. She was smaller in frame than he was, more slender and more shapely. Her lips were full, her nose small. Silky locks framed her face and draped loose over her shoulders and down her back. The soft flowery scent of her hair jolted through his spine, a sensation that warmed him. It set his heart pounding and left him staring at her in baffled confusion. He was puzzled by this odd reaction. She should be dead. He should have killed her.

Why hadn't he killed her?

Some distant warning went off in his head, dragging him back from his daze and reminding him to hurry. The mission, his mind muttered. His distracted glance flicked toward the empty sky, and a sense of urgency returned. His voice, normally smooth and deep, sounded loud in the quiet. "Obi sui obica mechee. Dinakip!" he warned, urging her to hurry.

The woman shook her head, not understanding him, but made no move to pull away. She said something with a breathless smile.

Torak knitted his brows in concentration, but her words didn't register. It sounded like an apology, which itself was odd if she recognized him. Her language was strange, certainly one he'd never heard before. He looked again at the sky. The Zahrá Che were coming. He needed to leave now. "Bokju bagogeek mu," he told her, trying a different language.

The female cocked her head in curiosity and repeated herself. It sounded like a question.

"Nud ekja?" he asked, trying again.

The stare continued.

Torak didn't have time to go through a list of languages, and hers wasn't registering. This area was dangerous. They needed to communicate now, so he could tell her to leave. Frowning in urgency, he touched her left temple and the base of her skull, intending to stimulate her language bundles just long enough to connect, and fired a pulse. A sharp snap of static energy sparked at the touch, and she flinched in surprise. Her eyes flashed blue, a bit brighter than he'd intended, and her breath caught. She froze, and her expression went blank as the element toojidium rewired her neurons to connect with his. Worried he'd used too much, he stared hard into her eyes and waited for her to recover. It took a moment, but the language centers in their brains finally connected. As their frequencies synchronized, the glaze cleared from her eyes, and her language flooded his mind.

It took a few more seconds for her to snap back, and she blinked sharply, entirely unaware of what had happened. "Oh … my," she said breathlessly, then focused unsteady eyes on him.

Torak knew why she'd flinched. Synchronization caused the ears to ring, but she hid it. "How about now?" he asked quietly.

With a sudden look of intrigue, she examined him closely. "Your eyes are white," she said in a murmur.

Her words processed in his mind.

Torak lowered his hand back to her arm and selected the correct words. They felt weird in his mouth, so he spoke slowly. "Who are you?"

Her face broke into a playful smile. "The woman who just made your heart skip," she teased, sounding winded and unsteady.

Torak noted a touch of humor in her dusty voice and thought it odd that she would jest with him of all people. Maybe, she didn't recognize him. She was correct, though. He wasn't sure how she knew, but his heart had indeed momentarily lost its normal rhythm. Entirely caught off-guard by this, he pushed his hood back, exposing his hair so that she might realize who she was joking with. Free from the garment, a scatter of loose, shiny black curls spilled down into his eyes and around his face, reaching nearly to his shoulders. There. Now she would recognize him. "Perhaps," he agreed almost cordially, "but that doesn't tell me who you are."

The woman's brows lifted, and she exhaled an amused huff. "Your future wife?" she said hopefully.

Wife?

Torak gave the word a moment to register.

Wife. Husband. Marriage. Union. There was no mistaking her meaning.

Instantly, the Zahrá Che were forgotten. A touch of uncertainty flickered over his features, giving him further pause, and he struggled to decipher the new language. Usually, he was faster at picking it up, but this language was complicated. More than that, her tone almost suggested a hint of flirtation rather than fear—another oddity. "My ... wife?" he began, still clutching her. With a note of suspicion, the tone of his voice dropped. "Do you know who I am?"

They were still staring. Still clutching.

"The man I just fell in love with?" she guessed.

Torak's brows lifted in surprise. He was entirely unused to being spoken to this way. If coincidence hadn't orchestrated this encounter, he would have assumed someone was setting him up, but that was impossible. Nobody knew his location. "Is there another meaning for this word 'wife'?"

She pondered the question with a coy blink. "There's only one that I know of."

"Really?" Torak was confused. Surely, she knew who he was ... didn't she? He decided she didn't. "It seems rather dangerous to say such a pledge to a man you know nothing about," he frowned, then wondered if perhaps she did know and was just mentally damaged.

"You can't be that bad," she argued in amusement.

"Are you so sure?"

She shrugged a slender shoulder. "Well ... no. You are dressed a bit like the Grim Reaper," she admitted, eyeing his garb.

Torak processed her newest words. Grim Reaper. Death. Harvester of Souls. Guide to the afterlife. Heaven. Hell. "Am I?" He glanced down at his attire, genuinely intrigued by the comparison. A trace of laughter brightened his deep voice. "So, what if I am this Grim Reaper? Does that make you my victim?"

His fearless companion considered this with a light chuckle. "I suppose that depends on what you're reaping," she teased.

Torak ran a few more words through his head and smiled as the language began to make sense. "I want your soul," he teased, "and ... your beating heart."

She winced playfully. "Ooh! Double whammy. Will this be an even exchange?"

Even exchange? Torak paused at the challenge, and his amusement faded a degree. He'd been joking, but ... was she? Perhaps this human knew precisely who he was and was making fun of him. His voice darkened in suspicion. "That is a bold request."

She shrugged. "But a fair one."

"You want an even exchange?" he double-checked skeptically.

"Naturally. Isn't that usually how that works?"

Again, Torak hesitated, entirely caught off-guard. *Was* she serious? He couldn't tell. "You do not know what you are asking," he warned, unsure now.

She cocked her head and chuckled. "You seem surprised."

But Torak was sincere. "I am. In a universe this vast, you are the first to make such a request, even in joke."

It was her turn to hesitate. "Joke?"

Another wave of uncertainty swept through him. *Had* she been planted? Nobody knew he was here; he was positive. There was no way she could be a decoy. Could she? Regardless, she was teasing him, and he didn't like it. "You know nothing about me," he said sharply.

"Yet."

Torak couldn't believe he was hearing this. Was this woman afraid of nothing? Okay, nevermind. He did like the teasing. "Are you always this reckless?"

"According to Rixton, yes," she giggled.

Torak attempted to glean what a rixton was. Perhaps it was a measurement. Some of her words didn't register yet, but that was normal with a new language transfer. Anyway, whatever it was, he agreed with its assessment. "An even exchange with me under those conditions should frighten you," he warned.

"It should, but it doesn't," she said with a bat of lashes.

"Do I not frighten you?"

"No."

A long look passed between them before she awkwardly released his arms and backed away. Twelve inches later, she bumped into a tree and gripped a low branch. "Is that what I should call you, then? Grim?"

"I have many names," Torak answered, dreading the moment she realized to whom she was pledging herself. She seemed fearless, a rather attractive feature, and he wasn't sure how to process that. It was charming, though.

"Which name do you prefer?" she asked, seeming genuinely interested.

"I am Tor—." Abruptly, he stopped, changing his mind, and the unspoken name hung on the air. He rather liked being spoken to this way by a beautiful woman and, suddenly, wasn't in a hurry to reveal his identity. A bit awkwardly, he corrected himself. "Tooji," he said instead, choosing the childish name his creator had used in his laboratory nursery. "To you, I am Tooji. What is your name?"

"Kinety. Emphasis on Net."

"Kin-**net**-tee," he repeated, trying the name out. "Kin-é-ty. As in Kinetic energy?"

"Yes," she smiled, impressed he'd caught on. "It's unusual, I know. Are you a soldier, Tooji?"

A flash of amusement lit his face, and he chuckled softly. "No," he assured. "I am the bad guy."

Kinety laughed aloud and gave him a bright smile. "Ah, that explains all the warnings," she said and gestured toward the campsite. "They're expecting you."

His amused expression faded sharply into a sober one. "The soldiers?" he asked, alarmed by the comment.

"Yes."

Torak's eyes followed her point, then returned, deceptively calm. There was no way the soldiers knew he was here. It was impossible. If they did, they certainly wouldn't be waiting, and she wouldn't be speaking to him so casually. Utterly puzzled, he asked, "Are *you* a soldier, Kinety?"

Entirely amused, she huffed a smile and lowered her lashes. "No," she giggled, tickled by the very idea. "Cowards don't make good soldiers."

The comment made Torak pause because the descriptor didn't match what he was seeing. He scanned her face, utterly intrigued by this charismatic humanoid female, then closed the small gap between them. "Are you a coward?" he wondered in blatant disbelief.

Kinety inclined her head. "I am."

"I disbelieve you."

Kinety leaned her shoulder against the tree trunk and eyed his attire. "Do you always wear cloaks?"

"Cloaks?" The word registered as clothing. Torak looked down at himself and the hooded Grim Reaper garment he was told was common among humans. A split second later, he realized he was dressed quite differently from her, and his heart skipped another beat. He worried that she was figuring him out but was careful not to panic yet. Humor had laced her demeanor to this point, so he mimicked her behavior. "Only when I sneak at night," he answered coyly but didn't bat his lashes.

It worked. She chuckled.

Torak chuckled with her, enjoying the light-hearted tone of his own voice. "Do you still not know who I am?"

Her smile widened. "The man of my dreams."

He recognized her comment as a compliment and laughed aloud. "Your … dreams?" he stammered, barely able to believe they were having this conversation.

She nodded.

Okay, she definitely didn't know who he was. Torak's heart pounded in relief, a realization that surprised him. For several seconds, he didn't know how to reply. The tingle surging through his stomach was new, as well. It was making his temperature rise. "Do you say this to all the boys?" he asked quietly.

Her laugh was genuine. "Actually, I don't."

Again, he didn't believe her, but his interest was entirely piqued. "Tell me," he said, gazing into her eyes, "what am I doing in your dreams?"

A charming grimace twisted Kinety's face. "Faaalling in love?" she supposed hopefully.

Torak laughed again, a rich sound strange even to his own ears, and angled his head, completely mesmerized by the strange encounter. He was floored to realize he was actually having fun, another sensation entirely unfamiliar to him. "With you?"

A guilty dimple puckered her cheek. "I hope so."

"Ah. If I am busy falling in love," he inched closer, backing her against the tree trunk, "what will you be doing?"

She accidentally dropped a glance at his lips but tried to hide it. "Trying not to wake," she said with a bounce.

By now, Torak was ready to sweep her off her feet and pledge his heart to her, but he stopped himself. There was no way this was real. Someone had sent her; he was sure of it.

His smile faded.

All at once, the nagging worry that he was being fooled returned, and his demeanor darkened. It was a trick. She wanted something. Subconsciously, he thumbed the ring on his finger. This ring—his star-fighter—was the single only thing he had to give and the one thing he never would. He'd kill anyone who tried to get it. His gaze, the intimidating one he reserved for his enemies, locked hers into place, and his voice dropped to a wary murmur. "Are you certain someone didn't send you?"

A touch of confusion flickered over Kinety's features. She looked away, a bit put off by the abrupt change in him and, ever-so-slightly, recoiled.

It was the reaction Torak expected.

Strong, gentle fingers tipped her chin, bringing her gaze back to his, and a look of skepticism furrowed his brow. "Who are you, really?"

Kinety forced a quick smile into her mesmerizing green eyes, and the tone of her voice lost its play. "I should go," she said quietly.

She tried to pass, but he stopped her. "You do not recognize me?"

"Should I?"

Torak gave his head a quick shake. If she truly didn't know, he wasn't gonna tell her. "No."

"They're waiting for you," she said, gesturing toward the camp behind her.

Something was different. He'd offended her.

Again, she tried to leave.

A spark of alarm zapped Torak, and his distracted mind scrambled to reverse the damage. He wasn't ready for the encounter to be over and struggled to think of a reason to detain her. He caught her arm. "Wait," he blurted, puzzled by his own reluctance to see her go.

When she faced him, he slid his star-fighter ring from his finger. If that's what she was after, she wouldn't get far with it, but he had to know if he was being played. The ring was black metal, extremely heavy, and wore a dull tint in the moonlight. Against every instinct he possessed, he dropped it into her palm. "Is this what you want?" he asked, ready to snatch it back.

Kinety blinked at the offering, then shook her head. "Thank you," she said, "but I can't take this." Politely, she handed it back.

She didn't want his ring?

Torak wasn't about to let her go now. Unsure what to think, he brushed her hair back, then slid his fingers over her ears and behind them. When he was satisfied her ears were natural, he examined her hands, touching them carefully. Shapeshifters rarely perfected their transformations. Characteristic mistakes were in the small details like ears and hands, but hers were clearly human. He knew because he'd been designed to look human himself. Her details matched his. She wasn't a shapeshifter.

Kinety blinked at him, puzzled by the inspection.

Torak released her hands and scanned her moonlit face. She was authentic, the encounter genuine. This woman had no idea who he was, didn't want his ring, and ... actually liked him. Odd. Even stranger, he liked her.

That changed everything.

Emboldened by the realization, he brushed her lips with his thumb. They, too, were real.

"What are you doing?" she asked, yet made no move to stop him.

Torak slid his hand behind her head. "Surrendering to a coward."

Kinety's eyes went wide.

Before he could stop himself, Torak lowered his head and touched his lips lightly to hers. He didn't know why he was doing this; he just was. Even better ... she was letting him. Any moment now, she would surely come to her senses and put a stop to this.

Surely.

A bit hesitantly, his lips lifted, then repositioned slightly for a more magical fit. Pressed against hers, they lingered, lightly puckered and unhurried, yet skittish—ready to flee at the first sign of resistance.

But she gave no resistance.

Sparkles, drums, fireworks, and embarrassment flamed Torak's ears while his heart thundered in his chest. What he was doing was completely against regulation, but he didn't care. A fine tremble joined the encounter, yet it wasn't his lips; it was hers. He could feel her heartbeat beneath his fingertips. The rhythmic sound thumped in his head. For a moment, it matched his own, thudding in sync with the beat of his pulse. As it did, another soft flash of energy sparked between them ... only neither noticed.

And then it was over.

"Your hands are trembling," he whispered, raising his head.

Indeed, they were. "I'm scaring me," she admitted truthfully.

A soft hiss whistled on the breeze, tossing a lock of her hair between them.

Torak tore his eyes away and glanced at the sky. He'd almost forgotten about the Zahrá Che. Wearing a troubled expression, he took one last good look at Kinety's pretty face, then released her. "Goodbye, my little coward," he said firmly and tried to pass.

Kinety curled her fingers into the cloth of his cloak, stopping him. "Don't go."

"You are distracting me from my mission," he scolded.

"Ooh, does that make me the good guy?"

Torak looked across his shoulder at her, puzzled again. "If we are in love," he said slowly, "should I not assume you and I are in league together?"

Kinety chortled in amusement. "I don't know about that," she countered. "Mortal enemies can be in love."

"Enemies?" he echoed with a note of surprise.

"Well, yeah. You're the bad guy," she reminded, then smiled.

Torak ran a finger over her cheek. "Yes, I am," he said, curling strong fingers around hers. Gently, he removed her hand from his sleeve, severing her hold, and slid his thumb over her knuckles.

"Tooji," she pleaded in a last-ditch effort.

Their eyes held again.

"Very bad." This time, he turned her palm up and slipped a flat stone into it. "You should leave," he whispered before vanishing into the shadows.

*****

Kinety didn't know what to think. Her feet crunched over the dusting of yellowing leaves sprinkled on the ground, but she barely noticed. Her mind was elsewhere. She walked down the dark hill in a daze, wondering what the hell had just happened. That had been the most amazing, most disturbing encounter she'd ever had, and she was still feeling its effects. That magical kiss had put her belly into a wild spin and set her heart pounding against her sternum. The worst part was that she failed to get Tooji's number before he told her to leave. After all that, he'd turned her down. That sucked, too, because he'd had an incredible effect on her. Her heart was still racing, and her gut felt heavy and constricted, making the short walk to the car seem like a daze.

It wasn't until she tried to open the car door that she discovered her keys were missing. She tapped her pockets front and back a second time just to be sure, but they weren't there. The wad of money was there and her cell phone, but no keys. Right away, she knew they'd either fallen from her pocket when her brother had flipped her over his shoulder or they were lying on the ground where the large Arnie had found her. She had to go back.

This realization earned a healthy groan for two reasons. If her brother caught her, he would assume she wanted attention and probably embarrass her. If she bumped into Tooji, he would surely think she was chasing him like some desperate floozy. He'd made his disinterest clear, so she definitely wanted to avoid him. Either way, she was going to look like a big dummy. But what choice did she have? In frustration, she ran her fingers through her loose hair, said a few unladylike words into the breeze, then marched back up the hill to find her keys.

Kinety was so engrossed in her thoughts that before she knew it, she'd crossed the dark field and was standing at the embankment. Whether she'd been quiet or not was anybody's guess, not that it would have mattered. The soldiers were making all kinds of racket now. She barely noticed, though. Her mind was still on Tooji and the bold tryst they'd shared in the woods. She'd never behaved like that before. Now that it was over, a tinge of shame warmed her cheeks.

Her keys glinted, lying on the ground where Arnie had found her.

As she picked them up, a brilliant flash of light and a sharp grunt startled her from her reverie. That's when she finally heard the noise —as in stopped and listened. A whirring hum, unlike anything she'd ever heard, filtered through the trees. It danced on the air, charging it and making the hair on her arms stand on end. Running footsteps, scrapes, and hushed barked orders filled the electrified air around the camp, growing louder and more frantic with each passing second. The sound beckoned her closer, and she wondered what kind of war games the soldiers were playing now that Tooji had arrived.

Another flash of light.

More curious than anything, Kinety squinted into the blinding lights and followed the sound of mock fighting. When she stepped through the trees into the camp, she laughed, marveling at how ridiculous the war game looked. She knew she wasn't supposed to be there, but this was hilarious. Two phony-looking spaceships hovered just above the ground on the far side of the clearing. Everywhere she looked, soldiers were either running or lying still in the dirt. What they weren't doing was fighting. For some reason, their weapons lay scattered on the ground in shiny, liquified puddles, appearing almost to smoke.

Stepping over the partially melted guns were phony-looking aliens in white uniforms. Black, almond-shaped eye shields peered out of soft helmets, adding a touch of Hollywood to the look. Small, skinny, big-headed creatures pointed weapons that emitted a curly buzz when fired. Two were shooting; one was transporting fallen soldiers onto the closer of the two ships. Another loaded a vessel on the far side. It wasn't clear how the aliens were lifting them, but the soldiers playing dead didn't move. Fortunately, there was no blood or gore on the ones going into the ships. The civilians she'd seen by the black van, however, were covered in rather realistic-looking gore. Too real.

Confusion set in.

Puzzled, Kinety focused on two very bloody, very dead-looking bodies sprawled around shattered equipment and wondered why there was no medical personnel field-training on them. Then, a whiff of sweet, iron-heavy blood hit her. Hesitantly, she scanned the clearing again. Another soldier fell.

This was practice, right?

In disconnected disbelief, Kinety watched as the third civilian near the van, still alive but wounded, stood from the ground in a daze and tried to speak to the nearest creature. The alien, who was bending over an unmoving soldier, lifted its white helmet, aimed its weapon at her, and fired. The civilian, a woman with short brown hair, flew backward and slammed hard into the van, buckling the side in a splatter of blood. Open-mouthed, she slid down to the ground, leaving a wet smear.

Kinety stared in horror.

Without warning, a large man dove, taking her to the ground in a tackle and scrambled frantically away from the clearing with her. In the chaos, she must have made a sound because his hand clamped hard over her mouth, silencing her. Frantically, he dragged her behind a rock toward the pile of belongings the soldiers had stacked

16

near their tents. Hurrying, the light-featured soldier—a man Kinety didn't recognize—grabbed a random military-issue duffel bag and snatched camouflage clothing from it, spilling its contents in his haste.

Kinety tried to look around the rock, but the soldier yanked her roughly back and stuffed her into the clothes, jerking his head up occasionally to look around only to speed up. There were no questions; there was no time. His panic was message enough. This was no war game. The aliens were real and killing anyone *not* in uniform. Catching on, she cooperated and quickly fastened the buttons on the oversized pants. He was just securing the buttons on her cover shirt when the soft crunch of a tiny foot stepped nearby.

A four-foot alien with almond-shaped black eyes—which looked much scarier up close—rounded the rock behind him, pointed a weapon, and fired.

A powerful concussion struck them both. The soldier bowed forward with a grunt, absorbing most of the strike, and took Kinety to the ground. He lay still, unconscious.

Kinety lay stunned, tangled in oblivion. The world, distant and confusing, blurred and buzzed around her. Magnetic energy pulled her upward into the air. The ground scraped away and spun, and an odd force stretched her flat. The floating sensation that followed was nauseating. She hovered, suspended on a cushion of air as little feet stepped up a ramp and onto a metal floor. The air chilled and hummed an audible pitch indistinguishable between high and low. In a dizzy whirl, she rotated face-up and landed on her back. Something sharp clamped hard into her left wrist, biting deep into her flesh. The stab of pain failed to produce a cry but did startle her from the delirium. Three seconds later, something bit her neck with a crunch. In a tumble of chaos, she was shoved aside into a pile of arms and legs, her face contorted in pain. With clumsy hands, she swiped at her neck with her nails, knocking the stinging teeth away.

"... *hmm hmm hmmm hm* ..."

Sounds buzzed and faded in her head, growing distant, until a body landed against her, jolting her again from the fog. The body was unmoving, heavy, and alive.

Through fluttering lashes, Kinety watched a blurry alien place a black chip on the soldier's neck and move away. From somewhere nearby, she heard the hiss of a pressurized something release. There was a shuffle of movement, and the body beside her was taken away.

"... *hmm hmm hmmm hm* ..."

Kinety tried to blink the blur from her eyes. Someone was singing. Her wrist throbbed painfully and heat radiated up her arm, but some primal instinct warned her to remain silent. As her vision fuzzed in and out, she watched the alien stuff the soldier into a tube-like canister. It snapped shut, and the empty canister beside it opened with a hiss. As if by magic, another body rose from the table, hovered, and moved away.

"... ba ba da da, zippin' through the stars ..."

Kinety watched through cracked lids as the alien opened its little hand, levitating the soldier horizontally, and walked him easily to the waiting canister. Then, the alien's little hand shifted, lifting the body vertically, and pushed the soldier into the tube. Behind him, the transporting alien came in with another load of unconscious soldiers and discarded them into the pile. The little creature quickly snapped wide genie-like bracelets onto their wrists with methodical haste and then hurried out through an opening in the wall.

"... na na na na, ba ba da da ..."

Kinety had seen enough by now to know whatever was happening was bad. Unsteady eyes found the door. Fighting powerful waves of dizziness, she tried to get up and realized she was on a floating platform. Her intention was to stand, but her legs were jelly. In a jagged blur, she oozed over the side, dragging a heavy body down to the floor with her. The two landed in a heap, with her on the bottom. In the chaos, she saw the platform and the alien vanish around the next row of canisters. Half dragging, half pushing the dead weight, she tried crawling on wobbly hands toward the exit. She'd made mere inches when the craft suddenly went dark. As it did, the fine vibration in the floor increased in intensity, humming through her and filling her head. It took effort to focus her eyes through the sound, but when she did, her heart sank.

The exit door was gone.

Without warning, an incredible G-force flattened her against the smooth metal floor, taking her breath and distorting her unorganized thoughts as the craft lifted straight up. When it slowed, she floated up off the floor. The world spun in a gyroscopic roller coaster, then took off like a shot, sending her and the heavy body tumbling together into blackness with a crash.

Chapter 3

A familiar hum worked its way into Kinety's groggy mind, beckoning her from the fog. She was alive, mostly, but that was as far as the good news went. The first unpleasant thing she noticed was the sharp pain in her left wrist as if her arm was actively occupying the space between a shark's jagged teeth. Accompanying that was a dull throbbing ache that pounded up the bones in her arm and the bloody wound on the left side of her neck. These, combined with the impressive impact headache she wore behind her eyes, made her instantly grumpy. The second source of irritation was the press of cold metal against one entire side of her body. A shiver or two might have helped the situation if she could have moved, but the crush of a heavy weight completely prevented that. The G-force was still there but steady and somewhat tolerable now. What number G, she had no idea, but the craft was flying and fast.

She had to get up.

Favoring her painful wrist, she twisted to her side and shrimp-scooted herself backward to get out from beneath whoever was atop her. Her heavy companion oozed to the floor. Free at last, she jimmied the soldier onto his back and, in the pale blue glow from somewhere nearby, recognized him.

It was Arnie.

Careful not to make a sound, Kinety covered his mouth and shook him, but he wouldn't wake up. There was a black dot on his neck. She scratched it off, earning a grunt, and shook him again, but he didn't wake. More than a little concerned at this point, she looked around and tried to unscramble her thoughts. The canister room was gone. She and Arnie were now wedged deep beneath some sort of ledge in a small space. The shapes around her were unfamiliar, but she was pretty sure they weren't supposed to be there. Vaguely, she remembered tumbling in, but the memory stopped there. Beyond their hiding place, some sort of hallway or walkway curved around the perimeter of the spacecraft, which wasn't large considering the radius—perhaps thirty feet in diameter. Bluish lights came from either side of the hall.

"... hmm hmm hmmm hm ..."

Carefully, Kinety poked her head out. She could hear faint singing but wasn't sure where it was coming from. To her left, she noticed the soft buzz and beep of high-tech computers blending with the occasional scrape of movement. To her right, she saw a lone alien at a small computer station with his ... or its ... back to her. Illuminated hieroglyphic-looking symbols covered the panel. The room, composed mostly of smooth walls, appeared to complete the entire back half of the aircraft. To her astonishment, the little guy inside resembled the typical alien image popular in comedies, only the skin wasn't gray. It wasn't fluorescent green either. It was pink. Pale, whitish pink skin stretched taut over a large, hairless head. Its dark eyes were quite large, with complex irises that resembled a high-tech motherboard, suggesting it wore computerized contacts. The slender, scrawny body was wrapped in a somewhat shimmery white suit made of unfamiliar material. And it had five fingers.

Fear rocked her insides.

Directly behind the alien, through a round hatch-like door, she saw another room—the one she'd crawled out of. Soldiers were no longer lying in heaps. Now, they were all packed neatly inside the vertical bio-canisters that lined the wall. The floating table was gone. This was nothing like the alien abduction stories she'd heard about on television. There were no experiments, but the fear was real. Why the mass abduction? Why had the aliens captured so many soldiers specifically, but not civilians? It made no sense.

"... zippin' through the stars ..."

In a typical fight or flight situation, Kinety might have opted for the preferable flight, but her spaceship joyride through space successfully removed fleeing as an option. Besides, her brother was in one of those canisters, and she was going to get him out of there. A quick glance showed Arnie hadn't moved, which meant she was on her own. Without giving herself time to think her plan through, she slipped out of her hiding place and crept behind the alien to the canister room.

Engrossed in its work, the creature didn't notice her.

Each bio-canister had a tiny window. Kinety peered into the first one she came to and found a soldier sleeping inside, but it wasn't Rixton. Neither was the next guy. Both had black things on their necks. In another, she spotted Yardley. He was asleep. One by one, she peered through the tiny windows and even recognized some of the men but couldn't find her brother. When she reached the last canister, Kinety checked behind her again to be sure she hadn't attracted the alien's attention.

She hadn't.

Unsure what to do next, she searched the canisters for a way to open them. She scanned the outside of the tubes for a lever or an eject button, but there was nothing. In frustration, she turned her attention to the small-framed alien at the computer and pensively chewed her lip.

His back was still to her.

On tiptoes, she crept to the edge of the open portal and peered around the ledge to see what he was doing. On a screen to one side of him—she'd decided the alien was a him—were color-coded depictions of the bio-canisters, each registering familiar vital signs over silhouettes with the wrist things blinking away. She could see the heartbeats, rate of respiration, and blood chemical symbols charted beside the devices on each left wrist. Though she'd never actually seen the symbols before, she knew that's what they meant. Puzzled by this, she examined the band on her own arm. It was made of thin metal, stretched five inches long, and had vertical grooves. It was smooth and lightweight on the outside, stylish even if one was inclined toward weird alien jewelry, but the inside was barbed with sharp shit.

The alien moved, startling her and sending her heart into her throat. Ducking back, she gripped the wall to keep from falling and mouthed more than a few silent curses. A few breaths later, she dared another peek.

"... *na na na na* ..."

On the large screen in front of him, a map of Earth's solar system appeared with a symbol marking their current position. He pinched the touch-screen, shrinking the solar system, then moved far away from their point in space and touched a cluster of stars in a constellation she recognized but couldn't identify. When rotated, the pattern of stars resembled a helix. Inside the helix, he selected a star cluster and expanded it until a binary solar system appeared. One sun was huge! Near the suns, he expanded again, bringing tiny planets into view, then counted four back. On the fourth planet, he zoomed in until three small moons were visible. A blue moon was selected and the word Gelphii, written in alien scrawl, appeared above coordinates along with its information.

Creeping silently, Kinety eased closer.

On Gelphii, the alien spun the moon, exposing a landmass, and chose the very tip of a curled peninsula. He highlighted it. Next, he touched the screen with the bio-canisters, highlighting a bubble around the men, then selected both the men and the Gelphii peninsula at the same time. Both began to blink and a trajectory formed through space between the selections until the two screens connected. The moment the two came together, a time-ticker appeared, and the light in the room behind her dimmed to red. A countdown began. It was then that Kinety realized what she'd just seen. The canisters weren't in a room, they were in a pod, and it was just programmed to go to the small moon Gelphii in the constellation Whatever.

Oh, hell, no!

Kinety's heartbeat pounded in her ears, and anger dissolved her fear. No way was she going to allow Mr. Bubblehead to send her soldiers to that moon. With a most unflattering snarl, she yanked the zipper down on her boot, snatched it off, and—

The alien whirled in surprise.

Whack!

—she lopped him upside the head.

The little alien went flying.

As fast as her fingers would move, she reversed the coordinates, doing in opposite everything she'd seen the little monster do, until the pod linked up with Earth. All she had to do now was get Arnie and get into the pod. Quickly, she stuffed her foot back into her boot, spun to get Arnie, and watched in horror as the pod door oozed shut.

"An Earthling is loose!" a voice cried in her head.

Pop!

The pod ejected.

The alien gaped at the missing pod, then at the screen. As he faced the dimmer light, the shades over his eyes lightened, adjusting instantly to the illumination in the fuselage. Furious, he climbed onto wobbly feet and, scowling in anger, snatched his weapon to kill her.

Before he could fire, there was a blur and—Crash!—Arnie and the alien flew across the small room.

"Two humans!"

As they landed, Arnie snatched the weapon in one hand and the alien's neck in the other. With a leap, he landed in front of Kinety, clutching his captive, as two armed aliens rushed in. In that moment, a blast of voices filled her head.

"Urik! The male is armed!"

"That's bad. Males are aggressive. Exterminate it, Jael, before it kills Deek."

Jael, the smaller of the two, aimed. *"Be still, Deek!"*

"Don't shoot me!" screeched Deek, kicking beneath Arnie's headlock.

"Jael, wait!" Urik, standing two inches taller, held up a hand. *"Kill only the male. Females aren't aggressive and have value."*

"This one is aggressive!" grunted Deek.

"Very well. Kill them both, Jael."

"No!" Deek cried, renewing his struggle. *"If you shoot the humans, you'll kill me!"*

"We can't take these things home with us," Urik barked, extending an incredulous arm. *"The route has already been calculated."*

Jael aimed back and forth, ready to shoot. *"Yes or no?"*

Kinety shrieked and stumbled backward into the computer panel, gripping her temples. "They're talking in my head!"

Arnie looked at her in confusion. "The aliens?"

"Yes!" she cried. "You can't hear them?"

"No." Arnie backed protectively against her, his collar soaked with blood from his neck. "Drop your weapons!" he shouted, shoving the barrel into the alien's temple.

Deek, cringing in fright, let out a high-pitched 'Eeeee' sound.

"Yes, Jael. Kill him," ordered Urik,

"Hold still, Deek!"

Deek squirmed, trying to duck. *"No. Don't shoot!"*

"I can kill him," insisted Jael.

"Eeeee!"

"Drop your weapons!" shouted Arnie.

Jael struggled to aim. *"Stop kicking, Deek."*

Urik set scrawny hands on skinny hips. *"This is a mess. How did the humans get out?"* he demanded in annoyance.

"I don't know! The vials were sealed," Deek grunted.

"Kinety," Arnie jerked a glance over his shoulder, "tell them to drop their weapons!"

Kinety flashed him a horrified look. "Me? I can't tell them!"

"If they're thinking into your head, then you can communicate with them," he countered with an uncanny note of reason.

Kinety shriveled from the angry aliens. Why was she able to understand them? "Drop the weapons," she whimpered.

At the recognizable sound of her speech, Urik jolted, Deek went still, and Jael's weapon went airborne. The startled aliens faced her with expressions that can only be described as the visual equivalent of a gasp.

Jael's weapon clattered to the floor. *"The female just spoke!"* he squeaked in astonishment.

Urik, still clutching his blaster, gave Jael's weapon a sideways kick, returning it to the awestruck alien. *"Pick it up!"*

"I thought humans only spoke human. This one speaks Zahrá Che!" Jael marveled, clumsily collecting his weapon.

"Humans are not telepathic," barked Urik. *"They cannot speak Zahrá Che."*

Jael pointed at Kinety.

Before Urik could argue, the ship jolted, and the artificial gravity switched off. Everyone lurched and tumbled slowly into the air.

"Eeeee!" Jael and Urik cried in unison.

Arnie dropped Deek and flapped his arms, his mouth contorted into a frown. Kinety toppled ungracefully into the computer panel. From the flight deck, alarms sounded off. Frantic lights blinked in warning, and an ominous whine hummed through the ship.

Arnie was the first to recover. By pushing off a wall, he launched through the air and quickly grabbed Kinety, but the aliens weren't worried about them anymore. In a panic, all three floated themselves expertly into the control room, no longer interested in loose humans, guns, or languages. The volume of their thoughts faded as they moved away. From the other room, their distant, high-speed thoughts muffled through Kinety's mind, blurring into a background mush.

Arnie bumped the ceiling, which knocked Kinety loose from his grip, and he glanced off in a different direction. Kinety caught herself above the computer panel, reeling.

Arnie gripped a contour in the wall, stopping himself, and struggled to make sense of what he was seeing. In annoyance, he swiped at the blood forming a blob on the side of his neck, glanced at the smear it left on his fingers, then blinked around the shiny room. "What just happened?" he demanded, trying to work his way toward her. "Are we on a spaceship?"

Kinety's expression conveyed the bad news.

A quick scan darkened his expression. "Where are the others?" he asked hesitantly, his deep voice a low rumble.

"I released them."

Arnie frowned at her and slapped clumsily at the edge of the computer panel to stop from floating away. "You did what?" he demanded, leaving fingerprints.

"You and I didn't make it into the canisters," she said, ignoring his look of confusion. "We both ended up on the floor. When the ship took off, we were thrown under a ledge in the hall, so we weren't counted with the others. That Deek guy—"

"Deek?"

"The alien you had in the headlock."

"You know his name?"

"—programmed the pod to go to some solar system, so I whacked him with my boot and reversed the coordinates before the pod ejected."

Arnie blinked at her, his lips curled in hesitation. "You did wh—wait ... where are the troops?"

"I sent them home," she said, motioning to the computer.

Blue eyes stared at her. "You know how to use their computers?"

"No. I saw the alien program it," she explained quickly. "I just did the exact opposite."

The large soldier actually paled.

A lone tear appeared but didn't roll down her cheek. Lost without gravity, it hovered at her eye, blinding her. Irritably, she wiped it off, then watched it float away. "I'm sorry I couldn't send you too. I only had seconds to reverse the coordinates. You and I won't survive," she said calmly, "but they will. That's what matters now."

Arnie groaned and smacked himself hard in the forehead. "No. No! No!" he growled and—Wham!—the gravity returned.

Both crashed to the floor.

Kinety raised her head slowly, positive she had just been shot, but Arnie remained face-down. He wasn't hurt, though. His grimace was one of frustration. "Why would you do that?" he muffled.

Kinety was certain she'd misunderstood the question. "They were going to another solar system," she explained as if to an idiot, "which meant they weren't coming back."

Arnie bit back a curse and folded beefy arms around his head.

"Wait. I'm confused," she said, easing painfully to a hip. "You act like I've done something wrong."

Arnie gave his blond head a slight shake, then swiveled a blue eye toward her from the floor. "You didn't know," he managed in a broken voice.

"Know what?"

"Our mission. It was classified. Your brother was telling the truth," he said, getting his elbows beneath him and taking a moment to rub his face.

Kinety shook her head, not following. "You were camping."

Arnie sighed patiently and sat up, then pressed the collar of his woodland camouflage jacket against his neck to stop the bleeding. "What happened here?"

Kinety shrugged guiltily and touched the angry wound on her own neck. Hers had stopped bleeding but still stung. "They put something on our necks. I took them off."

Bracing his elbow on a bent knee, he ran a hand over his head, winced as he touched a knot, and explained in a low voice. "If you've followed the news," he said a bit breathlessly, "you know about the soldiers disappearing."

She did.

Arnie studied her, then sighed and spoke in earnest. "The numbers are far worse than reported. It started with a few here and there, then suddenly it was by the hundreds. In all the cases, UFOs have been spotted, so special teams were quickly trained by space defense agents. There were ten camps set up across the country. Ours just won the jackpot. The soldiers you saw were dispatched as bait."

"My brother was bait!"

"Yes, but only to get the aliens to that location. The mission was merely to attract them, then let the Extraterrestrial Affairs agents stop the abductions through negotiations. Just in case, though, the teams were fitted with long-range tracking devices to help us locate the missing soldiers. If the missing men were close enough to Earth, we hoped to recover them. Nobody was forced. Your brother volunteered."

"No!"

"Something had to be done!" he argued hotly. "Would you rather him vanish like the others or have a fighting chance? Thousands of our men and women are gone, Kinety. They have families and sisters too. Those families want them back."

Kinety looked at the blank wall where the pod had been. "Thousands?"

"Thousands."

Stunned by the massive number, she exhaled in angry defeat. "So, I just … ."

Arnie ran his fingers through his short hair and dropped his head back against a blank wall. "You just rescued the rescue team," he said heavily.

"You have those things, too, right? Trackers and communicators?"

Arnie didn't. "I'm from a different unit. My job was to secure the area. If we make it to the missing men, I can defend them or lead a resistance, but I'm not trained to communicate with aliens or negotiate. All I can do is beat them up," he offered helpfully, then noticed her cockeyed fatigues, several sizes too large for her. He pointed to the high-ranking insignia sewn into the collar lapel. "Why are you in that uniform?"

Kinety looked down at her ridiculous attire. Self-consciously, she touched the oversized fatigues. "The aliens were killing anyone not in camouflage," she answered in a small voice. "A man dragged me behind a rock by the duffel bags and stuffed me into this. I was captured moments later. He was," she gestured, "in the pod I just sent home."

Arnie went still. "Wait. They *killed* the negotiation team?" he clarified in alarm.

Kinety expression was answer enough.

Arnie took a moment to process this, then asked, "So … who was in the pod?"

"Just soldiers."

"How many?"

"About twenty. The rest went into the other ship. I think they got everyone at the campsite."

Arnie stared at nothing for a minute. "Why would they kill the negotiation team?" he asked, struggling with the news.

Kinety shrugged. "Because they aren't interested in negotiations or civilians, only soldiers," she said in all obviousness. "Whatever they want the soldiers for, I don't think they're coming back. They were being sent out of the solar system … to a different constellation. Humans have barely reached Mars, Arnie. There *is* no rescue."

Arnie took the news hard. "Then our mission was a failure. I was wrong," he said heavily and exhaled in sour amusement. "You probably just saved their lives."

"I don't feel so good," she managed, brushing loose bangs from her lashes.

26

Before Arnie could reply, a series of frantic "Eeeee!" screeches came from the control room. Kinety and Arnie looked at each other, then hurried down the hall to investigate.

The flight deck looked like one big, futuristic computer, only smoother and somewhat ... liquid. There were panels of blinking lights, screens, and stations with little hover-seats in front of them. Running back and forth from station to station were three hyperventilating aliens in an all-out panic, their shaded almond eyes darkened black in front of the bright computers.

Kinety shared an alarmed look with Arnie, then asked in English. "What's going on?"

"It's Torak!" one of the aliens—she wasn't sure which—shrieked into her head.

She ducked in response, unused to the invasive sound, and peeked at Arnie. "Did you understand that?"

"I understood you," answered the soldier. "Did they answer?"

Kinety nodded. She wasn't sure why the aliens could understand her when she spoke normally, but it didn't matter just then. "Who is Torak?" she asked the aliens.

"The Annihilator, foolish human!"

"The Annihilator?" she echoed out loud for Arnie's benefit.

"Annihilator! Destroyer! Assassin!" It was Deek that turned around to glance at her, identifiable by the impressive bruise on the right side of his head. *"He'll kill us all!"*

"It's an assassin," she relayed to Arnie.

"He's located the pod!" Deek shouted to the others.

Urik, who was busy, answered. *"Cloak it!"*

Jael ran on scrawny legs, which was really cute, to another spot and worked frantically to follow Urik's orders. *"It is cloaked. He's already locked on!"*

"Destroy it! Destroy the pod."

Kinety rushed forward. "No!" she cried, hands out. "Don't destroy the pod! Jael!"

Jael ignored her.

As best she could, she relayed the broken conversation to Arnie. Jael tried something else. *"I can't destroy it!"*

Urik whirled, putting his back to the panel, and gripped it with both hands. *"How did he know which soldiers we were collecting?"*

"I don't know, but he's got the transport pod."

"Scramble the link, or he'll find the base."

Jael scanned the data in confusion and double-checked the information on a different screen. *"It isn't leading him to the base; it's leading him ... back to Earth."*

Urik stopped. *"How?"*

"Because it went the wrong way!"

"Wrong way?" Urik scowled at Deek.

Deek slung an angry arm at Kinety. *"She sent it back to Earth."*

"Then sever our link to it."

"I'm trying!" fretted Jael.

"Break the connection before he traces it back to us! Do it now!"

"It won't separate!"

"Then evade! We'll outrun him."

"We can't!" cried Deek. *"The wormhole opens in fifteen seconds. If we miss this one, we'll be stuck here until it opens again."*

"We don't have fifteen seconds," shrieked Urik. *"Open a com-link! Call for help!"*

The panel sparked, knocking Jael and Urik backward to the floor.

From his station, Deek whirled in terror and looked at the blazing screen with wide, unblinking eyes. It buzzed and crackled. *"It's too late,"* he panted. *"He's coming through!"*

Urik twisted his big head and gaped at the glowing panel. *"We're gonna die,"* he whimpered, scooting away from it.

The screen glowed unnaturally bright, and a humanoid shape began to emerge. An arm extended toward the main navigation screen, and a one-minute clock appeared.

They all blinked at it in horror.

The dark, silhouetted figure cleared into a dangerous-looking man with loose black curls that fell into deadly eyes. A crackle of blue electricity danced over his white irises. The unique irises, well-outlined in black, were large and unnaturally light despite the hostility contained within them. He glared at the aliens. "You have sixty seconds to tell me where the base is," he warned in a deep, ominous voice.

As he spoke, the counter began ticking down.

"Eeeee!" Deek screamed and ran to the far side of the flight deck, his breathing heavy.

Kinety rushed forward in relief. "Tooji!"

Torak jolted sharply at the sight of her, forgetting the aliens, and stared. "Kinety?"

Kinety beamed at him. Dark features, symmetric and well-placed, completed the masculine picture he'd painted in the moonlight. He was gorgeous, and she was thrilled to see him.

A wide-eyed Torak stepped through the monitor and into the flight deck, gaping at her in surprise. The ridiculous cloak he'd worn in the meadow was gone. Now, he wore a form-fitting black uniform that contoured tight over an impressive, muscular physique. The thick, compression material was shiny and sleek and nicely outlined his slender frame. A harmony of angels sang for Kinety.

Arnie looked back and forth between the staring couple. "You know him?" he asked her incredulously.

"Yes, I—"

Deek glared hatred at her. *"Vile human! You've killed us all!"* he cried.

"You led him right to us!" Urik screamed, startling Kinety from her eye-lock. He slapped wildly for his weapon and scrambled to point it at her. *"I'll kill you!"*

Alarmed, she staggered back.

Arnie aimed.

Torak sliced a hand sharply toward Urik and—Thwack! The tiny alien flew backward hard, as if struck by a sledgehammer, and crashed violently into a computer panel. The gun slid from abnormally long fingers and clattered to the metal floor by his feet. Then, slowly, the wide-eyed alien slid down after it, his chest caved.

Urik was dead.

Kinety covered her mouth.

Torak—actually a hologram of him—turned dangerous eyes to Jael, who also stood clutching a weapon. "Your death will be slower," he warned, his hand still outstretched.

Very carefully, Jael lowered the weapon to the floor and backed away from it, his fingers spread wide.

Torak shifted next toward the hyperventilating Deek, who quickly proved he was unarmed.

Arnie, who was now standing in front of Kinety, lowered his weapon, still pointed at the dead Urik. Warily, he removed his finger from the trigger and turned his attention to the holographic assassin, earning a lingering glare from the violent invader.

Kinety touched Arnie's arm, calming the bristle, and stepped around the soldier. "Tooji," she said again, looking in awe at the holograph. She could see right through him.

Through scattered black curls, Torak pinned electric eyes on her and sliced a sharp hand toward the timer counting down. It stopped. "And here I find my wife," he purred in low sarcasm. "Hello, wife."

Jael and Deek looked at each other in disbelief.

The erratic drumbeat returned to Kinety's chest, but she couldn't tell if she was responding to the magnetic pull he had on her or the repulsive violence he'd unleashed on Urik. The aliens' potent fear of him had already unnerved her. After seeing why, she didn't know what to think. Was this man the monster they claimed he was? Their concern certainly seemed valid. How could she possibly be attracted to such a man? Oddly enough, the powerful attraction she'd felt before remained just as strong even now, leaving an uncomfortable twist in her stomach. She could still feel the press of his lips against hers and the tingle that lingered long after. Heat seared her cheeks pink at the memory, announcing the internal turmoil to all.

Torak approached her. "Did you follow me?" he asked in a strange language.

Kinety spoke normally, knowing he spoke English. "No," she answered, stepping closer.

Arnie looked back and forth between them. "You can understand him?" he asked in amazement, but Kinety was too busy looking at Torak to register the question.

Torak's gaze trailed down over her, then paused on Kinety's lopsided fatigues. With a frown, he deliberately compared it to Arnie's bloody attire. "You lied to me?" he hissed, preparing to be offended.

Kinety recaptured his gaze. "Not a word," she swore.

The denial effectively dialed the villain's temper back. "Have you been harmed?" he demanded, noticing the blood on her neck and the clamp on her wrist.

Deek and Jael both shifted nervous eyes to her.

Kinety shook her head. "No."

Torak directed his next question to Deek, then Jael. "Why did you take her?"

A look of utter bewilderment twisted Jael's innocent face, and Deek shook his head emphatically, insisting he had nothing to do with it.

Torak accepted their ignorance and returned his attention to her. "Explain yourself," he said, inching forward another step.

Kinety paused awkwardly, trying to decide where the beginning was and how best to explain why she was onboard. "After you—we ... ," she began, then selected a different start. "I ... went back ... for my keys. There were two spaceships. Aliens were collecting soldiers and shooting anyone not wearing camouflage. Someone gave me this and ... ," she touched the crooked shirt. "I woke up on the floor and saw," she glanced at Deek, "him programming a computer—the soldiers were in tubes, in a pod. So, I reversed it and sent it home because he was gonna send it to—"

"Don't!" Deek threw his little hand forward. *"Don't tell him!"* he thought-screamed, startling her.

Torak slung his hand toward the little alien, instantly silencing him. Deek gasped audibly and clawed at his own throat.

Kinety jumped backward against Arnie.

"Send them where?" Torak asked her calmly.

"He'll kill them," Deek choked out desperately. *"He'll kill them all!"*

Arnie gripped her arm, ready to yank her back. "What's going on?"

Kinety fought the urge to get behind him. "Tooji wants to know where the pod is going. The alien says if he finds out, he'll kill our men."

"Then, don't tell him," warned the soldier.

Torak gave Arnie a warning glare and paced closer, keeping the conversation between himself and her. "Where was the pod going, Kinety?"

"Don't ... tell him!" the alien managed, struggling to remain conscious against Torak's energetic hold.

Kinety watched Torak, noticing for the first time how alien he actually looked. His pupils were normal, but the irises of his eyes were stark white beneath an electric blue haze or crackling aura that distinguished the iris from the sclera. The effect was freaking awesome and borderline god-like, but she wasn't about to say so. His dark hair was a bit longer than she'd realized in the meadow and scattered haphazardly around his head in a charming, silky mess. The ends almost reached his shoulders, adding a wild touch to his appearance, but that's where the warm fuzzy feeling ended. His physique, as impressive as it was, was actually somewhat intimidating and added potency to the air of explosive volatility he carried with him. He was dangerous, and now she understood why he'd laughed when she claimed to be in love with him.

Speaking of his temper, he was coming toward her with a rather perilous look on his face. The urge to recoil in fear was a strong one but pointless. She reminded herself that now wasn't the time to back down and stepped forward instead to face him. "Is that true?" she demanded, hoping it wasn't. "You'll kill them?"

His expression confirmed this. "This is not your war," he warned.

Kinety raised her chin. His eyes were magnetic, and it was hard not to get lost in them, but she managed. "Then don't involve my men," she countered angrily, sounding far braver than she felt.

"Your men?" Again, his attention dropped to her attire as if doubting her original denial. "How are they yours?"

Back and forth, all eyes shifted, following the spat.

Kinety reminded herself that she and Arnie were now on kamikaze suicide missions with pretty much no chance for survival, a fate determined the moment she'd ejected the pod without being on it. At this point, there was nothing to fear because the outcome had already been decided. There was no script, no prepared speech, and Kinety had no idea how to answer this jerk. She had no choice but to wing it and die like a big girl. Adding energy to her voice, she made as if to jab Torak in the chest and let it fly. "Those soldiers are supposed to defend humans from Earth. I don't know what this is about, Tooji, but I'm the only human here. That makes them," she pointed at Arnie, "my men! You have no business kidnapping them."

Arnie, standing silently beside her, understood only Kinety's words but followed the conversation. The two aliens remained absolutely motionless, watching the heated argument in awe.

Torak's eyes glittered at the accusation. "*That* crime belongs to your friends," he said hotly and slung the choking Deek away, "not to me."

Her glare blazed in offense. "Those little minions are *not* my friends!"

Torak raised his head, believing her at last, and turned to the panel. Quickly, he password-locked the route to Zahrá Che, sealing the coordinates, then linked a tracking signal to monitor the craft's location and communications. "Wait for me," he said, softening his tone significantly. "I will come for you."

But Kinety was too angry now to diffuse so quickly. Emphatically, she shook her head. "Why? Do you want me, or do you want information?" she demanded. "Because I'm not about to tell you where they are if you're going to hurt them, especially over some stupid war."

Anger flashed in Torak's eyes, and, for the first time, he raised his voice. "But you will allow them to be used as fodder in their stupid war?" he demanded with a point at the aliens.

Kinety paused, unable to respond. She had absolutely no idea what he was talking about. "Fodder?"

While he had the upper hand, Torak continued, still speaking alien. "The Zahrá Che," he jabbed a finger at the hated creatures, "are using the Terran as a cheat. I cannot allow that!"

Kinety didn't know what Terran was, but there was no time to ask.

Deek's voice broke in right here. *"We have no choice,"* he insisted. *"The Saphiridians have gone too far. The Gaki are slaughtering our people!"*

"Who are the Gaki?" asked Kinety.

In a scatter of black curls, Torak whirled on Deek. "You started this war!"

Deek cringed in fear. "Eeeee!" he screeched aloud.

Kinety stepped in front of Deek before Torak could kill the frightened creature. "Wait—you two are making my men fight your war?" she asked them both in disbelief.

"Why are you defending him!" demanded Torak.

Kinety slung her hand, silencing him. "Deek! Is this true?"

Deek blinked large, guilty eyes at her but didn't deny the charge.

Heat seared Kinety's cheeks. "They're *my* soldiers! They're supposed to protect me and the citizens of my world," she railed specifically at Deek, "not participate in some bullshit war you can't win on your own. And they aren't yours to slaughter, whatever your reasons," she said, rounding on Torak.

"I have a job to do," he said darkly.

Kinety's temper flared at Torak's tone. "Not if I can help it!"

The aliens went wide-eyed and ducked, certain she would die.

But Torak didn't kill her. Instead, he laughed, barely able to believe her audacity. "You are the *worst* coward I have ever met," he told her incredulously.

Kinety plopped her hands on her hips. "Tooji, I'm serious."

"So am I!" he railed.

Deek and Jael raised their heads, looked at each other, then continued watching in disbelief.

"Look," she said, trying to reason with him, "I don't care about your war. I just want my people back … unharmed."

Torak looked ready to snap her neck. "You cannot get them back, Kinety. You cannot do anything to save them, and I cannot allow them to be used against me. I will complete my mission … with or without you."

"Without."

And the fight was over.

Torak straightened abruptly and peered down at her, wounded by her reply. The expression lasted only an instant, however, before his features went hard again. His hologram flickered, indicating the connection was fading. "That is unfortunate," he said quietly.

A jagged break crawled across Kinety's heart, but she held her ground. "Please, don't hurt them," she tried again, her voice a mere whisper.

Another lingering stare formed between the two, reminding Kinety of the rendezvous in the meadow just before he'd kissed her.

He moved his hand as if to touch her face. "The bad guy," he reminded her, almost apologetically.

"Tooji."

The name struck home.

Torak's beautiful eyes narrowed on her in irritation. "Gaaah!" he growled, scaring the frightened aliens again. Angrily, he swept his hand, sending all the blasters skittering across the floor to Arnie, who stood in unblinking silence.

Deek and Jael covered their heads and curled into balls.

As Arnie picked up the weapons, Torak tore his glare from Kinety and thrust a hand toward Deek, pinning the hyperventilating creature firmly against a nearby panel. Confident he had the alien's attention, the unstable hologram clamped his teeth in hatred. "A vow," he warned, his tone deadly. "Tell your filthy emperor," he pointed at Kinety, "if she is harmed, I swear, there will be nothing but an asteroid belt when I am done."

Deek, panting in horror, gaped at the awful message.

Torak flickered again, and Deek fell to the floor. Glowering in anger, his electric gaze turned back to Kinety. "I will find you," he buzzed.

Kinety didn't answer.

An instant later, Torak was gone.

Chapter 4

Kinety stared at Torak's empty spot for several seconds before her knees buckled. Arnie hooked her waist before she could fall and faced the two gaping aliens, both staggering clumsily to their feet. They looked at Urik's dead body and then at the humans. Heavy silence stretched between the two species. There was nothing to say.

Much more relaxed now that he was the only one armed, Arnie led Kinety down the hall, claiming the back of the spaceship as theirs. After a quick check, they discovered that the spot they'd tumbled into during take-off was, in fact, a restroom of sorts. However, considering the tension between the two species, it was inevitable they would be left to figure out the details regarding its use on their own.

In the pod room, which Kinety and Arnie had decided to call it, the two Earthlings selected a comfortable-looking patch of floor. Both were zapped of strength and still unsteady after being shot by the alien blasters. Barely speaking, Kinety removed the thin camouflage jacket and made a makeshift bed for them to lay on. It was misshapen and lumpy but kept them somewhat separated from the frigid metal floor. There was no propriety, no formality regarding their sleeping arrangements. The two had no choice but to huddle together for warmth.

"What is a Terran?" she asked in monotone.

Arnie exhaled wearily. "It means of the Earth," he said with his eyes closed. "Terrestrial."

"Earthling?"

"Basically."

Neither was interested in discussing the topic further and soon both were asleep.

Sometime later, Kinety felt Arnie jerk awake and woke with a start.

Deek was in the room, glaring large eyes at them and clutching two clear pale blue blobs in his hand. The alien hesitated cautiously as Arnie rose to an elbow. The soldier merely watched him, though, so the alien crept closer. When it was clear he was in no danger, the unfriendly creature set the two blobs on the clothing mat by their feet. *"Eat,"* he thought to Kinety.

"Thank you," she said aloud.

He didn't answer.

"Deek ... where are we going?"

"Zahrá Che," he answered shortly.

"Za-RA-chee?" she enunciated, propping on a hip and brushing her hair back. "How long until we get there?"

"Eat," he snapped again and turned to go.

"Deek! Wait. Can we have blankets?" she blurted before he could leave. "We're cold."

The alien stopped, rather irritated by the request, then marched out. Moments later, two tiny white bodysuits, identical to the ones the aliens wore, sailed into the room and landed on the floor. A quick examination revealed compression garments designed to form-fit to whatever shape was put inside. Both stretched the suits over their clothes. This was Kinety's third layer of clothing. She looked rather lumpy now but didn't care. Warm for the first time since their abduction, the two sat on the cold floor and sampled the clear blobs of food.

As bizarre as it seemed, it appeared the blobs were actually chunks of nutritionated water that literally occupied all three physical states —solid, liquid, and gas—at once. There was no flavor, or so it seemed, because she'd lost all sense of taste and smell since arriving on the spaceship. It boasted a fluid consistency lighter than melted marshmallow and shook like jello, yet was heavier than air, drier than liquid, and possessed enough surface tension to mimic a solid. This certainly wasn't the most delicious meal they'd ever had, but they were glad to be having it. During their luxurious breakfast, the two sat against the wall and looked awkwardly at each other.

To Kinety, Arnie appeared well-groomed and healthy, with sun-bronzed skin and an unhurried manner about him. His voice was low, his presence astute and self-confident. He looked intelligent, he sounded intelligent. She was glad and sad that he was with her.

"The assassin," he began in a gruff voice. "You knew him?"

"Yes," Kinety admitted, then quickly corrected herself. "No. I met him."

"When?"

"After I met you, on the way to the car."

Arnie frowned. "In the field?"

Kinety nodded.

But Arnie wasn't convinced. Slowly, he shook his head, then sped it up. "No. Y'all had chemistry and shit. Are you part of the alien program?"

Kinety nibbled her blob, prolonging the eating experience since it gave her something to do with her hands. "What? No," she said, smashing a piece between two fingers to test the consistency.

"Are you a government agent?"

"No," she chuckled and ate the piece.

"A spy?"

"Nope. I'm a nothing. I can't even find a job," she snorted in sour amusement.

"You model. That's a job."

"Only when I need money. Rixton hates it. He thinks I'm too intelligent to be so wrapped up in looks and says I need skills, not a pretty face."

Arnie pondered that for a minute. "What can you do?" he asked, trying to find a comfortable position.

Kinety shrugged and made balls out of torn pieces of blob. "Not a whole lot. Rixton says I'm observant, but I don't think so. I always miss the basics because I'm so busy noticing stupid stuff. He thinks that's a skill, though I fail to see how. I can hack," she added with a glance.

Arnie's brows lifted. "Computers?"

"Mm hmm."

"Are you and your brother close?"

Kinety stuck one ball to another ball to see if they would cling to each other. "We don't get along at all, but we're close. He's my bestie."

"Is he?"

"Mm-hmm. I'd rather be hiking with Rixton than shopping with the girls or going on movie dates. He's probably tired of me, but I enjoy his company."

Arnie gave her a funny look and crossed his ankles. "That's unusual for siblings."

It was, and she knew it. "I like Rixton. He's overprotective but doesn't treat me like an idiot or an arm ornament. He teaches me survival skills and how to fight and fix things. Many men aren't attracted to that, so we spend a lot of time together."

Arnie's brow lifted again. "Are you telling me you can't find a boyfriend, either?" he chortled, thoroughly amused by this.

Kinety kicked his boot and ate a ball. "You laugh," she scolded, smiling, "but when they realize I can out-fight them and out-camp them and out-hunt them and out-mechanic them, they don't hang around."

Arnie paused, waiting for the rest. "Really."

"Yes, really."

"And?"

Kinety didn't know how else to put it. "And I also won't sleep with them," she admitted, eating the last of her playthings.

Arnie laughed.

"And then there's the brother," she added, on a roll now. "He runs them off pretty quick. I don't think in the land of men Rixton is particularly friendly."

"He's not."

"So," Kinety spread her hands and leaned forward now that she had nothing else to do, "what do you do for fun? Do you have hobbies?"

He almost shrugged. "I … weld."

"Weld what?" she prompted.

"Metal."

That was it. No elaboration. Nothing.

Kinety inclined her head for more, but he was done. She changed the topic. "How do you know Rixton?"

Arnie made a face and shrugged again. "Prior missions. Saved my ass a few times."

"Did he?" she said in interest. "He's mentioned you before but never elaborated."

Arnie sat there.

"Well?" she prompted.

Suddenly, he looked like he'd just been hooked up to a polygraph machine. "I trust him. One of the few," he added. "I consider him a brother."

Kinety waited again for more details but then realized that was it. It was apparent rather quickly that he wasn't used to chatting about himself, which wouldn't do at all. "You can't just stop talking now. I'm bored out of my mind," she declared, gesturing to the television-less room. "Say something. Ask something."

Amused, he propped against the wall. "Alright. The assassin. Tell me about him," he said, bringing the conversation back to its origin.

Kinety ran her fingers through her hair and fluffed it as she decided where to begin. "There's nothing to tell, really," she flubbed. "I saw him in the field—bumped into him actually … in a cluster of trees. He was larger than average, though not quite your size, and impressively muscular. He was in a cloak with his face barely visible beneath the hood. It was his looks that stopped me. Even in the shadows, he was handsome, but it was his eyes that did it. I've never seen eyes like that. I was too busy staring to realize I was staring. Then, he dropped the hood. Holy shit—it was waaay worse with the hood off! Dude. Was. Cute!"

Arnie chuckled.

Kinety's gaze dropped as she replayed the encounter in her mind. "At first, I couldn't understand him. He spoke in a different language. But then he touched me," she tapped her temple, "and suddenly I could understand him. I'm not sure what he did, but I still have a headache," she grumbled.

"Touched you?"

"Like this, on my temple and the back of my head. I saw a blue flash. At first, I thought I'd imagined it, but now I'm not so sure," she said with a wave. "I didn't focus on that, though. My heart was playing a game of hopscotch, and that was it—I wanted his phone number. I tried pretty hard to reel him in, but," she flicked a brow, "he rejected me."

Arnie grunted. "I didn't see that."

Kinety gave him a puzzled look. "Why do you say that?"

"What I saw wasn't rejection. You two didn't act like you'd just met," he said simply.

Embarrassment pinked Kinety's cheeks. "Our encounter was a bit out of line," she admitted, tucking a strand behind her ear. "Rixton would kill me."

Arnie folded his arms over his middle, probably more to keep warm, but the gesture fit. "Nothing to tell, huh?"

Kinety could only imagine how this was going to sound. When Arnie angled his head, indicating he was ready for the details, she traced her finger over the random camouflage design on her knee. "He introduced himself as Tooji, not Torak. When he asked who I was, I introduced myself as his future wife," she said with a blush. "I was teasing him, of course. The look on his face was hilarious. He seemed almost insecure, which didn't match his appearance at all. He asked if I knew who he was," she stalled here to wobble her head, "and I said, 'The man I just fell in love with.'"

Arnie gave her a funny look. "That was ballsy."

Kinety fluffed her hair, well aware of that, and giggled at the change in Arnie's expression. "It surprised him, too. He kept asking over and over if I knew who he was, then commented that it was dangerous to say such things to a man I didn't know. Normally I would agree, but I thought he was one of your guys, so I was playing with him. Rixton said y'all were waiting for the bad guy. Well, Tooji referred to himself as the bad guy, so," she spread her hands matter-of-factly, "I made the most logical assumption. I told him I was a good guy, which made us mortal enemies—kinda … playing along because I knew Rixton would never introduce us."

"I guess that explains why he was so confused," said Arnie.

"Yeah. Even with the misunderstanding, though, the whole encounter was short and sweet and silly, but," her voice dropped to a whisper, "kinda powerful."

Arnie waited for the rest.

Kinety plucked at a string. "I kissed him," she admitted with an awkward peek. "A perfect stranger."

Arnie's narrowed gaze was unreadable, his tone without inflection. "Did you?"

Kinety grimaced and wrinkled her nose. She was still bewildered herself and could only imagine how bad it sounded to her new acquaintance. "Yeah … and still bombed the interview. I'm just not very good with men."

"Why is that?"

"I don't know. Last time I liked a guy, I tried being shy and timid, and he left me for someone more interesting. This time with Tooji, I tried a different approach and ended up coming on too strong," she supposed. "It ran him off. He handed me this and left."

Arnie took the round object and rolled it around in his hand. "It's a rock."

Kinety sighed. "Alas, it is indeed a rock."

Arnie handed it back. "So, what happened earlier?" he asked, propping back against the wall again. "The argument."

Kinety glanced toward the front of the craft, knowing exactly what he was talking about. "Tooji wanted to know where our soldiers were, but Beep and Bop," she indicated the aliens, "said he would kill them if he found out. I told him if that was true, I wanted nothing to do with him. I was a bit rash, I guess. I mean … I know he's an assassin and probably psycho, but he was—is—reeeally attractive to me. It's almost magnetic. I didn't think I'd ever see him again, and then there he was and … I am so stupid, Arnie! Getting into a shouting match with him certainly isn't going to make him want me and sure as hell isn't gonna help save our boys," she fretted, then exhaled heavily. "I didn't handle that well. I kinda blew it."

"Want you?" Arnie echoed incredulously. "Torak is your enemy."

"Well, he did tell the aliens not to hurt me," she argued, hoping that meant something.

Arnie leaned closer, frowning now, and looped a thick arm over his knee. "If Torak's mission is to find and kill our men, then it's our job to stop him."

He was right, and Kinety knew it. Reluctantly, she nodded. "Apparently, we're hovering, waiting for a wormhole to open."

This surprised him. "We're not traveling?"

Kinety didn't think so.

"You can speak their language," he said, changing his tone to an accusing one.

She gestured in the affirmative.

"How?"

"I don't know."

"Can you read it?"

She frowned, remembering the symbols on Deek's computer. "I think so."

"How?" he asked again.

"I don't know," she insisted. "He touched me and it happened."

This interested him greatly and he paused for a minute, allowing some of the pieces to put themselves together. "You said you hacked Rixton's computer," he continued pensively.

Kinety fanned her fingers, watching the heat distortion and wondering what the hell was wrong with her vision. "Are your eyes acting funny?"

"No. Can you do it again? Can you hack another computer?"

Kinety's green eyes lit up. Hesitantly, she blinked at the screen Deek had used and lowered her hand. It worked similarly to technology on Earth, only more advanced, suggesting one had been reverse-engineered from the other. "Maybe."

Arnie pulled her up from the floor and took out his phone. Of course, there was no service. "See if you can figure out how to get a signal to Earth. If we're not moving, we may still be close enough."

It took a while to get the gist of the alien system. The unfamiliar symbols were new to her. It took concentration for the meanings to organize in her head, but once Kinety figured it out, a whole world opened up. "This is just like an internet," she said, looking through all the gibberish, "but universal rather than global."

"Find Earth."

That wasn't as easy because she had to locate it on the star map first, which took a while. The first thing she did was search through galaxies to find the Milky Way but wasn't sure where to start since there was no point of reference. So, she went into the recently archived files, which took forever to locate on the unfamiliar system, and did a search history. This brought her to the correct arm of the galaxy. From there, it was simply a matter of scrolling through and rotating the 3D star systems until she recognized a constellation. By the time she found it, she had developed a general understanding of the system and realized how easy it would have been to simply type in the name she wanted.

Already, home was very far away.

Each object in space had the known names listed, and the points of reference were the center of each solar system—typically the largest sun. Reference in deep space was relative to whichever solar system was chosen as the reference point and the numbers instantly adjusted, implying that there was no center to the universe. What she did learn, however, was that space was real darn big and that it would be very easy to get lost inside it.

Her headache continued in earnest.

Eventually, she located the star Sol and counted three planets back to Earth.

Arnie sat forward on the hover-chair. "Show me how to work it," he said eagerly.

Kinety showed him how to expand the screen and rotate the Earth. Focusing hard and moving quickly, Arnie located a military base near their abduction site and expanded it until a collection of streets was visible. He couldn't read the words or understand the symbols, but he knew exactly what he was looking for. Closer and closer, he zoomed until he found the building he wanted. When he stretched into the view they couldn't see inside, but lit symbols appeared scattered throughout the building. Some were moving.

"What is that?" he asked.

Kinety touched one of the symbols and began reading. "They're computers. I can see right into them. The ones that are moving must be cell phones. Oh, my goodness," she muttered, selecting an active computer and reading the screen, "I think this stuff is classified."

"Yes, it is," Arnie said in disgust, then waved his finger over the computers, attempting to select the one he wanted.

"What are you doing?"

"Trying to decide which computer belongs to my commander Colonel Nelson," he said and selected one. He glanced at the commander's badge embroidered on her jacket. "That's his uniform you're wearing, by the way. He was planning to join us."

"I'll be sure to dry clean it when we get back," she said, distracted by the strange keyboard by her hands. "These letters aren't in any language humans would know. I can understand them, but he can't. How are we going to communicate?"

Arnie scooted closer. "Go into his computer and pull up a keyboard. If we can control the computer remotely, I can type directly onto the screen."

Kinety created a link, and the contents of Colonel Nelson's screen appeared. "He's on it."

"Good. Take it from him."

Using her finger on the touch-panel in front of her, Kinety took the cursor from the commander, scanned his document until she found the letter combination SOS in a random word, and made circles around it to attract his attention.

There was a pause.

After a moment, the cursor highlighted the letters SOS from the Earth end of the link, and the letters went bold.

Arnie bounced in the seat beside her.

Moving quickly, Kinety located and summoned an on-screen keyboard, opened a new document, then scooted aside so Arnie could use it. Clicking one letter at a time, he introduced himself.

Captain Arnold Jagger, Black Frog, Team Two and hacker Kinety Dash. Alien abduction, two Zahrá Che ships, Pine Gulch Canyon. Apparent Objective: Collect Soldiers. Live soldiers in transport pods headed for alien war—extreme peril. Dash reversed ship #1 transport pod to Earth. We are separated from soldiers. Ship #2 unaccounted for. M

After a delay due to distance, the commander answered by placing the cursor beneath Arnie's text and rapidly typing back.

Pod recovered. All survived. Got satellite footage of entire abduction. A

Aliens took uniformed soldiers only, killed civilians. R

Reason? Y

Unknown. Hostile. Do not approach. H

Kinety Dash, the model? A

Yes. Sister to Sergeant Rixton Dash, abductee. After close encounter of Fifth Kind, she can communicate and read, unexplained. I cannot. D

Fifth?! Kinety Dash is civilian. A

Yes. Disguised in uniform, yours, actually. Outranks me now ;-) L

Tracker signals scrambled. What is your location? I

Unknown. En route to Zahrá Che, coordinates unknown. On ship with 3-1 aliens. Communication possibly temporary, using onboard system. Universal internet. Request Rank and ROE Release. T

Approved. T

Dash: Black. L

Confirmed. E

Where are soldiers headed?

Destination known. Message unsecured. EE

State soldier destination.

Commander? EEE

State soldier destination.

Arnie sat back. "We're being intercepted."

"How do you know?"

He pointed to the capital letters scattered throughout each message. "We're typing a nursery rhyme. Mary Had A Little Lamb. This message here," he tapped the one asking about the soldiers' destination, "should have been L, but it has no letter. I repeated mine twice, each time adding the letter I ended with. I'll bet you a nickel it's your boyfriend."

Kinety quickly severed the communication. "What is rank and ROE release?"

"It means I am not bound by military rank. I now outrank any soldiers I rescue. I am authorized to do whatever is necessary for their survival, and I do not have to follow Rules of Engagement with the aliens."

That made sense. She brushed her hair from her eyes. "You said 'Dash: Black' and the commander confirmed. What was that about?"

"You are now top secret and working for the government," he said and drummed his hands on the panel.

"Nice. A job." Kinety gripped her head in weary fatigue. "So, now what?"

"Give me your cell phone."

Kinety dug beneath the oversized fatigues to her original jeans and pulled her cell phone from her pocket. He took it and went straight into the advanced settings file. There, he inserted a code from memory and handed it back to her.

"What did you do?"

"I made it Wi-Fi charge compatible. We don't have cords, but we may still be able to use these."

"Really?"

"Our phones are made from outdated alien technology. Their computers should recognize them and charge the batteries automatically." Arnie pushed their phones forward. "See if you can connect these to this universal internet and to each other. I'm going to figure out how to use that bathroom," he said, standing.

*****

There was no way to measure time out in space. Years, months, days, hours, and minutes held no relevance anymore, at least from a classical perspective. By the end of three sleep cycles, Kinety was convinced an Earth week had passed. Arnie argued that their circadian rhythm would not yet have become that distorted and, therefore, only three days had passed. This argument lasted several days, or at least a few hours, and resulted in only one fistfight, some arm-wrestling, and several intense rounds of pea-knuckle.

Eventually, they chose to maintain the familiar method, since that's what they knew, and because Arnie was bigger. So, it was decided.

According to this logic, the wormhole opened on the third day. The warning came mere moments before entry when Deek arrived and instructed them to strap in. *"We're entering the wormhole,"* he thought simply and, with a swipe of his hand, produced the appropriate restraint equipment in a swirl of liquid metal.

Without further explanation, he left.

Arnie and Kinety looked at each other apprehensively, then sat down on the seats. Instantly, restraining material oozed over them.

Kinety tugged at the restraints. "Why do we need to—hoooly shhhhhhhh … !" she gasped as an indescribable pull smashed them into the smooth metal. Spaghettification streaks stretched everything into distorted waves. Color fragmented. Sound liquified. Their lungs locked. Time slowed. As if through sludge, she curled her distorted hand around Arnie's, squeezed for dear life, and blacked out.

When Kinety woke, she was pissed. After figuring out how to get out of the restraints, which took a minute, she marched into the flight deck and let the aliens have it. "You could have warned us, you little minions!" she barked.

Without acknowledging her, Deek reached sideways and turned off the gravity.

Kinety's hair and feet lifted into the air. With a yip, she slapped at a lip in the portal.

At the same time, from the other room, Arnie let out a "Woah, woah, woah!"

Instantly, Kinety's poise eroded. To hell with polite! To hell with diplomacy! She wanted results. Without a word, she floated toward the tiny restroom and gathered a few globs of water, which, by the way, were quite easy to carry in space. No cup was required. A simple, energetic launch at the back of a bulbous head was all that was needed.

Neither alien saw it coming.

Water droplets splattered against their heads and went everywhere. The aliens whirled, aghast at the assault.

Now, Kinety had their attention. "I said," she repeated, hovering in the air, "you could have warned us."

Deek gave her a sideways glare, fully intending to ignore her complaints. *You survived.*

"Look here, you little assholes! I have had enough of this. From now on, you will both treat us with courtesy or Arnie and I will move in here with you and teach you both some damn manners."

Jael deliberately ignored her. *"Shame there isn't an airlock between compartments."*

"Just ignore her. She'll go away," said Deek.

Kinety's green eyes narrowed. "Torak's warning to you was clear," she said from a sphere of floating hair. "Either you be nice, or I'll get on the radio and tell him you're being mean to me."

The aliens recoiled in horror. Behind an impressive glare, Deek's long, skinny finger shifted to the gravity button. Click.

Wham!

Kinety landed in a puddle of ankles and elbows.

In the back, a half-curse, a thud, and a grunt occurred—in that order.

Pissed again, Kinety raised her head and, through a curtain of tangled hair, found both aliens had turned in their seats to face her, giving her their undivided attention. Glowering, she climbed to her feet and pointed behind her. "That floor is hard and cold," she railed. "I want something soft to lay on—now!"

"There is no soft, hairy Earthling," snapped Deek in a condescending tone. *"This is a pod transport."*

"Then figure something out, or I will personally toss your little asses out of those seats and claim them."

The aliens balked at her foul language, but both knew she wasn't joking.

Entirely put out by the request, Deek's four-foot frame marched angrily to the blank wall she and Arnie had just unstrapped from. Scowling, he ran his hand down the smooth surface. As if by magic, a bunk appeared. Without a single word, the irate alien stomped his little booted feet out of the room, leaving his passengers to enjoy their good fortune.

"And warm it up in here!" she shouted after him.

When he was gone, Arnie flashed her a brilliant smile and gave her a silent high-five. For several seconds, they danced in quiet celebration. Happy with the results, both turned, smiling, and blinked down at the bed. Their smiles faded. It was roomy and spacious and could easily be described as luxurious … if one was a four-foot-tall, forty-five-pound alien with a bulbous head. For two humans, especially one Arnie's size, it was a microscopic loveseat.

Their happy expressions turned to awkward grimaces. They would have to share … but how?

Kinety, clutching a stiff back, stood over it. "That little roach!" she hissed. "He could have done that anytime."

Arnie didn't care. "Works for me," he said, lying diagonal across it. He took up the entire bunk.

Kinety scratched her head.

Arnie indicated a spot for her to arrange herself and shifted to accommodate her climb. Holding an arm aloft, he helped her on. She tucked herself around him well enough that she wouldn't fall off and tried to adjust for comfort. The first three or four minutes were excessively awkward, with much uneasy blinking and more than a few muttered apologies due to the intimate proximity. By five minutes, they were in place and neither cared.

Happily beyond that hurdle, the two spent the next few hours or years honing their new skill—alien manipulation. Clearly, the aliens preferred racial segregation, while the humans weren't as bothered by the intermingling. As a result, the humans found themselves with significant bargaining power. With Arnie coaching, Kinety managed to improve conditions considerably. Thus began the second half of their journey.

Now that their arrangements were more comfortable, it was time to get answers. Over the next forever, the ambitious abductees ended up with a second bunk, fresh suits, and a bit of basic knowledge about the war. Kinety had to ask it in pieces, but, eventually, they were able to determine this:

The Zahrá Che, which was the name of the planet, the people, and the language, were at war with the Saphiridians, a humanoid hybrid species, over a land dispute. Recently, the war had turned particularly brutal, causing the Zahrá Che no alternative but to employ the aid of Earthling soldiers to save their species. Torak, the annihilator, was Saphiridian.

That was it. Beyond that, Deek would not cooperate.

Chapter 5

On the fourth day after the wormhole, the ship began a descending orbit around the war-torn planet Zahrá Che. Deek hurried in with handcuff restraints for Kinety and Arnie to wear for the landing. Only, the idea didn't sit well.

"Here. Put these on," ordered the alien.

Kinety scowled. "No."

"Please."

"No."

"If they see you unrestrained, they'll think we've been hijacked."

"We have been hijacked."

"They might start shooting."

"Then tell them not to shoot."

"We have no communication."

"Use the radio."

"We can't, so they don't know we're coming."

"Why don't they know we're coming?"

"Because, obstinate Earthling, we've been hijacked. Wear the restraints."

"No."

The moment the craft touched down, a liquid hole opened in the outer wall. A squad of fierce-looking, heavily armed aliens in white suits and almond-eyed helmets rushed in. Deek and Jael were held at gunpoint and a team entered, weapons drawn. By the time the aliens reached the back room, Kinety and Arnie were holding the restraints and did, in fact, appear to be prisoners.

The two in charge gestured, motioning them forward to the flight deck. Behind the armed soldiers, an alien of apparent rank approached, his hardened face a mask of questions.

Right away, Deek stepped forward, hands raised in some salute. *"Sin Chin,"* he said respectfully.

"Why did you land on autopilot?" demanded Sin Chin, a split second before spotting Deek's guests. *"What is the meaning of this? Why were we not advised of passengers prior to your arrival? These Earthlings don't belong here!"*

Deek inclined his head and quickly informed the high-ranking creature of the event aboard the spacecraft, Torak's involvement, and Urik's death. After that, a cacophony of blended thoughts erupted, making the conversation hard for Kinety to follow.

"Torak?" the official echoed, clearly startled. *"Did he find the base?"*

"No."

"And the troops?"

"Our cargo was sabotaged, but Torak learned nothing."

"And he let you live?"

Deek paused for a moment, perhaps in shame, then pointed, leading all eyes to Kinety. *"Torak discovered his primitive humanoid companion aboard our craft."*

The aliens recoiled, and the mental chatter grew louder.

"Companion!" sputtered Sin Chin.

"Yes. When Torak discovered she was aboard," Deek's voice continued, *"he locked our destination and hijacked our communication. I attempted to get a message to you regarding our passengers, specifically that his wife was aboard. The transmission was intercepted by a public scanner. Torak also sent a message for the emperor,"* he said, passing a device to the superior.

Sin Chin read it and whirled, throwing his arms in horror. *"Inform the emperor! Quickly!"*

A guard rushed down the ramp on scrawny legs and vanished inside a nearby building. In tandem, the thoughts coming from the staring soldiers turned hostile. In a tangled myriad of thinking, Kinety picked up rabid anger, nasty insults, and more than a few quiet death threats. She and Arnie were surrounded and, at blaster point, detained atop a ramp while the aliens awaited instructions.

The telepathic noise in Kinety's head curled her lashes, and she had to focus to hear her own thoughts. "We aren't welcome here," she told Arnie.

Arnie nodded slowly. "I'm picking that up," he assured.

Kinety looked out at a poorly lit world. It had two suns casting double shadows across the structures of an aerial city. One sun was red and massive, the other tiny and white. Despite the two, it was cold. The dry air was thin. On it hung the odor of salt and dead fish with a background hint of iron. There were no clouds in the sky, only an orange haze. Noise from the city around them was muffled and sluggish without humidity to carry the sounds.

Zahrá Che was not a healthy planet. Even in the odd sunlight, everything here glowed, including Kinety's own fingers, which left a trail of heat when she moved them. "What the hell?"

Everywhere she looked, she noticed pale light and wondered why. All across the city, tall, thin spires or needles topped with large round, white globes reached high into the sky, each a cross between a water tower and a radio antenna. To Kinety, they looked like long, thin teardrops—just upside down. Another oddity about the globes was that they seemed to lean toward the sleek spaceships when they passed as if magnetized. These globes glowed the brightest, though this was only noticeable when one swayed, leaving a halo behind as it moved. In the distance, the layered, aerial city stretched far into the horizon, with about fifteen more antennas scattered throughout.

Just overhead, several spaceships hovered about Deek and Jael's craft, heavy with weapons and spaced at intervals around them. Kinety could feel the powerful rumbles more than she could hear them, which was weird. On the ground far below the platform where their ship had landed, scattered alien civilians moved about with unshaded eyes.

The ground rolled.

About here, Kinety noticed how dizzy she was. She was short of breath and quite unsteady. As the sensation washed over her, the cuff around her wrist blinked to life, stinging sharply at first, and heat rolled up her arm. Her breath returned in a wheeze. A few seconds later, the weakness faded. Her vision cleared, and the sting dulled to a tolerable ache. The cuff had worked its magic. Whatever magic that was had regulated the gasses in her blood so she could breathe the air. She was struck with another impressive headache on top of a throbbing wrist, which did nothing for her mood, but the sting of the cuff was suddenly welcome.

Arnie seemed to be experiencing the same thing. Inhaling shallow breaths, he busily examined his own cuff with a grimace before calming himself and drawing slow, deep breaths. A look passed between them, both very aware of what had just happened.

The messenger alien appeared moments later. *"His majesty will give audience,"* he called in a mental shout.

Kinety translated.

Arnie took her hand in a firm grip. "No matter what happens." he warned, "stay beside me."

Escorting aliens gave the abductees a satisfying push. In rigid formation, the two were ushered into an expansive building and surrounded by more glaring soldiers; these just as unfriendly. They were all nearly identical, with only very subtle differences distinguishing one from the other. Their mannerisms, personalities, and voices—Thoughts?—were where the true differences took place, yet even these were subtle. Everything about these creatures was symmetric, angular, and geometric, a style that spanned from their clothing to the architecture of the city to the decorations inside the building.

Kinety didn't know where to look first. Her mind whirred, busily comparing the details of this alien world to those in her own world. The building they entered was sleek, like the ship, with silvery blue tones. It had silent, pocket-style doors and windows that faded into white walls without panes or sills. There was a colorless floor made of … something. Whatever it was eluded her, though it was decidedly not linoleum. Metal? Wait … glass? This mesmerized her for a moment before Arnie tugged her along.

One alien separated from the receiving group, this one slightly taller than the others, and stepped forward to greet them. He and his troops wore red, silver-trim uniforms made of a different material than the white spacesuits worn by the fliers. The compression suits they'd worn in space were designed to distribute body heat evenly inside. She didn't know the purpose of the red uniforms.

Kinety forgot about the floor and stared at their glowing chests. These suits had different heat patterns, too. If these red ones had a functional purpose beyond fashion, it wasn't obvious. She was about to ask Arnie if he could see the heat emitting from them when an alien approached her. She noticed he walked with a silly kick-step and looked at his feet. He wore teensy little boots that cast a reflective shadow on the weird floor—like a gel shadow. It was weird.

"Savage Bride," he thought in polite disgust.

Kinety frowned up at the stoic creature, interrupted from her perusal. "Savage Bride?" she echoed, giving Arnie a questioning glance.

Arnie locked eyes on the speaker.

"I am Zodoo. Please know that the Savage Bride and her guard are welcome on planet Zahrá Che and will not be harmed."

Kinety made a face at Arnie. "His … name is Zodoo. My guard and I—the Savage Bride?—will not be harmed on planet Zahrá Che," she translated clumsily, then scanned the other glowering soldiers, taking particular note of the ones thinking they'd like to kill her. Their heat signatures were brighter around their skinny necks than the calmer ones with the warmest areas concentrated near the center of their chests.

Arnie barely acknowledged her. He was too busy studying the alien in front of them.

Kinety faced Zodoo. "My name is Kinety," she managed in awkward reply, then gestured to her companion. "This is Arnie. Where are our men?"

The unfriendly alien didn't glare, at least not outright. *"His Excellency Emperor Dinruk expects an audience. The Savage Bride is to be washed and prepared. Follow me."*

Kinety walked closer to Arnie. "He keeps calling me Savage Bride," she complained, falling into step behind the alien. "Do they think we're married?"

"Zodoo called me your guard, not your husband," he said, pulling Kinety to his other side when an alien got too close. "He isn't talking about me."

"Who does he think I'm married to?"

Arnie pondered this. "Do they mean the assassin?" he wondered beneath his breath.

"Tooji? Why would they think I'm married to Tooji?"

"Didn't he introduce you as his wife?"

"As a joke!" she clarified incredulously, then scowled at the ridiculousness. "He was being a smartass!"

"Do they know that?"

Kinety blinked at him.

A mass of Zahrá Che soldiers closed in behind them, and the two were ushered into a detoxification room. The restraints landed in a pile on the floor. To Kinety's delight, the washing process involved water. To her mortification, Arnie never left her side. Their honeymoon was undoubtedly over, even if he wasn't the husband the aliens were referring to. To Arnie's credit, she never once caught him peeking.

The toilets on planet Zahrá Che were the same as those on the spaceship, suction-style commodes that whisked waste away in a whoosh. The bizarre potties, however, were designed for little alien hineys, not human ones, and using them felt awkward. The showers were odd as well. A splash-capsule was sealed around the dirty person, and a blast of cleaning liquid coated the body from head to toe. After a quick self-rubdown—Splash!—another blast rinsed the first one away. This reminded Kinety of a cross between a dishwasher and a touchless carwash with an air mist at the end. The cleaning process took about a minute with very little water waste.

Past sopping hair, Kinety examined the nozzles, intrigued by the design.

As if it were the most natural thing in the world, Arnie pulled his clean Zahrá Che suit on, treating the alien uniform as if they were long johns, then replaced his hand-washed uniform over the top. His three weapons were tucked for easy retrieval, and he went respectfully about his business. As he retied his combat boots, Kinety noticed he'd donned the white space compression suit first, likely for warmth. This inspired her to rearrange the order of her own wet clothes the same way—the Zahrá Che compression suit first, her jeans and metallic shirt over that, and then the oversized camouflage uniform. When her own boots were tied, the two were led to a room with smooth walls and given a blob of water-food. If the attending aliens noticed that Arnie was in possession of three weapons, no comment was made about it. Rather, their thoughts seemed to prioritize more around their chores than their collective dislike of their guests. Kinety folded her arms, cold now that she was wet, and ignored them.

When they were finished eating, Zodoo returned, followed by another glowering squad of soldiers, each carrying blasters. They glared and bristled at Kinety as one might a spider. One low-ranking alien came at her carrying a white cloth and made to throw it.

Instantly, Arnie was between them. He snatched the fabric before she could take it, visibly uncomfortable by the soldier's hateful body language, and drew his weapon.

The aliens drew their weapons.

This alerted Zodoo, who quickly intervened. He glared at his naughty troops, who promptly lowered their blasters, then approached the wary Earthlings. *"Tensions are high. The soldiers are here for the Savage Bride's protection. The cloth is for warmth because your clothes are wet. Both of you, please sit,"* he said, gesturing politely to an expansive room with a small bench and a wide pedestal.

Kinety relayed this to Arnie. "Zodoo says the soldiers are here to protect us—"

"Really."

"—and the cloth is for warmth. He wants us to sit down."

Arnie passed the tiny blanket to Kinety but refused the sit offer, preferring to stand. Bristling at the little aliens, he motioned for her to accept the bench seat and took position beside her, his posture quite intimidating among the smaller soldiers.

Awkwardly, she pulled the cloth over her shoulders and folded her arms beneath the odd material. "What am I supposed to say?" she worried quietly to Arnie.

Arnie waved her still. "Just keep your voice strong," he coached, focusing on the guards.

A bit nervously, Kinety faced Zodoo, indicating she was ready. At this, he slid his hand down the smooth wall, and a large, bright light appeared above the pedestal. A figure blinked into view, then stepped through in a holographic glow.

Kinety squinted at the see-through Zahrá Che emperor, who stood bathed in pale light. Around him, the air shimmered like glitter floating on a breeze, but his heat signature seemed more external than central. He was slightly taller than the others and skinny, with weathered skin and a tiny little pot-belly. His eyes were shaded black, giving him an almost insectoid appearance, and his skin glowed an angry pink, distinguishing it from the pale aliens around her. He was older than the other aliens Kinety had encountered and wore metallic ornaments, including a winking breathing-bracelet on his wrist. His face possessed slightly more defined features, possibly from makeup, and his voice as it registered in her head was deeper and clear, giving him a potent air of authority. His approach, though diplomatic, appeared unplanned and unorganized, and his manner even a bit rushed.

"Wife of Torak," he said, his tone heavy with diplomacy.

Kinety leaned toward Arnie. "He just called me Wife of Torak."

"I am Emperor Dinruk. Welcome to—"

"His name is Emperor Dinruk," she relayed.

"—to planet Zahrá Che. I trust—"

"He welcomes us."

"—trust you have been treated well."

"Our treatment was tolerable, Emperor Dinruk," Kinety assured and cut to the point. "Where are my men?"

"The troops," he acknowledged, pausing to cough, then changed his tone to denote a more important topic. *"The Zahrá Che people are eager to begin negotiations—"*

"Negotiations?"

"—regarding the war. I have—"

Kinety twisted to Arnie. "He wants to negotiate—"

Emperor Dinruk slung his arm in exasperation. *"Somebody get a translator in here!"* he barked.

Zodoo whirled. *"Imbik! Quick! Find a translator!"*

Imbik whirled. *"Lugnit! Translator! Now!"*

Lugnit whirled and pointed. *"Peyink! Run!"*

Peyink dashed out of the room in a whisper of tiny boots. *"I need a translator!"* his vanishing thought cried.

Lugnit tapped his toe, waiting.

Imbik paced impatiently, waiting.

Zodoo faced the emperor, waiting.

Emperor Dinruk plopped skinny arms on tiny hips … waiting.

Kinety gave Arnie an apologetic grin. "They're getting a translator," she explained and waited.

Tiny footsteps returned, carrying Peyink, his fist high in the air. He thrust the translator into Lugnit's hand. Lugnit ran it to Imbik, who hurried it to Zodoo.

Zodoo handed it back to Imbik. *"Not to me! Give it to the Earthling soldier."*

Imbik hurried to Arnie, hesitated for an apprehensive moment, then tried to shove the tiny black device into his ear.

Arnie snatched it, startling the alien, who pointed awkwardly at Arnie's ear and then to his own. Arnie looked at the translator, which resembled a tiny hearing aid, then placed it warily into his ear canal. As he did, barbs engaged, embedding the thing deep against his eardrum and locking the item into place. He snapped his head to the side with a wince and made a tiny squeak before correcting his expression and raising his head. A slight twitch in his left eye and an increase in breathing were the only indicators that he was in pain, but even those vanished quickly.

"There. Now your guard can understand me," the emperor informed Kinety, then resumed in a diplomatic tone. *"The Zahrá Che are eager to begin negotiations regarding the war."*

Arnie's eyes rounded slightly as the emperor's spoken thoughts filled his head.

"I have what you want. You have what I want," the emperor continued, dropping the unwanted formalities. *"I think we can form some arrangement."*

Kinety gave Arnie another uncertain glance. "Arrangement? But I have nothing."

"You are Torak's bride. You have his ear," he corrected with a hint of impatience before visibly regaining his composure. *"It is my hope that you will speak to him on our behalf."*

Kinety shook her head in surprise, finally catching on. "What! Whoa! Wait! Emperor Dinruk," she exclaimed. "I'm afraid there's been a terrible misunderstanding. I have no power over Torak. I hardly even—"

"You have incredible power!"

"He won't listen to me."

His central heat signature lit up. *"He will!"*

"No. No, I mean nothing to Torak," she insisted, distracted again by the unusual glow. "I'm not actually his—"

The emperor slapped his hands down on whatever was in front of him with a whack and leaned forward. *"You're wrong!"* he shouted in a fit of temper.

Kinety stood abruptly, startled by the emotional outburst, and backed into Arnie, who gripped her arm. The cloth slipped from her shoulders, and she stood clutching it.

Arnie angled his back toward the aliens, unsure whether or not they could understand him, and spoke quietly. "I'm not clear about what's going on here, but my gut tells me it's bad," he murmured so that only she could hear him. "I don't give a shit who he thinks you're married to. You're talking to the top! Find our men."

"I don't know how to do this," she worried.

Instead of answering, Arnie turned her back toward the hologram. This time, Kinety didn't sit down. "Why me?"

"I believe you can be trusted. You defended our base against Torak," the emperor continued with a regal nod. *"For that, I offer my gratitude."*

Kinety worked to present a confident posture, which meant she couldn't hide behind Arnie. "I wasn't defending your base; I was defending my men," she corrected.

"Same thing."

"Release them."

"I will release the remainder of your men," the emperor gestured toward the window to his left, *"after you convince Torak to seal the portal."*

Kinety glanced at the window where he was pointing. "The remainder?" she echoed and flicked another nervous glance at Arnie.

"Keep your cool," he coached.

She turned back to the emperor, her phony composure barely in place. She ignored the thudding heartbeat pounding in her ears and focused on steadying her voice. "This is not our war. It's yours," she reminded him. "I want my men back."

"Then call off the Gaki," he insisted and, again, blatantly pointed left.

Kinety followed his point again, this time noticing the red sun visible through the window. She still had no idea who the Gaki was. "That is between you and Torak. My men—"

"Civilized conversation is impossible with Torak! We've tried, and he attacks us for our effort. He's killed thousands of my people. You are the only one who's ever stood up to him and lived. He's a monster, irrational, cruel! How you can tolerate such a man—"

"Wait," Kinety interrupted sharply, holding her palm up. "You're doing an awful lot of finger-pointing, Highness. Your Zahrá Che are the ones stealing soldiers who have *nothing* to do with this. You don't look so innocent to me."

"Self-defense," he said simply. *"This is war. After what Torak has done, how can you blame us?"*

Kinety stepped warily toward the hologram, her eyes glittering in suspicion. "What exactly has Torak done, Dinruk?" she asked, dropping the honorary.

He noticed, and his irritation increased. *"You know exactly what he's done!"*

"No! I don't. And right now," she pointed, *"you* look like the aggressor."

The alien glared at her. *"Indeed."*

"Easy," Arnie cautioned softly.

Kinety closed her hands around the blanket to hide the shake and dialed her tone back. "How do I know Torak is not the one defending himself?"

The emperor considered this and straightened, eager to answer that question. *"I have footage that proves otherwise,"* he assured and gestured to someone beyond the holograph.

Kinety stole a quick look at Arnie, earning an encouraging nod. As she turned back, the emperor's hologram vanished. In its place, a low-quality holograph without audio appeared.

In a spacious room, numerous Zahrá Che aliens in a green haze sagged in chairs and sprawled in huddles. From the left of the screen, in walked Torak, who stopped abruptly. The Zahrá Che turned, paused in recognition, and then freaked. The entire room erupted in a frenzy. One panicking creature darted in front of the camera, blocking it briefly. When the view returned, Torak was using a weapon to shoot unarmed aliens with one hand and using blue flashes of telekinetic energy with his other hand to knock the smaller people violently backward. All at once, a snarling group rushed him. Others climbed the walls. With a silent shout, Torak threw his arms wide, casting fire and slaughtering everyone inside. A billow of flame reached the camera, and the screen went black.

By the end, Kinety had backed into Arnie.
Another silent video blinked into view.

Torak's flickering hologram appeared inside a spacecraft. He spoke briefly to the crew, then vanished. Behind him, a timer registering mere seconds counted down. There was panic, a bright flash, and then a dark screen.

Next was a ground battle.

Torak in black, led a troop of humanoids in brown uniforms, presumably the Saphiridians, in physical and weaponized combat. Against the Saphiridians, the Zahrá Che physically stood no chance. Torak deflected their weapon strikes easily. With a wave of his hand, he redirected laser blasts, knocking the beams into nearby attackers and sending shooters flying backward in chaotic tumbles.

The fight was violent, bloody, and destructive. Torak's weapons, energy manipulation, and combat styles were unlike anything Kinety had ever seen. He obliterated anything in his path and mowed through the battle literally in a spray of blood.
In every silent video, Torak did appear to be the aggressor and an aggressive one at that. He slaughtered mercilessly, stepped over bodies without remorse, and was relentless in combat.
Kinety's heart hammered.
The emperor returned. Around him, the air sparkled, engulfing him in an almost surreal halo, which Kinety didn't believe for a moment. Though disturbed by what she'd seen, she was careful to keep her expression stoic. "The soldiers in brown," she said carefully, "those were Saphiridians?"
The emperor seemed bewildered by the question, then must have realized she honestly didn't know. *"Yes."*
"The Saphiridians are humanoid?"
Recognizing her ignorance as advantageous, the emperor switched his tone from one of a defendant presenting an argument against a bias to one of education. His manner became almost friendly, his

words more select. *"Yes. Our war is between the true-bloods and the hybrids."*

At her puzzled look, he explained, *"Long ago, the Zahrá Che created the Saphiridians as an experiment and terraformed a planet for them. The Saphiridians are hybrids—half-Zahrá Che, half-human using DNA from your own planet. We blended the two species, nurtured them, and allowed them to grow. Our intention was to create a legacy race without our flaws. Unfortunately, instead of gratitude, the hybrids turned on us and exploited our genetic experiments. They are a violent, war-like species, as you have just witnessed."*

"So, Torak is Saphiridian?"

"No. His loyalties are there, but he is not Saphiridian. Torak is an illegal hybrid motley—a chimera," he said, then explained. *"A Saphiridian scientist named Glarnt gathered DNA fragments from numerous species within the galaxy, then spliced them together to delete genetic flaws, resist disease, and enhance preferred characteristics. This was used to create an embryo, which was then incubated in a mixture of rare elements called torakonium. This was not a substance found in nature. Torakonium was created by accident in a Zahrá Che lab, an experimental blending of unstable metal elements typically used for superconductors and power condensers, but something went wrong. The botched mixture was disposed of improperly and, unfortunately, stolen by the Saphiridians, who mishandled it. There was an explosion, but Glarnt's fetus, infused now in this torakonium, survived. The child's atomic structure allowed him to detect, gather, store, and control numerous energies, including the toojidium that powers our technology,"* he said and coughed again.

Toojidium? Kinety caught the term and did a mental calculation, putting two and two together. Tooji.

"The exact composition of the stolen torakonium is unknown, so it cannot be recreated, nor can the result of the explosion. We've tried. Torak has a broad visual spectrum, including night vision, infrared, and regeneration capabilities. From inception, the boy was carefully weaponized. The Saphiridians created a war god, a combat genius. As a man, he has never been defeated and cannot be reasoned with. By design, he is immune to human emotion, incapable of compassion—an expert assassin. He was trained in combat and nothing else. All Torak knows is how to kill."

None of that matched the man Kinety had met in the meadow.

"With such a weapon, the Saphiridians have terrorized the galaxy. They are dangerous, ruthless tyrants. Their lust for power knows no boundary. When they want something, they release Torak and take

it. *Many species consider the DNA thefts an act of war and are allies to us in our fight."*

Kinety had an odd question. "Why is he mostly human?" she wondered. "What made them choose my species?"

"To keep him from breeding," answered the emperor. *"Pure humans perished with Tiamat, the original water-giant that created your planet Earth during a collision many millennia ago. The closest match to that species are Earthlings or Terran, your people. Earthlings are not true humans. They are considered trash hybrids due to the blending of pure human DNA with various Earth hominids, such as Neanderthal, but those flaws are easily removed to create a synthetic duplicate. It is frequently used as a base for new hybrid races with historic success."*

As the emperor spoke, Kinety and Arnie looked at each other.

"So, we're hybrids?" she clarified, gesturing to herself and Arnie.

"Yes. Earthling DNA is easy to manipulate and, therefore, highly sought after, but your species is not considered an attractive one because of the contamination. Torak, whose appearance is no accident, was intentionally left ugly. No sensible Saphiridian, or any other humanoid hybrid, would downgrade its bloodline with unrefined human DNA, especially with blood as tainted as Torak's."

Ugly? Nothing about Torak was—Kinety exhaled slowly. Rather annoyed by the dirty blood mentality, she took a moment, then returned to the esteem-lowering conversation. "Are there more like Torak?"

"No," assured the emperor. *"He's an anomaly—brutal, violent, and unstoppable. He possesses no known weakness. Even the Saphiridians fear him, yet they unleash him freely on my people. Nobody but Prime Joboba can control him ... until now,"* he emphasized, inclining his head at her. *"We're asking you to help us."*

Kinety laughed nervously, reeling from all this. It was clear by now that she would have to work miracles if she wanted her men back. Pretending to be diplomatic was not helping. The emperor was not simply going to hand them over, and Torak had made no secret of his intention. He was planning to kill the soldiers. That made him her enemy, not her ally. Realizing this, she tried to backpedal. "I don't know what you expect me to do," she told the glowing holograph, "but Torak's interest in me has passed. I mean nothing to him. I can assure you he won't listen to anything I say."

The emperor shook his head, unconvinced. *"Torak has Loquú."*

"What is Loquú?"

"It means universal language," he said with a wave, *"and Torak is the only being ever known to possess it ... until you."*

Kinety blinked at him. "Me?"

"You're using it now."

She shook her head. "I've never even heard of Loquú."

The emperor signaled. Seconds later, a recorded voice spoke in a choppy, guttural language:

"State your location."

Torak's voice answered. "I'm coming around the third moon. Visual in three ... two ... one ... target in sight."

"Engage total. Allow three survivors. We want witnesses."

"Engaging."

The voices fell silent and the emperor reappeared, his head angled speculatively. *"What did you hear?"*

"Someone talking to Torak," she shrugged, "giving him instructions."

The aliens in the room looked at each other.

Next, the emperor waved his hand to someone off-screen and floating words appeared.

LEBRIGIN. WOZZJOM.

Kinety waited for the words to vanish. When the emperor returned, she gave a small shrug. "What about it?"

"What does that say?"

She thought about it for a moment. "Lebrigin is similar to clean or area clear, but it's only part of the phrase. Wozzjom is a," she opened a hand and stammered to decipher, "stand-down alert or cancel depending on the inflection."

"Saphiridian transmissions are encrypted, their military writing classified, yet you can interpret both."

"Can't you?"

"No," he thought simply.

Kinety frowned at Arnie. He shook his head, assuring her he understood none of it.

"The only way you could have received such a gift is from Torak."

"How does that even work?" she asked.

"It is believed to be an energetic link into the language bundles in the brain."

Kinety stopped him. "That's impossible. I've never met the Saphiridians."

"You linked with Torak. You know what he knows."

That shut her up. Stunned, she fell silent.

"This is not something Torak would share with any but his companion."

Why would Torak have done that? Kinety leaned subconsciously against Arnie, very aware of the heat crawling up her neck. It was her heat signature that was rising now, which was weird because she could see it.

"Did you not agree to this union?" wondered the emperor.

She gave a guilty pause, unsure exactly how to explain that she had—kinda—but she'd been joking. She'd only known Torak a combined total of fifteen minutes, the end of which had seen a complete unraveling of their short relationship. Dumbfounded, she blinked at the emperor, which was her answer.

"Torak has also publicly claimed you as his companion. Do you deny this?"

"No, but he was being sarcastic."

"Did you deny it when he announced it?"

"Well, no … but—"

"Your union is legal."

Kinety's mouth opened and closed a few times. "Does Torak know this?"

"Torak threatened to obliterate my planet if you were harmed," the emperor assured in disgust. *"It does not appear to me that he takes your relationship lightly."*

Kinety was dizzy.

"It is my humble request that you use your union to suppress the Saphiridian attacks on Zahrá Che civilians, thus reducing our reliance on Earthling soldiers for battle," he said imperially. *"Convince Torak to close the portal, and I will no longer need your people to stop the Gaki attacks. At that time, you may take custody of the remainder."*

She stared at him.

"And know this," the emperor said emphatically. *"The Zahrá Che are not your enemies. Our plight is desperate, our plea sincere."*

The glowering aliens surrounding her certainly didn't support the emperor's claims, but Kinety inclined her head anyway, acknowledging the declaration. She had no idea when or if she'd ever see Torak again, but that didn't matter now. Her moment had arrived. "I'll speak to Torak on your behalf … on the condition that you stop taking soldiers from my planet."

"Our lives depend on—"

"No!" Kinety's voice echoed inside the building, silencing the startled monarch. It startled her too, but she continued. "No more!"

The emperor gaped at her.

"You keep your aliens and your spaceships," she jabbed a finger at the wide-eyed alien troops, "away from my planet Earth. No more Earthlings—I want your word."

Silence.

Her voice dropped. "You promise me," she insisted, "or I'll join the fight against you."

All eyes shifted to the monarch.

It was clear at this point in the conversation that Emperor Dinruk lacked the ability to fire death lasers from his eyes, which was good news for Kinety. The threat, however, worked. *"Fine,"* he agreed, then snapped angry eyes at Zodoo. *"Ready her ship and prepare a public statement. I want her removed from the planet immediately and sent to base four. When she arrives, she may bzz, bzz with Torak through video."*

Zodoo inclined his head. *"The ship is ready, Excellency."*

"Where are you sending us?" she demanded.

The emperor turned back to his Earthling audience. *"To a secure bzz, bzz, bzz. Bzz Torak cooperates, he gets bzz. You get your bzz bzz bzz ... ,"* he buzzed.

The connection broke.

"That ... is not going to happen," vowed a whispery voice.

Distracted Zahrá Che whirled to their computer stations in alarm. The aliens screeched in fright and worked frantically to clear the signal.

"Zodoo! The dome has been disengaged. We have incoming!" warned one. *"A Saphiridian fleet has breached our northern perimeter!"*

"How long until they arrive?"

"They're here!"

The emperor's image flickered into jagged static. *"Get the Bride off the planet, now!"* his distorted voice ordered.

Outside, a warbling alarm screamed through the city.

Before they could recover the emperor's holograph, the signal was hijacked. With a flicker, a blond alien with a slightly large head, a snub nose, and humanoid features appeared. His uniform was brown, labeling him as Saphiridian.

"It's Prime Joboba!" cried a Zahrá Che alien to Zodoo, who worked furiously to clear the channel.

Arnie's fingers curled around Kinety's arm. With increasing pressure, he began easing her backward.

Joboba's brown eyes swept the room through the signal distortion until they zeroed in on the two humans. "Is that her?" his guttural voice asked to someone beyond the holograph.

Kinety recognized the voice. It was the same one from the Saphiridian recording—Torak's handler.

Arnie's grip tightened.

A disembodied voice replied, "Identity confirmed, Prime."

Barely veiled hatred sparkled in his brown eyes. "Engage!" he ordered through white teeth.

Kinety was yanked backward, spilling her blanket. There were three seconds of silence, and then—an enormous explosion destroyed the building, splitting two walls and fracturing the floor. Aliens went flying. Arnie took Kinety to the ground.

"They're after the Savage Bride!" someone shouted. *"Don't let them get her!"*

"Stun her!" cried Zodoo. *"Get her to the ship!"*

Lugnit spun to his hip, aiming his blaster at Kinety. Arnie kicked the bench, knocking it into him just as the alien fired a stunning shot. Lugnit toppled beneath it. The holographs vanished in a vacuum of silence, and the large room went dark.

Clutching his weapon, Arnie dragged her quickly away from the chaos, then pushed her into a crawl toward a billow of dust. The aliens descended on the spot they no longer occupied, furious, and scattered to find them, their telepathic voices screeching into Kinety's head.

"Soldier!" a voice hissed. "This way!"

Arnie whirled, recognizing the language, and spotted two alien heads poking from a split in the broken wall, barely visible in the haze. Braced to fire, he neared, clutching Kinety. "Identify!" he warned quietly.

A gloved hand waved them closer. "Sergeant Orlando. Bravo 153rd. We're human," he said and slid the white helmet off, revealing the blessed sight of a black man with a scruffy chin. On his neck, he had a round, puckered scar, right where Kinety and Arnie's were. "Hurry!" he urged, beckoning them through the rubble.

"He's human!" Kinety squealed and scrambled for him. The squeeze into the broken wall was a tight one, but the man pulled her roughly through, then reached past her for Arnie.

"Park! Where are you?" Orlando called quietly.

"Right here." On the unlit backside of the broken wall, the second human, this one Asian, produced two helmets with almond-shaped eyes and two white alien compression suits. He, too, had an angry, puckered scar, which looked almost purple. "Put those on. Hurry," he ordered, guiding them into a maze of debris.

Arnie and Kinety squeezed into the compression suits—her fourth layer—disguising their camouflage clothing. Just then, through a smaller crack in the ruined wall, they saw four Saphiridian soldiers in brown uniforms drop into the building through a jagged hole in the ceiling.

Kinety hesitated, wondering if Tooji had sent them to rescue her. In a spray of heavy firepower, the four Saphiridians spread out, firing indiscriminately at the Zahrá Che. Through the smoke, two quickly found her discarded blanket. One roared in anger, the other began shooting the abandoned cloth.

Kinety jolted sharply, confident now that rescue hadn't been the plan.

"They've escaped. Find them!" one Saphiridian ordered, no doubt speaking into a radio.

Arnie yanked Kinety's helmet down, and the group hurried quietly away. In a series of blurs and bumps, they darted through the rubble of the broken building until the hazy daylight appeared through a small gouge. Their companions went there.

Park, the smaller of the two, poked his head out first, then slid through. "We're clear. Go! Go! Go!" he hissed, ushering them out of the building.

Arnie gripped Kinety's hand and dashed out after the men, leading her away from the Saphiridian attack. Like crazy people, they ran— not away from the fleeing Zahrá Che citizens but toward them. Arnie's grip tightened when they reached the crowd, indicating his discomfort among the hostile aliens, but he followed, completely trusting their fellow humans.

Kinety kept up. Looking through the alien eye-shields felt weird, but they worked like polarized sunglasses, making everything crisp and easy to see, even in the shadows. Eventually, she adapted.

Sticking close to the Zahrá Che crowd, the disguised humans moved away from the battle using hand signals and keeping a low profile. Careful to avoid attracting attention, both men pretended to search for cover and mimicked the behavior of the Zahrá Che fighters on the ground, waiting for the moment when they could separate.

Overhead, a fleet of twisted-iron, steampunk Saphiridian airships thundered into the sky. Sleek, mirror-silver Zahrá Che ships intercepted them, firing silent lasers and maneuvering masterfully through the air in swarms. The rugged, blocky vessels returned fire with deafening, destructive pulses. They chased the sleek Zahrá Che ships, which vanished at random, turned at zero-point ratio, and responded with far superior precision against the brute strength of their aggressive enemy. In a thunder of energy fire, something nasty hit one of the water tower antenna things.

It exploded.

The concussion was massive, knocking all four humans to the ground. As they skidded to a stop, a high-pitch whine split the air. In a shower of fiery sparks, a wounded Saphiridian battleship crashed into the side of a building. Screaming Zahrá Che citizens dove for cover. In the chaos, the humans snatched the fallen Zahrá Che weapons, then separated from the reeling crowd. Running hard, they ducked into an alleyway and looked back. Almost in unison, all of the Zahrá Che citizens hid.

Park looked up. "Shit! Get the compression suits off!" he shouted, peeling his away and tossing his helmet aside with a scatter of sandy brown hair. Overhead, a mirrored Zahrá Che ship appeared, seemingly out of nowhere, and the bottom of the craft opened up. In a controlled fall, Earthling soldiers in camouflage descended. "Hide!" he cried, shoving them faster.

Kinety saw the human militants land on the ground and spun. "Arnie! It's them! Our troops," she cried, taking off. She ran for them, waving her arms. "Over here!"

Arnie tackled her backward.

A soldier rounded on her and fired. The shot missed them by inches, and he charged.

"Run!" cried their rescuer. "They'll kill you."

The group dashed around a corner and ducked behind a pillar.

Arnie pressed his hand against Kinety's chest, pinning her to the pillar, and peeked. "Why is he attacking us?"

Park pulled them into a different alley and pointed to the scar on his neck. "The chips. On their necks," he rushed, checking behind them. "It programs them to kill anything not in uniform—human military camouflage. Get her out of that compression suit!"

In a flurry of grabbing hands, Kinety was freed from the white suit. Arnie tore at his clothing next. Tossing it aside, he peeked around the corner, waiting. He held a hand up for silence as the soldier advanced and braced. Seconds later, a camouflaged blur dashed past.

Arnie sprung and grabbed him, disarming him quickly. In a flurry of powerful moves, he knocked the chip from the soldier's neck, caught the startled man in a headlock, and dragged him backward.

As the soldier's senses returned, he panicked.

"Stand down! Stand down!" Arnie growled into his ear. "I'm a friendly!"

The soldier stiffened, slowing his struggle, and blinked in breathless confusion. Streaks of blood rolled down his chest from the wound. "Where am I?" he panted, looking around at the bizarre landscape. "What the fuck is this?"

Arnie returned to Kinety.

"There's a ship coming!" warned Park.

Orlando pointed at a massive duct. "Into the gutter. Run!" he ordered and dragged the confused soldier toward the large round culvert.

Chapter 6

It was hard to breathe. Once inside the underground canal, Kinety collapsed, gasping for air. She wasn't used to running through a war zone or being shot at and didn't care for either. Her bracelet stung, working hard to keep her alive in the unfamiliar atmosphere. Breathing through the sting, she struggled to stand. "Where's my brother?" she wheezed at the soldiers in exhaustion. "Where's Rixton?"

"What is his last name?"

"Dash. Rixton Dash."

Neither man had heard of him.

Arnie caught her and, clutching her possessively, faced their rescuers. Inside the subway, pale lighting lit the tunnel. Thick walls muffled the battle outside, giving the fight a distant feel and the humans a much needed break. "Who are you?" he panted.

Orlando extended a distracted hand for a quick shake. "I'm Sergeant Lamont Orlando," he said, introducing himself again. "Infantry. Go by Orlando. That's baby Lieutenant Park Hyun Bin, pilot in training," he said, gesturing to his companion and ducking at the sound of a nearby explosion. "He looks like a K-pop idol but can't hold a musical note with a bucket. Let's hope he flies better than he sings."

Dust billowed in, clouding the air.

Arnie shook Park's hand. "Korean?"

Park inclined his head and peeked out the culvert. "Half. And don't listen to him. I am an amazing singer," he said with a slight accent. "I also study languages. I'm fluent in seven, so far. Once you learn a few, it gets easier. The building blocks are the same. Still working on the flying. You can call me Park."

"I'm Captain Arnold Jagger, Black Frog, Team Two. Call me Arnie. This is Kinety. Find me another human, Park," Arnie said, stepping away and joining them at the edge of the culvert. "Orlando?"

Orlando cracked his knuckles, ready to play. "Oh, yeah. I'll take one."

"Get ready," Park said, dropping his voice to a whisper and pointing in separate directions. "We got two headed this way. There and there."

Arnie gestured Orlando toward one and pinned eyes on the other. "Get the chip," he whispered.

Orlando braced.

Arnie glanced sharply at Park, then gestured toward Kinety, effectively placing him on babysitting duty.

Park nodded, backing toward her.

Orlando dashed out one way. Arnie vanished in the other direction.

The bleeding soldier beside Kinety watched the impromptu operation in utter confusion. "Where are we?" he asked again. "How did I get here?"

"We're on planet Zahrá Che," she said quietly. "You were kidnapped. What's your name?"

The soldier paused as if unsure, then looked down at the name sewn onto his uniform. "Marshall," he said, then stared out at his bizarre surroundings in disbelief. "What day is it?"

"I don't know," she said with a shake of her head.

Arnie returned moments later carrying a barely conscious soldier with blood gushing from his neck and put him beside Marshall. "Stop that bleeding," he ordered, turning as Orlando dashed back into the culvert, shaking his head. "What happened?"

"Couldn't reach him," wheezed Orlando. "He nearly killed me. We can't stay here. If they're dropping soldiers, there's gonna be a battle."

Another explosion rattled the ground.

"A battle?" Arnie peered out. "Is this how you got here?" he asked Park, gesturing toward the discombobulated soldiers beside him.

"More or less."

Kinety moved to the edge of the culvert but couldn't find the red sun. The haze was too thick now. "Where are the others?"

Park didn't know. "We're it. We got separated from them and have no idea how to get back."

Arnie's newest soldier sat up in alarm, instantly in a panic as his brain kicked back on. Disconcerted, he slapped at the blood on his neck and crab-kicked backward before Park brought him under control.

"We're friendlies! We're friendlies!" Park repeated forcefully until the message reached its target.

The man, whose name tag read Norelo, stiffened and went still. "The brownshirts!" he hissed, looking wildly around for Saphiridians. "They're killing us!"

Park shooshed the man and vigorously rubbed his shoulder to stimulate his focus. It worked.

Finding no brownshirts, Norelo slowed his scan. "Where am I?"

A blast of dust swept Kinety's hair, and she caught herself. "Planet Zahrá Che," she answered.

Orlando noticed the commander's badge on her uniform and jerked upright. "Commander!" he said in confusion.

Park spun and saw it. "You're a colonel?"

"No," she managed, ducking a spray of shrapnel. "I'm a civilian."

The men looked at the scar on her neck, then at each other.

"I thought only mouthy soldiers were being taken," said Park, jabbing a thumb at Orlando. "They're taking silly-vilians now too?"

Kinety leaned forward, squinting into the dust. "No. It was an accident. I need to orient. Where was the building?"

Orlando stepped behind her. "The one you were in? That way. The first explosion came from over there. We moved that direction after the exit and then came around. Crash is there," he said with a point and tried to pull her back. "Clock is ticking. We gotta get moving."

"Wait. We need to catch the rest of our soldiers," Arnie said, looking for more.

"It's too late," said Orlando. "If any of the brownies, the little aliens, or our guys see you, they'll kill you. We learned that the hard way."

"We can't just leave them," Arnie argued.

Orlando stopped him. "Whatever those chips do muddles the mind, puts it into autopilot. The humans charge into battle like berserkers, killing everything, but are picked off like insects. Most that were dropped are already dead by now. Human soldiers don't survive the battles. If we hunt them, we will be too."

This wasn't the news Arnie wanted to hear, but he believed Orlando.

Park frowned at Arnie. "Why weren't you two with the other captive humans? How did you get here, anyway?"

"It's a long story," Arnie assured, his mood rapidly souring.

From where Kinety stood, she could just see silhouetted rubble smoking through the haze. "What are those spires?" she asked, pointing to the tall teardrop needle things.

"Those tall things? Some sort of power source, I think," said Orlando.

Kinety ran the positions through her mind, then pointed to her left. "We have to go that direction," she said, then faced the unfamiliar men. "Does this tunnel go that way?"

Billowing smoke and destruction darkened the sky, bringing with it an eerie silence. The shooting had stopped. Arnie noticed this and warily took Kinety's arm. "What's that rumble?"

Park pointed a different way. "No. This tunnel veers off in the other direction, but Orlando is right. We gotta go. C'mon, you can tell us on the way," he said, waving them into the gutter.

Kinety stepped out of the gutter. "That's the wrong way. We need to go that way," she insisted, pointing.

"Why?" asked Orlando.

"Because that's where the soldiers are. Is there another gutter?"

"We'd have to find it, but we can't do that until dark," the black man argued. "How do you know where they are?"

"That's the direction the emperor pointed—toward that red sun. How long until it gets dark?"

"We're in a binary solar system. Two suns. The days alternate between red and blue. We've only seen dark once since we arrived here about ten days ago," Orlando said, glancing at his watch. "Wait … you spoke to the emperor? The alien emperor?"

Kinety squinted into the distance. "I see another gutter," she said, pointing it out. "One hundred yards, tops. Arnie?"

"It's too far," warned Orlando. "That rumble is them dropping brownies. We've gotta go!"

But Kinety was determined. "Our men are that way, and they're in trouble!" she argued, pointing to the gutter she wanted. "We have to go—aaaah!"

From nowhere, a Saphiridian soldier clutching a Zarah Che blaster snatched Kinety off her feet and took off. As he ran, he reported. "U five seven two, I have Torak's female. Southwest quadrant, grid thirty-seven," he said, putting the blaster to her head. "Zahrá Che in pursuit. Request immediate extraction—oof!"

In a flying tackle, Arnie took the brown-clad Saphiridian down, killing him as they impacted the ground. The blaster discharged, incinerating a hover vehicle, and all three rolled, spilling Kinety. Finishing his roll, Arnie landed on his feet, hauling her up with him into a hard run. Orlando and Park raced beside them, firing on the move and shoving Marshall and Norelo along.

Overhead, screaming starships, both Zahrá Che and Saphiridian, raced for them and the battle resumed. The silver Zahrá Che ships targeted the airborne invaders, while tiny citizens concealed around the city opened fire on the ground troops. Looking entirely out of place, glossy-eyed human soldiers in camouflage roared bloody murder and fired on the Saphiridians, who returned fire on the charging combatants.

Around the corner of a building, another Saphiridian appeared. "Female in sight, Torak. Grid thirty-seven, heading to thirty-six." He aimed his blaster right at Kinety. "The Zahrá Che are attempting to eliminate the target," he said and fired twice at her.

Arnie yanked her left, dodging the shots by inches, and dove behind a round structure. "Aren't those Saphiridians?" he panted, skidding on his hip, then scrambling to his knees. "They act like they're trying to kill you!"

Kinety struggled to catch her breath. "The one that grabbed me … ," she wheezed, "requested extraction because we were being chased by Zahrá Che—only we weren't—then tried to shoot me. And that one by the building … said the Zahrá Che were about to eliminate me … but he's the one who fired," she stammered.

Arnie peeked out. "That makes no sense," he said, checking for more.

Two more shots rang out, striking the metal thing in front of them and melting one side. Arnie shoved her to the ground and twisted to shoot as more Saphiridian soldiers came from the other side, all firing. Several dropped. In the sky, Zahrá Che fighters zipped back and forth, killing the Saphiridians soldiers shooting at Kinety. The larger steampunk vessels took out the zombified human soldiers and the scattered Zahrá Che snipers.

Suddenly, a metallic black starship, unlike any others in the sky, screamed into view.

All at once, the Saphiridian aircraft lifted straight up into the air, the Zahrá Che vessels scattered, and the snipers vanished. At the same time, the Saphiridian soldiers who'd been trying to kill Kinety did an about-face and aimed behind themselves as if creating a protective barrier between the other shooters and the humans.

Arnie and Kinety looked at each other.

As the black starship circled overhead, it released a blue pulse, knocking everything in its path backward. With a spin, the fighter reversed its arc and dove, spraying the ground between the humans and everyone else with a wall of fire, nearly incinerating Park. Arnie lurched to grab him and yanked backward. Both fell and ducked the heat.

More Saphiridian troops thudded down from the ships above and hit the ground shooting.

A glossy-eyed human rounded a street corner and charged, taking two Saphiridians down before Orlando intercepted the soldier and tackled him sideways. They landed together on the ground, fighting. Orlando hooked a leg around the man, pinning him, and scratched the bolt from his neck in a spray of blood.

The black starship screamed overhead, shooting and dodging return fire.

Beneath a spray of crisscrossing laser shots, Arnie yanked both men behind the weird round structure and reached to help Orlando stop the bleeding. While his back was turned, a soldier in brown grabbed Kinety.

"U six five four! Extract!" the Saphiridian shouted.

Kinety shrieked and scrambled to reach Arnie but came away with only a clump of dirt. Before she could grab him, she felt a tingle and, in a blink, she was gone.

Arnie let out a roar of rage as she disappeared.

Park yanked him. "Run!" he shouted, looking past with wide eyes and pushing the others in panic.

Orlando yanked his new soldier up and hauled him into the nearby tunnel. As the group disappeared inside the smelly culvert, a

Saphiridian airship lined up with the culvert opening and fired a massive pulse, obliterating the entrance.

*****

Kinety, frizzy-haired and covered in dirt, landed inside a Saphiridian spacecraft in a sparkle of electrified flesh. "Arnie!" she cried, flailing for him, but he wasn't there.

Her captor dropped her to the floor. "Target acquired," he said and stepped calmly away as if it was time for lunch.

Kinety spun, breathing heavily, but Arnie didn't appear. It didn't take long to realize he wasn't going to. Frightened, she looked at the Saphiridians surrounding her and saw mainly their backs. Men and women in brown uniforms manned different panels along the outer walls of the hollow craft. The vessel's interior measured maybe forty feet in diameter and was as ugly on the inside as the outside. She scrambled backward. However, none of the crew appeared to have any interest in her alarm. They ignored her, turning the ship toward space and leaving the battle and the Zahrá Che planet behind. "Put me back!" she called out, but nobody cared.

As the craft ascended, artificial gravity gripped her, pinning her to the floor, and she felt the distinctive pull of acceleration. Air vents in the wall hissed on, calming the sting of her bracelet. "Put me back!"

When the crew failed to acknowledge her, Kinety stood and hurled the clump of dirt in her hand at the back of the nearest head. A woman with a round face whirled, glaring in hatred.

"Put me back," Kinety snarled at her.

A very slender, human-looking man with fancy red rank and a slightly oversized head spun patiently to face Kinety and grinned. Clearly, this was the one in charge of the vessel. "Welcome aboard Saphiridian Combat Vessel 654. I am Third Level Flight Superior Darplano. I imagine you're wondering what all this is about. I can assure you that all your questions will be answered shortly."

"Put me back," she snapped. "My men are down there!"

"I have orders to transport you to safety."

The woman Kinety had struck called over her shoulder. "Superior Darplano. I'm receiving a signal from Torak. He wishes to beam in, Sir."

Darplano inclined his head. "Open conduit."

A screen beside the woman lit up, and Torak's silhouette appeared. When it cleared, a holographic image of him stepped through. Scattered, sleek black curls that looked almost wet fell haphazardly into electric vampire eyes. The tips at the back just reached his shoulders, sharp in detail despite the transparency of his image. His skin, clear inside the hologram, was bronze and smooth over the pipes visible behind his impressive physique. Instantly, he singled her out and approached. "Kinety!"

Kinety's pulse leapt at the sight of him. "Tooji!" she said in breathless relief and hurried past Darplano. "Arnie's down there!"

Torak scanned her for damage and stopped inches away. "Are you hurt?" he worried, studying her face.

"No. Arnie's down there," she said again.

"Why are you dirty? Did they harm you!"

"No," she managed, trying unsuccessfully to straighten her dusty clothes. Self-consciously, she touched her messy hair. "There was a fight. They took me," she babbled, indicating the crew around her. "Arnie is still down there. I have to go back. They're shooting at my soldiers!"

"What? No! You cannot go back," he said incredulously, then stopped. Abruptly, he remembered their audience. After a quick glance around, he grew visibly angry and switched to a sharper tone. "You have caused enough trouble as it is!"

Kinety frowned at him. "What?"

"Where is she!" demanded a familiar guttural voice.

Kinety looked past Torak's see-through image to a blond head on a nearby screen and recognized the brown-eyed Prime Joboba—the same man who had interrupted the emperor. Only this time, the glare of hatred was gone, and a look of outrage contorted his features.

"Is this her?"

She paused at the question. Hadn't he already identified her?

"It is," answered Torak.

"How widespread is the news," asked the Saphiridian leader.

Superior Darplano stepped forward. "Galaxy-wide by now, Sir."

The digital blond head shifted back to Kinety. "Torak?"

"A misunderstanding, Prime," Torak said.

"I figured so. I've already called an emergency council meeting at Jag Mosrog space station. Darplano, take her there. I'm on my way."

Darplano inclined his head amiably, accepting the order, and walked away with his hands folded behind his back. Torak's hologram gave Kinety one last lingering look and vanished. Prime Joboba disappeared from the screen next, leaving her standing alone in the middle of a crowded Saphiridian spaceship.

*****

The men dove, covering their heads as violent debris sprayed the metal walls around them. When it was over, Arnie pushed to his elbows, growling in frustration, and threw a rock at the blocked exit. "I lost her," he gritted through his teeth. "I lost her! Goddammit!"

Park helped Orlando's newest soldier stand. "On your feet, Wesley," he said, noticing the man's name.

"Where am I?" asked Wesley, holding pressure on his bleeding neck. "Who are you?"

"Friendlies. We're on planet Zahrá Che," Park explained, then looked up at the sound of scraping on the far side of the barrier. "We were abducted by aliens. They're chasing us. We've gotta go."

Arnie slapped the ground with a curse and gripped his head. "Fuck!"

Orlando stood, glaring at Arnie, and jabbed an angry point at the rubble. "Who is she?" he demanded. "What the hell was that!"

Park beckoned the group into motion. "We talkie while we walkie. Let's go."

Arnie snatched up his weapon. Clamping his teeth in anger, he got up. "That was Kinety. The night we were taken, she attracted the attention of an alien called Torak. He's dangerous, a destroyer or assassin or something. They call him the Annihilator. The two hit it off before she learned who he was. Now, he's claimed her as his wife," he said, angrily dusting debris off his arms and neck, "and it's caused a shit-storm."

"You mean that crazy motherfucker in the black ship?" asked Park, zipping his finger wildly through the air.

Arnie's brow knitted. "I'm guessing. He fights with the Saphiridians, the ones you're calling brownies," he said over his shoulder. "The emperor said he's a blend of spliced alien and human DNA genetically created by the Saphiridian or some shit. They've weaponized him."

Orlando scowled. "If this Torak is so fired up over Kinety, why were the Saphiridians trying to kill her?"

"Good question," said Arnie. "She said they were talking rescue, but it looked more like an assassination attempt. When Torak showed up, they turned and protected her instead."

Park slowed to a stop, then did a double-take at the larger man. "Wait. How do you know what they were saying?"

Arnie tried to beckon him back into motion, but Orlando stopped too. "I am not taking another step until you tell us what the hell is going on," he said with mounting suspicion.

Arnie shook his head. "We don't know either," he said, then slumped against the culvert wall and exhaled.

Park stepped closer. "How are you able to communicate with them?"

Arnie tapped his ear. "I can't. I'm wearing a Zahrá Che translator. *She* can. Torak," he said, gesturing upward, "did something called Loqúu when they met. Now, she understands all of them. The emperor called it a universal language. Like I said, they think she's his companion. Apparently, that's a big deal."

Orlando grimaced at the ridiculous story, then pulled a piece of alien food from his pocket. "That's the biggest load of bullshit I've ever heard," he said, tearing it into pieces and passing it out. He offered some to Arnie.

Arnie, who'd eaten within the last twenty-four hours, declined. "Even after talking with the emperor, we still don't know why our soldiers are here. What do you know?"

Park squinted into the dim waterway. "I remember the attack on Earth and the little aliens with blasters. I was hit. I woke on a transport ship—in a tube. I think the ship was struck because my tube was shattered and sparking. I got out and found a fried microchip on my neck," he said, touching the puckered scar beneath his ear. Leaning sideways, he pulled the chip from a pocket and handed the burnt device to Arnie.

Arnie examined the black piece and touched his own scar. The front of the chip was flat, maybe an inch in diameter. The back side had barbs underneath it—just like his sharp-assed translator, just like the breathing bracelet biting into his wrist. It was definitely Zahrá Che.

Park continued. "The aliens were busy fighting, so I tried to get the others. I managed to free Orlando here. I no more pulled him out, and the ship flew over a plateau in the middle of a rocky desert. All at once, half of the soldiers in the tubes woke up and started banging on the glass."

"The microchips were disabled?" asked Arnie.

"Looked like it," said Park. "Each soldier had a weapon. The ship's floor disintegrated like liquid mercury, and the awake half dropped into a portal or something. It was slow, like a controlled fall. I almost fell. I couldn't tell what was at the bottom, but I heard screaming—grown men screaming like terrified women. Before the floor liquified shut, I saw something come out of the portal—a blur. Aliens on the plateau freaked. Our spaceship circled, shooting, which is probably why the floor remained open. Whatever it was slaughtered a shitload of the aliens before they killed it. I only saw billows of dust, but it was bad. Whatever it is, our men are inside with it."

Goosebumps lifted on Arnie's arms. "Do you know where the portal is?"

Park crinkled his forehead, thinking back. "Only that it was on a plateau—a steep one. Two of the sides just drop off. I saw the red sun low in the sky," he remembered, then continued his story. "Orlando didn't wake up until I pulled the microchip off his neck. Then the other side woke—their eyes opened, anyway—and we were deposited beyond the borders of Paradise City," he said, gesturing around them.

"Beyond the borders?" echoed Arnie.

"An energy dome protects the city."

"How long after you left the plateau did you land?"

"Three minutes, tops."

"It has to be close," said Arnie.

Orlando made a face. "Not necessarily. We were in a spaceship."

Park went on. "Outside the city, those big clunky ships swarmed the sky, and goofy-looking aliens in the brown uniforms tried to break through the dome using bombs and lasers. Mirrored spaceships appeared out of thin air and dropped our soldiers into the attack. Right away, those ugly-ass aliens turned on them. They were blown up, shot with lasers, and physically attacked. We got the chips off a few soldiers. Those survived for a few days, but that was it. There's no shelter, no hiding place, no food, no water. The brownie attacks are frequent and violent. There's no medical, either, so those who don't die right away usually succumb to their wounds. We have no idea who we're fighting or why, only that we are."

"How did you get into the city?"

"Three of us—me, Orlando, and a guy named Jake—found our way into the city through the sewage system looking for food and medical supplies, but it was a maze down there. The stuff we needed was hard to find."

"Other day," Orlando said, chiming in, "that blurry something Park described came out of one of the sewers. Wasted a shitload of aliens before they killed it."

"What was it?" asked Marshall.

"I don't know, but it vaporizes its victims—slowly. They're scared of the sewers. If the blur gets into the city, the aliens on the ground vanish into their buildings and seal the entries. Same day, those ugly brownie-fucks came for another attack and saw the blur outside the dome slaughtering our troops. The whole fleet retreated. Whatever it was obliterated the last soldier camp. I don't know what it was, but it shredded our men."

"It was invisible?" Norelo asked, peering into the dim sewer tunnels.

Park nodded. "So far, we haven't seen anything in the sewers. We take turns sleeping now but haven't gone back outside. Since then, we've watched two more soldier drops beyond the dome," he said, his voice heavy with regret. "Today was the first one inside."

"You said there were three of you," Arnie recalled. "Where's Jake?"

"Went out one day looking for food and got caught by a blur. Those little alien bastards panicked. Orlando and I escaped inside this sewer, but Jake was killed. Nobody has come looking for us. They're completely empty," he said, gesturing up and down the tunnels. "The aliens never come down here, probably because of the blur."

"How long have you been in the city?" asked Arnie.

Park shrugged. "About ten alien days without a clue what to do," he guessed. "We can't communicate a word with these creatures. The suns rarely set, so it's hard to move around. We can't read. We can't travel. They're hostile little fucks too."

Orlando gestured in agreement. "We've been sitting here wringing our hands, scavenging for food, until today. We heard a big commotion outside. Went to see why and saw you and Kinety coming off the ship in cuffs. Mugged a few aliens, took their clothes, and went after you," he said firmly. "Most soldiers don't survive the drops, but some do. They just wander off, killing things until they're killed. We have to find where they're storing them."

Arnie pointed into the gutter in the direction Kinety had specified. "They're that way," he said, standing, "and we're going to find them. Break time's over."

*****

Tucked against the wall between twisted pipes, Kinety watched the Saphiridians go about their business. At first, it seemed that they paid her no attention, but, after a while, she detected sneaked peeks and random glances. It wasn't long before the murmuring began. Again, she was not welcome.

"… don't look at her …"

"… looks just like him …"

"… why we can't just … ," one whisper said in guttural tones, "… make it look like an accident."

"… your mouth! If Torak …"

Kinety's skin crawled, and, for several scary moments, she wondered what they would do with her. Horrible images built in her mind, tightening a clamp of anxiety around her throat. Strangely enough, however, the assassination attempts had ended.

And Tooji … or Torak—Kinety didn't know what to think about him. He didn't want her—that was clear now—and that was fine. The two weren't compatible. In every way, he was her enemy, but the attraction she'd felt toward him was real, so it hurt knowing he'd been toying with her. Frightened, she leaned against the dingy wall and stared at the bulky construction of the spacecraft. It creaked and rattled, sounding as if the bolts would snap at any moment, and she wondered if it was powered on jackhammer juice. Loud bangs and groaning pops startled her and made her breath catch. It reminded her of a poorly built submarine that had sunk too deep in the ocean. Her only consolation was that nobody else on the ship seemed even remotely concerned. Telling herself this, she turned from the unfriendly crew and pressed her temple against the cold metal wall near an air vent.

Now more than ever, she felt alone and vulnerable and didn't like it. Without Arnie, she was a trembling mess. Since all this began, he'd been there. She had a friend. Now she was alone, and a heavy knot of worry descended into her belly. How in the world would she ever find her soldiers now? Without Arnie, how would she ever find her brother? Without either, how would she ever survive this? She was lost somewhere in the universe with no ally. No contact. No communication.

Except for her phone.

Kinety snapped out of her gloomy thoughts and blinked wide eyes. With the faintest sparkle of hope, she pulled her phone from her pocket and clicked it on. Instantly, it linked up with the ship's computer and began to charge. Careful not to draw attention to herself, she shifted her bent leg to block the phone from glancing eyes, snapped a few pictures, and quickly typed a message.

Arnie?

For several minutes, she stared hard at the screen, waiting for him to reply, willing him to check his phone, but there was no answer. Discouraged and bored, she began sifting through her settings to see what her phone could do. It took some advanced adjustments, but eventually she was able to connect to the universal internet through the spacecraft's link.

The first thing she did was search for information on the bracelets because she was curious as to how they worked. According to the rather complicated description, the 'Armlets' were composed of programmable matter that was injected directly into the bloodstream to recover and maintain the stasis of the organism recorded at baseline, which is automatically programmed upon initial introduction. There was more to it than that, but that was the gist. Her second search was about Tooji, which led her to the element toojidium, the blue power source used by the Zahrá Che.

As she learned about both, she accidentally found Saphiridia, which it turned out was in the same galaxy but on different ends of a star cluster. Saphiridia orbited only one star, Zahrá Che orbited two. According to the documentation, the planet Zahrá Che was in its last phase of survival due to the expansion of one of its binary suns and had already experienced a global evaporation event that had drained its oceans. The red giant star Kinety had seen while on the planet had an active alert on it, warning of its impending demise. According to the notes attached, the dying star had lost nearly all of its outer layer, which had been promptly collected by the white dwarf star hovering close by. This process would eventually trigger a supernova. The danger zone was outlined in a highlighted area, which stopped well before reaching the Saphiridian end of the constellation.

Kinety was perplexed. Why in the world would the Zahrá Che spend this valuable time fighting in some stupid war? They needed to get off the planet, she thought to herself. Next, she focused the information on the power source common for these two species. She understood only about a quarter of the explanation but gathered this: The power was toojidium energy—a term the emperor had used—which came from a vacuum between all other energy fields. Apparently, the spires, called power capacitors or skypods, collected, stored, and freely shared this fancy power drawn from absolutely nothing everywhere in the universe. The spires were indeed magnetized, which she had suspected after seeing one lean toward a vessel. All the ships had to do was hover near one of the round resonance chambers to recharge their fluorite octahedron crystals, which came in lovely shades of green and purple ...

*****

Hours later, the men reached a five-point junction with four open tunnels to choose from. Overhead above the center junction was an access hatch that opened into the city above. Arnie waved for silence. Clutching their weapons, they eased into the intersection and checked to be sure the tunnels were clear.

They were.

Some tunnels curved off, breaking the line of sight, but each seemed quiet. Curious, Arnie paused beneath the hatch twenty feet overhead. "I'll go up and see which tunnel to take," he said, stepping onto the ladder. "I'll be right back."

Orlando peered apprehensively into the tunnels. "I get nervous when I can't see down the canals. Let's make this fast."

With Park watching from below, Arnie climbed to the top and poked his head up just enough to see the glow of the red sun. That was all he needed. "We need to go that way," he said, pointing to the correct tunnel.

"Can you see any food?" Park asked, unaware of the tentacle reaching for his ankle. "Or bicycles or skates, or how much further because we've been walking for close to ten thousand miles. My feet hurt. We should be reaching Neverland by—aaaah!"

Arnie looked down just as the tentacle yanked, taking Park to the ground. Instinctively, he jumped, landing on top of him just as the appendage snatched him into a tunnel. With blinding speed, they were heaved along the ground and dragged through a corridor.

Arnie struggled to hang on. "Orlando!"

Orlando shouted and ran after them. Park and Arnie crashed hard into the curved wall and zipped around a bend.

"It's got my foot!" Park shrieked, slapping wildly for something to grab onto. There was nothing. "Get it off! Get it off!"

"Kick it!" shouted Arnie.

They both kicked at it, trying to scrape it off Park's ankle, then spotted more slithering quickly toward them.

"Babies!" screamed Park. "With teeth! Oh, my God! Aaaah!"

"Keep kicking!" Arnie locked his arm around Park and slapped at his leg pocket, very aware of the tentacles wrapping around his own ankles. Carefully, he worked his fingers inside. Tentacles grabbed at his wrists and legs, rendering them nearly immobile, but he focused on his task.

"Shit! Shit!" Park shouted in alarm, panicking. "A drop-off!"

Ahead, Arnie saw a gap in the floor, bulging with squirming appendages. Whatever it was stretched up from below, encouraging him to hurry. With a yank, he snatched his wrist free of the tentacle and pulled the only weapon he had—a grenade—from his pocket. Dodging more appendages, he yanked the pin and hurled it into the worm pit. "Brace!"

The grenade exploded.

Flesh splattered against the curved ceiling and rained down in plops. Arnie and Park slid to a slippery stop ten feet from the edge and ducked the barrage of splattered gore.

The smell was indescribable.

Arnie shook the goo off and looked. He wasn't sure what he'd just killed, but the explosion sounded wet. Breathing heavily, he blinked down at the severed tentacles lying beside their legs and exhaled in relief.

With slimy hands, Park frantically unwound one from his ankle, eyes wide, breathing erratic. "That really stinks," he gagged.

"*That's* why nobody comes down here," Arnie panted, scrambling backward and pulling Park to his feet.

A wide hole was ground into Park's fatigues from his thigh to his hip and another from his elbow to his wrist, with damaged skin just visible beneath. Arnie had a match on his opposite hip and could feel cool air from his shoulder down his backside to his knee. A sharp sting buzzed along the back of his arm and on the side of his butt in complaint, but he was glad to be feeling it. A bit wobbly, they backed away.

Orlando and the others rounded the corner at a full run, weapons drawn, and blinked in horror at the gore. "Are you alright?" Orlando asked, reaching warily for Park.

Park stuck a finger in a hole. "Dude, our clothes are trashed. Your pocket is gone."

Arnie jolted at this. "Shit!"

In a panic, he patted himself and felt his phone, safe in an undamaged pocket. Grimacing, he pulled it out and turned it on, worried he'd broken it, and saw an image of Saphiridians on a dingy spaceship above a message from Kinety. "Yes!" he whispered.

Vaguely aware of the hands pulling him away from the splattered mess, he quickly texted back.

Kinety! Where the hell are you? I'm in the tunnels with Park and Orlando. You okay? M

I'm okay. Sitting alone. Saph unfriendly but not bothering. They scare me. Saw Torak in hologram. Upset about wife rumors. Heading to some council at Jag Mosrog space station to explain. Torak meeting me there. A

Bad feeling about this. R

Me too. I'm studying ZC. Head toward the red sun. It's a red dwarf and unstable. Oceans evaporated. Still water underground. There's a purple plant with a fat, prickly stem and a blue flower. All but flower edible. Tastes bad raw but holds sterile water. Portal on Gimeg Plateau. I sent an aerial view. Follow the airships. Boys are there. Y

I'll find them. H

Tell Rixton I forgot to pay the mortgage. A

You'll tell him yourself. Keep marking your location. Stay in touch. D

With a heavy stone in his gut, Arnie switched his phone off and put it away. He'd relayed the messages as they came, so the others were already updated on the information, but he was uneasy. Powerful waves of uncertainty crashed over him. He had no idea what to do next. He'd lost Kinety. He was trapped on a dying planet orbiting a collapsing sun, heading for a destination he knew nothing about, hoping to save men who may not be alive. Pessimism wasn't a typical part of his demeanor, but the reports coming in were grim. He was worried. On top of all that, he had no weapons and no knowledge of the opponent he was supposed to fight. For the first time in a long time, he felt afraid, though saying so wouldn't help. Quietly, he followed the others into the correct tunnel at the five-point junction, and the weary group continued their trek, each lost in his own thoughts.

For the next few hours, they walked without incident, without conversation, until a draft chilled them from their musings. They all noticed the cold breeze at the same time.

"We made it," Park said, speeding up toward the open end of the tunnels where water used to drain into the sea—only the sea was no longer there. "We have reached the … ."

Standing together at the edge, they looked out over a sloped drop-off into a massive, colorless wasteland that stretched into the horizon. In the sky, a tiny, bright white sun hovered far in the distance. Closer, a red sun sat large and swollen on the horizon and seemed almost to crackle with fire, though it failed to produce much heat. Despite the size and nearness of the red sun, the light was dim and unsteady and cast a hazy glow on the empty nothing. Few plants remained along the ocean bed and, from what they could tell of the rest of the planet, there were no trees left. Boulders and rocks littered the dry, uneven ground and debris gave the landscape a cluttered look. This is the wasteland they had to cross.

Park looked stricken.

"Kinety told us the oceans evaporated," Arnie reminded gently.

"Yes, she did," Orlando agreed, giving Park's shoulder a comforting squeeze. "We've just never seen a planet die before. C'mon, kid. Let's keep moving."

The climb down was treacherous. At the base of the cliff, the brittle ground morphed into large cracks that broke deep between sections of dried crust. Arnie had seen this type of dried crust many times during the summer months at his home—broken squares of hard, dry dirt sitting atop the moist crevices that split between them. It was exactly like that, except on a massive scale. Now, he was the ant winding its way through a maze of crust. The ocean bed smelled of salt and long-decomposed bodies. Here and there, crumbling bones of unidentifiable animals and fish gave testimony to the deteriorating conditions of the planet.

Park averted his gaze from the worst of it.

Arnie's vision adjusted quickly to the low light. Inside the cracks, the terrain was harsh and unforgiving but shaded from the dual suns overhead and the cold blowing wind. The walls on either side changed shapes, adding interest to their journey. The dryer cracks were wide, the muddier ones more narrow, and none were level. The uneven ground where they walked ranged from powder dry or sandy to soupy mud and boasted a slight roller-coaster effect that quickly grew tiresome. The crusty flattops often reached well over their heads but occasionally dipped down to waist-level. Some cracks, usually in the deeper areas, were narrow enough for the group to walk along the top of the crust and hop across. Other times, they squeezed through unforgiving openings or crawled around blockages. Scary-looking insects and small animals that made little biological sense scurried in alarm as they passed, then chittered or buzzed in irritation. Before long, all six were exhausted.

Finally, with the cliff shrinking behind them, Arnie called a halt for the day.

"It definitely looks like an empty ocean," Orlando grumbled, sweeping his gaze across the vast, smelly nothing. "Where are we going again?"

"Toward the red sun," Arnie said, selecting a ten-foot-wide flat between shallow blocks of crust. "We're looking for Gimeg Plateau."

Park collapsed in exhaustion. "How are we supposed to find a plateau when we don't know where we are?"

Arnie pointed to the spaceships zipping through the air overhead. "We follow the ships. I'll know it when I see it. Kinety sent a photo."

Orlando leaned his head back against the dirt. "I can take first watch."

But Arnie refused and sent his new friends to bed. He was too anxious to sleep, and his mind was racing. Deep in thought, he stared off, worrying about Kinety and replaying the awful story Park had told.

Chapter 7

A heavy thud reverberated through the spacecraft.

Kinety, sans eardrums, woke with a violent start. After several moments of breathless confusion, she remembered where she was and was sorry she'd woken. Ugly Saphiridians were everywhere. The hustle and bustle suggested the homely hybrids were docking.

Yay.

She shook life back into her filthy hair and, waiting politely to be remembered, watched the crew secure the vehicle. There was no way of knowing how long she'd been asleep, but she had to go to the bathroom … bad. Only, they all appeared to have forgotten her. A few minutes later, several crew members headed her way.

She started to get up.

They passed her without looking, unsealed a door, and exited the craft. Others busied themselves elsewhere, writing reports, organizing cargo, et cetera.

Kinety sighed in annoyance and sat back down, a bit worried she would make a mess if she waited too long. Nobody was paying any attention to her, though, so while waiting for something to happen, she sent a quick message to Arnie, letting him know she had reached her destination and sent a map. That done, she climbed to her feet and waited some more to be acknowledged now that they'd arrived. Again, that didn't happen. The entire crew pretended she wasn't there, each carefully avoiding eye contact and remaining far too engrossed in their duties to notice her. Finally, it dawned on Kinety that nobody *wanted* to take responsibility for her, which did nothing to improve her already low opinion of the Saphiridians.

Disgusted by their behavior, she took the hint and stepped out of the ship into a docking tube. This led to a corridor with a transparent exterior wall that opened to a mass of docking spaceships and bustling cargo activity. Beyond the port, the nothingness of space peered in, stirring a pang of homesickness. Pale, distant stars arranged in unfamiliar constellations were barely visible beyond the light of the space station. It reminded Kinety how far she was from home and how small Earth was in this vast universe. But … there was no time to lollygag. She really needed to pee! Encouraged, she moved on, looking eagerly for anything that resembled a restroom facility.

Eventually, she found one and slammed through the door in a swish of enthusiasm. It looked different than human restrooms, but the idea was the same. There were holes to relieve oneself into, some on the floor, some on benches, and another in the wall. A wash basin—she hoped it was a wash basin—stood against the opposite wall in front of a digital mirror. When she stepped close, water flowed. She took her time in the alien restroom, using the opportunity to wash herself and finger-brush her teeth. She ran wet fingers through her tangled hair to rid it of dust and spot-washed the military uniform she was wearing. When she was as clean as her little … water dispenser thing … would allow, she searched for any other reason to remain in the washroom but could find nothing else to do. Wait! She could stretch.

She was stalling.

A few yoga stretches later, Kinety was ready to go. To where was still a mystery, but she couldn't hide in a restroom forever. With a stiff upper lip, she stepped into the cold halls of the massive space station crowded with random alien races. This time, she paid attention to them, her curiosity piqued. The intelligent life in this place screamed diversity, spanning animals, insectoids, humanoids, and … other. Their heat signatures were muted inside their compression suits, but the electronic items scattered around their bodies glowed with pale light. Odd. Kinety had never noticed heat patterns before. Now, she saw them everywhere. In fact, the glow was so constant that it had normalized in her vision. The brightest glow came from electronics—she didn't know why. The glow, however, reminded her that she had a cell phone.

Kinety brushed a lock behind her ear and took her phone out. With a mischievous lip-bite, she started a video and arranged it in her pocket so the camera lens could record. Smiling at her own brilliance, she turned eagerly into the chaos. Uniformed flight crews passed in groups, their demeanors businesslike and sober. But that isn't what stopped her. It seemed that not all of the aliens she encountered were warm-blooded. She tipped her head, then stared at one cluster with translucent skin, like scales on a fish. Were they fish people? Their temperatures suggested it, and she wondered what planet they were from. Those with colder blood wore a thin line of heat along their skin and appeared less comfortable inside the space station, yet were entirely civilized and intelligent. The see-through people were incredible to look at. She could see their pulsating organs, the food in their stomachs, and globs of poop hovering close to the exits.

Kinety ungawked her eyes and looked away quickly, unsure how private that last part was.

Most of the aliens were humanoid, a few not so much, and the majority walked on two legs. Some slithered. She tried not to stare, which was hard until she started pretending she was on a Hollywood movie set. It was childish, yes, but it allowed her mind to wrap itself around the indescribable weirdness. After that, she adapted and even inclined her head and smiled as two very tall, very thin blond people went by. They were beautiful, slightly haughty, and spoke in angelic tones.

Amazing.

The two aliens gave her an odd look as they passed, but she was already offering a politely muted gesture to the next creature. Only … this one looked like a wet spider with acne. She startled and averted her gaze. It wasn't her intention to be rude, but she had no idea what it was and wasn't sure which eye to look at. A dog in a Halloween costume, she assured her short-circuiting mind—a slimy one. Suppressing a shudder, she moved quickly past.

"… the Savage Bride," the thing snorted, oozing by.

She paused at the comment, startled by the Halloween-spider-dog's unfriendly tone. Choosing to ignore it, she continued on, assuming the creature was just naturally grumpy, probably due to its own awkward biology.

Okay, now she was being ugly.

Chastising herself, Kinety left the docking section and entered a maze of endless corridors. Here, traffic was heavier, giving her even more to look at. And look, she did! She passed iridescent creatures with narrow bodies, bug-eyed aliens with large heads, obscenely small … things? … in a heated argument, and slimy somethings with large muscles and jagged teeth—all with different heat signatures. So, were the heat distortions in her vision a side-effect of space travel? How cool was that! Pondering this, she hurried by and found herself at an elevator.

Two lizard men—men?—slowed when she stepped out onto a new floor. "… Torak's wife … ," one sneered.

Slightly alarmed, she hurried past and found herself at a food court that stunk to high heaven. The smells were a bizarre mixture of rancid, sweet garbage, fried swamp mud, and spicy wet dog. As nasty as the combination was, her stomach growled, insisting she try the nearby delicacies before deciding. Her gag reflex, however, encouraged otherwise. Curious, despite her aversion, she angled toward the odors for a peek at bonafide alien food.

And was sorry she did.

Piles of slimy, pulsating masses lay in smelly, oozing goo. Some creatures were dead and certainly rotting. Other items appeared more like plant material, though the insects crawling over them made her mouth water for reasons other than hunger or interest.

Kinety passed the displays with a warning burp and stopped at a water tank with pods sitting at the bottom. An accidental whiff reminded her not to stand too close, and she doubled back with a gag. Still, the pod was interesting, and she wondered what it was. Fat white petals or seeds coiled tightly around the outside of an unopened flower. They were beautiful and unique, and she tried to imagine what they would look like opened.

A walrus man with a fleshy mustache slithered over. He blinked an eye down the length of her before snatching a pod from the water with his finger-flippers and plucking a white petal thing from it.

Kinety stepped closer, eyeing it. "Is it a seed?" she asked.

"Hahaha! No." Expertly, the walrus person held it upright and gave it a firm pinch. Spider legs sprung from the underside, kicking wildly and oozing green stuff from its center. The walrus thrust the bug forward, offering it to her. "Try it."

Kinety recoiled sharply and—Whack!—bumped into a green person-oid with stubby spikes on its head—wait … her head. The female-maybe thing whirled in offense and proceeded to scold her in a voice that sounded like she … or it … was vomiting.

The walrus laughed again … or barked … in hilarity. Amused, either way, it popped the squirming spider into its mouth and turned to a different customer, crunching the kicking legs beneath his fleshy mustache.

Kinety clapped a hand over her mouth and hurried away from the food court with a deep gag.

Deep breath.

Exhale.

Deep breath.

Exhale.

Relieved to be away from the area, she slowed her speed. Breathing carefully, she struggled to control a powerful wave of nausea. It was the crunch that had done it, and it echoed even now in her head. On the bright side, she was no longer hungry. What she needed was a distraction.

Kinety hurried along, searching. It took a few minutes to find a good one, but she maintained her delicate composure until she found herself at a shop. Instantly, her mood brightened. "Oh!" she cried, increasing her speed.

Nearly beside herself, she swept inside and eyed the weird items on display. Guessing what each was for was fun for a while, only there was no solution to the riddles. She would have found humor had someone been there to solve the mysteries, but the standoffish patrons in the store were careful to keep their distance from her.

Whatever.

Kinety had too much to look at to worry about them. There were fat things with beaks and clothes that fit over no body part she could identify. Furry items dangled from hooks, glowing squares of computerized glass sat on a shelf, and bowls of shiny round rocks cluttered the floor.

Kinety was glad to see the rocks. She knew what rocks were and, desperate for something familiar, tried to touch the pretty stones. That is, until they squealed and moved away, startling her. With a yip, she snatched her hand back and blinked at the bowls. Those weren't rocks. Heart banging, she carried her curled hands and wide eyes back into the hallway and hurried away from the odd store, giggling at her dumb self.

A beautiful woman with scaly, iridescent blue skin and green eyes swept by with a scowl as she exited, reminding Kinety of a human fish. She smelled like one too. Kinety lifted her brows and shuddered, thankful Earthlings didn't smell that way.

More aliens brushed by, making faces and giving her nasty looks.

"That's her," one said to the other.

Another tutted in offense to a companion. "Oh, the nerve! She looked right at me."

Kinety wandered aimlessly through the halls, pretending to ignore the ongoing comments and thoroughly forcing herself to enjoy herself. She was on an alien space station. These creatures were amazing, comfortable in their own skin, and appeared to belong here. Who cared what they thought? Their voices, speech patterns, and languages spanned every sound imaginable, from beep to vomit to growl. To her, that was amazing. Each had its own scent and gave off a unique energy, approachable or otherwise. Best of all, they were real.

All noticed her.

"… just as ugly as Torak is …"

Kinety's smile slipped at that. It had long since occurred to her that Torak wasn't particularly popular here, which seemed odd considering these were his fellow … creatures, but she hadn't anticipated the depth of dislike. They hated him. She pretended not to understand that last insult and hurried along, acutely aware that they all seemed to know exactly who she was.

"… at her makes me shudder …"

"Ew, ew! There's two of them."

"… females are just as bad as the …"

Clearly, the word had spread about her relationship with Torak—whatever that was. Also, of all the species present, it occurred to her that *she* was the one who stood out most. There were no other humans.

"Ignore her! Don't look at her."

The comments were getting ruder.

"Oh, gross! Look!"

" … it's the female …"

Kinety's brow furrowed after that one, a creature with transparent skin and freckles talking to a bobble-head doll-looking beast.

Almost everybody she passed had some human-looking trait—at least two legs, two arms, two eyes—including the Saphiridians, which were everywhere. Yet, none were actually humans—only her. With this uncomfortable realization, Kinety began actively scanning the traffic for Torak.

"… how she could marry him. That is just …"

And on she walked, listening to the horrible comments until she could stand it no longer.

"… the thought of Torak mating makes me want to …"

That did it.

Finally overwhelmed, Kinety shook herself and searched for a place to separate from the crowd. Several more insults passed before she found an open door to an empty room and slipped inside, breathing deeply. The room was dim, though not dark, and quiet compared to the unpleasant corridor. Strange-looking furniture was neatly organized around a spacious floor, but she didn't feel welcome enough in this place to sit. Instead, she rested her elbows over the back of a padded chair and gripped her head.

Breathe in. Hold. Breathe out.

Keep your cool, Arnie often said. But it was hard.

As she composed, her memory flashed back to the moment she'd met Torak when she'd claimed to have fallen in love. It was no wonder he'd been so surprised. Now, she understood why he'd kept asking if she knew who he was. Everyone here hated him.

Kinety suddenly had the strongest urge to text Arnie and siphon a bit of strength from him. Right now, she was running dangerously low on confidence and could have used the power boost, but this wasn't the time. She was supposed to be somewhere and probably needed to get there.

Deep breath. Exhale.

Composure restored, she shook her hair out, straightened her posture, and spun face-first into the largest lizard she'd ever seen. "Aaah!" she yelped and backpedaled against the chair she'd been leaning on.

The seven-foot-tall reptilian towered over her, wearing only a cape on his otherwise naked body. He stood upright, exposing external ribbing on his chest, and had a central ridge that curled back over the crown of his head. His unfriendly face was somewhat humanoid, with a slightly snout-ish nose and tight lizard lips. Shiny, see-through green-white skin stretched taut over an obscenely muscular body in a mottled pattern. He had catlike eyes, elongated gold irises, and vertical black pupils with blotchy red sclera that looked dangerously like that of a venomous snake. And … he could speak.

"Sooo … you're the lucky girl," he hissed slowly, his language reptilian, "who's won the heart of the beast. Tell me," he stepped closer, peering at her intently, "does he fuck like he fights?"

On instinct, Kinety tried to slap the creature. The lizard caught her wrist with one … four-fingered claw with webbing and grabbed her shirt-front with the other. With a yank, he snatched her sharply forward until she was inches from his scowling face. The vertical pupils in his snakelike eyes lengthened as they peered hypnotically into hers. As he did, broken images of her first meeting with Torak flickered through her mind:

Torak lowered his mouth to hers.
"Do you know who I am?"
Kinety passed her eyes over his handsome face. "The man I just fell in love with?"
He smiled. "To you, I am Tooji."

Kinety struggled to get away from the lizard, but he held her still, locking her gaze. The chair scraped behind her as he came forward again, eager to see more.

Torak was kissing her.
"What am I doing in your dreams?"
A charming grimace twisted her face. "Faaalling in love?"
Torak laughed aloud. "Do you say this to all the boys?"

Breathing in choppy breaths, Kinety concentrated on her limbs. She wanted to claw this lizard's eyes out, slap the shit out of him, or scream for help but was too startled by the invasion to move.

Torak dropped his ring into her palm. "I want your soul and your beating heart."
"What are you doing?"
"Surrendering to a coward."
Torak's lips lifted, then repositioned over hers where they lingered, light and unhurried.
"Is there another meaning for the word wife?"
"Tooji."
Torak looked at her intently. "I will find you."

Unable to get away, Kinety gritted her teeth and focused instead on the slit of the lizard's eyes. For a moment, she almost thought she saw a flash of blue. As if by magic, she began to force the vertical pupils wide, breaking his lock on her, and pushed her way inside his mind.

Oknok sank sharp, venomous fangs into the Saphiridian's scalp to hide the bite, then found a knife and stabbed the dead body. Leaving, he tucked the weapon into someone else's pocket.

"Please stop! Oknok, stop! You'll kill us all."

Oknok shoved the controls forward. "I'm taking that ship. I don't care who dies."

A female lizard screamed beneath Oknok, struggling to keep her clothes on. "Information like that will cost you more."

"It's just a job. No hard feelings." Oknok shoved a wrapped body into the water.

The lizard jerked backward, trying to break contact with Kinety.

Oknok laughed as a frog-skinned alien was dragged away. "I didn't kill Ubnar! I'm innocent! I didn't do it."

Jagged mountains on a broken moon glowed in the sunrise. "Hide the crystals here. Nobody will find them."

Oknok looked down at upturned, panicking faces. "Sink it. No witnesses."

With a gasp, Oknok shoved Kinety away, scraping the chair against the floor. She staggered backward in a scatter of hair. He gaped at her in horror. She stared back, wearing the same expression. Realizing what she'd just seen, the lizard grew angry, and his skin darkened brown. With an offended hiss, he snapped two small fangs down from the top of his mouth.

A shadow darkened the dim room.

Kinety glanced past his head and saw Torak standing in the doorway. Her pulse leapt.

Oknok noticed the shift of her gaze, and his fangs vanished. A quick glance over his shoulder instantly altered his demeanor, and his skin faded back to green. "Torak."

In his hand, Torak opened a circular blade with a hinge. "What are you doing?" he asked quietly, stepping inside.

"Your wife was lost. I frightened her," Oknok hissed politely, "… by accident."

Torak stepped between them, his deadly gaze pinned on the lizard. "Did he hurt you?" he asked Kinety, his tone dangerous.

Oknok took an involuntary step back.

Kinety brushed scattered hair from her eyes. "Uh … ," she stammered, then gave her head a quick shake, "… n-no."

Torak broke the eye-lock. "Get out," he warned.

Oknok gave Kinety one last glance, then hurried away.

Kinety watched him go, then exhaled sharply in relief. Catching her breath, she looked up into Torak's beautiful face and lost herself in it. The mystique of his eyes was dazzling. She'd forgotten just how magnetic he was in person, and a powerful recurrence of her initial response to him came flooding back. A moment later, she was in his arms with her heart galloping in her chest. They locked around her, strong and warm, and she felt the press of his lips against the side of her head.

But the reunion didn't last.

His arms relaxed and she lowered herself from her tiptoes. He was close enough to kiss her again, and she wondered for a moment if he would. He didn't, though. Instead, he touched a strand of her hair and gazed down into her face.

Kinety admired his strange, vampire eyes. In the light and up close, they were beautiful. He was beautiful. She wondered if she should kiss him. "Tooji."

Torak tried twice to say something but then deliberately didn't. Rather abruptly, he lowered his hand as if snapping out of a trance. In a flat voice, he blurted, "Why did you not wait for me? You cannot go just wandering through a space station by yourself."

And ... the spell was broken.

Startled, Kinety unlocked her eyes from his and looked away in embarrassment, chastising herself for doing it again. Torak was her enemy, and he didn't want her, she remembered as a bonus. Pink-cheeked, she stepped awkwardly away, adding distance from the suddenly uncomfortable embrace, and adjusted her hair into her face to hide her shame. "Because I wasn't told to," she answered over her shoulder.

Torak paused, noticing her abrupt discomfort. For a guilty moment, he almost reached for her but didn't know what to say. Frustrated, he clamped his teeth and turned away, struggling to reign in his temper. After several seconds, he turned back and took her by the elbow. "Come on," he said, pulling her out of the room. "The council is waiting."

*****

Torak led Kinety to a crowded room and stopped in front of a table that outlined a curved wall. Sitting at the table was a myriad of different species, each one clearly high-ranking and representing a specific race. This was evident by the unyielding, high-brow expressions they wore on their important faces and the emblems on their angular clothing.

Right away, she recoiled from their disapproving stares and instinctively stepped closer to Torak. If he noticed, however, he didn't acknowledge it. Instead, he stood rigid beside her, his face stoic and unreadable. Behind them, aliens of unidentifiable species crowded the benches, either waiting their turn or to watch what was bound to be a terrific show. Kinety didn't know, but plenty were crowding into the room.

Prime Joboba marched in next and stood against a far wall. His short blond hair was neat over his large head, his uniform crisp. The glare he gave to Kinety enhanced the snub of his nose, which she found quite unattractive. Moments later, the council motioned for silence and gestured the beginning of the hearing. In the resulting quiet, all eyes turned to Torak.

"Torak, Master of War," Torak said, introducing himself in a common alien language, "and Kinety, citizen of Earth, requesting a formal annulment of public marriage."

Torak's blunt request struck Kinety like a blow. She'd known it was coming but hearing him say it made her chest tighten and her stomach sour. Embarrassment heated her ears.

An aged Saphiridian woman in formal brown clothing peered down her own snub nose at Kinety. "Public marriages are almost impossible to annul, Torak. How did this happen?"

Torak answered her directly. "Gossip and baseless rumors, both characteristics of Emperor Dinruk, have spread across the galaxy. This is a political tactic I have no interest in. This woman does not belong here."

Unshed tears stung the backs of Kinety's eyes. She wasn't sure why, but his apathetic words hurt.

"Do you deny your public claim to this Earthling?" asked the alien beside the Saphiridian.

Kinety stared. This one looked like a poorly drawn human caricature. She didn't know what humanoid this guy was blended with but definitely liked the ape-descended variety better.

Torak turned his head to the new speaker. "It was a sarcastic remark. A misunderstanding," he answered. "The Zahrá Che misinterpreted it, intentionally or otherwise. Nothing more."

Never in Kinety's life had she felt so unwanted.

"This council sees no reason to deny your request for annulment, Torak, and encourages the public to accept. Open voting will begin at the close of this session," said a green person of unclear gender.

"Kinety of Earth," it said in the same alien language, "can you understand me?"

"Yes."

"Do you have a benefactor who can claim custody of you?"

Kinety knew better than to look at Torak. He'd made his feelings clear. "No," she said, speaking barely above a whisper.

Prime Joboba stepped forward. "The council must be aware that this Earthling was caught consorting with Zahrá Che and should be considered a sympathizer."

Kinety glared back, startled by the accusation. "Is that what you call it?"

She was ignored.

The haughty judges put their odd heads together and whispered before the green council-thing spoke again. Moments later, the green person sat up straight and looked at her. Its eyes darkened. "What skills do you possess, Earthling?"

Kinety hesitated here. After hearing the rude comments about her unpleasant appearance, she was certain 'Taking sexy photographs' would not be well received by her captivated audience. Hacker of prehistoric computers wouldn't be much better. Preferring to avoid unnecessary ridicule, she cleared her throat to find her voice. "Just … domestic," she stammered, suddenly mortified by the truth of that reality.

The unimpressed looks on their faces hammered that shame home. The snickers behind her didn't help.

"Mm hmm," the green thing said in distaste.

Being pretty had always been enough to get Kinety by, but now that this was negated she suddenly felt worthless and incompetent. Rixton had warned her. It was a shame, too, because she was extremely intelligent. She'd wasted years of her life being cute instead of investing in anything of value in herself. Her looks, the only thing she had, certainly hadn't been enough to hold Torak's attention and, without him, the 'alone' sensation she already felt sank deeper.

The realization hurt.

The next speaker, this one with an elongated skull, shifted his imperial gaze to Torak, completely dismissing Kinety, who had clearly demoted herself in his esteem. "This council sentences this unskilled sympathizer to the service sector," he said in a regal tone. "I am confident a benefactor can be found to refocus her attention."

From the audience, numerous hands lifted into the air.

Kinety blinked at them in horror. "What? No! Put me with my men," she said emphatically. "They're at the Zahrá Che portal on Gimeg Plateau."

The official addressed her outburst with a short glance. "Their situation is a grave one. Your life is worth more elsewhere," he said flatly. "Request denied. Put the Earthling female up for auction."

Kinety shook her head, growing angry now. "I want my men," she informed the hard-headed council. "I'm not serving anybody. Return me to Gimeg Plateau."

"No," said Torak.

Kinety faced him, stricken by yet another betrayal. "What do you mean, no!" she argued. "The Zahrá Che need you to close the portal at Gimeg Plateau. They'll give me my men if you—"

"No." Torak focused electric eyes on some spot before him, refusing to look at her. "Where is the location of the base?"

Kinety snapped her head back and looked away from him, annoyed that this was still all he cared about. "What do my men have to do with that portal?" she demanded instead. "What is so bad that I can't go there?"

Torak didn't answer.

A female voice behind them filled the silence, speaking an odd language in muted, secretive tones. "She's as stupid as she is ugly. It isn't domestic skills they need at ground zero," she muttered to her companion. "What an idiot."

"Why in the universe it is so fashionable to breed with human females is beyond me," replied her companion. "This one is ugly enough to scare the Gaki."

Kinety whirled on the females, both dark-haired, snub-nosed Saphiridian civilians with tight lips. "Perhaps you two should concentrate on your own glaring flaws before pointing out those of others. I don't find you ladies particularly attractive either, and you're both severely lacking in class. Perhaps that's why nobody wants to breed with you," she supposed.

The startled women blinked at Kinety.

Torak took her by the arm and yanked her forward, ending the spat. With a hiss, he warned her to be quiet, wearing a look of alarm on his handsome features.

Prime Joboba stepped forward again, his eyes rounded in outrage. "Torak, did she just … ?" he began with a point.

The council members passed startled looks between themselves, then blinked back to Kinety, suddenly interested in her again.

After a tense silence, a man with enormous, furry ears spoke slowly. "How exactly did you arrive on Jag Mosrog?" he asked in the gurgly Saphiridian language.

Torak's eyes widened ever so slightly, and he looked like he might shoosh her.

Kinety frowned at the unexpected question. "Saphiridian Combat Vessel 654."

Soft gasps filled the room.

Another official using a different language asked, "Who was in command of that ship?"

Kinety wasn't sure why everyone was whispering. "Third Level Flight Superior Darplano and his unfriendly crew," she answered in annoyance, unsure where this was going.

Torak rolled his eyes closed and exhaled.

"She speaks Loquú!" someone said in awe.

At the declaration, every eye turned to Torak.

Torak corrected his expression. Very deliberately, he did *not* look at Kinety.

The big-eared councilman stood angrily and slapped six-fingered hands onto the table. "Explain this."

"It was accidental," Torak said calmly.

"Was it?"

He didn't answer.

"Torak?"

Torak's electric white eyes cut sharply to the man. "I do not have time for this," he warned, reaching the end of his diplomacy. "I have no interest in this human!"

The man stood upright, perturbed by the sharp tone, and angled his head. "Very well. We'll take blood samples and incarcerate her."

"No. Send her home," Torak said firmly.

"If you refuse claim to her, Torak, then you have no say in her fate," the man argued.

Torak's tone went deadly. "I said … send her home."

The entire council looked at Prime Joboba, who inclined his head in agreement, then shifted their glaring eyes back to Torak.

"No!" Kinety broke in, looking between them. "Send me to my men!"

The councilman nodded at Joboba in agreement, ignoring Kinety entirely, and spoke to an alien in a brown uniform standing near the back wall. "Summon Deep Space Cargo Transport 87. Get blood samples to storage and return the Earthling to her planet."

Without another word, Torak spun to leave.

Two more aliens in brown uniforms rushed forward to collect Kinety and energetic murmurs filled the room.

Kinety jerked away from the men. "You can't send me home!" she cried to the uninterested council. "Send me to my men!"

The brown-suits pulled at her.

She yanked free. Her voice, small and broken, shook. "Tooji!"

Torak stopped at the name.

Startled, Joboba spun to look at her, then at Torak.

Kinety pushed the grabbing hands away and stood silently behind him, stunned by the horrible turn of events. Staring at his back, she tried one last time. "Tooji," she said again with a crack in her voice.

Without answering, Torak walked out of the room, abandoning her to her fate and leaving her trembling where she was. This time, when the brown-shirts beckoned to her, she followed them, head high, brows higher.

Prime Joboba stared after as she passed, his eyes narrowed to slits.

As Kinety and her escorts disappeared down the hall toward the docking stations, Oknok hurried by and squeezed through the door toward the council. "He's lying!" he barked, attracting the exiting crowd's attention. Amid their puzzled stares, he stepped forward into the center of the room. "Torak is lying."

"Oknok?" one councilwoman said, expecting a good reason for his intrusion.

Joboba paused in the doorway.

The lizard passed deliberate looks to all the officials, one at a time. "I performed a mind-tap on the human female before the hearing," he said, earning a satisfying silence from the crowd. "Accidentally, of course."

"Oh?" said the councilwoman. "And what did you see?"

"Everything."

The council looked at each other. "Torak has publicly denied claim to her," one reminded the lizard.

With dramatic slowness, Oknok shook his green head. "He lied. I don't know why, but in every way that human woman is Torak's wife," he informed everyone. "I saw it."

"Perhaps he changed—"

"He handed her his ring!" interrupted Oknok vehemently.

Gasps, then … silence.

Oknok continued, addressing everyone now. "He gave her universal language. Not even the experts have that. No genetic experiment before or after him has ever succeeded in recreating Loquú—not even close—yet he gave it freely to the human Kinety."

The council members stared at the lizard, then at each other as hushed murmurs of surprise danced through the room.

"I didn't see for sure," the lizard said heavily and circled to look at new faces, "but I suspect that Torak's wife may already be with child."

*****

Prime Joboba didn't wait to hear any more. Seething, he marched to the docking port to be sure Torak's fighter had separated from the space station, then stormed up to Superior Darplano. "Kill that woman!" he demanded, so angry he could barely speak.

"You can't just kill her," Darplano argued aloud, then looked around to be sure nobody was listening. Whispering, he said again, "You can't just kill her. She's a public figure now."

"If she has Loquú, that means she can speak Saphiridian military code," Joboba raged, jabbing a finger toward the cargo ship's docking station, "and can read it."

Darplano looked around again, trying to signal to Joboba to lower his voice. "She can't do anything about that from her primitive solar system," he said, trying to calm him.

"The Zahrá Che found her once; they can do it again. By now, they know she can translate. They'll have her before she ever reaches her solar system. I'm not taking any chances. I want her dead!"

"This isn't about the language, is it?" accused Darplano.

Prime Joboba glared at the inferior officer. "Did you see him stop when she called out?" he said, barely above a whisper. "If he falls in love with her, we'll lose him. And then what!"

This time, Darplano didn't argue. Prime Joboba was right.

Joboba's eyes glittered dangerously. "She'll ruin everything. Kill the bitch!"

"Sir ... if Torak finds out ... ."

Joboba smiled. "He won't because you're going to be smart about it."

Superior Darplano watched as Kinety's cargo ship separated from the space station. "And the crew?"

Joboba looked the inferior officer in the eye and cocked a brow. "What crew?" he wondered, then spun on his heel and strolled briskly away.

Chapter 8

The hatch of Deep Space Cargo Transport 87 thudded shut with a loud bang. The vibration shuddered across the floor, earning a shiver from Kinety. A high pitch whir split the air, and the vessel separated from its docking station with a bang.

Kinety gripped the restraints holding her in her seat and closed her eyes, waiting for the fear to pass. After separation, she felt a moment of weightlessness before the onboard gravity kicked in. The sensation nauseated her already twisted stomach, but the upholstery was safe. She hadn't eaten in ages, and there was nothing for her to vomit. If there had been, she would likely have done the honors at the space station food court. Eventually, the spaceship smoothed out and quieted as it picked up speed. When she was able to open her eyes again, she stared unblinking at the grotesque mechanical contours and rickety emergency pods rattling against their bolts.

She felt wretched.

Overwhelmed with her distressing situation, Kinety hung her head. She was afraid and couldn't see a way out of this. For the first time in her life, she was truly alone. All she knew was that her fate, once in Torak's hands, had been cast aside. He wasn't interested in her at all and was now gone from the picture. To be fair, he had warned her. Nobody else on that space station cared a whit about her troubles—they'd proven that—and the crew escorting her now had not an ounce of interest in her plight. They were following orders, delivering a useless piece of mail.

A tear rolled down her cheek.

She'd failed. Arnie was on his own with the soldiers. Whatever happened now, only he could determine whether they lived or died. Soon, Kinety would arrive on Earth and continue being just as cute as she was when she left … and just as useless; only Rixton wouldn't be there. It was hard coming to grips with such a truth, and a knot of anger stirred in her chest. With all her heart, she resented herself for failing, for being in the way of others who were far more competent. With an angry sniff, she wiped her cheeks and glared at the crew, hating them for doing their jobs, hating them for not caring that she was upset, hating them for not bending to her charm.

But then …

Like a slap upside the head, Kinety realized what she had just done. She'd fallen into the exact same way of thinking that had put her where she was. Here she sat, busily blaming everyone else in the world … universe … when it was her own shortcomings that held her restrained in her seat.

Another tear fell, this one with less self-pity.

Why couldn't she do something—because she was a girl? Right now, there was no man standing by to rescue her. Of course not. The men weren't there to rescue her because *they* were the ones needing to be rescued.

And here she sat … crying.

Kinety looked again at the crew. If Rixton was here, what would he do? She took a moment to imagine how he might have handled being told to go home and shut up. The words 'Fuck you' came to mind.

She stared hard at the Saphiridians. Almost as if her brother was speaking into her head, she heard him telling her to be a man. He said that often when she was grossed out about a bug in her hair or a scary climb over a deep ravine. And he was saying it now. Only, this time, it was the real deal. As she watched the crew going busily about their duties, a fine tremble began in her belly. Not one crew member paid her the least amount of attention. She was obviously no threat to them and wasn't even cuffed for the journey. The only thing she had ever been good at was being pretty.

And she was pretty, even if they didn't agree. They, however, assumed she was harmless. That was their mistake.

Kinety was not harmless.

The tremble radiated outward, adding warmth to her limbs. As she heated, her gaze shifted to the life pod, then to the twisted pipes against the walls around her. There was a small, aluminum-looking tube on the floor near her feet that would do her no good. Beside her seat, a long-handled lever with some unknown purpose was locked into place and bolted at the fulcrum. This showed more promise. The construction behind the lever was supported against the skin of the ship, and whatever it was would hold just fine without the handle in its position. All she had to do was loosen the bolt, and the handle would become a weapon, but she had no tools—only her hands.

Another tear.

It was because she looked so harmless that her hands were not bound, she realized, and studied them. Perhaps she could use them.

The aluminum tube lay beside her foot.

Kinety looked again at the crew.

Black widows looked harmless, didn't they?

There were six of them.

The tube smiled.

Kinety smiled back. It was up to her now. Any decision, she warned herself, any choice made from this moment on, she had to be willing to die for.

And she was.

Ten minutes later, the folded aluminum tube snapped in half from the strain, but the bolt was loose. The heavy lever, easily two feet long, popped off into her hand. After another minute, six bewildered crew members writhed in pain as she helped herself to their weapons and boarded the life pod, looking just as harmless as she did before the beating.

*****

Well away from Jag Mosrog, Torak shut down the engines of his star-fighter and hovered, gripping his head and hating himself for his unbelievable stupidity. With a growl of rage, he slammed his open hand into the panel and dropped his head back in misery. He'd hurt her. That's the part he couldn't get over. He'd actually hurt her, which meant this whole time she'd been sincere. With unblinking eyes, he stared out at the spaceport, hoping like hell he'd betrayed her enough to make the galaxy news.

He truly hoped so.

The problem was now he couldn't clear the memory from his head. The way her breath caught when he'd announced he didn't want her, the crack in her voice when he'd walked away.

Far below, a cargo ship flashed against the docking port, preparing to leave. Torak knew without being told it was hers. Against his better judgment, he switched on the communication link and listened as Deep Space Cargo Transport 87 separated from the space station. For several minutes, he monitored the crew transmissions and watched as the ship shrank into the blackness of space.

Disgusted with himself, he turned the opposite way and sped off, refusing to look back. By now, word would be spreading that the rumors of Torak having a wife had been false. He could imagine their disappointment as it was revealed that he publicly rejected any association and simply left her. His hope was that his haters would be sympathetic to her after such a humiliation, which would direct their hatred toward him where it belonged. He was used to it. He'd been hated his whole life.

A stab.

In a universe of people who despised him, Kinety was the only one who didn't … until now. Now, it was truly universal and, to be honest, he hated himself just as much as they did.

Another curse.

Usually, he tried to avoid listening to the news, which thoroughly enjoyed trashing him at every turn, but today he deserved it. Today, he wanted to hear how awful he was, and he wanted it to hurt. The nastier they were, the better too. He could handle a bruised ego far better than he could a broken heart, he thought in desperation. He'd never had one before, and it was fucking killing him.

Gritting his teeth, he switched the signal to the news transmission and sat back, bracing to receive his just due.

"… to recap this special bulletin. The lies! The theater! The deception! Why did he do it?" said the animated reporter. "Our analyst has some insight."

"This is clearly based on speculation," squeaked a new voice, "but the accuser Oknok has a very valid point. Lying *is* a behavior untypical of this individual, yet the situation merits nothing less. It is my professional opinion that he is panicking, and I don't blame him. Now that word is out," he chortled ominously, "it's liable to start a new war!"

"I just—I just—can't even," stammered the announcer. "There are no words! I just—let's hear the clip again. I'll think of what to say in a moment. I'll just play the segment again for our listeners."

Static carried over the air, followed by the murmur of voices, a combined sound that irritated the hell out of Torak. Grimacing in disgust, he reached to turn the noise off.

"He's lying!"

A reptilian voice barked, silencing the background chatter almost instantly.

"Torak is lying."

At the sound of his name, Torak's hand froze.

"Oknok?" a surprised female voice said.

There was a shuffle of feet. "I performed a mind-tap on the human female before the hearing," the lizard's familiar voice said. "Accidentally, of course."

"Oh?" said the councilwoman. "And what did you see?"

"Everything."

Torak went rigid, staring at the communications panel.

"Torak has publicly denied claim to her."

Oknok's voice was insistent. "He lied. I don't know why, but in every way that human woman is Torak's wife. I saw it."

"Perhaps he changed—"

"He handed her his ring!" interrupted Oknok.

Gasps and then … silence.

Oknok continued to a dead-silent audience. "He gave her universal language. Not even the experts have Loquú. No genetic experiment before or after him has ever succeeded in recreating that—not even close—yet he gave it freely to the human Kinety."

Torak shook his head. "Oknok, stop," he mouthed in horror.

Hushed murmurs of surprise crackled over the air.

"I didn't see for sure," the lizard said heavily, "but I suspect that Torak's wife may already be with child."

"No! No! No!" Torak roared in fury and yanked the controls hard to turn around. "Aaargh!"

Engines screaming, he rocketed at full power back toward Jag Mosrog. As he streaked through space, Torak checked the call number for a direct link to the craft still well within range. Only, there was none. Frowning, he called over an open line. "Deep Space Transport 87, come in."

No answer.

Shifting frequencies, he tried again.

"Deep Space Transport 87, come in."

Static.

Torak tried several more methods, but there was no answer. Growing concerned, he shut down noncritical systems and rerouted power to his thrusters. Streaking through space, he summoned his live star map, desperately searching the flight path for Deep Space Transport 87.

It was gone.

"C'mon, c'mon," he whispered and switched screens, but his searches were all in vain. The cargo ship was not on its projected path. "Where are you!" he shouted and snapped out of the star map entirely. Almost frantic, he linked to the space station and found the cargo ship's last recorded ping, which registered the craft as far off course. His breathing shallowed as he turned toward it.

When he arrived, the cargo transport wasn't there.

Nothing was.

Torak's heart pounded. Open space stretched wide before him. He spun his craft, searching the blackness, but there was nothing there. With a trembling hand, he switched his search criteria from signal to debris and began looking for rocks.

Nothing.

After expanding his search of the area, he finally found a dead signature floating out in the open. No power. No signs of life. With trembling hands, he shoved the controls left, racing for the unregistered object. Long before he reached the unresponsive craft, he knew it was Deep Space Transport 87.

A cold wire wound itself through his insides.

When he had a visual, he slowed to examine the outside, which showed damage from improper boarding. "What have I done?" he whispered, staring at it.

The transport was no longer traveling but, rather, holding its aimless position in space. He performed an energy scan, then double-checked to be sure he was alone in the region.

A bad sign.

Minutes later, he stood over the slaughtered bodies of the Saphiridian crew. Kinety was gone. Whoever had attacked them had taken her.

Torak clenched his fists. When he found out who it was, there would be no mercy, he vowed, glaring at the carnage. As he looked, he noticed a lingering glow in the panel. It was fading as the last of the computer's energy drained. Calmly, alarmingly so, he set his hand on the recorder and surged it enough to activate the computer's memory of the last ten minutes. The image was glowy and grainy, and the audio staticky, but it was enough.

In the fuzzy holographic images, a shaken crew crawled up from the floor, wiping bloody noses and clutching stomachs.

Grimacing in pain, one Saphiridian reached for the panel to call for help. After slapping at it twice and getting no response, he raised his head, frowning in confusion, and tried it again. "I can't call out," he said, switching to a different method.

"What do you mean you can't call out," grunted another, busily pulling himself up to his feet.

"I mean, it's dead," said the first.

A third man reached the panel, this one with an impressive black eye, and tried to help. "Everything is down."

"That's impossible," a wounded female said, "unless we've been hit by a pulse."

The crew looked at each other.

"The only way we'd be hit by a pulse is if we were being … attacked," the first said.

"Attacked? By who?"

Bang!

The crew whirled and gaped in alarm at something beyond the holographic view. "What in the world?"

"What is this!"

"Aaaah!"

Torak watched the men go flying and fall violently into their current positions. Whoever killed them had either been lost in the static or careful to stay out of view. There was nothing else to go on —no voice, no image, no distinctive attack pattern.

There was also no Kinety.

Torak tried to pulse the memory further back, but the recording was gone. Concentrating hard, he ran the footage through his mind, trying to recall some detail. It had started out with the men crawling up from the floor.

Frowning, Torak looked at the dead bodies and realized he was not looking at the result of a single attack ... but a second. Closer inspection of the nearest body showed strike wounds—linear, non-fatal strike wounds.

His heart sped up.

Torak looked around for evidence of a previous attack and found a bloody cable lever lying on the floor. That cable lever should have been—he pivoted—on the wall beside the passenger restraints. Below unretracted restraints, clearly where Kinety had sat, was a folded piece of metal tubing. It was broken and damaged in the center as if it had been used as a wrench to unscrew—Torak looked below the seat—a bolt.

His breath caught.

Slowly, he turned to look at the dead bodies again, this time noticing only the strike pattern—a right and a left, two per crew member, and all at the right angle. It was Kinety. She'd attacked the crew, which meant ... wide-eyed, he spun to look behind himself.

A life pod was missing.

Yes!

Kinety was alive—Torak exhaled in relief—and ... he knew exactly where she was going. Only—if she arrived on Zahrá Che in a Saphiridian escape pod, they would shoot her down. "Shit!"

Torak took off in a dead panic.

*****

Kinety couldn't control her hands; they were shaking so badly. Horrified by what she'd done, she concentrated on breathing deeply to slow the flow of adrenaline. At present, she was close to overdosing on it. That was bad because, at the rate she was going, she'd need more sooner than later. No need to be a man. Today, girly had served her well. Ha! Take that, Rixton.

Now, the pod ...

First thing, she summoned planet Zahrá Che on the map and programmed her course. Once she was going in the correct direction, it was time to learn how to fly. She had plenty of time to learn, too, because it was going to be a long flight. Then, with wildly shaking fingers, she maneuvered the controls, learning how to work the patchwork bucket. No doubt she'd be charged with some alien version of assault and battery, mutiny, piracy, destruction of property, and certainly grand theft spaceship, but she didn't give a shit. She was a criminal now, an ugly one according to the hybrids, and had just gotten dumped ... publicly.

Nope, she didn't give a shit.

Once she got the hang of the controls, Kinety checked the map carefully for debris, then began searching the Zahrá Che planet for Gimeg Plateau. When she found it, she programmed her destination into the computer, which automatically directed her toward a wormhole, increased her speed to max, and pulled out her phone. There was no signal. In frustration, she tucked it away and began searching compartments for something to eat—which ended up being freeze-dried something with a side of blob. She was careful to not inquire about the contents of either, not after her trip to the space station food court. Kinety didn't want to know what it was, so she pretended she was eating chicken. It tasted more like what she thought frogs or crickets would taste like than chicken … but it was chicken. When she was finished mystery munching, she settled down for a well-deserved shudder and a nap.

Hours later, a high-pitched beeping sound woke Kinety, and she quickly slapped at the panel to make the noise stop. A few random buttons later, the screeching was blessedly silenced. When her vision came fully into focus, she didn't know where she was, at least not right away, and had no idea how long she'd been asleep. The good news was she'd found a small bathroom, and it was time to use it. Groggy and a bit unsteady, she availed herself of the facilities, entirely unaware of the alarmed Zahrá Che patrol ship moving to intercept.

When Kinety returned to the pilot seat, the planet Zahrá Che was very large in the window. About here, she began looking for some sort of automatic docking feature because she didn't have the foggiest notion how to land her tin can. Surely, with the technology in this galaxy, the spaceships knew how to land themselves.

When she didn't find a docking button, she formulated a landing plan. It couldn't be that hard. Slow down, touch down—easy peasy. Carefully, using her rookie navigation skills, she programmed Gimeg Plateau as her destination, set the course, then activated the command. That way, when she arrived, all she had to do was slow the pod down. She just needed to find the brakes, she thought, checking the floor near her feet.

*****

Torak tried again to contact Kinety through the radio, but her entire communication panel was off, and a scan of the onboard signals showed the imminent collision alarms were muted. On top of that, a Zahrá Che battleship was barreling toward them, preparing to intercept the life pod.

Torak pinged an identification signal to the approaching Zahrá Che planet patrol and connected to the communications signal. As expected, the patrol vessel was attempting contact.

"Alert: Your craft is entering restricted territory," said the robotic warning, cycling through several languages. "Identify yourself, or your approach will be considered aggressive." When she didn't answer, the automated message changed. "This is Zahrá Che battleship 36. You have been intercepted. Acknowledge!"

Torak angled his craft between the massive spaceship and the racing escape pod and braced to fire. Right away, the weapons on the large ship began to prime. "Torak in escort," he said quickly, careful to make his presence appear as unthreatening as possible, considering he was aiming at them. "Pod approach is nonaggressive and emergent. Request stand down."

There was a long pause.

"Do you copy?"

Right then, a station near the back of the massive craft opened and dogfighters began pouring out, not as an attack yet but in tight formation, which was bad. There were far more than he could handle alone. Torak glanced out his side window with a curse, watching Kinety's pod streak away. It was going too fast, but he couldn't chase it yet, not if he was about to fight. He shifted his position, staying strategically between the alarmed Zahrá Che battleship and the pod, and started backing in the direction he had to go.

"Do you copy!" he barked as pleasantly as he could manage, trying to rush them.

After another very, very long pause, the Zahrá Che ship canceled the warning loop, and a thought transmission responded. The weapons remained primed, but the ship slowed its advance. *"Copy."*

Torak spun his fighter. In a blast of thrust, he darted after the blazing pod. It was much too far away now for him to catch up, even at the speed he was reaching, but its course was easy enough to calculate. Without a doubt, Kinety had programmed a direct lock on Gimeg Plateau, but she hadn't adjusted her flight settings from deep space to planetary approach, which meant she was coming in like a comet. At her current rate of acceleration, she was about to obliterate the entire mountain.

The escape pod entered the atmosphere at a sharp angle and caught fire.

Torak's fighter screamed after her, very aware of the small Zahrá Che patrols scattering away from the portal below. Again, he scanned the pod, searching for a way to hijack the craft. Flicking his gaze back and forth between the window and his computer, he isolated a link into the vehicle, rerouted control to the power system, and fired a microwave pulse into the accelerators.

In the distance, the dry ocean bed came into view and, with it, Gimeg Plateau.

The schematic image flashed in alarm, receiving the destructive power surge, and the life pod's engines went immediately into emergency shutdown. Right away, he could see her craft begin to slow, but it wasn't enough.

Just then, the Zahrá Che warning loop returned, cycling again through several languages. "Alert: Your craft is entering restricted territory," said the robotic warning. "Identify yourself, or your approach will be considered aggressive. Alert: Your craft …"

Ignoring the transmission, Torak focused again on the link into Kinety's pod, switching on anything not fried enough to slow it down. Remotely, he activated emergency flaps and reverse thrust, then worked to get into the guidance system, but the connection was unstable.

He was catching up.

The fire went out around her vessel, and the plateau loomed, large and clear just ahead of her. She was seconds from impact with her craft angling sharply toward the steep walls of the plateau.

There was no time to reconnect.

Impact in 10 … 9 …

Torak flew his craft above her, collecting energy from the air into his open palm.

7 … 6 …

With a twist, he spun his fighter over hers, throttled his power, and dove toward the pod.

3 …

Carefully, he fired a restrained blue pulse, knocking the escape pod down into the dry ocean bed. It hit, throwing dirt, sand, and debris high into the air as it scraped.

Before it could bounce up and tumble, Torak fired again, shoving the slowing pod down into the ground. A violent arc of mud and steam sprayed outward as the pod carved a gouge into the soft muck and slowed to a stop. Torak yanked his craft up, avoiding his own impact, and found himself facing two incoming ships. One immediately fired on him, and he spun out of the way.

They weren't Zahrá Che.

Recovering, he looked back with a hiss. Who in the hell was attacking him?

The fighters split. One fired on him again, providing a distraction, while the other darted toward Kinety's steaming wreckage below.

The craft looked reptilian.

"Fucking Oknok!" With a shout, he pulsed the one charging him, knocking the fighter sideways, and engaged the second to redirect it away from Kinety. Just as it spun and turned to fight, there was an explosion overhead. Torak looked up and saw the sparkle of silver Zahrá Che fighters glittering in the sky around tiny gray spots, indicating a confrontation with an incoming fleet. In bursts of fire, the two forces swirled and darted around each other, blasting lasers back and forth in an all-out dogfight.

As Torak chased his target, he noticed the first craft he'd struck regaining control and opened his palm to collect more energy.

Chapter 9

Kinety blinked her eyes open and lifted her woozy head. She was on the ground, or rather *in* the ground, if the mud pressed against the windshield was any indicator. She didn't remember getting there, which meant she'd blacked out. Her head hurt again. Clearly, the auto-land feature in this tin can needed some repairs because that was a hard landing. She could tell by the impact headache thudding inside her skull. Moaning wearily, she moved all her parts just to be sure everything still worked, then dug her phone out and texted Arnie.

Marco A.

Polo! L

I just landed. I

Holy shit! Was that you? T

You mean the one who just landed in the mud? Yes. T

We're on our way. L

I'm climbing out. E

Relieved he was coming, Kinety looked around to see if her stash of dried mystery food and packaged blob was still beside her. She had nothing to carry it with, so began stuffing all she could into her pockets. Next, she gathered the weapons she'd swiped from the cargo crew. Once she was loaded like a pack mule, she maneuvered her way up to a hatch and crawled through the small opening at the top of the vessel. The air that greeted her was cold and stunk of stagnant mud.

The armlet woke angrily.

Bruised and a bit banged up, she stood for a moment on top of the blackened spaceship, growing accustomed to the sharp sting buzzing her arm, and steadied herself. All around her stood the mud walls of the gouge she'd cut into the ground. The top of her landing site was bone dry and crusty, but water pooled in swirling pockets around the nose where the pod had cut the deepest. Steam hissed where it touched. She looked down, realizing that the skin of the steaming craft was hot enough to heat her toes through her boots, which encouraged her to get moving.

The only way out was up the tail-end of the pod, so she started up.

Kinety tossed her brown hair into the cold wind and climbed upward out of the gouge until she could see above the dry ground. Eager to find Arnie, she crawled up the side of the unnatural ditch and stood on top of the crust. Behind her was the Gimeg Plateau. She hadn't missed it by much, but everywhere else she looked there was nothing in any direction, just vast open emptiness. Cupping her hand beside her mouth, she called out long and loud, "Maaarco!"

From a short distance away, Arnie's small, disembodied voice called back from between the deep cracks. "Pooolo!"

Kinety bounced in excitement. She couldn't see him yet, but he was near. "Marco!"

The response was closer and accompanied by running footsteps. "Polo!"

She laughed, immediately enjoying herself. "Marco!"

Arnie's head appeared in the distance, a bright smile on his dirty face. Orlando and Park were with him. "You flew that?" he called, jogging forward to rest from his earlier sprint.

"Yeah," she bragged. "It's idiot-proof."

Arnie laughed. "Yet, you crashed anyway! What's up with that?"

"No, no, no," she corrected arrogantly. "It was a hard landing."

"Very hard!"

"Yes, but any landing you walk away from is a good one."

He was about to yell again when his smile vanished. With a jerk, he drew his blaster and pointed it right at her. "Don't move!" he shouted and fired.

Kinety froze in surprise.

A huge lizard, coming at her with incredible speed, took the shot, flipped backward with a sharp grunt, and sprawled on the ground mere feet behind her.

She shrieked and backpedaled in horror.

Arnie charged forward. "Kinety, get down!"

Before Kinety could register the warning, she heard a crackle of thin wings, and a massive, flying insect that looked freakishly like a humanoid grasshopper grabbed her by one arm and a shoulder. Its sharp claws plucked her from the ground and lifted her high into the air. "Arn—aaaah!" she screamed and dropped her weapons.

Arnie charged after.

Park jerked his blaster up.

"No!" shouted Orlando. "You'll hit her."

Cursing loudly, Park lowered his weapon and took off, following the insect.

*****

Torak narrowed his eyes on the insect and took off after the creature but couldn't shoot it down. If he struck it, Kinety would fall. He had to wait.

The insect looked back, very aware of who was giving chase, and headed for the plateau.

A voice shouted through the communicator. "Torak!"

It was Prime Joboba.

Torak grimaced, concentrating as the ground began to slope upward. "What?"

"You're needed in the Yekuon system where one of the Zahrá Che bioweapons laboratories has been located. A battle with the defending Zahrá Che is ongoing, and Saphiridians are taking heavy losses because we weren't operating at full fleet," he added in an accusatory tone. "Where are you?"

Halfway up, the bug reached a small, flat stretch of land, and Torak had his chance. He zipped his craft overhead to one side, sliced sideways, and dove for them. "I will be right there."

The insect recoiled sharply toward the cliff, bracing for the blow, and sliced sideways into a rocky outcropping. Just before it struck the side, the creature dropped Kinety on the ledge and tried to catch itself. She hit the slope, rolled twice, and slid to a stop where a narrow section of ground leveled out.

"Also," Joboba continued, "a team of scouts will assist your search for the human storage facility. Report to the Daka Space Port Armory immediately following—"

Click.

*****

Kinety was slow to get up. When she raised her head, she saw the insect tumble to stop fifty yards away. In a panic, it spun to its feet, gnashing its mandible, and spotted her. Frightened, she scrambled backward on all fours and looked around, but there was nowhere to go.

The wounded insectoid scurried forward toward her, clacking its jaws, but then froze suddenly, staring at a point just past Kinety. With a slow crunch, a pair of black boots stepped around her toward the large bug.

It was Torak.

In his hand, he opened a round blade with a hinge and waited for the creature to make the next move. The insect wagged its antennae in a non-threatening manner, lowering its head, and quickly backed away. Torak closed his weapon, watched for another moment, then swiveled to face Kinety. Eyeing her carefully, he approached, unsure how she would receive him. Without speaking, she turned her face away from him. For the first time, she had no interest in looking into his beautiful eyes.

"Are you hurt?"

Kinety shook her head.

In that moment, all the things Torak wanted to say vanished from his mind. Standing over her, only one thing registered. "You are the *worst* coward I have ever met."

Finally, she looked at him.

In silence, he lowered his gloved hand to help her up.

Kinety ignored his hand, refusing the offer, and stood by herself. Dusting her hands on her pants, she muttered, "What are you doing here?"

His gloved finger tipped her chin, and she glared at him past wounded lashes. "Making your heart skip," he teased softly.

Kinety's heart hammered at the comment, but the memory of his rejection was too fresh. He was her enemy. As hard as she tried, though, she couldn't take her eyes away from his. His irresistible irises, outlined in black, held hers like a magnet. Right then, she wanted nothing more than to throw herself into his arms—but she couldn't. He'd made himself and his opinion of her quite clear. She was done with him.

When she didn't respond, Torak tucked a wild strand behind her ear.

Uninterested in round two, she dodged the unwanted touch.

Awkwardly, Torak hesitated, then dropped his hand. A long pause hovered in the air before he spoke again; his tone was back to normal. "You cannot be here."

"I'm not leaving," she said.

"Dammit, Kinety! You cannot save them," he said, slinging his hand angrily toward the portal.

"Then I'll die trying," she vowed.

"Kinety!"

"I'm not leaving without my soldiers."

Torak shifted his weight in frustration, visibly reigning in his temper, and set his hands low on his hips. He wasn't good at negotiating, especially with a female, less so with one he liked, and he struggled to find the right words. "Kinety … I did not mean— you do not understand—"

"I understand enough," she interrupted angrily.

"I was just trying to … ," Torak stopped, looking sharply past her.

A mirrored patrol ship slid around the plateau.

Next, Torak snapped his gaze to the six humanoid Earthlings racing toward the plateau through the cracked crust. One was the soldier Arnie … and the patrol had spotted him.

Torak frowned. If Arnie died, there would be nobody to take care of—he glanced at Kinety, then cursed. In annoyance, he rushed past her. "Wait here!" he called back and produced his star-fighter with a pop.

Kinety watched him jump into the black vessel, which appeared from nowhere, and vanish inside. With a high-pitched scream, Torak's black fighter intercepted the silver patrol vessel, engaging it in a dogfight.

Above her, a slower Zahrá Che vessel appeared and stopped directly over the plateau. As it hovered, a loud thud split the air, startling her. From where she stood, she could only see the bottom of the craft. There was a heavy whine and, as she watched, a liquid hole opened in the floor, revealing loaded tubes with alarmed soldiers inside. Right away, she knew what she was looking at.

The soldiers dropped.

"No!" she cried and raced to the side wall of the plateau. Like a madwoman, she began rock climbing up the sheer side. Rixton always insisted she use harnesses when they went rock climbing and had never really trained her in freestyle, but that wasn't about to stop her now. Overhead, she heard unbelievable screaming—men screaming like women—and climbed harder. Gritting her teeth, she spider-crawled up, forbidding a single tear to fall as she moved. The sobs were there, however, spurring her faster. Panting through her teeth, she heaved her body frantically over the side and found herself facing the insect again. It looked like a cross between a grasshopper and a praying mantis but stood much taller than her.

A faint hint of blue flashed in Kinety's eyes, making her head hurt worse, and clicky sounds filled her mind.

"Bride," it clicked.

Warily, she braced to defend herself. She didn't want to fight but was ready if she had to. "Let me by," she warned, looking around the ground for a weapon.

The insect stepped carefully forward, twisting its head to angle a bulbous eye at her, and spoke in a series of clicks and pops. "It is true," it chirped. "The Savage Bride can speak."

Kinety responded by clicking her tongue. "Let me by," she said again and tried to circle around it. "I just want to reach my men."

The insect blocked her, clacking its mandibles. "You can stop this," it insisted in a hissy chitter and gestured one of six legs to a disturbance in the air just behind it. "The Gaki."

"What are Gaki?" Kinety followed the gesture to a large, shapeless distortion, almost like a bubble of invisible water that sat in the air. From it emitted an odor that could only be described as death. It had to be the portal the emperor had spoken of, and her men were inside. "How?" she rushed, eager to go.

In one of its many claws, the insect produced a tiny vial. "Kill the queens."

"Why don't you kill the queens?" she ticked angrily.

"My kind can't sneak in. They hear our wings, so we cannot get close to the nest. The Zahrá Che are weak and cannot fight. They cannot run. Other species cannot even touch the vial, so potent it is. None of us have the strength or stealth of an Earthling, and our blood makes Gaki breed faster. This is why the Zahrá Che use your soldiers to fight the Gaki."

Kinety eyed the vial. "What's in it?"

"A plague. My people have tried many times to communicate with your race, but we failed. They kill us when we approach. You are the first, Wife of Torak. Only you can stop the Gaki."

"What do I do?"

"Gaki cannot swim. Use the water to stay alive," it clicked, placing the vial on the ground. "There's a tributary a few miles in, beyond the nest. Put this where the waters converge near the waterfall. It will eliminate the Gaki."

"What about my men?"

"There are never survivors, but they fight well until death."

"None?"

"One may enter Neontak but not exit. Those already inside will die there. Only you can save those yet to enter," the bug chirped, backing away from the vial, "and billions of Zahrá Che lives. Help us, Bride."

Kinety noticed a movement just beyond the creature, but when she looked nothing was there. "Tell me … what is this all about? This war. Why are they fighting?"

"Long ago, the Zahrá Che created the Saphiridian hybrids, terraformed a planet for them, and allowed them to thrive in a neighboring solar system. The Saphiridians did thrive and more. Eventually, they began expanding and soon claimed every viable planet that could be terraformed as their own. But there was one that was different—Neontak," it said, indicating the portal. "It needed no terraforming. The ecosystem and air composition were already established. Recently," the bug gestured to the red sun, "the Zahrá Che sun started to die. To save their species, they need a habitable planet, fast. They asked the Saphiridians for Neontak. The Saphiridians refused. Desperate, the Zahrá Che tried to take the planet by force. When the Saphiridians found out, they released the Gaki into Neontak, preferring to destroy the ecology of a beautiful planet rather than let the Zahrá Che have it; so selfish are they. War broke out."

An odd prickle crawled over Kinety's skin, making her shudder, and beneath her feet she felt a tremble in the ground. Another glance showed nothing to explain it. "Why can't they just share?" she asked.

"The Zahrá Che and Saphiridians need different atmospheric compositions and water chemistry to fit their needs and cannot coexist due to political and cultural incompatibility. The Zahrá Che have a large population and not much time, so they fought dirty. The war escalated quickly, and a new portal was opened from Neontak into planet Zahrá Che to infect it, too, with Gaki. Now the Saphiridian attacks are almost daily, and we don't know how to stop the Gaki. Millions died before we found a temporary solution—your soldiers. The war is between the Zahrá Che and the Saphiridians, but many true-blood species support the Zahrá Che, while the hybrids support Prime Joboba."

Behind the bug, the air began to buzz.

"Where does Torak fit into all this?"

"Torak is nothing but a—"

The insect noticed the buzz suddenly and whirled in fright. With a choked cry, it threw its wings open to fly away. Before it could jump, the air exploded and a cloud of dust billowed from the ground, circling around the insect in a tornado of spinning dirt that rendered its wings useless. At the center of the circle, the insect screamed horribly and went down in a blur.

Kinety jolted in alarm.

Inside the ring, the shrieking insect clawed wildly at the ground beneath a spray of green blood. The circle began to shrink and, piece by piece, flesh was torn from its writhing body.

Cold, black fright seized Kinety's insides.

Soon, the spinning circle closed in and what was left of the insect's body vanished beneath a pile of squirming, naked creatures, and the dust cloud stopped. It had been eaten alive.

Was *that* the Gaki?

Wide-eyed, she stepped back.

It was a mistake.

One creature, a skinny, lanky thing about three-and-a-half feet tall with razor-sharp claws, spun toward the crunch of gravel beneath her foot. Sharp jagged teeth protruded from its mouth, still wet with fresh insect blood. Its beady red eyes zeroed in on her. With a buzz, he vanished. The buzz signaled the rest and about twenty more turned, each vibrating itself invisible.

Kinety whirled to run and crashed face-first into Torak. "Tooji!" she cried, launching the vibrating creatures into an instant frenzy. Dust billowed in a circle around them.

Torak shoved a gun into her hand and spun her around so she stood against his back. "Too late. We are surrounded," he said calmly and looped his free arm firmly around her middle from behind. "Listen carefully."

The circle began to close.

Kinety's breathing grew loud. "Tooji!"

"A Gaki attack is geometric. It appears as if they are moving counterclockwise, but they are actually lining up. They buzz themselves invisible. The ground vibrates as they swarm; pay attention to it," he said, holding her back tight against his. "The pattern is entirely organized. There is a rhythm to it. The alpha will strike first. His antipode, the creature exactly across from him in the ring, will strike immediately after, so will come at your back. A small step to the right will turn you into the next attack. They go in order, so we have to kill them in order. Listen to it. When the vibration frequency pitches, the dust will break."

"The alpha will attack from the front," she repeated breathlessly, "then one will attack from the back. Turn to the right."

"Not necessarily from your front. Alpha is usually the tallest, but you do not know where he will strike from. That is why you need a partner. When the dust breaks, that is how you find him. Every attack includes the opposite," he said again. "They go in order one at a time, which means the Gaki to *his* left. Turn toward the attack, fire straight ahead, and wait for me; we step right together."

"Tooji!"

"They are lined up. Wait for the attack," he coached firmly.

"What if I miss?"

"Do not miss."

The dust broke just to her left, startling her. "Aaaah!" she shrieked, turning into it, and fired barely in time.

A grotesque creature jolted crazily and dropped at her feet, kicking and writhing. It had pink skin, a long, narrow face with tiny, beady eyes in enormous sockets, a large, oblong head, and a ridiculously muscular jaw. Unmoving red pupils surrounded by yellow reflective sclera stared ferociously at Kinety as it died. Sharp piranha teeth lined the inside of its partially open mouth.

Behind her, Torak fired and shifted her one step to the right just in time for another break in the dust. Kinety yelped sharply and fired, nearly missing her turn. She had to calm herself.

He fired.

They turned.

Desperate for something to hold onto, Kinety slid her arm back around his middle the way he had her. The gesture seemed small, but it simultaneously gave her courage as well as synchronized their movements.

The circle began to tighten.

Fire. Fire. Step.

Fire. Fire. Step.

"What are they?" she managed.

"Gaki. They are like insects. They have a hive mind and low intelligence," he said over his shoulder. "They are mine."

"Yours!"

"Yes. I stole five queens from planet Fareh-Nombie and created a portal into Neontak for the males to follow," he said, firing.

"Why would you do that!" Kinety tripped over a body, fired, and corrected her footing.

And the pattern changed.

Torak fired twice and struck one jumping out of turn, knocking it away when it would have fallen on him.

Kinety squealed, taking a glancing blow from one on her side as she fired.

"Faster!" he ordered. "I fire. Step. You fire. Step."

She yelped, nearly missing another, then synchronized again.

"The Zahrá Che were using bioweapons against the Saphiridians, so I opened a portal to Neontak to occupy them while my people fought to create a vaccine, antidote, anything. It worked until the Zahrá Che started stealing soldiers to fight their battles and to thin the Gaki. Now, they monitor Neontak. Invisible transport ships hover nearby. When Gaki swarm near the portal, the Zahrá Che drop abducted soldiers until the herd is either defeated or fed and turn away from the portal," he explained. "Get ready."

The dwindling Gaki altered the pattern again as the ring closed in.

"Same time," he said, taking a bigger step. "Shoot. Turn. Shoot. Turn."

The pile of bodies at their feet made turning difficult.

When only a few Gaki remained, Kinety's weapon emitted a sound and failed. Torak whirled, hooking his arm around her to get her out of the way, and spun with her pinned against him, firing in both directions. Four shots later, the fight was over.

In the distance, a mirrored Zahrá Che patrol ship appeared through the smoke of burning wreckage, spun in the air, and darted toward them.

Torak saw it.

Stunned, Kinety scanned the piled Gaki carcasses, visible now, and realized the horrible fate she'd just escaped. Wide-eyed, she twisted in Torak's arms with a sob and slammed her hands into his chest, knocking him back. "You son of a bitch!" she choked.

Torak quickly took her malfunctioning weapon from her hand. "We have company."

She pointed to the dead Gaki. "My men are in there with that?"

Torak opened a panel on the side and, with a click, reset her weapon. "The Zahrá Che are killing my people," he said, as if that made it okay, and summoned his fighter. It expanded with a pop. "Come with me."

Kinety snatched both weapons from him. "Go to hell!" she shouted and whirled. Close to panic, she grabbed the vial from the ground and ran for the portal.

"Kinety, no!" he shouted and tried to follow, but the Zahrá Che patrol vessel opened fire.

Chapter 10

Kinety pushed through the Neontak portal, which felt as if she was walking through unwet water, and stepped from the cold, arid climate of Zahrá Che into the hot, swampy world of Neontak. It was like stepping through a wall of liquidy mud but emerging dry on the other side, a sensation difficult for her brain to process. The new planet was painfully humid and the heavy air hard to breathe. On it hung the sweet odor of fresh blood and a lingering stench of decomposing flesh.

The band on Kinety's arm winked frantically, telling her the air was not suitable for breathing. An injection of some synthetic material sludged into her vein, giving her a dose of who knew what. Almost instantly, her breathing recovered. It stung her arm up to her shoulder, working hard to keep her blood chemical levels within normal limits, but her attention didn't linger there. She needed to find her men. There were footprints everywhere she looked, yet it was dead-silent here.

Clusters of bizarre three-toed footprints stamped circle patterns over the ground. Elsewhere, familiar combat boot prints cut scattered trails into the brush, linear, which hid their numbers, well established, which suggested many. Quietly, Kinety crept around a puddle of stagnate water to follow the trails, stepping lightly and rolling her footsteps to stifle any noise. Here and there along the way, she found torn fatigues, wristwatches, fingers, and unempty boots. There was blood everywhere. Her chin quivered at the sight, and sadness squeezed her heart.

In the distance, rapid blaster shots rang out. This was followed shortly by a high-pitched screaming as some unfortunate soldier was torn to pieces and eaten alive.

Kinety fought the urge to crouch down and cover her ears. "Focus," she coached in a soothing whisper. "Focus."

The soldier trails moved up toward higher ground but split often to who-knew-where. She chose a random path, entirely guessing.

Another blaster shot rang out.

Next ... the screams.

Kinety breathed through it. Beyond the swamp, she reached the base of a rocky hill and looked down at the valley below. It was vast and open and teeming with Gaki. While she could, she focused on one group in particular, noting their mannerisms, behavior, and appearance more closely now that they weren't trying to attack her. They looked like underdeveloped orcs or skinny malnutritioned goblins with no hair. They did, in fact, behave like insects, with each group following one central male figure, usually the largest.

There were too many to count.

Their skin ranged from light to dark pink and stretched sallow over their skeletons. Their faces were sunken into narrow, oddly shaped skulls with large eye sockets. Low-intellect expressions altered their long, ugly faces. They did appear to communicate with each other, however—sometimes aggressively, other times in apparent humor. Tiny red irises darted watchfully from massive beady eyes that opened to only slits despite their enormous sizes. The yellow sclera reflected the faint light from a single sun barely visible through an overcast sky. Thin lips stretched over the sharp, jagged teeth packed in mouths that hung open when not in use. Some were naked; others wore rags, which didn't necessarily cover genitalia, as if merely to ward off a chill despite the heat. Females and males were mixed. Small children appeared to wander on their own, attached to no parent or adult in particular. A few were pushed around and either responded to it with aggression or merely moved to a different position.

Kinety shuddered and eased away from the edge to find the soldiers. As she backed up, she bumped into someone. A hand clamped sharply around her mouth and groped her throat for a bolt that wasn't there. There was a soft "Shhh" against her ear, and her head was turned toward the face of a man she didn't know. He had curly brown hair, an unshaven chin, and big, alert brown eyes. An angry wound puckered the side of his neck.

It was one of the soldiers.

Kinety threw her arms around him. The stranger hugged her tight, then set her back. Very aware of the Gaki below, he put his finger across his lips and beckoned for her to follow. On silent feet, they crept higher into the rocks where a bunch of frightened soldiers were hiding. There were nine in the group, some fully bearded, some scruffy, some with fresh stubble. None were clean-shaven. All had wounds on their necks, most still bleeding. Several rested with their backs against the stone, staring off with dazed expressions while they caught their breaths. One soldier gripped his head and rocked back and forth. Two were on guard, watching opposite directions. Another, covered from head to toe in someone else's blood, sat bathing himself in dirt, frantically trying to scrub the smell off.

They all faced her when she entered, each noticing her badge, and several beckoned her eagerly into the huddle.

"Commander!"

The man who'd come for her squatted in the center of the group and spoke quietly. "Please tell me you know what the hell's going on."

Kinety waved the men close. Her hands and her voice shook almost uncontrollably, so she spoke slowly. "I do, and I'm going to help you. What is your name?"

"Clapper. Those things are eating us. They detect blood like sharks. The only way to hide is to sacrifice anyone who's been contaminated."

"What the hell are they?" one demanded.

"We've taken heavy losses," whispered one of the guards.

Kinety looked down below but didn't see any more humans. "How many men just got here?"

"About fifty. There aren't that many left. A whole shitload of them just got wasted."

Kinety forced down a swell of emotion and focused. She couldn't dwell on harsh facts just yet. She'd made it here. She had a job to do. "That's because they weren't trained to fight them," she said.

"You can?"

"Yes. Listen to me," she said firmly and beckoned all but the two on watch closer. The man who was rocking began to whisper to himself. "What's his name?" she asked.

"We don't know. He's Chinese."

Kinety reached out her hand and looked him in the eye. "Can you understand me?" she asked in English.

He said something in Chinese.

When he did, Kinety saw a faint flash of blue, earning more headache on top of the beauty she already had. Wincing, she thought about what she wanted to say and sounds appeared in her head. She formed them. "Can you understand me now?" she said in clunky Chinese.

Instantly, he stopped rocking and gawked at her. Close to tears, he lowered his hands from his head and answered in his native language. "I understand you," he exhaled, scooting toward her. "I understand!"

"What is your name?"

Tears filled his eyes. "Zhang," he struggled to say.

It took a moment to process his words, but she got it. Understanding him almost clearly, Kinety reached for his hand, inviting him into the huddle, and promised to explain everything. He squeezed her fingers in a death grip, positioning himself by her side, and let loose two streaks of silent tears.

Speaking quietly, she told the soldiers what she knew. "They're called Gaki. They're land piranhas with insect minds. They attack in geometric patterns. I can show you how to fight them, but I'll have to go down there to do it."

"Why?"

"So everyone can see."

The men didn't want her to go. In unison, they protested. "They'll eat you."

"They're going to try," Kinety countered, nodding.

"Where are we? Why are we here?" one of the men asked, pushing forward.

"They're coming this way," said one of the watchers in alarm. He spun to look at the dirty man covered in blood. "They can smell him!"

The group instantly began to panic.

"Throw him down!"

Two tried to grab the bloody man.

He scrambled wildly to Kinety.

Kinety squatted over him. Like a snake, she grabbed Clapper by the shirtfront and caught another man by a finger. Sharply, she twisted it back, successfully gaining his undivided attention. "Listen to me!" she barked, keeping them in the huddle, then spun to another man. "Be still!"

"They're coming!" the watcher hissed again.

The panic was contagious, and Kinety worked hard to keep her cool. "The Gaki must be fought in pairs," she told the men, who finally stopped to listen. "You can't fight them alone. I'll show you how, but I need a partner."

"You know how to fight these monsters?" asked Zhang in Chinese.

She released the man's finger. "Yes," she nodded sharply, then continued to the others, "but if they're coming, I don't have time to teach you. You'll just have to watch. I can draw them away, but I need a partner."

"It's a suicide mission, Commander," another man pleaded. "They'll slaughter you!"

Kinety spun to him. "Yes, and every one of us here will be dead in three minutes unless you all learn how to fight them. Right now. Nobody gets sacrificed!" she said with authority.

They stared at her in blank disbelief.

Below, another victim screamed in terror, this one female.

Instinctively, the men reacted.

Kinety sharpened her tone. "Every minute we waste talking, someone else dies," she barked, determined to keep their focus. "I'm scared too, but I'm going down there, and I'm gonna show you how to do it. It has to be done in pairs. Which one of you is going to keep me alive?"

A black man stood. "I will, Commander. I'd rather die fighting," he said with a quiver in his chin. "Name's Cassius."

"Which way are they coming?" she asked and gave Cassius one of her blasters.

The watcher pointed.

Kinety took Cassius by the hand and pulled him the other way. As they walked, she whispered, describing as quickly as she could what he had to do. "They'll surround us while they line up. They vibrate, so the swarms are invisible, but they attack from the front and back at the same time. Listen to the buzz. When you see the dirt break, you fire. If you don't see it first, then I will and will turn you toward your attack. Shoot only the attacker. Too fast, and your weapon can't charge for the next attack. If you die, I die."

"Oh, my God," was all he said.

Right away, she smelled them, and her insides shook. "We have to get out in the open, so the others can see us. I'll call out instructions," she explained, leading him down. "Stay with me."

"This will save our boys?"

"God, I hope so." Kinety pulled him out into the open and saw movement too fast to identify. "We've been spotted," she said heavily.

Cassius's breathing increased.

Before she could lose her nerve, she called out in a pitiful squeak. "Soldiers!" she attempted, then squawked again. "Soldiers!"

Her voice cracked, alerting nobody.

Cassius took a deep breath. "AttenTION!" he bellowed loudly. His strong voice echoed. "Eyes HERE! CommanDER!"

Horrified eyes peered from every nook and cranny, and startled Gaki whirled in delight.

Kinety called out. This time, her voice bounced against the rocks. "They're called Gaki!"

She paused to breathe.

Silence, thick with disbelief, hung frozen in the air.

Kinety's skin prickled. "Watch me!" she shouted, sensing their approach. "Watch me!"

The ground trembled.

"Oh! Ohh, I want my mama," Cassius chanted softly over the buzzing air.

They were coming.

Kinety could feel the panic in her throat. Forcing her voice, she called out. "Get a partner! Back to back," she instructed, hooking her left arm backward around Cassius. He did the same, his wrist trembling violently against her waist.

Right on cue, a circle formed around them, this one much larger than her first with Torak. "Gaki attack in order! The attack is geometric. It has a rhythm," she shouted, adding false strength to her voice. It bounced off the rocks surrounding the valley. Here and there, heads poked up. "Front and back at the same time. Alpha strikes first, then his antipode."

The ground around her trembled as the disorganized ring increased in size. A tear streaked down Kinety's cheek. She squeezed her lids to clear the blur. "They attack in order," she shouted.

Behind her, she could feel Cassius's heavy breathing. She was close to hyperventilating herself and paused to catch her breath.

"Keep calling, Commander," Cassius coached, tightening his supportive arm around her.

In the distance, Kinety saw Zhang and focused on him. "They buzz to communicate, like bees. Listen to the buzz. When it pitches, the dust breaks. Turn into the attack with your partner at your back. You fire! Your partner fires! Step right together," she called with a crack in her voice. "You fire. Your partner fires. Step right!"

Cassius's fingers curled into a fist, clutching a tight wad of her shirt as the circle of billowing dust organized around them.

Kinety was crying now. "They're ready, Cassius," she said breathlessly, squeezing him. "Wait for it … wait …"

The buzz pitched.

Cassius yelled suddenly, jerking her around, and fired.

Kinety saw her dirt break and fired, then turned him firmly to the right, almost too far. "Smaller steps!" she cried, nearly missing her second shot.

He corrected with her and fired. She fired.

Kinety and Cassius quickly found the pattern. Gaki began landing at their feet. When the pattern shifted, they coordinated. "Faster!" she called out, letting her audience know that the pattern had changed. In the distance, blaster shots began ringing out. Moments later, a long, blood-curdling scream pierced the air, followed by a second who clearly died fighting. "It's not working!" she fretted.

Cassius's arm tightened, turning her faster. "It is!" he argued firmly. "They died as a team. They're fighting. Our boys are fighting!"

More rhythmic blasters joined the cacophony, adding chaos to the valley.

Kinety's ring lasted forever. When it was over, she sagged against her trembling partner. "Cassius?" she whimpered.

"I think I wet my pants," he said, assuring her he was okay.

Kinety chuckled through her tears. Holding tight to each other, they stepped warily away from the dead bodies. As they moved, she saw Arnie, Orlando, and Park standing on the hill, all filthy from their climb up the plateau. They'd seen everything.

"Arnie!" Kinety tried to go to him, but when she stepped out of the array of carcasses, the air charged with vibration and her skin prickled, notifying her that they were surrounded again.

"Oh, shit! Cassius," she cursed, and the two crashed into position again.

"We got this! We got this," Cassius crooned, calming himself as much as her.

This attack started from the side, nearly knocking them over, but Cassius stepped hard, breaking their fall as Kinety fired.

*****

Above them, near the rocks beyond the swamp, Torak watched in breathless silence. Every strike launched at Kinety stopped his heart. He was ready if she missed. No way was he about to let her get hurt. But she hung on. She was clumsy at first, yet held her own and worked well with her partner. Around them, everywhere Torak looked were rings of attacking Gaki, fallen bodies, and weary soldiers. Lone men partnered quickly, forming teams of first two, then three. Soon, larger groups gathered between the more confident fighters, with standing men huddled tight at the center and the shooters stepping protectively around them. For what seemed like an eternity, the rhythmic pops continued, and soon fewer screams echoed through the valley. Occasionally, a lone Gaki would crouch as if lost from its pack and look around in confusion. These were picked off quickly by snipers.

Torak stepped forward, pushing a branch aside to see better, and watched as the fighters in one ring fell out of sync. One took a sharp hit from the side and went down, but a sniper killed the beast, taking the downed man's position from afar. The man, visibly shaken and bleeding, crawled quickly back to his feet and resumed the fight.

Torak exhaled in relief … then shook himself, startled to find his heart was pounding.

Over an Earthling soldier.

And just like that, the soldiers were winning. In a swirling mix of emotions, he released the branch, unsure why he was responding viscerally to an enemy's victory. The realization embarrassed him, and he glanced around just to be sure nobody had seen.

It was time for him to go.

Tightlipped, he scanned the valley again for Kinety, who had moved. He lurched forward a step in alarm, then spotted Arnie near a group of men. He was hunched over a rock, looking for anything to shoot. With skill that impressed even Torak, Arnie sniped moving targets. He picked them off with astounding precision, keeping stray Gaki off wounded, lone, or occupied fighters.

Torak liked Arnie.

W-well … not like as in *like*. Arnie was his enemy. He was just … capable. Leaving Kinety with a rival that was capable was … utterly stupid but better than just allowing her to die in a Gaki attack he himself had fashioned for the explicit purpose of killing his enemies, which included … Earthling soldiers … like Arnie.

Torak grimaced in self-disgust and shifted his stance in annoyance as his prized Gaki littered the ground. He didn't like Arnie. The soldier was clearly skilled, however, and had demonstrated well that he could and would take care of Kinety.

The attacks were slowing.

Because of Kinety.

Like a punch in the gut, Torak realized what he'd done. Everything was different now that his human wife had blabbed that classified information to her men and taught all of them how to fight the Gaki. Why had he shown her that?

Dumbass.

Annoyed, Torak scanned for Kinety and, this time, found her. The paired fighters were lowering their weapons, and the snipers guarded the perimeter as wary soldiers crept into the valley, forming a crowd. As if drawn by a magnet, groups of scruffy-faced men began working their way toward her. Some stopped to fight loners, but the Gaki numbers in the region had just been obliterated now that they faced educated opponents. Wounded Gaki scurried away, keeping the snipers busy.

Kinety was standing in a pile of carcasses, her weapon by her side. Dirty, beautiful, and weeping softly, she surveyed the soldiers coming from every direction. There were more than sixty, looking haggard and hungry. The soldiers, combat-stricken and confused, gathered around her.

Without meaning to, Torak felt a sense of pride. But then …

"Look out! Watch out. Coming through," called Arnie's familiar annoying voice as he made his way to her. His camouflage uniform was shredded along one entire side from shoulder to knee, showing a bare back and nearly all of one leg.

Kinety met him but said nothing.

Arnie set his hands low on his hips. "That's the stupidest thing I've ever seen anybody do," his distant voice boomed through the valley.

Kinety completely agreed. Mentally exhausted, she sagged against him, more than happy to let him hold her up, and dropped her head —rather intimately—against his impressive chest.

Torak felt a rush of jealousy and clamped his teeth. Arnie had Kinety. No biggie. He could just leave her with his enemy, he decided with a tick in his jaw. She'd be fine. It was time for him to leave. He'd only be gone a few hours, one night tops. Then he would figure out a way to make her want him again and not Arnie. Just one night, he told himself, turning to go.

One night.

Chapter 11

In the valley, Kinety rested her head against Arnie's dirty chest and listened to the chatter. Mindlessly, she looked at the scattered heat signatures, which seemed weak in the Neontak heat. Her exhausted mind, however, did nothing with this information. The mood was jovial, artificially so, perhaps, or maybe short-lived, but the humans —all bearing ugly wounds on their necks—had just pushed through the unsurvivable odds for the first time. She'd made it. She'd done what she set out to do ... and it was all thanks to Torak—her mortal enemy.

As she watched the soldiers celebrate, noting with a heavy heart that none were familiar, she let her conflicted mind wander back to Torak. The man had her entirely confused. If he hadn't come when he did, she would have been killed at the portal, and all these men would have died. Why had he shown her how to fight the Gaki? Why ... if he disliked her so much? He'd made such a spectacle telling the universe he didn't want her, so why had he come?

Kinety didn't know if she would ever see Torak again. There was certainly no reason for him to come back. If she was honest with herself, she'd say that was for the best, but she *did* want to see him again ... to thank him, at least. She owed him that. For now, she would try to forget her handsome alien and the sting he'd left behind. She'd found at least some of her soldiers and wanted to be with them. It was time to put her wounded heart away and figure out what to do next.

All around her, voices blended together.

Through the noise, a single voice called out. "Dorkymodo?"

Kinety froze. With a catch in her breath, she twisted, scanning the unfamiliar faces. Only one group knew her as Dorkymodo.

Just then, there was a break in the crowd, and her brother rushed forward, looking thin, unshaven, and worn. His glasses were missing, and he was filthy, which was unlike him. A nasty gash split his forehead near the temple, and an angry scab darkened the side of his neck. He'd been on Neontak for days and was still alive.

Kinety hesitated, barely daring to believe her own swimming eyes. "Rixton," she managed, struggling to find her voice. "Rixton!"

Rixton's unbridled look of surprise said it all. In disbelief, he spread his hands.

With a cry, Kinety threw herself into his arms. Clutching him, she screamed long and hard, then dissolved into deep, wracking sobs. Together, they dropped to their knees, clinging to each other. Around them, a slow, gentle round of applause began, congratulating the reunion.

The land was out of balance. Because of the Gaki, unnatural in number and not indigenous to the planet, the entire ecology had been thrown out of whack. The carnivorous and voracious eaters behaved like a plague, consuming anything live with mindless greed. There were no land animals of any size left, which had left a gap in the natural food chain. Because of this, the insects were indescribable. Without small animals to thin them down, they swarmed the weary humans in hungry packs.

In the crowded valley, Rixton waited, knowing he would have answers to his questions soon. While the chaos dwindled, he sat near Arnie and Kinety, visibly shaken by all he'd seen, and stared at the thick army of bugs.

Kinety wanted to sit with her brother, but Arnie had other ideas.

"That uniform you're wearing," the large soldier said, eyeing her baggy clothing. "I want it. I'm tired of my ass hanging out, and I'm covered in worm shit."

Kinety gladly removed the oversized clothes and handed them over. "If you ruin these, you'll have to go naked," she warned, adjusting her compression suit over her jeans and metallic silver shirt. It was hot on Neontak, but she felt better wearing it because the suit regulated temperature. Besides, there were far too many insects here, and she didn't want them biting her.

Right there in front of God and everyone, Arnie stripped his old clothes away and donned the new ones. That's how he discovered the unidentified food and blob she had stuffed into her pockets. "Aw, hell yeah!" he laughed and redirected her focus back to the soldiers. There wasn't enough to go around, so he used a knife to cut what they had into pieces while Kinety passed it out.

"Orlando!" Arnie called, slicing a piece of blob on a rock.

Orlando hurried to answer, then spotted his new rank. "Oh, *you're* the Commander now?"

Arnie glanced at his new insignia and stood a bit straighter. "Yes. I just promoted myself. Now there are two of us. Get a team and get these Gaki bodies out of here."

"How would you like them disposed of?"

"Bonfire."

A bright smile lit Orlando's face. "Yes, Sir."

As he rushed off, a large group gathered around Kinety, pushing and shoving to get information with their food.

Arnie acknowledged their questions while the soldiers worked quickly to clear the gory debris. "Let me get these men fed, and then we'll talk," he told a group of eagers. "For now, I need two men with loud voices positioned at the edge of the valley. Let's begin calling out for survivors."

While Kinety served the men, she chatted with Zhang, who refused to sit until she did. Zhang, who she discovered had been there the longest, had come with an entire group of fellow soldiers. After much trial and error, he and his men had found a plant that was safe to eat and a place to get water, but the Gaki had decimated them. He was the only survivor and was struggling with that fact. He was better now with someone to speak to, and flat refused to leave Kinety's side. As a sniper by trade, Zhang vowed emphatically that his services would be available to her for the duration of their stay and probably forever.

Kinety didn't know what to say. Embarrassed by such a pledge, she pushed her filthy hair, caked with Gaki blood and dirt, from her green eyes and smiled at her new ally. He was lonely and emotional and needed someone besides just her to talk to. "That's sweet of you, Zhang," she said sincerely and spotted Park. With a wave, she beckoned him over. "Park, do you speak Chinese?"

"Not well. I'm still learning that one, but I do speak Hangul," he said, looking past her to Zhang, then spoke in his native Korean language. "Do you speak Hangul?"

Zhang sat up with a brightened expression. "Ne!"

Park slapped the man's hand and introduced himself.

Thrilled, Zhang scooted himself near Park and enjoyed a decent conversation for the first time in forever with his new best friend.

Kinety got back to work.

A tiny voice, far in the distance, cried out. "Hello?"

Arnie snapped his head up and tucked his knife away. "I need a rescue team!" he called, summoning an armed group of men. "Come straight back and report."

In a tight cluster, the search team hurried off to find the straggler.

Finally, they were ready. "Briefing in five!" Arnie hollered, giving the soldiers time to close in. "Commander, you ready?"

Kinety stepped close, her face contorted into a grimace. "What do I say?"

"Tell them what happened. Everybody here has a right to know everything. The more they know, the better chance we have of surviving. They'll have plenty of questions, and you have to answer them," he said, messing up her hair.

Kinety shrieked and tried to fix her frizzy tangles.

When the soldiers gathered and were seated, Arnie stood at the front of the group and introduced himself. "I am Captain Arnold Jagger, Black Frog, Team Two," he announced in a powerful voice. "I go by Arnie. You may call me Arnie. I have been officially released of rank, which means, regardless of your rank, I am in charge until we finish this shit sandwich. Beneath me, the hierarchy stands. I have also been released of Rules Of Engagement, which means I have the authority to do whatever I deem necessary ensure your survival."

"So, you have legal permission to be an asshole," teased someone in the crowd.

The comment amused Arnie. "That is affirmative!" he confirmed. "Just so I'm clear, casualties are no longer permitted. The more of you fuckers I bring home, the better I look, the fatter my bonus. If you plan to die, you come to me and ask for permission. I'll tell you no, and you can bitch to your friends about how mean I am. Hooah?"

"Hooah!" some soldiers shouted in unison.

Another group balked. "That's, hoorah, motherfuckers!"

"Oorah!"

Arnie smiled. "I have with me Kinety ... or," he gestured to the insignia on his new fatigues, "the Commander. This is her shirt."

A loud cheer and thick round of applause went up.

Arnie gave a slow nod and joined. When the appreciation quieted, he continued. "Sit tight, and your Commander will explain what the fuck we're doing here. Let's be patient. You all have questions; she'll answer what she can. If she doesn't know, she doesn't know. Suck it up, buttercups."

A soldier raised his hand, attracting Arnie's attention. "Um ... is that Miss November?"

Kinety winced and touched her hair self-consciously, mortified by how she must look. And smell! Nevermind ... she didn't even want to go there.

Arnie gave a crooked huff. "She was Miss Last November. Today, she's Miss Commander. Kinety?" he said, stepping aside.

Kinety gave Rixton's knee a squeeze and stood. Omitting the more personal details of her meeting with Torak, she started at the beginning and told the soldiers how it all began. "Like you, we were kidnapped by the Zahrá Che. On Earth, the night my group was taken, I inadvertently encountered one of the key participants in this war, a villain to the Zahrá Che, known as the Assassin or the Annihilator. His name is Torak ..."

This intro led to the aliens and the war. Speaking loud enough to be heard, she covered the basics of the conflict and the human soldiers' particular involvement in it.

"I don't know where we are compared to home, but it took us seven days and a wormhole to get to planet Zahrá Che," she pointed toward the swamp, "on the other side of that portal."

"Shouldn't we get the hell out of here?" someone asked.

Kinety wasn't in a hurry for that. "The portal to leave here leads to planet Zahrá Che, home of the aliens who took us. Their war is raging. Their planet is dying, so there's nowhere for us to go. We're not ready."

There were murmurs of agreement and disagreement.

Kinety gave them a moment, then went on. "An attempt was made by our military to negotiate with the aliens on Earth, and trackers were installed on the last batch of soldiers," she pointed to Rixton, "but the plan was a fail. Our negotiations team was slaughtered, and Arnie believes the trackers are useless now. We're too far from home for a signal, so our people can't help us. It is not our job to participate in this alien war, but our fight is far from over," she continued. "You men and women are here on Neontak for two reasons. First, to fight because you're good at it. Second, humans—who they refer to as Earthlings or Terran—are considered a trash species. We're fodder. We, as a group," she gestured to all of them, "are not the only humans here. There are more of us. Many are sent into battle against the Saphiridians. We have three survivors from that group," she said, indicating Marshall, Norelo, and Wesley. "That's it. The rest of the captives are being held elsewhere, waiting to be brought here to fight or feed the Gaki—however you want to look at it. We've thinned the herd for now, so I don't expect more soldier drops any time soon. It's just us. Now that we're together, we have to find a way to reach the others."

"Do you know where they are?" someone asked.

Kinety glanced up at the sky. Rainclouds were forming in the distance, warning that it would soon rain. "Yes. I know where they are. I just don't know how to get there yet."

Rixton was confused. He narrowed heavily-lashed green eyes and scowled at his sister. "Wait, how do you know all this?" he asked, voicing the question on everyone's mind. "And when the hell did you learn to speak Chinese?"

Kinety ruffled her hair and made a face. "Apparently, by accident, Torak gave me Loquú, which means universal language. It—How do I explain this?—downloads the language when I hear someone speak it. After that, I'm ... kinda fluent. I don't understand slang or some of the objects and phrases, but I can understand any language ... and can answer. When I speak, my brain tells me what sound to make and interprets what I hear. I'm slow and it feels weird talking, but so far I can communicate in every language I've encountered," she said, indicating Zhang.

Park translated and Zhang inclined his head.

Rixton's laugh held little humor. "Universal language? Can you read it?"

Kinety wrinkled her nose, unsure how else to explain. "Yes. I can read anything Torak can read and now," she gestured again to Zhang, "... I think I can read Chinese."

Rixton blinked at her, waiting for the punchline.

Kinety gave him a glare, telling him to shut up, then faced her silent, unsatisfied audience. Awkwardly, she grimaced at them. She had no choice. Pink-cheeked, she cleared her throat. "The reason I know all this is because Arnie and I," she indicated him, "never made it into the tubes. So, when the pods ejected, taking the soldiers to storage, we were left on the spaceship with the Zahrá Che aliens. That ship was attacked by Torak—until he recognized me. Torak and I had an encounter—"

"Argument," corrected Arnie.

"—argument," she amended with a dimple, then sobered. "A very public one. There was a misunderstanding, and now ... I am known as the Savage Bride, Wife of Torak—"

"The hell you are!" snapped Rixton.

"—which means I was temporarily treated as an important political figure—a diplomat, I guess."

Kinety tucked a strand of hair behind her ear. "Because of that, I met the Zahrá Che emperor. During that meeting, the Saphiridians attacked. I was arrested and brought before the hybrid council at Jag Mosrog Space Station, where Torak requested an annulment."

"Was it annulled?" demanded Rixton hotly.

"I don't know."

"Did you even have a ceremony?"

"No. It's different here."

"Different, how?"

"Details, woman!" Park interjected, clapping his hands and tossing them high.

"Well," Kinety dipped her head, "Torak called me his wife, joking, actually ... and it stuck."

"He *said* it!" Rixton clarified.

Kinety scuffed the toe of her shoe in the dirt and nodded. "He ... claimed me."

Rixton stared at her, pissed.

"The council said the public would vote," she told her brother. "I don't know the results, but I assume it was annulled."

"So, it's the hybrids against the Zahrá Che?" one man asked.

Kinety wagged her head. "I've only gotten bits and pieces," she reminded the crowd, "but the politics appear to be the hybrids against the true-bloods. The war, specifically, is Zahrá Che against Saphiridian. This planet is called Neontak, and it belongs to the Saphiridians. The Zahrá Che wanted to colonize it before their own sun dies, but the Saphiridians said no. Zahrá Che tried to steal it. The Saphiridians summoned the Gaki, basically land piranhas, from planet Fareh-Nombie to stop them. The Zahrá Che brought us here to save themselves. Beyond that ... ," she shrugged.

It started to drizzle.

Arnie stepped forward, retaking the briefing. "Now, you know what we know," he said, signaling an end to the chat. "We'll let that soak in for now. It looks like the sun is about to set. We need to focus on a nighttime protocol while we have the light to do it. The lingering details we can worry about later."

Kinety retook her seat beside Rixton and exhaled. There was nowhere to go to get out of the rain, so she wrapped her arms around her knees. In a gesture uncommon for him, he lifted his arm and let her not only touch him but actually snuggle against him. It felt weird … like she was snuggling with her brother, so Kinety made him suffer for the grossness and kissed him too. Rixton wiped the slobber from his cheek in disgust and thumped her upside the head to make her listen to Arnie, who was talking.

"… since the pucker-factor has been brought under control," Arnie was saying. "It's time to break into squads and embrace the suck. You, I want a headcount. Run the numbers twice. Fighters, partner up and set up a combat outpost perimeter. Let's get a watch started in four-hour increments. I need a team to begin working on traps to find dinner. There won't be many animals on land with the Gaki about, so we'll need to catch whatever we can from the swamps. Officers, I need you all up here."

*****

Joboba stormed into the room and slammed his hands down on a computer panel. "Where is she!" he yelled.

Embarrassment pinked Superior Darplano's cheeks pale. "We don't know, Sir. When we arrived, the cargo crew was unconscious, and there was no trace of the female."

His brown eyes glittered dangerously. "Did she escape, or did someone get her?"

"We saw no evidence of an outside attack."

Joboba pinched the bridge of his snub nose and chuckled. "That means she escaped," he seethed through his teeth. "Go get her!"

Darplano passed looks between his crew. "We have no idea where to look for her. She could be anywhere."

Joboba exhaled, then faced the idiot. "She *told* you where she was going. She told everybody!"

"You mean Neontak?"

"Yes, Neontak."

"But … there's Gaki," argued Darplano.

Prime Joboba snatched the Superior up by his shirtfront. "Good!" he hissed, then shoved him away.

It took a moment for Darplano to catch his meaning. Understanding, he gave his head a sharp dip, then spun on his heel.

Rixton waved his hands in frustration, then held up Kinety's rock. There was nothing even remotely special about the stone. It was a smooth, somewhat flat disk, perhaps two inches in diameter and less than an inch thick. It reminded him of a little spaceship. "Wait, wait, wait. You're censoring something. Why did he give you a rock?" he asked, brandishing it.

Kinety tried to take the rock, but Rixton kept it from her. "Start at the beginning."

Annoyed with the butthead, she snatched the stone back and wiped rainwater from her face. It was her rock, and she meant to keep it. Tucking it away, she told the truth.

Rixton was slow to answer. "You kissed a strange man you bumped into in the woods at night?"

Kinety scraped bark off a twig with a fingernail. "I didn't mean to."

For a moment, Rixton appeared to short-circuit, but he pushed through it and ran his hand through his short, dark hair. It stuck straight up in the rain before plastering back down on his wounded forehead. "So, is Torak friend or foe?"

As Kinety scraped, the twig cracked. "I don't know," she answered and looked at her brother. "The Saphiridians were trying to kill me, but Torak is the one who taught me to fight the Gaki."

"Did he?" Rixton lifted a brow. "When did he do that?"

"Today."

"At Jag Mosrog?"

"No. Before I crossed the portal." She examined a pebble and decided it looked like any other pebble. "After I landed, Arnie and I were playing Marco Polo when some insect thing just grabs me and flies away. It dropped me on the side of the plateau. Next thing I know, Torak is there. Some Gaki came out of the portal. We were attacked, and he taught me to fight."

Rixton frowned. "So, Torak knows you're here?"

Kinety selected a different stick to play with. "Yeah, I … kinda took his guns," she said with a grin.

"And Torak is Saphiridian?" Rixton clarified.

"No. The Saphiridians are half-Zahrá Che, half-human, and wear brown uniforms. Torak is a human-based creation with a blend of different alien DNA infused with energy, some sort of biological-elemental experiment. When he survived, the Saphiridians weaponized him. He wears black and looks like us."

"Geez. There are more aliens?" Rixton asked with a grimace.

"Oh, yes. I recorded a video on Jag Mosrog. I'll show you when it stops raining. Torak's in it. There are more aliens than I could count. Lizard people. Walruses. In fact, it was a talking grasshopper that got me today," she said and pulled out the vial. "He—it … gave me this."

"What is that?" Rixton asked, looking at the vial.

Kinety was quick to tuck it away. "A virus, I think. The bug said if I put it in the water, it'll kill the Gaki and save our soldiers."

Suspicion clouded Rixton's features. "Put it in what water?"

She peered off in the distance. "A tributary a few miles in. I guess the nest is there. I'm supposed to kill the queens," she said.

Rixton pinned her with a stare. "Absolutely not!"

"If it'll kill the Gaki," she said firmly, "I don't have a problem with it."

"I do," said Rixton. "If it's a virus, it could kill us too. It's not an option."

"But Rixton—"

He held up a hand. "You don't release a bioweapon if you don't know the consequences … and you don't know. That could destroy the entire ecosystem on this planet. We also don't know who our enemies are, so we can't trust anyone … especially talking grasshoppers. Let's bed down for the night. The sun is going down."

Chapter 12

Kinety woke a few hours later to the sound of hushed voices and the soft light of two pale moons in a clear black sky. She had to pee. By habit, she reached for her phone to look at the time, then realized that was pointless and put it back down. The soldiers around her slept quietly, some likely for the first time in days. Arnie was one. He lay face-down beside Kinety with his forehead on his forearm. His breathing was deep and slow, the rhythm of exhaustion. Rixton slept on her other side with a blaster beside his hand.

Neither moved when she sat up.

The paired guards, placed at intervals around the camp, all noticed her. Kinety quickly singled out Orlando and Park and jabbed a finger toward the woods. Orlando spoke quietly to Park and stood.

"How long is this gonna take?" Park asked, making one eye larger than the other.

"A couple hours," Orlando teased, "and don't be asking questions."

Park gave him a thumbs-up and sealed his lips.

Smiling, Orlando motioned Kinety to the edge of the camp and waited while she stepped carefully around the sleeping bodies. "That was some mighty fine shootin' you did yesterday," he whispered when they were far enough away from the others. "Didn't get a chance to say so."

"It all seems like a blur now, but thank you," she smiled and hurried behind a bush.

Kinety finished quickly and dusted herself off. "What was the latest headcount after they found that guy in the hole?"

"Seventy-seven. Four females, including you. We got a few therapy issues and plenty of PTSD going on, but we'll be okay now," he said, lingering while they talked.

Kinety wasn't in a hurry to go back to sleep and stepped toward a clearing to look up at the moons. One was larger than the other and slightly lopsided. "It stinks on this planet. The rain didn't help," she complained, then sighed. "Do you have family back at home, Orlando?"

Orlando followed her gaze and nodded. "I got a daughter. Never married her mother. I'm sorry about that now. I've been thinking about her."

"You can propose when we get home," she said with a matter-of-fact shrug.

Orlando shifted his weight and made a face. "Nah, she already found someone else. I let her get away. I do wonder what my little girl has been told. I'm sure she's wondering where her daddy is."

Kinety lowered her lashes and scanned the dark landscape. "The media has been open about soldiers vanishing but denied knowledge about the disappearances. When I left, they were saying two thousand, but Arnie says the actual numbers are far worse. There's plenty of speculation and some rather accurate conspiracy theories. The most popular rumor was there was a secret war going on between countries because ours wasn't the only country affected. How long ago were you taken?"

"Month-and-a-half ago, I believe, if Arnie's watch is still accurate. Park was longer. Two months. I think I woke once before being transported here, but I can't tell if my imagination is involved."

"What did you see?"

"Tubes. Standing upright. Just a big sea of tubes. It was cold, and I felt like I was floating—kinda, banging around, I guess. That's it," he said, taking her by the shoulder and guiding her across toward the camp. "Come on. It's time to get you—"

Zzzip!

"—oof!"

A quiet blaster shot struck Orlando in the back, knocking him hard into Kinety. In a spray of blood, she crashed to the ground beneath him with a pained grunt. Stunned, she blinked, unsure what had happened.

She was wet.

Trembling violently, Orlando pushed his bloody weapon into her hand, choked, and slumped to the ground.

She looked at it, then pulled her legs from beneath him.

"Orlando? Orlando—oh my God!" she exhaled quietly, shaking him and looking wildly around in confusion.

Nearby, Kinety heard a thunder-crunch of heavy feet. Instantly silent, she scrambled backward into the bushes and pressed herself against the trunk of a fat tree. Seven seconds later, four large Zahrá Che soldiers in white compression suits clomped into the clearing. Through the leaves, she could see the pale glow of heat distributed evenly across their bodies.

One bent over Orlando, then stood. "It's not her. Find her!" he ordered, sending two in one direction and then hurrying off with the other.

Park's alarmed voice pierced the quiet. "Kinety?"

Sobbing in silence, Kinety held her breath, unable to answer as the searchers stomped through the brush. When she dared, she tried to dart back toward the camp.

"There she is!"

Zzzip! Zzzip!

A tree in front of her disintegrated.

"Aaah!" she shrieked, spun the other way, and took off into the woods.

The chasers charged after her.

"Kinety!" someone else called out.

A spray of blaster shots burst haphazardly around her, sending her scrambling for obstacles. Sharp voices and blaster fire erupted from the camp, followed by barked orders and a barrage of chaos. Judging by the noise, a whole bunch of someone was holding her soldiers back. All around her, heavy feet crunched over the uneven ground.

Kinety tried to make it back down, but footsteps crashed behind her.

Zzzip! Zzzip!

Ducking sharply, she darted into a cluster of broken rocks, tripped over a pile of bones, and slid down a steep embankment on her hip. At the bottom, she landed hard but stifled the grunt. Grimacing in pain, she backed quietly away from the drop-off and dashed into the woods below to hide. As she clung to a low branch, winded and hurting, she startled at the strong odor of blood clinging to her and remembered the Gaki. Working frantically, she tried to remove the compression suit, which was futile. Orlando's blood had soaked through to the metallic shirt she wore underneath. There was no time to remove either.

"Down there!"

The sound of voices spurred Kinety on again. Somehow, she had to get the bloody clothes off, but getting the suit over her heeled combat boots would take a minute, and she couldn't stop. She knew she was getting too far away from the camp, but her men were pinned and calling out for help would only alert her pursuers. She had to make her way back on her own. Desperate to return, she tried to circle around.

Zzzip! Zzzip!

The crown of a young tree exploded near her head. Kinety whirled the other way, and the chase was on again. Everywhere between her and the camp, she heard the vigilant searchers and spotted faint glimpses of heat. With strategic effectiveness, they were separating her from the soldiers. Noise from the fight echoed loudly through the valley, no doubt waking the Gaki. Aware of this, Kinety's stomach soured. If she met them alone, she was in trouble. She tried to hide.

But the moment she found a spot, the odor of blood wafted powerfully around her. No hiding place would be safe from the Gaki —like sharks in bloody water. Hiding was not an option. She had to run.

Below her, the trees thinned, and a pale beam of sunlight cast a linear glow across the predawn sky. In the distance, through a break in the trees, she saw the reflection on a river. With a glimmer of hope, she headed down into a valley toward the water, away from the camp.

As she dashed between trees, the odor of Gaki soured the air. They were coming.

A small meadow with smooth contoured ground opened up at the bottom of one hill. Across the meadow to her right, she saw a distant familiar figure in a form-fitting black uniform. "Tooji!" she panted breathlessly and turned toward him.

Darting this way and that, she hugged the treeline, heading for him. As the sky lightened, she hurdled fallen logs, scaled rocky hills, and sailed over creek beds, terrified the Gaki would jump out at her, praying Torak was still there when she arrived. As she neared the meadow, she began noticing dark pieces of something scattered on the ground. With nearly every footstep, something light in color crunched noisily beneath her feet. Whatever it was, there was a lot of it. Slowing to a stop, she picked up a piece of the dark bit and squinted at it. In the purple glow of early morning, she identified it and her heart stopped.

Shredded camouflage clothing.

Wide-eyed, she scrutinized the white things, long and broken, round and scattered, and recognized them too. She'd stumbled into a vast massacre field full of human skeletons. Horrified, she clapped a hand over her mouth, catching an untimely scream, and started backing away.

Across the field, something moved.

Kinety jerked her head up in alarm, and a prickle danced over her skin. They'd found her. Terrified, she whirled and raced in the other direction, ducking, slapping branches, and tripping over vines. At the bottom of the sloped ground, she leapt across a deep, narrow ditch and slid down the far side to a rocky outcropping.

She could smell the river.

Just as she rounded the blunt side of an eroded hill, a gloved hand snatched her backward, and she fell at a pair of booted feet.

"Tooji!"

In an instant, she was in his arms, gripping him with all her might. "They're coming!" she hissed against his neck in alarm. "They're coming! Get ready!"

"Get into my spaceship," he ordered, pulling her roughly toward the dark vessel barely visible through the trees. "I will get you out of danger."

Kinety yanked away. "What? No! We have to fight!" she whispered, checking her blaster settings.

He tried again to pull her. "There are too many to fight!"

"I'm not leaving without my men," she argued.

The ground began to tremble.

"It is too late for them! Hurry!"

"I'm not leaving," she said again, giving him a shove.

A branch snapped.

Near panic, he yanked her into motion, nearly throwing her to the ground. "Run!" he shouted, looking over his shoulder.

She stumbled and caught herself on a rock. "No! We have to fight!"

"We cannot fight Gaki!" he screeched, jerking her over the rocks.

Kinety threw herself down and recoiled from him. "Let me go!" she cried, then scrambled backward when he came after her. He reached for her, but she kicked him in the side, knocking him away.

Torak dove and clapped a gloved hand over her mouth to silence her, then yanked her roughly with him toward the craft.

Kinety clocked him upside the head with her blaster, knocking him back again, and tried to go the other way. "Arnie!" she screamed.

In an instant, Torak was on her. Strong fingers ripped her compression suit, tearing it off her shoulders and away from the jeans she wore underneath, his fingers pinching and scratching.

Kinety fought to get away.

Torak growled in frustration and reached for his knife.

Crying aloud, Kinety spun to her back, fighting him, and grabbed the hilt. As they struggled for the knife, she head-butted him in the face, snatched it away, and kicked out of the suit. He fell backward, giving her time to add distance. Dropping the blaster, she used the knife to slice the ankles free and tugged hard to get the pant cuffs off her boots. The suit came away in his hands, and she scurried backward.

Hissing, he wadded the torn clothes and tossed them angrily aside. With a leap, he was on her again, clawing at her, tearing at her bloody metallic shirt, and dragging her violently toward the craft.

Kinety couldn't reach the blaster. She picked up a rock instead and whacked him with it.

Torak jerked sideways and, with a rip, came away with her shirt. Growling, he hooked his fingers around the waistband of her jeans and hauled her back down.

Kinety punched him twice, freeing herself, then braced a knee on the ground. With a shout, she kicked him, sending him flying backward, and grabbed her fallen blaster. In a blur, she scrambled to her feet. All around her, the air buzzed. Wearing only a lavender bra and bloody jeans, she ran hard for the river, crying aloud. "Arnie!"

The river sparkled in the first rays of sunrise.

Kinety was almost to the bank when a massive ring of dust formed around her. She screamed and slid to a stop, unable to go any further. In one hand, she held Orlando's bloody blaster and in the other Torak's knife, neither enough to fight with. "Arnie!" she cried, spinning alone inside.

Sobbing loudly, she scanned the bottom of the ring as it organized around her, searching desperately for a break in the dust.

It broke.

With a cry, she fired, killing the one in front of her, then spun, slashing the knife backward across the face of the next attack. She reversed and fired, barely catching the next strike. The body struck her slowing her turn with the knife.

Another Gaki jumped.

A blast from nowhere knocked the creature backward.

Kinety yelped in fright, then spun to face the next attack.

"Aaargh!" With a chaotic war cry, an unfamiliar man in faded camouflage came screaming over the spinning ring and crashed hard into Kinety. The attacking creature went flying. His arm locked sharply around her and he fired three shots, killing out of order. The intrusion disrupted the pattern and, for a second, the attack stopped.

In a flurry of yanks, Kinety and her partner were back to back with his strong arm holding her in place.

Weak-kneed with relief, she hooked a trembling arm backward around his middle. They spun together in the center, bracing for the next break. To her horror, the ring expanded. "What are they doing!"

The man's dark blue eyes swept the circle. "Adding more," he said in a low voice.

Kinety looked past the ring to the water, just beyond the circle. Right then, the ring broke in three places. They fired together. A blaster shot from far in the distance took out the third.

They didn't know which way to step.

"We are not going to make it," he said calmly, barely catching a strike from the side.

Kinety fired.

A third Gaki crashed into her, knocking her hard into her companion. They both stumbled, and she fired again, point-blank.

The sniper got the third.

"They can't swim!" she cried, trying to keep her feet beneath her.

A Gaki out of turn got the man's blaster.

The sniper knocked the creature back, but her companion was now unarmed. With a powerful pull, he yanked her up. "Over the top," he grunted and threw her like a javelin.

Kinety stretched in surprise, suddenly airborne over the ring, and sprawled ungracefully on the other side. A split second later, he followed. Legs high, he hurdled the swarm and came down with a

Gaki latched hard on his bleeding arm. Growling in pain, he snatched it by the neck with one hand, ripping it and a chunk of skin off. With the other hand, he grabbed Kinety and stumbled back. The creature in his hand kicked and snarled, flapping its arms and struggling wildly to claw him. The ring dissolved in a cloud of dust, and the vanishing Gaki spilled over each other, trying to dogpile their prey.

The sniper, far in the distance, continued to fire, picking the animals off. Her companion pulled her backward into the water, using the Gaki in his hand to knock the attackers away while she fired. They splashed in and sloshed deep.

Kinety dove, adding distance, and surfaced far from the shore. Her rescuer slung the dead animal in his hand to the bank, then sloshed backward into the deeper water with Kinety. Rabid Gaki, wild-eyed and salivating, skidded to a stop at the edge. Several fell in and thrashed in the water.

And the snipers opened fire.

Gaki scattered like roaches.

With a splash, Kinety's partner heaved an arm around her middle and let the current take them away. When they were safe, he angled toward the bank at the next bend, touched the bottom with his feet, and pushed Kinety into shallow water. She stopped before reaching the shore, though, feeling safer in the water than on land. He stopped beside her and scanned the area. "That was close," he puffed.

Kinety turned her face away from him and sank to her knees in the shallow water. She tried hard to stop the tears but couldn't. Orlando was dead, someone was trying to kill her, and Torak had attacked her. And ... she'd almost been eaten alive. As embarrassing as it was to lose her cool in front of this stranger, there was no stopping it.

He sat down awkwardly in the water beside her. "Are you hurt?" he asked.

Kinety shook her head and wiped her eyes. No," she said, realizing how awful she must look to this stranger, and tried to smile. It failed. "I'm fine. Thank you ... for coming when you did."

Their eyes met and held.

A warm sensation spread through her and, startled by it, she quickly disconnected the look. It took a moment to recompose, but she managed. A minute or two later, she wiped her cheeks again and cleared her throat. "What is your name?"

"My name ... ," he answered with some effort, "... is Kek."

"Kek?"

He hesitated, then wiped a bead of water from his face.

When he didn't answer, Kinety managed a small smile. "Is that a nickname?"

147

Kek inclined his head. "A nickname. Yes," he agreed, watching her closely. "And you are?"

"I'm Kinety," she said and turned eagerly toward a thunder of footsteps.

"Kinety!"

"Over here, Arnie! I'm okay."

Arnie rounded the corner at a full run, weapon drawn, and splashed into the water. He grabbed her arm and pulled her to her feet. A quick check confirmed her negative diagnosis before his attention switched to the stranger.

Kek looked at the weapon, stood from the water, and then looked at the man.

Arnie noted the camouflage uniform and lowered his gun. "Where's your partner?" he asked, winded.

"I am alone," Kek said, noticing Arnie's hand around Kinety's arm.

"I told you during the briefing everybody has a partner. No exceptions."

Kek paused. "I ... missed the briefing."

"But, you knew how to fight the Gaki?"

"I saw that part."

Arnie inclined his head. "Let's get back to camp. We'll find you a partner."

"Where's your partner?" asked Kek.

"Behind me," Arnie answered flatly. "I'm a faster runner."

Kek faced Kinety. "Do you have an assigned partner?"

"Well ... no."

Kek gestured, naming himself as her partner, and raised his brows expectantly at Arnie.

Arnie opened his mouth to argue, then scowled at the newcomer, cornered by his own rules. Annoyed, he pointed to the soldier's sterilized fatigues. "Where is your name tag?"

Kek followed the point, then blinked Arnie's uniform, which had a name sewn above the chest pocket. "Er ... I appear to have misplaced it."

Kinety made quick introductions. "Arnie, this is Kek."

"Kek?" Arnie cocked his head. "Is that a nickname?"

"A nickname," Kek affirmed.

"That was a nice jump back there, Kek," Arnie informed him. "Good job."

At the second thunder of feet, Kek shifted his gaze. Seconds later, Rixton and Park came around an outcropping of rocks.

"Rixton!" Kinety said, rushing to him.

Park stopped on the bank, frowning hard, and looked upriver. "Where's Orlando?" he asked in alarm.

Rixton shoved his blaster into the back of his pants, sloshing toward the group, and yanked his shirt up over his head. When he got there, he grabbed Kek's hand, startling him, and gripped his fingers into a handshake. "What happened?" he demanded, pulling the shirt down over Kinety's head.

Kek watched Rixton cover her, then blinked down at his hand.

Kinety wiped her eyes, which were filling again, with her new t-shirt. "Orlando took me to use the bushes. They killed him," she said through fresh tears. "I'm so sorry, Park."

Park's face contorted at the news.

Arnie's lips bunched, and he stifled a curse.

"I tried to get back to the base, but they chased me this way," she finished.

Rixton scowled warily at the swirling water and hooked his arm around his sister. "We don't know what's in this water. Out," he said, guiding her to shore.

Kek followed, awkwardly watching the men. On the shore, Park put his back to them, keeping watch and randomly wiping his eyes, while the others sat on scattered rocks.

Kinety sat on the ground beside her brother's rock and hugged her knees.

"What happened to your clothes?" asked Rixton, shirtless now.

Kinety scraped angrily at her own cheeks. "They shot Orlando in the back. He fell on me. I was covered in blood which attracted the Gaki. I was heading for the river when I saw Torak in a clearing," she said in a stronger voice.

Kek, who'd been looking down at his bite wound, tuned in and looked at her.

"Torak was here?" asked Rixton.

She slung her hand toward the woods. "Over there. He tried to force me into his spaceship, but I refused. It got physical," she sniffed. "He tore my compression suit off me in the fight. I told him I didn't want to go, but ... he wouldn't quit. He even pulled a knife on me," she said with a catch in her voice and held up Torak's knife.

Arnie listened to the story with a slanted scowl. "Torak ... did that?" he asked hesitantly.

Kinety nodded.

Kek took the knife from her and examined it. When nobody was looking, he dropped it into the water.

"I got away, but then was surrounded ... alone. Then, Kek arrived." Kinety turned swollen, red eyes to her new partner. "That jump was amazing," she said with a wet chuckle.

Arnie slapped Kek's hand and folded his fingertips into a squeeze. "That's because he's a badass. I wouldn't have reached you in time."

Kek looked down at the second handshake.

Kinety faced her brother. "We're close to the tributary now," she said meaningfully.

Rixton noted her change of attire. "Do you still have the vial?"

Kinety pulled it from the front pocket of her jeans and examined the clear amber liquid. "I kept it in here. The other clothes were too baggy," she said, displaying it.

Kek's light blue eyes locked on the vial. "Where did you get that?"

"A grasshopper wants me to put it into the water by the Gaki nest," she answered.

Rixton sliced his hand through the air. "No. I already told you," he said definitively. "There's no guarantee we won't be affected. The last thing we need now is to kill off our own men with that shit. Put it away."

Arnie looked upstream. "The Gaki are evolving. They're changing their tactics now that we're fighting back."

Rixton peered the same direction with a worried look on his face. "I saw," he said heavily. "We all saw."

"Who was sniping?" asked Arnie.

"Zhang," answered Rixton. "The moment he realized Dorkymodo was missing, he started climbing."

Even Arnie raised his brows, admiring the Chinese man's skill. "Boy is on the team."

Park picked up a rock and threw it across the surface of the water, bouncing it. "I'm beginning to hate the fucking Zahrá Che," he declared with a sour huff.

Kinety shook her head. "That wasn't Zahrá Che."

The men frowned at her.

Park pointed vehemently over his shoulder. "That was Zahrá Che!" he argued hotly. "We all saw them. White suits, white helmets, big black eyes. They pinned us in the camp while they chased you around, murdered my buddy, then took off."

Kinety continued shaking her head.

"Did you get a look at who was after you?" Arnie asked her.

Kinety glanced back toward the woods. "Well … no, it was too dark. I mean—I saw the suits, but … it wasn't them," she insisted, facing Arnie. "When we were taken from Earth, the Zahrá Che stepped with tiny feet. Light, quick steps. These were heavy."

Kek was watching her.

"Are you sure?" asked Rixton.

"I'm positive. And they spoke."

Rixton missed the significance. "Spoke what?"

Arnie answered for her. "The Zahrá Che are telepathic. They can scream, but they don't speak out loud," he said, furrowing his brow pensively. "The Saphiridians do."

Kinety gave a pitiful chuckle. Feeling more confused than ever, she gestured in exasperation. "I had hoped that I'd misinterpreted the hybrid aliens' attitude toward me, but there is no mistaking it now. It was them. They meant to kill me but got Orlando instead."

Park stared out at nothing.

Kinety dropped her wet head into her hands and pushed her fingers into it. After taking a moment to calm the quiver in her chin, she brushed her messy hair back, bracing elbows on knees, and rubbed her hands together. "There's a huge massacre site at the base of the bluff," she continued with a glance at the rocky hills. "We've lost a lot of men in this disgusting place. We have to do something, Arnie. We've gotta find whoever is left and get them out of here."

"How?" asked Rixton incredulously.

Arnie and Kinety looked at each other. "We steal a spaceship," they said in unison.

Kek's brows climbed high on his forehead.

"Just so you're aware," Arnie said to Rixton, who was watching Kek, "Zahrá Che ships are sleek, silver, and nearly silent. They're very agile and quick but lack power. The Saphiridian ships are clunky, loud, patchwork metal—very steampunk. They're slow but pack a wallop. Either ship will do."

"Sooo, who's going to fly the spaceship?" wondered her brother.

If autopilot and auto-land counted, Kinety outranked all the others —combined—in experience … and she could read alien. Realizing this, she spread her hands and sat up straight. "Me," she shrugged.

Kek, who'd long since backed out of the conversation, made a face and scratched his ear.

Rixton drummed a beat on his thighs, specifically noting Kek's close proximity to and focus on Kinety. "That sounds solid. While you two hash out those details, the rest of us will figure out how to defend ourselves because we'll get picked off sitting around a campfire. We need defenses and a refuge for the next batch that comes in."

Arnie inclined his head. "That's my department. What do you have in mind?"

"Walls."

Kinety pointed at Rixton. "The Gaki can't swim!"

"Okay … then a moat," said Rixton. "We move the camp here to the river and start cutting a moat. What do we have to use as shovels?"

Park skipped another pebble. "Rocks," he said without enthusiasm.

Arnie stood up and clapped his hands together. "Works for me," he said, walking off to mark a perimeter.

Rixton hauled Kinety up and abruptly pulled her into a walk beside him. "Let's get the others."

Kek marched to Arnie and thrust a furious finger past him. "Who is *he*!" he growled through his teeth.

Arnie faced the soldier, a bit surprised by his venom, and followed the point. "*That is* Rixton."

Kek glared. "Rixton!" he hissed hotly.

Wearing a peculiar look on his face, Arnie approached the smaller man, deliberately blocking Kek's view of Kinety's retreating back. "Yes, Romeo, his name is Rixton. That's her brother," he said, diffusing the man's hot temper.

Kek's expression flickered. "Brother?"

"Yes, and they're close," warned Arnie.

Kek stole another peek. "Are you sure?" he demanded.

"Quite sure," Arnie assured.

Kek took a moment to absorb this, nodded, then peeked again, this time with a curl in his lip.

Arnie snorted in amusement. "If you've got the hots for Kinety … *Kek*, you'd better get real sweet on Rixton or you don't have a snowball's chance in Hell with her."

Kek hesitated, not understanding the comment.

"Aside from your astoundingly *vulgar* romantic timing," Arnie continued with emphasis, "they're always together. You'll get nowhere with *her* unless you intend to make friends with *him*," he said, indicating the taller sibling.

"Friends!" Kek spat in disgust.

"Best besties."

Kek blinked at him.

Arnie gave Kek a firm thump on the shoulder, wrapping up the annoying conversation, then pointed him toward a natural dip in the ground. "You can start by finding rocks and digging an impressive moat," he said, picking up a sharp-edged rock and handing it over.

Kek took the rock, then scowled at Arnie's back as the blond strolled away.

Arnie rolled his eyes heavenward. "That awkward moment when your science fiction horror thriller becomes a romantic melodrama," he grumbled to himself. "This is why we don't bring smoking hot models into the field."

Chapter 13

The camp was moved to the nearest edge of the river, and a meeting was called. Kinety, Arnie, Park, and Rixton positioned themselves on a large boulder near the shore where they could see out over the sea of faces. Park faced backward, watching the water with swollen eyes. Zhang, who'd come down from the bluff when he'd seen Kinety coming, climbed onto a high outcropping nearby and scanned the terrain, eager to pick off stray Gaki.

Kek stood against the smooth cliff-face below Zhang with his arms and ankles folded, slightly separated from the others.

Kinety glanced at Kek, catching his eye, then faced forward again. It was time to focus. When the soldiers had gathered, she stood up on a low bulge. Her heart was heavy, but now was not the time to get watery-eyed. She had a job to do. "Our numbers were at seventy-seven this morning," she said, speaking loud enough to be heard. "What is our new headcount?"

"We're at seventy-four, ma'am," answered an officer. "We lost two in the battle and your friend Orlando."

Hearing his name did it. Kinety rubbed her throbbing temples for a moment and breathed deep, but it didn't help. Unable to fight the sting of tears, she ruffled her frizzy hair from her face and gestured Arnie up. "I can't."

Arnie traded places with her. "The Gaki can't swim," he told the soldiers, coming right to the point. "Therefore, we are investing in real estate right here against the river. Besides being useful for obvious reasons, like washing, it will also protect us from Gaki *and* sparkle beautifully at sunset. Before you ask, the answer is: No, you may *not* swim in the river. We don't know what the fuck's in there," he said, pausing for a round of groans. "Today, we will all engage in some mandatory, back-breaking fun. Are you excited to participate?"

"Hooah?" whimpered a few wary soldiers.

"Me too," he said with a sharp finger jab. "I've set up a perimeter —there, there, there, and there. I need four teams. Ma'am," he pointed to a female officer, "organize this. Team One. Guards. You'll be watching the camp and escorting anyone in need of supplies beyond the perimeters. Snipers, find your spots and stay awake," he said, pointing to strategic locations around the camp. "Team Two. Landscaping. You'll be outside carving a moat—"

Groaned curses fouled the air.

"—with rocks," Arnie continued with an enthusiastic nod. "Team Three. Construction. I need you outside dropping logs or inside building shelters—sturdy, log-cabin style. We don't have nails.

Team Four. Service. You'll prepare food, boil and distribute water, provide camp clean up, and medical. Pick your team, stay busy. If I catch your ass not having fun, I'll kick it. Let's get to work," he said, gesturing them into action.

*****

Kinety followed the landscaping group and selected the sharpest, flattest rock she could find. On her hands and knees, she began digging, pulling the dirt behind her where it would be used to form the inner raised walls of the moat.

Kek chose the spot just beside her.

Though she pretended otherwise, she was very aware of him and had to concentrate on not peeking. He was very attractive, with pleasant, symmetric features, but strangest of all … he smelled like a flower. His hair was an unusual mix of sun-bleached brown and dark blond. The sides were pulled back tight and secured behind his head in a tiny, sticky-outy ponytail with loose tendrils that fell into his face. The ends brushed against the tops of his shoulders. His nose was adorable. Dark lashes rimmed striking blue eyes. His chin was strong and slightly scruffy, which accentuated almost pretty lips.

Kek was definitely good-looking, but that wasn't particularly unusual in a camp full of military men. He was fit and muscular, a fact all too apparent when he, like the others, pulled his shirt off while he worked. Kinety appreciated that, but something else about him niggled the back of her mind. Something about his manner soothed her. More than that, he intrigued her and it wasn't evident why. She'd never noticed magnetism with any man before. Now, suddenly, it was everywhere. Was she that lonely?

Kinety paused to wipe her brow and glanced to see what he was doing. Incidentally, she noticed the dull black metal band he wore above his impressive biceps, just below his equally impressive deltoid.

Kek caught her looking and made it a point to catch her gaze. His digging slowed. "How long are we to stay at this camp," he asked, sitting back on his heels.

Kinety gestured past him toward the portal, even though she couldn't see it, indicating the spaceships flying around Gimeg Plateau. "Only until we can steal a ship to rescue the others."

Kek tried to keep his amusement from his voice. "Steal a spaceship? Are you not thinking that is a bit dangerous?"

She shrugged and resumed scraping at the ground. "I'm certainly not going to sit around here and safely wait to expire," she said, scoring a large rock from the dirt. "I've seen the ships flying overhead on Zahrá Che. There has to be a way to hijack one. We just need to figure out how to go about it."

Kek almost laughed out loud. "That plan sounds a bit reckless for such a small human group," he said.

Their eyes met again.

Only, Kinety wasn't teasing. "Perhaps," she admitted, "but I doubt any of us will survive long anyway. No point getting scared now."

"Then why rescue the men?" he challenged.

"Because we shouldn't have to die in their war," she said, a bit sharper than she meant.

His amusement faded, and he resumed his digging. "What do you know of their war?"

In her mind, Kinety gathered all the tidbits she'd collected. Brushing loose hair from her eyes with her wrist, she looked out at the strange landscape, which was actually quite beautiful. "I know both sides are guilty of terrible things, but I don't know the whole story. It's a land dispute. This planet is called Neontak. I've only gotten bits and pieces, but the Zahrá Che, the little guys that captured us," she clarified, "are trying to take it from the hybrid Saphiridians. The Zahrá Che appear to be the original aggressors, which they seem to regret now. At least, that was the impression I got from Emperor Dinruk."

Kek's expression went still. "Emperor Dinruk? You spoke to him?"

"Yes."

He stopped digging. "Where is—," he began, then ended the question abruptly. Switching demeanors, he resumed working the ground and spoke in a normal tone. "Do you know where he is?"

Just then, a large spider-looking thing with wings landed on Kinety's hand and bounced. As it bounced, it sang like a cicada. She yipped sharply.

"*Do not* slap it," warned Kek with an outstretched hand. "It will fly off of you on its own. They do not bite, but they do chase."

She recoiled but waited, and the bug flew off. "No," she shuddered, tossing her rock aside and shaking her hand. "We spoke through a hologram."

"How did you get audience with him?"

Kinety shifted her knees to a more comfortable position. "For a short while, I was known as the Savage Bride, Wife of Torak," she relayed, flashing rounded eyes.

"Torak?" he echoed.

"The villain," she reminded him. "He's on the Saphiridian side. Apparently, his job is to torment the Zahrá Che."

Kek scraped a deep gouge. "Are you not married anymore to this man?" he asked with a grunt.

"Oh, no. Torak didn't care for the rumors and set them straight pretty quick," Kinety said with a chuckle to hide the sting that was still there.

"So, the emperor saw you because he thought you were Torak's wife?"

"Yes." She worked another rock out. In her aggression, she did something that, with a blue flash, made the stones roll away from her hands by themselves. Startled, she jerked back, then checked to be sure Kek hadn't seen. When she was certain he hadn't, she continued digging. "Torak is the Zahrá Che villain. I, personally, didn't see the monster they described and argued in his defense, so the emperor showed me videos of some of the things he's done—terrible things. Shows what I know."

For a moment, the blue in Kek's eyes faded. "I would not trust anything the Zahrá Che showed to you," he warned, blinking them blue again. "I-I mean … they are the alien ones who kidnapped us, right?"

"Yes."

"So, what did this Emperor Dinruk want?"

Kinety made a face. "He asked me to negotiate on his behalf. I agreed on the condition they stop taking our men from Earth, but when I tried talking to Torak, he wouldn't listen. I knew he wouldn't. The marriage was a misunderstanding."

"How so?"

Kinety hesitated, wondering if she was telling this stranger too much. "It's a bit hard to explain," she grimaced.

Kek motioned to the un-dug moat they'd barely put a dent in, implying he had all the time in the world.

He was right.

She gave a half-shrug and huffed. "I met Torak on Earth," she said with a glance.

Kek adopted a look of interest, prompting her to go on.

Kinety's digging slowed as she remembered. "Oh, he was something," she said with a dreamy look on her face. "Absolutely gorgeous. Strong. And the way he … ," she stopped, remembering suddenly who she was talking to, and cleared her throat.

Kek pushed a mound of dirt to the edge of his crater. "The way he what?"

Kinety had no intention of telling him what and started digging again. "When I met him, it was … he was—I can't even describe it —magnetic?" she supposed, then continued. "I introduced myself as his future wife," she admitted with some embarrassment. "I was teasing, of course. I didn't know he was a notorious assassin or a villain or the most dangerous person in the galaxy—whatever. I thought he was a human with really cool eyes and was hoping to score a phone number."

Kek lifted his brows.

"Anyway, I saw him again when he hijacked the Zahrá Che spaceship and, returning the jest, he called me his wife. He was being sarcastic, but I think the Zahrá Che took him literally. That's the only thing I can think of to explain the assumption. I don't think the Zahrá Che use much humor."

"They do not," Kek said, then wobbled his head. "I-I mean … they probably do not. Did you tell the emperor that it was a mistake?"

Kinety plucked a large hunk of mud from the ground. "Yes. I told him I didn't have Torak's ear," she said, turning to face him, "that I wasn't his companion, but he was insistent. He almost had *me* convinced that Torak wanted me, that he would come for me, and seemed almost to expect it, but," she paused here, "that isn't what happened."

Kek's brows flickered.

"The Saphiridians did come," she clarified. "At first, I thought maybe Torak sent them to rescue us but … it was the opposite. They attacked us. I was arrested and brought to the council where Torak promptly and publicly 'denounced' me," she said with air quotes. "I worry what will happen to our soldiers when the emperor finds out. Surely, by now, he knows I was rejected," she said, more to herself than him, then smiled. "That sounds like quite the story, doesn't it."

Kek wasn't digging anymore. "I am certain Torak had a good reason to reject you."

Kinety laughed, a short, unhappy sound. "Someone like Torak probably has a harem of beautiful women at his disposal, which is reason enough," she grunted, giving the ground a good scrape.

She didn't see Kek shaking his head beside her or the befuddled look on his face.

"Either that, or I just bombed the audition. It would have been over by now, I suppose, but I stole a Saphiridian spaceship. That seems to have made them pretty angry," she remarked offhandedly. "That's who came after me this morning."

Kek's rock scraped faster. "You do not think it was the other … aliens? It looked like Zahrá Che to me."

Kinety was certain. "Nope. It was the Saphiridians."

Kek tossed a handful of dirt. "Maybe … whoever … was after all of us."

Her hands slowed their digging, and she sat back on her heels. "I don't think so. It seemed like it at first, but," she paused, putting her thoughts together, "they accidentally shot Orlando instead of me. When they realized it, they said so and chased me. I heard them talking. It was Torak's people."

The blue in Kek's eyes faded a few shades. "If Torak wanted you dead, you would be dead," he snapped.

Kinety slowed her digging, puzzled by his tone. "Have you heard of Torak? You said you missed the briefing."

"I have ... heard enough," he said awkwardly. "If he is like you describe him, I do not think he would let someone else do it.

"He wouldn't."

Kek reigned in his temper, knowing it would get him nowhere, and focused on the hole he was digging. "Then why would he send his people to do what he could do himself?" he asked in a softer voice.

Kinety shook her head. "That's the part that makes no sense," she told him. "It was Torak who showed me how to fight the Gaki. We'd all be dead now if he hadn't ... ," she shook herself and forced a smile. "I'm sorry. I didn't mean to get into a deep discussion. I was just rambling."

Instantly brighter, he made an I-don't-mind face and gave a light-hearted shrug. "I cannot imagine anything more boring than digging a moat. You may as well ramble."

Kinety shoved her pile of dirt away, fully prepared to shut up, and shook the blood back into her hands.

"What would you do if Torak came back for you?" Kek asked a few minutes later.

Kinety gave it some thought but didn't answer. Instead, she looked away and tried to make herself look busy.

But Kek was waiting. "Do you want to see him again?"

"No," she said, giving her head a shake. "I saw him this morning, and he assaulted me."

A muscle ticked in Kek's jaw. "That is what you said."

"Torak has no interest in me," she emphasized. "He wants information. If he gets it, he'll kill our soldiers so that the Zahrá Che can't use them to stop the Gaki. I just have to reach them before he does."

"Where are they?" he asked.

"Far away," she said shortly and wiped her brow.

"So ... tell me about Rixton."

"Rixton? He's my brother. My best friend. My hero," she said with a short smile.

"Your hero?"

She nodded, eager to change the subject. "Our parents died in an accident. Rixton had just finished boot camp when it happened—maybe a month," she said, gazing off. Her voice took on a distant tone, and her green eyes glossed in memory. "He'd finished top in his class and just been offered entry into some fancy, hushy-hushy Intel unit. They had just sent him to begin training at some super-secret base. It was a big deal, and he was pretty excited. I was underage. When Rixton was told I would be placed in foster care, he gave up his prized position, started local training for some job he had no interest in, and took custody of me. Then, he used his entire education fund to purchase a little house and gave up everything he'd ever wanted in life to take care of me," she said, returning to the present. "That makes him my hero."

Kek, who had paused to listen, abruptly started digging again. "What about you? Are you his hero?"

Kinety's hands slowed. So far, the answer to that was a resounding no, but she was determined to change that. If they could survive and if she could find a way to rescue the other soldiers, *then* she would be Rixton's hero ... but she wasn't going to tell Kek that. Instead, she politely waved the question away. "I'm tired of talking about me. Tell me about you. You were bitten. Is your arm okay?"

"Bitten? Oh." Kek angled to hide the nearly healed wound and made a face. "It is good. Arm is good." Unable to bring anything about himself to mind, he scooted away to work a new area, ending the conversation.

*****

Prime Joboba paced back and forth with his hands folded behind his back. Every fifteen seconds or so, he would snap his brown eyes at the blank screen just to be sure it hadn't come on without him realizing it. When he saw it still dark, he would grit his teeth, curse, and spin on his heel to resume his furious pacing. "It's one woman! It can't be that hard!" he railed to the silent room.

The crew on his ship concentrated on looking busy. Though each was certainly in agreement with him, they were far too engrossed in their tasks to engage in delightful conversation.

Finally, with a crackle, the screen blinked on, and Darplano's head appeared.

Joboba whirled, scattering his blond hair, and nearly tipped himself over. He stuck out a foot to balance, then rushed forward and gripped the panel. Arms spread wide, he leaned toward the screen. "Is she dead?" he demanded hotly.

Darplano pursed his lips and pulled his ear in embarrassment. "We managed to separate her from the camp and push her toward the nest, but her men ... ," he grimaced, not wishing to relay the rest.

"Then kill the men!" Joboba growled in all obviousness.

Darplano screwed up his face. "We couldn't. Torak was there."

Joboba, who was about to say something, stopped and stared at the man. "Torak is in the Yekuon system," he informed him.

Darplano shook his head. "He was there. We retreated when we saw him because we didn't want to get caught."

Joboba's shoulders dropped. "And what, please tell, was Torak doing?"

"Fighting, Prime," he said respectfully. "It looked like Torak was trying to drag the bride to his fighter, but she wouldn't go. The two fought."

"They fought?" Joboba clarified.

Darplano bobbed his head vigorously. "Yes. Quite violently, but she disarmed him and got away."

Joboba exhaled and chuckled. "She disarmed ... Torak?" he double-checked.

"Yes, Prime."

Joboba was reaching his limit on stupidity. "*Nobody* disarms Torak, Superior Darplano, and one does not simply fight Torak off. If he'd wanted her in his ship, he would have picked her ass up and carried her. It wasn't him!"

Darplano drew himself up in certainty. "We all saw—"

"It was a shapeshifter, you fool!" Joboba snapped, then curled his lip thoughtfully. "Someone else is after her. Someone who doesn't want her dead. Why would someone not want her dead?" he asked himself with mounting concern.

Darplano paused a moment before answering, then offered a careful reassurance. "If Torak has no interest in her, Prime, then there's really nothing to worry about," he soothed.

Joboba froze.

Every hand in the spaceship went still and a long, stagnant pause hushed through the flight deck.

Hesitantly, Joboba turned to look at a woman at the station beside him. "Pull up a location on Torak."

The woman tried a few different methods. "I can't zero in on his location, Prime."

"Find him!"

With a nervous jolt, she worked faster.

But Joboba was already pacing again. "If she's captured, she'll be used against Torak as a distraction ... or worse," he worried, horrified by the thought. Disturbed by the direction his thoughts were leading him, he pointed to a man at another station. "We have four shapeshifter species," he barked. "Find out which one is showing nonaggressive interest."

The man immediately got to work.

Joboba faced the screen and glared at Darplano's staring face. "I don't want this woman anywhere near my war god. She's dangerous, and I want her gone. Infiltrate her troops and Make! Her! Dead!"

Joboba slapped the screen off. Jaw cocked, he spun to the woman at the first station, still frantically searching and shaking her head as she looked. "Where is Torak!"

*****

Kek took his aggressions out on the ground, cursing his own temper. He was pissed, though. He still hadn't gotten the location of the base, but he had seen the assassination attempt—or at least the end of it. There was no way the Saphiridians had threatened her. No way! But she was right about the Zahrá Che footsteps and speech. It wasn't them. So, who could it have been?

Anger singed his insides.

And who had tried to take her? Only a shapeshifter could have impersonated him, likely to kidnap her. But why the assault? Were they trying to turn her against him? If the shapeshifters were involved, she'd eventually be fooled unless he revealed himself. Dammit! He was busy. The Saphiridians were in the middle of a war. He didn't have time to babysit a woman, especially one who had declared herself to be his mortal enemy.

Shit.

There was more. Not only had the public rejection not worked, but it had also sensationalized the news—Torak had a woman. In the eyes of the galaxy, his and Kinety's union, legitimate or not, was valid and legal, which indeed made her—Kek peeked at her profile —his wife.

Shit. Shit.

As he worked, the phony blood regulator on his wrist spun. While Kinety wasn't looking, he straightened it up and gave it a thump to relight the lights. He'd wired them to stay on, but without blood flow to charge the power crystals, they kept failing. He'd broken the barbs off before applying the armlet because he didn't need the damn thing. His body adapted automatically to atmospheric abnormalities, though sometimes the toxic combinations turned his skin slightly green or orange, depending on the composition. The armlet was all part of this ridiculous disguise and rather uncomfortable, but not nearly as uncomfortable as the camouflage uniform he was wearing. Its original owner had died in a Saphiridian battle. Who knew why the name tag had been missing.

Speaking of names, apparently Kek had been a poor choice for one. It seemed simple to him. *Kinetic energy* velocity measured in *kilograms* per second. He couldn't get more Earthling than that! They loved acronyms. Isn't that what Kinety's name was referring to—Kinetic Energy? He thought for sure he'd blend right in with Kek. That's why he'd chosen it. Hell, Arnie's name was referring to the Argon and Nickel elements—Ar Ni e—right? These Earth

161

humans were all over the place. Maybe he should have gone with something simpler, like J'Rod or Zok.

Earthlings.

His next organized thought was an expansive flash photo collage of all his enemies—and he had many … not just in this galaxy either. The fake Zahrá Che attack and the shapeshifter made two in one day, so her location was obviously known. Another attempt could happen at any time. That was bad. How in the stars was he supposed to keep her alive?

And Joboba? Huh! That wasn't going to go over well.

Now was not a good time to smack his own forehead, so he pinched his temples instead. The best thing he could do was to leave and let her face her fate. A simple retaliation by him on whoever got her first would end the matter and allow him to focus again on the war. That, of course, would be the simplest way to handle this, except the idea wasn't sitting well with him. In fact, the mere *thought* of someone harming her infuriated him. There was no way he could leave.

Kek ran his fingers through his artificially lightened hair. By now, he should have had the location of the base. This farce as an Earthling soldier was only supposed to last a couple of hours. All he had to do was leave. But, if he left, she would die.

Dammit.

Why should he care if she died? She meant nothing to him. He hardly knew her. He should leave.

She'd be dead within hours. He couldn't leave.

Wait. She wasn't actually his wife. It was propaganda created by a manipulative race and pumped out to the galaxy and believed by everyone in it … which made it official.

He needed to go.

Arnie was here to protect her, and he was armed with puny blasters that wouldn't save him from a gleshmog. Unless Torak convinced her to go with him—wait … no. She'd already refused him, even though that hadn't been him. And—he ran his fingers down his unfamiliar face—if she found out he was deceiving her, she'd believe whatever garbage the emperor told her, especially after thinking he'd assaulted her.

She would hate him.

That last thought earned a twinge. From what Kek could remember as far back as his memory stretched, she was the first person he'd ever met who didn't hate him, including his own people. They tried to hide it, but there was fear there. Kinety wasn't afraid of him at all. From the first moment, she actually did appear to have an attraction, which completely baffled him. That had never happened before. Ever. He wasn't sure what was wrong with her, but he certainly didn't want to jeopardize that good fortune any more than he already had. This meant she had to live. For that to happen, he had to stay.

It was impossible. He had a war to fight.

Kek shoved a blast of energy sideways into the ground, loosening a large swath of dirt beneath Kinety's hands. The Earthlings were right. A moat would keep the Gaki out, but he wasn't going to kneel here and scrape the hard ground with rocks. Another blast in the other direction loosened the ground beneath other digging hands, and he watched as they began easily rolling it toward the edge. Just to be nice, he fired off a few more. There. He was done. Soon the moat would be too. He really, really needed to leave now. Deciding to come right out and say so, he stood abruptly and faced his damned wife.

When she blinked her pretty green eyes up at him, Kek towered over her ... and lowered his hand. "Come with me. I will show you how to tell which plants are edible."

Kinety wiped her face and stood without help. "Oh! You can tell?" she said, dusting off her hands and scanning the dense vegetation enthusiastically. Oblivious, she wandered off.

At first, Kek was pissed by the snub and set his hands on his hips in irritation, then remembered he looked like someone else. Good! This was good, he thought with a sniff and a scowl. That meant she wasn't fooling around with other men. They were off to a promising start.

Good.

Chapter 14

By late afternoon, the moat was taking shape, and a pile of branchless logs were scattered over the ground. Kinety's buddies had all gathered to rest and sat waiting, half in anticipation, half in dread, for an unappetizing pile of roasted plants to be served to them. The days were longer here, and they'd all noticed it. The Neontak sun hovered low on the horizon, adding colored light to the lavender sky. A loud hum came from the trees, the evening song of the flying cicada spiders. Clean after a splash bath at the river, Kinety sat on the ground beside her brother with her ankles crossed and her back against the stone wall of Zhang's outcropping. Arnie sat near Rixton, who now wore a torn shirt he'd found on the ground, and the two talked shop. Park and Zhang, already served, busied themselves by playing with their food as they ate it.

Kinety sat quietly, enjoying being not dirty. As her hair dried, she folded her arms over her knees and peered at the sunlight reflecting in the water. Her hair, usually loose and fluffy around her shoulders, hung heavily along the sides of her head and down her back. Her face was bruised, either from the branches or the fight, and she looked pale from lack of food and water.

Kek, who could barely keep his eyes off her, hovered nearby but kept to the shadows for the moment. He still wasn't fitting in. Something about the way he was speaking wasn't blending with the others. In the dark, he added another dab of flower oil to his skin. He hated the way it smelled but knew Kinety would recognize his scent if he didn't. Stinking like a bouquet, he tucked the tiny bottle away and eavesdropped, paying close attention to the nuances of the Earthlings' casual speech and relaxed banter. They used contractions, such as don't and I'm, and preferred a shortened sentence structure that he needed to match better. He detected a lazy usage pattern and frequent use of sarcasm, which all seemed to enjoy. When he thought he had the gist of it, he stepped into view and found Kinety surrounded. Shifting his unnaturally blue eyes back and forth at her friends in annoyance, he scowled. They stayed ridiculously close to her, and it irritated him.

Friends.

Kek chose that moment to become one. "Mind if I join you?" he asked and sat beside Kinety without waiting for a reply. He gave her a wink, then faced her awful sibling. In the same manner of greeting he'd seen other soldiers use, he stuck his hand out at Rixton. "Name's Kek. You must be the brother," he said, trying out his new shortened sentence.

Rixton accepted the handshake, then lifted his brows as the newcomer continued to pump his hand up and down. "Kek," he said, taking his hand away. "Is that a nickname?"

"A nickname," Kek grinned.

"Rixton," he offered, then waited expectantly to see what the man wanted.

Kek blinked back, unsure what to say next to his new 'friend.' Silence stretched between them and, right away, it was evident Kinety's sibling wasn't very friendly.

Arnie wiped his face with a filthy shirt and scowled at the half-dug moat, then accepted a leaf-plate full of cooked yuck from a food server. Using two fingers, he lifted the plants and examined them. "So tell us, Kek," he said, stalling the first bite, "how did you enjoy your day with Miss November?"

Kek paused, not understanding the question.

Park, whose mouth was full, stopped chewing and gaped at her. "*You're* Miss November!" he muffled in surprise.

Rixton helpfully closed Park's jaw with a clack of teeth, earning a few laughs.

"I thought you looked familiar," Park said, trying to select the least nasty piece of food. "You were in the white bikini and matching snowboots, weren't you?"

Kinety wrinkled her nose. "Weren't they cute?" she smiled. "I got to keep the boots."

"Did you keep the bikini?"

"No."

Kek tried desperately to catch on. "Miss November?" he echoed, recognizing some significance to the title but unsure which response was expected. "You mean the month?"

The men blinked at him, then at each other.

"Swimsuit Magazine, November Issue," Park said slowly to the daft idiot. "She's a bikini model."

Kek tried not to look lost. "Oh … bikini."

To everyone else, Park spun his finger by his temple, then told Kek, "Yes. Arnie's little girlfriend was the centerfold."

Arnie curled his lip at the food. "Are you sure this shit is safe?"

Kek had no idea what the hell they were talking about, but he didn't care anymore. "Kinety is not Arnie's girlfriend. She is spoken for."

Kinety ignored him. "Zhang and Kek found some edible plants," she was telling Arnie. "We picked a bunch. Kek and I both gagged some down already."

"How long ago?"

"Couple hours," Kinety assured.

Arnie made a face of disgust, took a deep breath, and swallowed the stuff. "Mmm!" he marveled in delight. "Tastes like a cheeseburger!"

"From the grill," gagged Rixton.

Park burped and put his knuckle to his mouth to keep from vomiting. "Reminds me of cold, frothy beer," he assured with his eyes closed.

Rixton shouldered his mouth clean, as if that would help, then sent an annoyed look at Kek. "Until further notice, Romeo, I am the only one here who will be speaking for Kinety. Until I say otherwise, she is unavailable," he said and stood. "Break's over, and I see a pile of logs. Let's go start a shelter so we have someplace to sleep tonight."

"Romeo?"

Park got up. "Yeah," he chimed in with a thumb jab over his shoulder. "Get in the back of the line."

The faux blue of Kek's eyes faded. "Is there a line forming?" he asked dangerously.

Kinety tossed a clump of dirt at Rixton and stood. "*Romeo* wasn't talking about himself," she said, dusting her bottom. "I told him about Torak."

Rixton ignored her and walked away with Park.

Arnie narrowed his eyes on the fuming new guy, then chuckled. "If Torak was interested in an opportunity, then his first step would be to stop sending his buddies to kill her," he informed the newbie with a lingering stare. "But no worries. He made himself very clear ... he's not interested. Let's get back to work," he said, jabbing a point in the direction he wanted them to go.

As they moved away, Kek seethed, clamping his teeth and glaring a hole into the back of Arnie's head. Knowing when to shut up wasn't one of his strengths, and he worked hard at it now. With effort, he reminded himself that he didn't look like Torak, which meant Rixton and Arnie weren't letting anyone bother Kinety. Good! This was good, he thought, and deliberately didn't kill the big Arnie bastard. He wanted to, but he didn't. And the Saphiridians weren't trying to kill her, his mind bellowed behind curled lips. Why did they keep saying that?

*****

The work was endless, the workers silent. As the sun lowered, day two, they worked together to erect the walls of their building. The Gaki had only attacked twice but had run off before finishing the second fight thanks to Zhang.

After a while, Kek could stand the mindless focus no longer and scooped up some mud to help Kinety. He didn't care what they

167

talked about so long as they did. "Tell me, what exactly are your plans once we get where we're going?"

At the question, Arnie's head shifted toward his shoulder to listen. Paying attention, he dropped his notched log into place, closing the gap between them and bringing the building up another level.

Kinety glanced at Kek. "I already told you, silly. We're going to steal a spaceship and rescue the men."

She had, but Kek couldn't think of anything else to talk about. "After you take it by force, do you know how to fly it?" he asked, dropping a glob on the next log.

"Ooh," chimed Park, who was on the wall setting log ends into their notches and whistling cheerfully, "he's right. We'll have to hijack it. My favorite thing!"

"How do you know that's your favorite thing?" asked Arnie.

"Hey!" snapped Park with a point. "I'm planning ahead."

Rixton busily gouged a notch into the next log. "Do you think we can get the aliens to bring us home?" he asked without looking up. "Which ones are the good guys, anyway?"

Kinety snorted. "Neither. The Zahrá Che are selfish and certainly couldn't be bothered with us once they get what they want. The Saphiridians will kill us. They've made that clear. We'll have to get home ourselves."

"How?"

Kinety was slow to answer. She didn't want to give them false hope but supposed leaving them with nothing to fight for was just as bad. The men needed a bit of morale. "I ... know how to program the pods if I can get my hands on one. I've flown a small ship, but it was mostly on autopilot," she answered honestly.

Park stopped whistling. "Where is home?" he asked with a quick glance up from his work. "Not that I'm in a hurry to cut your vacation short, but I'm pretty funned out."

"The wormhole is about four days away from here and isn't always open," she said, feeling a sudden wave of homesickness. "We were on the ship for a week."

"Where is here?" he asked.

That, Kinety didn't know. "I never saw where Neontak is, only where they were storing the men."

"Where is that?" asked Kek.

Arnie stopped abruptly. "Not here," he answered for her and paused for a drink. Using a cup someone had made from a broadleaf, he took a sip. "This looks almost tall enough. Rixton, how many logs do we have left?"

"Two. This one's almost ready," Rixton said, digging the last few chunks out of his newest notch.

"Break time, " called Arnie.

"Hallelujah!" Kinety finished stuffing mud between the two logs, set her goop aside, and slumped against the log-cabin wall in exhaustion. Eyes closed, she puffed her cheeks and let her muddy fingers hang. It wasn't the heat that bothered her, especially with the sun setting, but the humidity. It made the air hard to breathe, and she was tired. The day was mostly over, but there was plenty of nighttime left to work. She just needed a minute in the shade.

When she opened her eyes again, a young soldier with dark hair and a hooded brow was standing in front of her holding a cup of water in his hand. Kinety looked at it in surprise, startled that she hadn't heard him approach. He inclined his head, offering it to her. Beside him, another soldier stepped forward, clutching a small bouquet of flowers.

Kinety was touched. "Thank you," she said, reaching for the water. Thwack!

Kek's knife landed deep in the man's throat, knocking him backward. Water sloshed to the ground as he fell, writhing and grunting horribly.

Kinety shrieked in fright, alerting the entire camp, and spun to see Kek's hand recoiling from the throw. In the next instant, Kek's muddy blaster was pressed against the temple of the soldier holding flowers.

Everyone turned.

Without speaking, Kek yanked Kinety away from the frozen man and shoved her into Rixton's arms.

Arnie approached carefully and eyed the dead body. "What is this?" he asked Kek.

Kek's voice was calm, deadly. "Their pupils are vertical," he said, giving flowerman's temple a shove. "They aren't from Earth."

Flowerman hissed and glared at Kek, exposing the vertical pupils. Arnie noticed the pupils of the dead man and yanked Kek's knife from his throat. As he did, he spotted the cup lying nearby. Steam wafted up from the spilled water, leaving a splatter of burnt grass.

"That's not water," said Kek.

Arnie faced the flowerman. "Kinety, tell him to drop the flowers," he said, stepping closer in threat.

"Drop the flowers," Kinety translated.

With an animal hiss, the alien lurched for her.

Rixton yanked her backward and fired, killing him, and Arnie slashed downward. With a grunt, the man fell facedown into the spilled flowers beside his severed hand.

From the scattered bouquet, one of the pretty 'flowers' opened into a horrid scorpion-like insect with impressive fangs and a long whip-tail. Kinety shrank from the creature, horrified that someone would give that to her, and turned into her brother's arms.

Kek stepped on the bug.

Trembling, Kinety looked at the burnt grass, no longer steaming, and the cup of water. She'd almost taken it.

Kek lifted the dead man's hand from the ground and held it out for the others to see. It was scaly on the back and almost webbed. Next, he folded an ear down, exposing green-tinged skin and more scales. "Reptilian," he said.

Arnie motioned for Park to follow and shouted. "Atten-hu!"

The staring soldiers quickly lined up and stood rigid.

"Show me your hands, ears, eyes!" he ordered, moving quickly down the line with Park guarding his back.

Just as they reached the end, Park thumped Arnie and pointed to a pile of bushes beyond the camp. "There's more!" Busted, the head of a third figure vanished from the trees and ran.

Park darted by Arnie to give chase.

Kek intercepted him. "Park! Wait," he said, stopping the Korean, and held up his hand for silence. Looking out, he directed everyone's attention to the buzz on the air, then shifted back toward the empty bushes.

As they waited, the distracted perimeter guards retook their positions. A full, silent minute passed before a horrid, hissing scream filled the late afternoon air.

Arnie exhaled heavily and dropped his weapon by his side. "Everybody in this camp needs to know everybody else in this camp. If you don't," he said wearily, "you need to find out why. Right now! Be aggressive! They're after the Commander," he pointed at Kinety, "and we can't let them get her. Hooah?"

"Hooah!"

"Hooyah!"

"Oorah!"

Soldiers crowded around the dead bodies, each getting a good look before they were cleared away.

Messy-haired and muddy, Kek approached Kinety, who stood watching from the shadows. In his dirty hand, he held a fresh cup of water. "Here. It's clean."

Against her will, her heart made a pitter-patter she hoped he hadn't noticed. It was in opposition to her current mood and annoyed her. Awkwardly, she watched him, unsure what to say, and gave the water an unappetizing glance. "No. Thank you."

Peering down at her, Kek took a drink, then deliberately placed the cup in her hand. "Now, it's muddy."

Kinety managed a weak smile. Feeling better, she drank, eyeing him over the rim. This was the second time he'd saved her life, and she wasn't quite sure what to think about that. She liked Kek, and she could tell he liked her. He was certainly good-looking enough, but she had yet to clear Torak from her mind. Something about Kek actually reminded her of Torak, which wasn't helping. In fact, it made it worse. It wasn't fair to Kek, who was a sweetheart, but being near him made her long to see her Tooji. This meant she could have neither. With a sigh, she wiped her mouth and gave the cup back to him.

In exchange, Kek handed her a bark-tray of mud, and they got back to work.

*****

By sundown, Kinety needed a break—just a few minutes. Arnie flopped down beside her and knuckled her thigh. When she cracked an eye, he stuffed a cup of water into her hand. "How you doing, Commander?"

"I'm good," she smiled wearily. "Doing good."

"New guy irritating you?"

Kinety looked at the new bathing pool her brother and Kek were enjoying. She chuckled and took a drink. "He's good company."

"We can let you rest," he offered.

Kinety shook her head and forced her eyes open. "We can't stop," she insisted through her fatigue. "If you work, I work."

Arnie didn't like it but didn't argue. "If you need a moment alone, I can take you."

Kinety flashed a pair of dimples at him. "Honeymoon's over, eh?"

"Stop your bitching," he teased, hauling her up. "Come on."

*****

Well into the night, the group worked by firelight, adding large leaves and branches with mud layers between to form a roof. Kinety tied her hair back and blew out her cheeks but was careful not to complain in front of the men. Doing so would slow the group, and there was just no time. Their soldiers were waiting on Gelphii. They needed her, but the ones dumped here on Neontak had to have a refuge. The shelter had to be built strong and the survivors provided with a safe haven before a group could be formed to go find the others. Perhaps she was psyching herself up, but the urge to get to Gelphii drove her like a cattle prod. On and on they built, each hour a lifetime, until, finally, the ground began to wave in front of her. The lack of sufficient food and water and poor sleep caught up to Kinety and, eventually, she could fight it no longer. Her knees gave out.

Kek caught her on the way down. Before Arnie could get there, he lifted her into his arms and propped her against his chest. Her head rested on his shoulder with her forehead against his neck, and she slept.

Rixton scowled, noticing Kek's secure grip on her, then gestured for the others to keep building. "We're almost done," he called out and handed up more mud.

Kek moved away from the group and searched the ground for a good spot to set her down, but it was covered with bark and dirt and branches. As he looked, he noticed Arnie coming. He would have preferred if Arnie stayed and worked with the others, but the irritating soldier stopped beside him. He didn't particularly want to talk with the larger man, but the soldier apparently had other ideas.

"How long do you intend to keep this up?" asked Arnie in a low voice meant to stay between them.

Kek nearly dropped Kinety.

Arnie, who'd expected the reaction, stopped and faced the phony human squarely. "Your shapeshifting skills are impressive, Torak, but when you get angry the fake blue in your eyes fades to white. Don't let her see it. She'll recognize you."

Kek's surprise shifted to annoyance and, right on cue, the blue faded. Angry electric white eyes glared at the irritatingly perceptive soldier. He didn't ask aloud, but the expression was unmistakable.

So Arnie answered, his gaze steady. "I suspected at the river. You confirmed it yesterday. Every man from my planet knows what a bikini is," he informed him quietly, "especially when she's in one. Why are you here?"

Kek, very aware of the woman sleeping in his arms, imagined ten different ways he could kill this sub-human male but refrained. He certainly wasn't going to tell Arnie the real reason why he was still here. His brain kicked into high gear. He was here because … uh … uh … . "I need the location of that base," he said, giving the man the answer he expected.

"You won't get it. Good job with the lizards today."

Annoyance didn't begin to describe the look in Kek's gaze. "Who is Romeo?"

Arnie gave a snort, amused by the question. "Don't let her see you get mad," he warned and walked away.

Kek's fingers tingled. He wanted nothing more than to throw a blast of energy at the smug little mogulwoop, but adjusted Kinety's body against himself instead. Seething inside, he resumed his search for someplace to set her down. The truth was, he didn't know why he was here, with the enemy, on a pointless build. He had things to do and certainly didn't have time to be standing off with aggressive Earthling males, looking for lizards, or fooling around with a silly alien female who refused to tell him what he needed to know.

Then, he remembered the encounter on Earth, the way she'd looked at him—without fear, without hatred. Entirely ignorant of his past or his sins, she'd seen him as a man, not a monster, and was attracted. To what specifically, he didn't know, but she'd been drawn to him. He'd felt it the moment he saw her, the powerful, magnetic pull. It was a sensation he was unfamiliar with, and it took him entirely by surprise. He never expected it to last. He thought once she learned who he was it would vanish in an instant, so he wasted no time deluding himself. He'd slipped a rock into her hand and left, fully expecting to never see her again.

Unable to find a spot on the ground, Kek propped against a rock and braced his elbow beneath her, then tucked his foot to support her weight on his thigh.

For him, the kick to the gut didn't come in the meadow on planet Earth; it came on the Zahrá Che pod transport when, even after realizing who he was, the way she looked at him didn't change. She still saw him as a man, even as he tried to assure himself he was mistaken. Her heart rate increased, and her eyes lingered despite her anger and their heated argument. The attraction had survived his identity, remaining untainted and without fear. He couldn't have been more surprised if she'd slapped him. The same thing had happened on Jag Mosrog. After that, he could focus on nothing else, and their encounters spun round and round in his head—her kiss, the pleasant smell of her, the feel of her hair in his fingers. It was no wonder he was behaving so foolishly. In front of every world, he'd humiliated her and made a spectacle of himself. Now, here he was, in disguise, carrying her around in his arms, ignoring the other things he had to do.

Why *was* he here?

Arnie had asked, but Kek didn't know. Staring up at the two moons, the soldier's warning danced around in his head. Kek was worried about what would happen when Kinety found out he was deceiving her. He didn't like the disguise. She definitely wasn't responding to him like before. So, was that because she thought he was someone else or because the attraction to Torak had begun to wane? Not knowing was bothering him. Could the attraction have faded? Could she truly have taken his rejection that hard? He'd only been trying to protect her. She was totally convinced, though. Ironically enough, nobody else was—only her.

His stomach twisted.

What if the spark had died? The thought of her looking at him with hatred in her eyes, or worse—fear—felt like a stone in his gut. He wanted her to smile at him, kiss him, look at him the way she had before but didn't know how to make it happen again, especially dressed as another man. The banter in the Earth meadow had been fun but was glaringly absent between her and Kek. Would it return when she knew the truth? If Arnie's warning had merit, which was likely, the answer was no.

Two facts remained: If he left now, his enemies would kill her, the only woman he'd ever wanted. If he stayed, he risked alienating the only woman who'd ever wanted him. Either way, he would get no information about the base.

A conundrum.

Then his mind drifted the other way. What would he do now if she did give him the location? The whole point was to destroy the base, entirely and completely. That was his mission. Finding that base would end the war, but was it worth the cost? If he killed her men, she would hate him. The very thought earned a shudder. For the first time, he began to question his unwavering loyalty and devotion to this war. Fighting was his life, everything he knew, yet suddenly it left him feeling empty. Deep down, he didn't want to fight it anymore and wondered if there was another way.

Kek tried to imagine other scenarios. He couldn't move all those soldiers himself without being seen as a traitor, and the Saphiridians certainly wouldn't cooperate. Their hatred of the Zahrá Che ran too deep. Yet, to stay the course would result in Kinety's unbridled hatred, a possibility he couldn't bring himself to consider.

Troubled by these thoughts, Kek rested his cheek against the top of her head, committing the feel of her in his arms to memory when a warning sensation jolted him back into reality. Abruptly, he raised his head and blinked around. Something was sneaking in.

"Tsst," he hissed sharply, signaling to the others.

They halted and turned to look at him.

Kek locked eyes with Arnie, concentrating on their surroundings, then held up two fingers. He pointed them to the left at a group of trees just in front of Rixton, who quickly drew his blaster. Next, he held up three fingers and pointed them to the curve of the rock wall just beyond the unfinished moat. Park backed against the log wall of the unfinished building, mouthing big curse words and bracing for a fight. A single finger, Kek pointed upward to the rock cliff, just over Arnie's head, then slid his eyes sideways toward his back. Very carefully, he withdrew his own blade, then signaled he was ready.

Arnie let out a sharp whistle, startling everyone in the camp. At the shrill sound, a pack of thick, knee-high creatures with fur and venomous snake fangs ambushed them from all sides. Their back legs were long and muscular, for powerful leaping, with thick tails to aid in height, and their front claws razor-sharp for tearing flesh.

It was a swift attack, well-coordinated and violent. When it was over, the men backed together, breathing heavily and gawking in surprise at the dead scavengers.

Kinety moaned, blinked sleepily at Kek, then dropped her head onto his shoulder and went back to sleep.

"Who's hungry?" panted Rixton.

Kek scowled down at the dead bodies and blanched. "No ... I've never cleaned an animal," he said, turning away in disgust.

"It's time you learned. Give me your knife," Rixton said with a point and opened his hand to take it.

Hand over his impaler?

Kek looked at the waiting hand, then at the carcass. Awkwardly, he reached for the long blade and handed it ... to his enemy. It was an odd sensation, simply handing his weapon away, but he managed it. Watching the sub-human warily, he took careful note as Rixton made a cut.

"I started it. You finish. Here," Rixton said, handing the knife back. "Be a man."

"This is disgusting," Kek complained, taking it.

Rixton pointed to a spot on the carcass. "Put the knife there and slice this way but don't puncture the stomach. You'll ruin the meat."

"My hands are slipping."

"Get a good grip—yeah, right there," coached Rixton, "slice and pull at the same time ... yep, yep ... easy does it. Good, now drop the contents onto the ground. We don't want them."

Kek gagged. "Like that?" he managed, trying to turn his nose away from the smell.

Rixton knuckled his arm and pointed at the cleaned carcass. "Good job, city boy," he praised, then showed him exactly how to quarter the sections. "You can either cut along this line here and cook the pieces or leave the carcass whole and use a stick to turn it."

Kek watched closely as Rixton taught him how to skewer the dead animal.

Nearby, Park returned with a disgusting-looking something to burn.

"What is that?" asked Arnie. "You can't find wood?"

"I ain't gonna tell you, and then you don't have to worry about scary dreams at night," said Park, "but there's more. We're building with wood, not burning it."

Arnie knew when to stop asking questions. "Go get more. I'll get the fire lit."

As Park walked off, singing in off-key Korean, Arnie cut his eyes to the side. "Hey, Kek, come help me with this fire."

Kek stepped over Kinety's legs, checked to be sure Park and Rixton weren't looking, and snapped his slimy fingers over the burn pit.

"Thank you," Arnie sing-songed.

Joboba still couldn't locate Torak, which was souring his mood further by the minute. Frustrated, he paced back and forth in front of three rigid crew members standing at attention. "Let me get this straight: You answered a distress signal from Zahrá Che sympathizers—"

"Mantis," one specified without moving.

"—Mantis," Joboba echoed slowly, "and broke formation to rescue them?"

"Affirmative," answered the unblinking leader. "Their situation was critical."

Joboba's eyes glinted in wonder. "Was it?"

This time, the crew leader didn't answer.

Joboba straightened and clasped his hands behind his back. "I wonder … do you always rush to aid our enemy?"

"No, Prime. The Mantis are neutral and not considered our enemy."

Joboba whirled as if struck and blinked at the woman. "If they're not with us they're against us, and the Mantis aren't with us."

Again, the crew leader didn't respond, and Joboba stepped close. "That's an enemy," he whispered, then straightened. "It was a brave rescue, though, wasn't it? Dangerous. That took guts. How many lives did you save?"

"Fifteen, Prime," the woman answered nervously.

"Fifteen!" Joboba thought about this for a long moment before a message notification pinged on his computer. He looked at it, then spun to face the crew members. "We'll finish this later. Go wait in the auxiliary," he said, gesturing them to the back of the spacecraft with a dismissive wave.

With a respectful nod, all three hurried away.

Joboba strode to his panel, and the screen blinked on.

It was Darplano.

"Is she dead?"

Darplano fidgeted his finger in front of him. "We couldn't reach her."

Joboba slapped his hand on the panel. Behind him, a wall slid shut, sealing the auxiliary chamber. "Why not!"

"Because the escapees have built a camp. It's guarded, and she doesn't come out."

"Then go in!"

Darplano tugged on his ear. "I hired shapeshifters to do just that, but they were caught and killed. We just can't get close to her, Prime. She's too well protected."

Joboba gnashed his teeth and released the bolts on the auxiliary chamber. Instantly, warning lights began flashing. "Protected by whom?" he asked over the warbling alarm.

Darplano ignored the three crew members banging frantically on the auxiliary chamber window behind Prime Joboba. "The soldier Arnie we saw before, Kek, Park, and her brother Rixton."

"Brother?" Joboba paused thoughtfully. "We could use that!"

"If we get illusionists involved, we could just make her come to us," offered Darplano.

"The Goblasi!" Joboba said with a snap. "They'll want to be paid. That's all for now, Darplano. I need to make a call."

Darplano gestured just past his superior. "There are crew members in the auxiliary pod," he warned.

Joboba slapped the jettison button, ejecting the unpressurized chamber. "What pod?" he asked and severed the link with Darplano.

*****

By the next day, a small village had sprung up from nothing. There were huts and cooking camps and trails that were already forming between the buildings. It was rustic, but it was home … almost. Here and there, some groups applied final touches, some sought out food or a bath, others lounged in the shade for a well-deserved rest.

Arnie's team, however, was still going. Next on their agenda was an outhouse.

While the team worked, the men in the camp passed Kek's blade around, using it to shave their beards, much to his horror. With a whimper, he turned away, unable to watch.

"So, Kinety, how did those scrawny-ass aliens move all us big, burly men around," Park asked, passing his log along and selecting another. "We're twice their size."

"You are not burly, Park," Kinety corrected.

Park snapped his head up and angled his head at her, making one eye bigger than the other. "Focus, woman!"

Kinety smiled. "It appeared as if they were using some sort of antigravity power," she remembered. "They held their hands flat like this," she demonstrated," to make them move lying down, then lifted their fingers to stand them up. A microchip was placed on our soldiers' necks, here," she touched the wound on her own neck, "and they were stuffed into tubes with absolutely no effort at all."

Park couldn't even imagine something so amazing. "Ohh, to have that kind of power," he marveled and looked at the rocky bluffs around them. "I would make art with all these rocks, just to confuse future archeologists and historians," he said with a fantastical wave of his hands. "Wait, that's already been done. Give me a minute."

"No. No. No," argued Rixton. "Not antigravity. Telekinetics! That would make the drive to work much more entertaining. And I would push your rocks over."

Laughter.

Kinety tossed sweaty brown hair aside and spoke over her shoulder. "What kind of power would you want, Arnie?"

"Telepathy."

"No, you don't," she assured, raising a knowing finger. "Telepathy is really weird. I don't know if I'll ever get used to it."

Just then, a series of high-pitch screams split the air. Everyone whirled, weapons drawn, but froze instead as a group of wet, naked soldiers tore out of the bathing pool, slapping wildly at themselves and waving their arms.

Behind them flew a swarm of flying spiders.

In a mad rush, the shrieking soldiers bumped into each other, unable to outrun the creatures, then dashed toward the river and dog-piled into it.

Kek laughed aloud.

"You're telepathic?" asked Park in wide-eyed wonder.

"No, silly. The aliens are. Trust me," she said with a huff, "you don't want telepathy."

Arnie had no choice but to trust her and concentrated on choosing another superpower to adopt. "Okay … whatever it is a genie does," he decided. "When I want something, just—bam! There it is."

Rixton gave him a fist bump, and Park danced in agreement. "Yeah!"

Kek laughed at the ridiculous conversation. "Ready, Arnie? One, two, three, lift."

Arnie slid his log between the ends and stacked two short logs at the notches. When it was set, he whacked Kek with an elbow. "What superpower would you like to have, Kek, if you could have one?" he asked, eager to keep the enticing conversation alive.

Kek gave the blond a sharp look, warning him to shut up, then looked at Kinety, eagerly waiting for his answer. "What superpower?" he echoed thoughtfully, then flashed Arnie a bright smile. "A venomous bite."

"You don't already have that?" asked a super sweet Arnie.

Everyone laughed at the crack.

Kek glared at the mouthy soldier. Curling his finger, he beckoned Arnie over. "Come over here and find out," he offered in his most charming voice.

"Uh, uh!" Arnie crooned. "I don't like being bit."

Joining in the fun, Kek redirected the question. "What superpower would you like, Kinety?"

Kinety batted innocent lashes at him. "The gift of persuasion," she said sweetly.

Kek's brows lifted in surprise. "You mean the eyelashes don't work?" he teased, earning a second round of fist bumps from the boys.

"Not on me, they don't," said Rixton. "Hand me that mud, Dorkymodo."

*****

By the following afternoon, a deep moat had been carved, foundations were in place, and support buildings were in the works. The mood was more or less pleasant among the homesick stranded. Scattered here and there were pockets of laughter, singing, and chatter that kept the mood jovial and helped pass the time. Focus was placed on soldiers suffering from depression, PTSD, and anxiety by villagers with more positive outlooks. These strugglers were kept distracted with humor and ultimately worked the hardest during the day. At night, new friends would gather and grieve together, reminisce, and tell stories of home and heroics. Games were popular, and apprenticeships had already begun between helpful trades, especially in areas of survival, entertainment, carpentry, and field medical skills. 'Support your people,' was Arnie's message. 'These are your people,' he said often. 'We take care of our people.'

The town was to be named, but the vote had been delayed because the suggestions were still coming in. Grand discussions during mealtimes were held over the topic with much noise and entertaining faux arguments. So far, the most popular candidates were: No Gakisville, Dotdotdot-Deedeedee-Dotdotdot Town, Aliens Ain't Realsburg, WhereDaFuckastan, Shit Sandwich Station, and Savage Bride Canyon.

Kek wasn't an Earthling, yet even he could see the humor and fun that went into the exercise. He didn't remember when he'd laughed so hard ... or if he ever had. His favorite, of course, was Savage Bride Canyon, but its close second WhereDaFuckastan made him chuckle intermittently throughout the day. Besides, it contained his new favorite bad word. He'd discovered its derogatory meaning of 'fuck' only after asking Arnie how one word could have so many different uses. It was quite handy.

During the hottest part of the day, Arnie marched through the camp, banging two fat branches together. He was impressively shirtless, sweaty, and sunburned. A day or two's growth of dark blond facial hair scruffed his chin, blending him in nicely with the rest of the men in the camp. "Hear ye! Hear ye! Follow me to the tree!" he bellowed, successfully interrupting every conversation and halting every task.

Every eye turned next to Rixton, who strolled alongside him carrying an armload of long vines and fibrous plants. All over the unnamed camp, puzzled soldiers set down their mud, their sharp rocks, and their logs.

Kek stood, wiping sweat from his forehead, and gathered his unruly hair into the ponytail it had escaped from. Glad for the interruption, he followed Kinety into the shade.

"Why are we gathering at the tree?" wondered a panting soldier, filthy from digging the moat. "I'm busy."

Rixton dropped his pile of sticks, and Arnie stood proudly over the mess, fists on hips. "Why, 'tis break time."

"Which is code word for—?" prompted a suspicious female officer.

"Rope-making class," Arnie announced proudly. "Here. Take a stick."

Despite the grumbles to the contrary, the sweltering camp swarmed every inch of shade beneath the massive tree.

Kinety stretched her shoulders and picked a spot against the trunk, just as relieved to be out of the heat. Her jeans were stained, and a hole had developed at one knee. She still wore Rixton's shirt, which was knotted high around her waist. Her boots were scuffed and muddy, and her hair spilled from a loose bun she'd fashioned atop her head.

She was adorable.

Kek could barely keep his eyes off her. Working hard not to ogle her, he sat nearby at the base of the tree, his face drawn in inquisitive amusement, and watched as Arnie passed out sticks.

"To make rope," Arnie began, "you want fibrous branches from high up in the tree to avoid branching buds. Find only strong sticks. No gray stuff. Flatten it into two halves, like this," he said, demonstrating so that all could see. "You want these fibers. Grab those at the thick end. Give that a try and we'll continue."

"Hey, Arnie," one soldier called out as he worked, "I got a question. How are we not getting sick? The viruses and bacteria are different on this planet, and we should all be at least mildly affected by them."

In unison, almost every hand went still, pausing to hear his reply.

Arnie opened his mouth to respond, then stole a subtle peek at Kek.

Kek glanced helpfully at the fake band on his wrist but noticed with a start that the lights were out. Easing it out of sight, he lifted his brows at Arnie as if also interested in his answer, then covertly zapped the band to reset the dead batteries.

"The … bands," Arnie annunciated, knowledgeably indicating his. "We already know they regulate the gasses in our blood so we can breathe, so I imagine they also provide … synthetic—?" he glanced back at Kek, who disguised an affirmative gesture, "—antibodies and immunities. Just a guess. It's alien technology. Makes no sense to me, either. Okay, you all got your fibers? Hold them like this. Get a good grip ..."

The curious onlookers, satisfied with the explanation, returned to their ropes, their hearts once again at ease.

Kek was slower to resume the mind-numbing exercise. Instead, he passed his faux blue eyes around the quiet soldiers. The soldiers were better groomed now, and many of them nearly clean-shaven. With polite respect, they hung on Arnie's every word, following his lead and absorbing his lesson entirely, and Kek marveled at it. This wasn't the cowed fear of a tyrannical officer with the power and/or desire to punish poor behavior. In fact, as crazy as it sounded, these people almost appeared to admire him.

Kek had never seen troops admire a leader before. Leaders were in place to issue orders and squash dissenters. For that matter, he'd never seen a leader talk with his troops, much less joke and play with them. Arnie did this as a tactic, he was sure ... and it worked. Hell, Arnie even bantered expertly back while the troops made fun of him, all while easily securing his position at the top and maintaining absolute control over the camp.

How different Earthlings were from the Saphiridians!

Merely disagreeing with a higher rank had resulted in countless Saphiridian executions. The troops knew better. It was confusing to watch ... this, and Kek struggled to wrap his mind around such *pleasant* behavior in the military. In fact, it was contrary to everything he'd read about the Earthlings, who were categorized as a war-loving, oppositional species. These were having fun despite everything. In the beginning, he'd assumed Arnie was merely using reverse psychology but had since begun to wonder if that was the case. Unless he was excellent at pretending, it appeared that Arnie actually cared about his fellow soldiers. Was that even possible?

The troops certainly seemed to like him.

Kek glanced covertly at Kinety, who was getting gripping assistance from her brother. Her concern for the soldiers also seemed genuine, but why? What benefit did she get from coddling them?

Kek felt a pang of jealousy, though he wasn't sure why. Forehead wrinkled, he twisted his rope. For the life of him, he couldn't imagine a reason for her fierce guardianship. They were just troops. Well ... that's how they started, he admitted to himself. Now, they were all becoming friends.

Well into the lesson, two men set their ropes down and, navigating the crowd, approached Kinety beside the tree.

Arnie, who was busy instructing a few rows over, turned mid-sentence, instantly alert. "Marshall?" he prompted, leaving his demonstration to join them. "Norelo? What's on your mind?"

Marshall didn't answer right away. Instead, he dropped to his knees beside Kinety and gestured Norelo down. Kinety and Rixton lowered their ropes.

"Commander," Marshall addressed Kinety when he spoke, his tone deliberate and direct, "we want to go back."

Kek's eyes rounded and snapped to Arnie, certain he would be furious that the request was put to someone else … but he wasn't. Rather, Arnie remained silent, allowing Kinety to respond.

Kinety glanced at Norelo, earning a firm nod. "To look for survivors?" she assumed.

Marshall held her gaze. "Yes. The Gaki have been brought under control here," he explained, "but nothing says the battle drops have stopped on Zahrá Che. In fact, I would imagine they've increased."

"Why so?"

"The purpose of the Gaki was to distract the Zahrá Che. Without that distraction, the Saphiridians might see that as a relief and will likely increase their ground attacks. Currently, there is nobody there to defend our soldiers or to guide them here," said Marshall.

The man was right. Kek shifted his gaze to Kinety.

"The chances of you surviving that are slim," she warned, though her tone wasn't discouraging.

Norelo chimed in. "We have no expectations of surviving this mission. None of us expect to see Earth again, and we've come to terms with that. This sentiment is unanimous across the camp."

Kinety looked out at the sea of faces, none of which denied the comment. In fact, the entire camp had again gone silent, following the conversation and nodding their heads in quiet agreement.

"The three of us," Norelo pointed to Marshall and Wesley, "should already be dead. We're alive because of Arnie. If the purpose of our survival has only a temporary value anyway, I want my last mission to be spent paying that gift forward. You were right, Commander. We have no business dying in their war. I cannot sit here, safe and cozy in my new cabin, knowing our slaughter is ongoing. We intend to rescue as many as we can and guide them here before those fuckers take us down."

Kinety and Arnie made eye contact. Both agreed.

"All three of you?" she asked, motioning to the third battleground survivor.

"No. Wesley has been selected as our designated survivor," said Marshall. "He will stay here. Norelo and I want you to send us back."

Kinety looked back and forth between the men. "Why are you asking me this?"

"You mean, why are we jumping the chain of command?"

Laughter.

"You were insane enough to confront the Gaki for us when the odds were against you," he said, indicating the listening soldiers, "so I know you'll understand why we have to do this."

"I do," she assured, "but Arnie would need to approve that."

Marshall inclined his head politely and grimaced. "Arnie already said no. I was hoping you could convince him to cooperate."

Arnie circled the group in mock offense, glaring sidelong at the ballsy soldier.

So, Kinety batted pretty lashes, intercepting the large leader's ire. "If they were to bring back more soldiers," she presumed, thoughtfully formulating the calculations in her head, "that would add to your 'total rescued' numbers."

Arnie considered this. "How many are you planning on bringing back?" he asked Marshall with a greedy squint.

"I don't know. We would get as many as we—"

"All of them! Sir," interrupted Norelo loudly.

"All of them?" Kinety gave her head a tilt, impressed by those numbers. "Thaaat *would* make you look pretty good, Arnie."

Arnie looked suspicious. "How good?"

"You might get a bigger bonus," she supposed.

"The military doesn't give bonuses," he countered, plopping unfooled hands on hips.

Rixton leaned toward Kinety, half-smiling, and mumbled under his breath.

Kinety's argument resumed. "Ah, but they do give medals," she reminded him.

"A medal?" Arnie pondered this judiciously, then returned the conversation to Marshall and Norelo. "What are your qualifications?"

Marshall shook his head. "My resumé wouldn't impress you. I was on weekend duty for filing an ID-one-OT complaint on the first shirt when I was taken."

"Are you on weekend duty often?"

"Yes, Sir. Last time I was in a bar fight … ahem."

"So, you have no search and rescue training?"

"No, Sir. I'm a troublemaker."

"You're gonna be in trouble if I don't get a medal."

"I'll get your damn medal."

"And you, Norelo?"

Norelo shook his head. "I'm a mechan—"

"He's my apprentice!" Marshall interrupted.

"—uh … student troublemaker," Norelo finished, earning another round of amusement.

Arnie shifted his glare to Kinety, assuring her he'd deal with her later, then peered out at the staring faces. "Do we have any other *trouble*makers interested in a soup sandwich dangbang?"

Kek's head cocked in doggie-style confusion as the words failed to register, but Kinety saved the day.

Puzzled, she leaned toward Rixton. "What is a soup sandwich dangbang?"

"Pointless suicide mission," he answered, barely glancing up from his rope.

A hand near the back of the group shot up. "I am," called an eager female soldier.

"What are your qualifications?"

"Just basic training, Sir—"

Arnie exhaled and pinched his temples.

"—but I have three letters of reprimand," she added.

"I was search and rescue!" shouted another man. This one dropped his rope and stood.

"Was?"

"I got kicked out."

Arnie slung his hand in appreciation, then clapped, encouraging a round of applause.

Kek laughed at the utter ridiculousness.

"There we go. Four troublemakers," Arnie announced. "Let's put your broken skills to good use. You have ten minutes to gather whatever you need for the mission. If you have cell phones, bring them. Meet me by the rock. The rest of you get back to work. Break's over! Hey ... take your ropes with you!" he barked and motioned Kinety to her feet. "Get up, partner. You started this; you get to help with the logistics."

Zhang was already on his feet.

Kek, who wasn't about to get left behind, dropped his rope and stood with Kinety, his mostly blue eyes sparkling with merriment. Baffled by Arnie's unorthodox method of leadership, he gathered with the Troublemakers at the rock, then watched them inspect their weapons and run an inventory of their personal items. Their names and information were recorded by the camp's designated historian, along with messages to loved ones before the group headed to the portal.

Only Norelo had a cell phone. "Why do you need a cell phone?" he asked, handing it over to Arnie.

"Our phones are no good on Neontak," Arnie said, taking it, "but they work on Zahrá Che if we can connect them to the universal internet. Kinety can even configure it to read in English, but you won't understand half of what you find."

"You just want to read my text messages."

"Gross. I'm not into poetry," teased Arnie. "Your text messages are safe."

"Hey! My poetry is from the heart," Norelo informed him.

Marshall shuddered. "Your ass-whooping will be from the heart if you start reciting that shit …"

As they walked, the group joked and goofed off, ribbing Arnie, who was still threatening them over some medal he intended to receive. For him to get it, their mission had to be successful. The banter amused Kek, but he found it weird. Even as the Troublemakers headed for their suicide mission, they seemed almost giddy, eager to die for their fellow Earthlings, and Kek struggled to wrap his mind around the camaraderie. Saphiridians never banded together, certainly not in friendship, and leaders didn't take suggestions. Without batting an eye, they would sacrifice unfortunate soldiers and carry on.

In a more serious tone, Arnie gave the team instructions. A team leader was selected, and the four members were paired. Warnings were made and landmarks described until they reached the portal. Warily, the group stepped into the dry, uninviting Zahrá Che world, but the plateau was vacant. The sky was red and dim, the smelly air cold. Instantly, their armlets winked to life, biting into their arms with jagged intensity.

Kek was glad he didn't have to worry about that. His body adjusted automatically to available atmospheres. He'd never appreciated this detail, however, until now.

Favoring his throbbing wrist, Arnie programmed Norelo's cell phone to charge automatically, then handed it to Kinety. She sat on the ground and, within moments, the phone was connected and a map of the area showed on the screen. She gave it back to Arnie.

"We're here on Gimeg Plateau," he said, pointing the group's attention to the map. "The city is here across the ocean bed. Use the purple plant as a food supply to get across. Collect some and keep it on you. You'll reenter the city through the sewer system here …"

As Arnie coached the team, Kek peeked at Kinety and found her looking out into the distance with laser-focus precision. Frowning, he followed her gaze to a pale glow barely visible in one of the cracks. The heat signature, only discernible because of the cool air on the dying planet, was moving between—wait!

Kek did a double-take and followed her gaze again, just to be sure the heat signature was what she was looking at. Without a doubt, it was. How had she spotted that? Humans from Earth didn't have infrared vision.

Working quickly on her phone, Kinety pulled her thermal camera up and panned it over the dim ocean bed. Two more signatures came up, making three. She touched Arnie's arm, interrupting him, and got up. "There's someone out there," she said, pointing, and handed him her phone.

Arnie took it. The glow, visible only on the phone, was absent without it. As he scanned the red horizon, Kek motioned, attracting his attention. With a subtle gesture, he pointed out two more, these walking together. "Are they human?"

Kinety, who was squinting at the most distant glow, shook her head. "I can't tell," she said, scanning for more.

Arnie lifted a brow at Kek, who the question had actually been for.

Kek, distracted by Kinety's ability to see them without the camera, snuck an affirmative nod to Arnie.

Arnie handed Norelo's phone to Kinety again. "Find the thermal imaging on this. The Troublemakers are gonna need it. Troublemakers! Look there and there," he said, using Kinety's phone to scan. "Do you see the heat signatures?"

They did.

"Those are humans. Split up. Two of you go that way, two that way. Approach carefully. That microchip shit may still be on their necks. They will kill you. Remove it. They will experience panic, confusion, and time loss. The recovery takes some time. Expect it. Help them through it. Send them here. I'll have someone waiting at the portal to escort them into Neontak. Afterward, you four can meet up again and continue on your original mission."

"Yes, Sir!" they responded in tandem.

"What about that one?" Kinety said, pointing to the signature closest to them.

"I'll go," said Kek.

Arnie gave his blond head a quick shake. "I can't leave Kinety, and you don't have a partner."

"Zhang is here," she reminded.

"Without Kek, that isn't enough. We're not leaving you," Arnie said firmly.

Kek caught Arnie's eye. "I'll be fine," he assured, holding his gaze meaningfully. "He's not far. The air isn't buzzing, so there's no Gaki."

Arnie held his gaze, silently asking why.

Kek raised his brows, insisting.

Kinety started to protest, but Arnie silenced her with a hand. "Go ahead, Kek. I'll send someone to wait at the portal for you to return. Troublemakers," he said, turning to the two teams, "make good decisions."

They all gripped hands and hooked thumbs.

"Go," Arnie said, sending them off. "Bring them home."

Marshall faced Kinety. "Thank you for everything, Commander," he said, taking her hand.

"You come back," she said softly.

"I'll be back. By the way, I have a poster of you in my garage. You were in the boots."

Kinety wrinkled her nose. "Weren't they cute?"

"Not as cute as the bikini. See ya," he smiled.

With that, the Troublemakers were gone.

Arnie slapped Kek's hand hard and folded their fingers into a firm grip. "Hurry back."

Kek faced Kinety and a long, lingering look passed between them. She looked like she wanted to say something but stopped herself, so he shifted his gaze back to Arnie. "I will," he promised and went over the side to the nearest ledge.

Arnie ushered Kinety and Zhang quickly back into Neontak, urging speed so a new team could be sent to wait at the portal.

By the time Kek returned with his confused, glossy-eyed soldier a few minutes later, the new team was already waiting. Once the wandering soldier was safely in Neontak, Kek returned to the Zahrá Che side of the portal and faded back into his own skin. Torak sagged heavily against the rocky cliff, utterly drained of energy. Weak-kneed, he lowered himself to the ground and took a moment to draw power from the atmosphere. With an exhaled grunt, he squeezed his eyes, blinking the blue away, and rubbed them for a minute or two. They were tired. Being Kek was exhausting. As he recharged, he sat with his eyes closed and chuckled softly to himself. "WhereDaFuckastan."

Chapter 15

Rixton was suffocating.

Kinety ran, trying to reach him. A flash of blue knocked her backward, and she landed with a cry.

Rixton couldn't breathe.

Scrambling wildly, she clawed past unfriendly aliens, flailing for her brother …

Kinety jolted awake, reaching for something that wasn't there, and sat up in her pallet. Sleepy-eyed and breathless, she blinked into the dim dawn-break, quite unsettled by the bizarre dream. It was just a dream. Relaxing heavily, she exhaled in relief, then frowned at her next thought. That was a dream, right?

Unsettled, Kinety rolled to an elbow and gave herself a moment to wake. A quick check proved everyone in their little cabin was safe and asleep. Park. Zhang. Arnie. Kek was still gone. Rixton was gone. Where was Rixton?

She rolled to a hip, alarmed by his absence, and pushed wild hair from her eyes. His space, just beside hers, was empty. Had he gone to the bathroom? Twisting, she wondered why he hadn't taken a buddy, then remembered they had an outhouse now.

Frazzled, she rubbed red, sleepy eyes and waited for him to return. While she waited, she rested her head against the log wall and peered out the open door to the pale streaks stretching across the dark sky. She was sore and not looking forward to another day of hard labor, but there was still work to be done. The camp was coming along, though, and a routine was beginning to appear amid the chaos. Soon, the moat would be deep enough to add water, and the soldiers would have someplace safe to wait while she and a team went to find the others.

Rixton still wasn't back.

Kinety had to pee. After giving her eyes another good rub, she got up, wishing she had an allergy pill. A sharp tap on the outhouse door proved it was empty. This, too, puzzled her. She was quick with her own business and went to check the yard, but Rixton wasn't there. The night guards were in place and appeared entirely unbothered. Growing irritated, she wondered if anyone else was awake this early but saw nobody else moving about the quiet camp.

Rixton wasn't by the moat. He wasn't by the supplies or the water bucket. She looked by the river and didn't see him there either. Growing alarmed, she looked out. There was no way he left the camp without a partner. He knew better. Zhang, Park, and Arnie were all three inside sleeping, so where was Rixton?

Just to be sure she wasn't losing her mind, Kinety peeked inside the cabin, hoping she'd missed her brother and that he was back inside, but Rixton's pallet was still empty. Hers, of course, was empty. Arnie was sleeping. Zhang was sleeping. Park was gone.

Where was Park?

Kinety checked the outhouse again and found it empty. With mounting concern, she turned to check with the guards and saw Park walking alone toward the portal. "Park!" she called quietly, but he didn't hear her. Quickly, she hurried into the cabin, snatched her blaster, then darted out after him alone.

Zhang opened his eyes with a jolt. Right away, he saw the three empty pallets and Kinety's missing blaster. "Arnie!" he hissed in alarm.

Arnie sat up sharply. One glance at the empty cabin, and he was on his feet. "Where are they?"

Zhang scrambled into his shoes, muttering in Chinese, and grabbed his blaster.

Arnie skidded to a stop in the doorway, clutching his, and saw Kinety running for the portal. "Kinety!" he called out, waking the whole camp.

She didn't hear him.

The two guards turned, and Arnie pointed at Kinety. "Where is she going?" he bellowed angrily.

The soldiers followed his point. "Who?" they wondered, then blinked at him in confusion. In a daze, the guards stared off, eyes glazed and slow-blinking.

"Shit!" Arnie banged on a random building, startling all inside. "Get up! Get up! Get up!" he shouted.

A sleepy soldier popped out. "What's wrong!"

"The guards! Something's wrong with the guards," Arnie pointed, shoving the man toward them, and took off beside Zhang. They hurdled logs, rocks, and inclines in a mad dash for the portal. On the far side of the valley, they crested the hill just in time to see Kinety hurry through to Zahrá Che.

On the other side, they cursed in horror as Kinety dashed through the orange glow of planet Zahrá Che toward a fifty-foot triangle spacecraft hovering near the edge of the plateau with its ramp down. The air was cold and dry and dust billowed beneath the craft, camouflaging the aliens standing outside it. In front of her, Rixton and Park both entered the spaceship as if in a daze. Kinety dashed up the ramp after them, and all three vanished inside.

Zhang skidded to a stop and dropped hard to a knee. Squinting, he aimed his blaster. Arnie charged past him, running like an Olympic sprinter to catch up.

Kinety's armlet bit into her with shark teeth, but she didn't care. "Rixton!" she cried, fighting a wave of dizziness as she adjusted to the hazy atmosphere. "Park!"

Staring aliens crowded the base of the ramp. As she dashed past them they swarmed, ushering her into the spacecraft and blocking her exit. Blaster shots flashed around her. One alien shrieked and spun wildly before falling off the ramp.

Kinety didn't care. Like a madwoman, she charged through the door.

Another alien fell, this one backward.

She leapt over it.

The spaceship interior blinked and winked in an array of odd, transparent technology. Seven more of the alien creatures, each dressed in silver compression suits, operated the clear computers, these bare-headed and speaking rapidly to each other as she skidded into the flight deck.

Ahead of her, Park and Rixton stood in front of a tall, gray-skinned alien with a bulbous head and sharp, angular features. He—it—wore an ornament on its head. The alien resembled the Zahrá Che in general, only taller, heavier, and with beady black eyes.

Kinety's eyes flashed blue, connecting her brain to the language.

"It's her!" said one. "The Savage Bride!"

"Launch!" cried another.

With a jerk, the alien wearing the head ornament snapped intense black eyes from Rixton and Park to Kinety. "Sleeeep," he purred.

She shoved her blaster against the alien's forehead, stopping him from advancing. "Rixton!" she cried, grabbing her brother. He wasn't blinking. "Park!"

Neither acknowledged her.

The alien twisted its head slightly. "Sleeeep," he crooned, looking deep into Kinety's eyes and stepping forward.

Warily, she yanked Rixton backward by the shirt and stepped protectively in front of Park, her weapon trained on the freaky alien. "Who are you! What have you done?" she demanded, physically backing the men away.

"It's not working," he said to someone else and tried harder.

A second alien hurried forward to assist and narrowed focused eyes on her. "Sleeeep," they both insisted.

"Back off!" she shouted, pointing her blaster at the new one.

An alien spilled through the door, its back bowed, blood spewing from its mouth. It skidded across the floor and rolled into a wall.

"She's immune," cried an alien.

In an instant, Kinety was surrounded by four more aliens, each trying to stare into her eyes. She snapped her weapon at all of them in warning, dragging Rixton and bumping Park backward with her shoulder. "Rixton," she said sharply, rattling his arm as she worked the uncooperative men toward the exit. "Park, stop looking at them!"

A frantic alien toppled into the doorway, its arm outstretched. "Seal the door! Seal the—oof!"

An outer door, composed of staggered, interlocking panels, started sliding shut. Kinety whirled, grabbed a hover-chair, and shoved it between the closing doors.

"Get us out of here!" cried a shrill voice.

"I can't!" shouted a reply. "Something's holding us down."

Park stumbled over a hover-chair, knocking Kinety down, and fell beside her. The jolt woke him. He gasped hard, panting in lungfuls of air as if surfacing after a deep swim. Startled, he scrambled backward in a panic and blinked confused eyes around the spacecraft in surprise. "Where are we?" he wheezed between confused puffs.

"Launch! Now!"

The floor beneath them trembled.

Kinety shoved him toward the grinding door. "Get out! Get out!" she shouted, practically dragging Rixton.

"I can't launch!"

"Then go sideways! Get off the plateau!"

An alien jolted forward, reaching for Kinety.

She fired, killing it, then aimed at the others with a trembling hand as the ship jerked sideways. Through the open doors, Gimeg Plateau began to shrink.

"Something's holding us down!" fretted the alien at the controls. "We're moving, but I can't lift off."

Rixton's knees buckled, dropping him onto Kinety. Awkwardly, she caught him. His lips were blue, his eyes unfocused. "Park, get out!" she shouted, giving her heavy brother a whack to the temple with her blaster. "Rixton! Wake up."

Rixton jerked hard, taking Kinety to the floor with a gasp. Writhing, he struggled to breathe.

"Rixton?" Park cried, grabbing him. "Holy shit!"

The door panels whirred, smashing the hover-chair. It buckled, succumbing to the pressure.

Park pinned Rixton and blew hard into his mouth.

"Out! Out!" Kinety shouted, shoving them toward the whirring door. "Get him out!"

Arnie's arm and head appeared in the crack of the door. Snarling, he fought the pull of the speeding ship, trying to pull himself inside.

"Arnie!" she cried, fighting to reach him.

Park turned to heave Rixton out, but an alien grabbed him and forced eye contact. Instantly, he froze again. Staring wide-eyed and unblinking, he obediently kicked the chair, trying to free it from its clamp. The hover-chair twisted, threatening to pop out as the whirring doors fought to close.

Arnie growled, pinned at the waist now.

"No!" In a panic, Kinety stomped the chair back into place to stop the doors from closing. The ground blurred past the narrowing crack as they skimmed the dry ocean bed.

With a snarl, Park tackled her backward, knocking her hard into a nearby wall. Her knees buckled and she dropped, unconscious.

Arnie landed hard on the floor, roaring, and—Wham!—knocked Park off her. Park crashed to the floor with a gasp. With a violent kick, Arnie leapt, knocking two aliens backward into a pile of others, and took Park's attacker to the floor.

Something exploded.

A powerful concussion rippled through the ship, knocking everyone off their feet in a deafening blast. Kek flew in through the sparks, roaring in fury.

Confused aliens shrieked in alarm and scattered.

Kek kicked a nearby alien violently backward, sprawling it against the panel across the room, then twisted to grab Kinety. With a heave, he yanked her against him, dropping her forehead onto his shoulder. Holding her tight, he slung his hand, caving the chest of another and knocking it into a group.

The aliens panicked.

Arnie grabbed Rixton, whose eyes were rolling back, and blew hard into his mouth. "Look at me!" he ordered, slapping his cheek, then saw Park. With a jab, he cracked an elbow into the stunned Korean. "Dammit, Park, stop looking at them."

Park fell sideways with a curse and inhaled sharply. "I don't like these aliens," he wheezed, his eyes rounded wide. "They're assholes."

The alien in the headgear yanked a panel open—

"Kek!" Arnie shouted.

—and whirled, aiming a blaster at Kinety.

Kek thrust his hand, knocking the lead alien backward in a violent flash of blue. The leader struck the wall, eyes open, chest caved. The other aliens shrieked in horror and dove for their weapons. Pissed now, Kek slung his hand in a violent arc.

A small, sonic boom sent all the aliens flying. Arnie and Park ducked sharply, stunned by the noise. Instantly, the flight panel began flashing and emergency alarms sounded.

The aliens spun frantically to regain control of the craft.

Holding his ears, Park blinked at Kek and sat up.

Kek's hand crackled with blue energy as he backed toward the exit with Kinety. He sliced his hand toward the exit panel, frying the controls in a melt. The whining door relaxed, dropping the hover-chair and opening to reveal the crusty ocean bed below. With a flick of his fingers, a countdown clock blinked onto a cracked glass screen. "Jump!" he barked, jerking the wide-eyed Park to his feet and throwing him toward the exit.

Fifteen seconds.

The remaining aliens shrieked and clawed at the controls, desperate to stop the clock.

Twelve seconds.

Arnie heaved Rixton up. In two steps, they were out.

Nine seconds.

One alien spun and gaped at Kek. "It's you!" he mouthed in horror.

Six seconds.

Kek wrapped his arms around Kinety and jumped. They hit the top of a square of crust and rolled over the side. In a crumble of dirt, they slid down the steep wall into the soft crack below.

The explosion was massive.

Kek hooked his arms around Kinety's head and ducked as fiery debris rained down around them. After the sparks faded, he gripped her face and frantically tapped her cheek. "Kinety!" he worried, rattling her shoulder to rouse her. "Kinety!"

She woke, confused and unsure what had happened, and blinked up at him. "Kek?"

"Are you hurt?" he asked, breathing heavily and brushing hair from her face with shaky hands. "Did they hurt you?"

A waft of smoke fouled the air, and Kinety remembered with a jolt. In a panic, she spun away from Kek and scrambled to her feet. "Rixton!"

"He's over here," Arnie called.

Kinety followed his voice at a run and landed on her knees beside her brother. "Rixton!" she cried, throwing her arms around him.

Completely confused, Rixton glowered at his clinging sister and pulled away. "Where the hell are we? Where were you going?" he demanded, scanning their smoky surroundings.

Kinety exhaled in relief and slumped against the crust wall. "Don't do that again," she said breathlessly and dropped her head into her hands.

"Where are we!" he asked again, this time angrily.

Arnie scowled at the red sky and the unfamiliar landscape. "We're on Zahrá Che ... some-fucking-where."

Park pointed at Kek, who was approaching, and started to get up. Wide-eyed, he wiggled his fingers. "Did you see—the-the blue—?"

Arnie pushed Park back onto his butt by the shoulder, silencing him with a look, and raised his brows. "I saw it. That explosion was huge. They must have bumped into the ground," he said meaningfully.

Park blinked at Arnie for a second, then glanced at Kinety, then at Kek, then again at Kinety. In that instant, he remembered the bizarre story she'd told that first day on Neontak about the alien assassin Torak with the magical powers who had accidentally claimed her as his wife. Fragments of information sifted through his mind, settling into place—Kek's jump into the Gaki ring, his claim that she was spoken for, his violent reaction to the aliens with the gifts. In a moment of eureka, he figured it out. Another look at Arnie confirmed that the leader already knew.

With a stammer, Park took the hint, then fingered a goose egg on his head. "Geez, Arnie! You cracked … my … ," he began, then stopped short. A jagged memory crackled through his mind, and he snapped a sharp look at Kinety. "Did I hit you?" he whispered.

Kinety shook her pounding head. "It's okay. Are you alright?"

Park paled, remembering. "It's not alright! I attacked you," he realized in apologetic horror. "Kinety!"

"It wasn't you, Park!" she argued, holding her hand up. "It was them. Their eyes were hypnotic. They told you to kill me."

"Who were they?" he demanded, glaring at Kek.

Kek deliberately didn't answer, reminding the Korean that his identity was a secret.

"It doesn't matter," said Arnie. "They're dead. Are you okay, Park? Your nose is bleeding."

Park sniffed and brushed his hair back, knocking debris from it. "No, I'm offended," he snapped, dusting himself off. "They just looked at me and made me do whatever they wanted. What's up with that? Who does that?"

Kinety touched her brother's shoulder. "Rixton?"

Rixton gave her a quick wave. "I'm good. I'm good," he said in annoyance.

"Why did you two leave camp?" she demanded. "You know better."

Rixton jabbed a finger at Kinety. "I was following you! What the hell were you doing wandering off on your own, Dorkymodo?"

"That wasn't me," she said, closing her eyes and pinching her temples. "It was an illusion."

"What do you mean it wasn't you! I saw you leave," Rixton argued.

Arnie shook his head. "Whatever you saw wasn't her."

Park made a face and pointed at himself. "No, *I* followed Kinety."

Kinety pulled her dusty hair around her shoulders and straightened her back, which was sore now. "You both followed an illusion. They attempted to hypnotize me, but it wasn't working."

Rixton circled his finger. "How did their hypnosis work on us but not on you?"

Kinety had no idea. Shrugging, she looked up at Kek, who was watching her. She'd woken in his arms, which made no sense … unless he'd jumped with her. "When did you get here?"

"He followed me," Arnie said, answering for him.

Kinety wanted to thank him, but the words didn't happen. The eye lock was too tight.

Still frowning, Rixton looked back and forth between her and Kek.

Kek approached slowly. "We should get moving," he murmured.

"Which way is back?" she asked, lifting her lashes as he neared.

Kek tipped his head the correct direction, then lowered his hand to help her up.

Before she could take it, Rixton hauled her up by the arm. "Let's go," he said and pushed her into motion beside Arnie.

*****

Kinety stumbled to an ungraceful stop beside Arnie. At his look of surprise, she straightened herself and fell into step. "Apparently, Rixton wants me to walk with *you*," she said in acute irritation, "not Kek."

"Oh?" Arnie glanced back and saw the two men glaring at each other in hatred. "What's going on?"

Kinety snatched a chunk of dirt from the steep wall and crumbled it with her fingernail. "With Rixton? I think he wants to talk to Kek. Probably to run him off. Actually, I don't care. The whole thing is bothering me. All of it."

Arnie peeked at her in amusement. "This sounds serious. Let's have it."

Kinety stumbled a bit, still dizzy. "I think Rixton may be right. Maybe I shouldn't spend any more time with Kek."

Arnie caught her arm until she straightened. "Why? I thought you liked him. Did something happen when you two were alone?"

"Yes—I mean, no! No. He didn't do anything. It was … ," Kinety gripped her dirty hair and exhaled. "It's me. I don't know what's wrong with me, Arnie. I've been following him around and laughing with him and sitting too close and—I mean, I can tell there's something there, but then … ."

Arnie already knew. "But, Torak."

"Oh, my God. Every time I see him, I get all flushed and my heart pounds. My knees go soft, and … he doesn't want me." Kinety grimaced and huffed in frustration. "I've never behaved like this. Now, all of a sudden, I'm just throwing myself at all these men."

Arnie's eyes narrowed in amusement. "By 'all these men,' you mean Torak and Kek, right? Or is there someone else on your radar?" he asked, flexing his muscles and biting his lip.

Kinety laughed and gave him a backhanded whack to the stomach. "Stop making fun of me. I'm serious," she whined, then gave him a pitiful look. "I feel like an ass."

Arnie wasn't quite sure what the problem was. "It sounds like you prefer Torak," he shrugged, steadying her again.

"My enemy."

"Your enemy."

"Yeah, well, I've met him a whopping three times—four? He's already announced to the galaxy he doesn't want me, and ... he's an alien," she said with a sour laugh.

"If there's chemistry, who gives a shit?"

"Well, Kek, for one," she answered incredulously, "who's human."

Arnie scratched his ear. "Mmm. There's that ... ," he agreed with a wince. "What else is good about Kek—besides ... that?"

"Kek makes my heart go pitter-patter," she said with a blush.

Arnie made an 'oh' face, paused, then asked, "If Kek makes it pitter-patter, what does Torak do?"

"Stops it."

Arnie didn't chuckle ... out loud. It was hard, but he held it in. Instead, he nudged her shoulder, speeding her up when she slowed, and recovered his step beside her. "I think Torak has more claim than Kek. He came first and, well ... you are politically married."

"The marriage was annulled. Besides, Torak is worried about war, not me," she said with certainty and kicked a pebble. "I really like him, but he was pretty clear about not feeling the same, and Kek reminds me too much of Torak. I refuse to be in love with two men."

Arnie had never been good in matters of love and romance, but it was evident that this conversation was taking a nosedive. "I think you're reading too much into this. Let's just take a step back and—"

"You know what? You're right," she interrupted with a springy bounce, "I don't have time to be worrying about men. We have to find our soldiers and figure out a way to get home. I should just wash my hands of them both."

Arnie opened his mouth to argue, then smiled. "Good idea."

*****

Rixton waited for Kinety and Arnie to walk off with Park far in the lead. When the others were a good distance away, he faced Kek, glaring.

197

Kek felt the blue of his eyes fade a few shades. Unamused, he shifted his irritated gaze to Rixton. "Was that necessary?"

Rixton stepped close. "That'll give us a few minutes," he said, his tone direct.

Kek waited impatiently for him to elaborate, but he already knew where this was going. Rixton, too, had figured it out.

Rixton watched his sister gather some more distance beside Arnie, then twisted his brows at Kek. "Torak—is it?"

Kek's eyes went white and the electric blue current snapped into place around his irises. "That's right," he answered and started walking.

Rixton kept pace beside him. "Nice," he said dryly. "You mean to tell me Kinety hasn't figured this out yet?"

"Not yet."

"Why are you in disguise?"

"She thinks I'm her enemy."

"Are you?"

Kek huffed in sour amusement. "Yes," he admitted, his voice low.

Rixton sent him a sideways look. "Why are you here?"

Sparks crackled between the men.

"I want information, for one," admitted Torak.

"By now, you already know you're not going to get it," Rixton presumed correctly. "Let's discuss the other reason."

Kek would have preferred knocking the guy over but didn't. He was supposed to make friends with him. Best besties, Arnie had said. "I have a few enemies," he seethed, not knocking him over.

"A few?" Rixton accused, then pointed over his shoulder to the spot where the ship had blown up.

"Goblasi, from Janosethi. Mind masters."

Rixton waited for more.

"She's made herself pretty popular," said Kek.

"Ah. So, you're here *guarding* her," Rixton inquired skeptically.

Kek ignored the tone and didn't answer.

"They almost killed me, and they tried to kill Park. Were they about to kill her?" Rixton asked with another jab behind himself.

"They ordered Park to do it."

"I want it to stop!" Rixton hissed through his teeth. "Disassociate yourself from her."

Kek's hands tingled. One blast and the mouthy sub-human would be quiet. "I tried," he retorted slowly, "at the council. It didn't work. All it did was make her a media sensation."

Rixton stopped mid-stride and faced the larger man. "The attacks are coming daily, and they're getting worse. There has to be some way to stop this."

Annoyed, Kek stopped. He reigned in his temper, struggling to tolerate Kinety's brother, then tried a different tactic. "We should appeal to the Saphiridians," he said carefully. "See if they'll offer protection."

Rixton recoiled. "Protection?" he echoed, refusing to even consider it. "The Saphiridians can go to Hell! They're slaughtering our people! They tried to kill Kinety!"

"They wouldn't," he insisted, "not if *Torak* has spoken for her."

Rixton was unamused. "Torak the Assassin?"

Crackle. Crackle.

Kek glared down at him. "That's right."

It was Rixton's turn to huff. "You dumped her."

"I tried," Torak snapped. At Rixton's intensified glare, he amended, "It was for her own good. I was trying to protect her from my enemies. My appeal for annulment was denied. By majority consensus, the citizens of the galaxy have decided that Kinety is my wife. The marriage is legal."

"What about divorce?"

Torak laughed and indicated the smoking crash. "There is no divorce," he said and started walking again. "My enemies have already adopted her. There have been too many attempts since the annulment trial to assume otherwise."

"I know of three."

"We're at seven," corrected Kek.

"Seven!"

"Seven," Kek confirmed. "Kinety barely escaped from the cargo ship that was returning her to Earth from Jag Mosrog. Right after she ejected, the ship was attacked—probably reptilian. There were no survivors. That's one. When she landed on Zahrá Che, two fighters attacked her escape pod—definitely reptilian. Two. The mantis that gave her the vial and tried sending her on a suicide mission was three. The Zahrá Che on Neontak missed her and killed her friend. Four. A kidnapping attempt by a shapeshifter disguised as me. They want her alive—I don't know why—was five. The shapeshifters in the camp with the poison were six. The Goblasi today makes seven," he said irritably. "She's also had audience with the Zahrá Che Emperor Dinruk as a negotiator. Clearly, my attempt to annul didn't fool anyone. Neither will divorce. Kinety is my wife."

Rixton scowled but fell silent, letting this soak in. Seven! For a long time, the men walked together without speaking, at least until Park, Arnie, and Kinety reached a blockade in the gap between pieces of broken crust and had to turn around. Kek blinked his eyes back to blue as the group reversed and watched Kinety as she passed. Maintaining their formation, they migrated around the block to the next gap.

A series of mixed emotions skittered through Rixton's head. Part of him wanted to tell this jackass to take a hike and leave his sister the hell alone, but some primal instinct stopped him from doing that. Without having to be told, it dawned on him that this man, this alien, was the real reason they were still alive and likely would have a hand in the continuation of that—an idea he was rather vested in. Realizing this, he dialed back the attitude. "So. Are you as bad as they say?" he asked.

Torak huffed in amusement. "Depends on who's saying it," he answered simply.

"Who else knows?"

"Arnie. Park, now."

Rixton inclined his head. "Well," he said cordially. "Let's hear it."

"Hear what?"

Rixton spoke carefully so the daft idiot could keep up. "The truth. You were on Earth for a reason. What is it?"

Kek half-smiled. The guy was irritating, but if they were going to be best besties, then killing him would be counterproductive. "Alright," he agreed and came right to the point. "My mission is to eliminate all of you. Kinety is in the way."

Rixton made no reaction. "Why?"

Kek watched Kinety walk ahead of them. "Recently, the Zahrá Che began infecting my people with biological weapons—plagues, viruses, and neurotoxins. Wiped out millions. The Saphiridians needed time to find a cure and quarantine, so I opened a portal from Neontak and let the Gaki keep the Zahrá Che busy. Then we attacked, bringing the fight to them. It was very effective and nearly ended the war. The Zahrá Che can't fight physically and stood no chance, so they began stealing Earth soldiers who could do that for them. I went to Earth to put a tracker on the next batch of fighters, which were supposed to lead me to the base where the fighters are being stored. Once I find the location, it is my job to annihilate them and end the war."

Rixton gave his head a nod. "Enter Kinety."

"Yes. There were two ships on Earth. Your sister was captured by mistake, got loose, and saw the Zahrá Che program the transport pod with my tracker on it. She reversed the coordinates and sent the pod back to Earth. She knows where the base is. Only she and the Zahrá Che know the location. I've tried everything to find them. The transport ships are cloaked invisible and programmed to self-destruct if accessed. I can't go near one, and I can't holograph in. So far, she's refused to tell anyone the location, even Arnie. But now that she has her army," he glanced toward the plateau, "it's time to get the others."

Rixton slowed, letting the weight of the approaching situation settle in his mind. "And it's your job to kill them."

"It's my job to kill them," Kek confirmed. "Kinety's soldiers."

"Does Kinety know this?"

Whether Kek wanted to admit it or not, he was beginning to enjoy himself. "Oh, yeah. Torak is obligated to the Saphiridians to complete the mission," he answered and lifted his brows. "She knows this and doesn't care much for the idea. "

"Naturally."

"And now she thinks I attacked her, so there's a trust issue."

"Are you sure that wasn't you?" teased Rixton.

Kek glowered at the smaller man, refusing to answer such a stupid question. "If she catches me, she'll want me to go, but I can't leave her. That's why I'm in disguise."

"Don't complete the mission."

Torak angled his head slightly. "Would you betray your people so easily?"

Rixton shrugged. "Then, we'll do it without you."

"If I leave, she'll be dead within hours, and all of you with her. You've seen them come after her. Soon, they'll step up their game. Once this group of Neontak humans is gone, the Zahrá Che will happily feed the rest of your men to the Gaki."

Rixton stepped over a pile of fish bones. "Kinety said the Zahrá Che defended her against the Saphiridians. They protected her."

Torak kicked a rock with his toe and watched it tumble. "Kinety's association with me is known throughout the galaxy. Harming her, regardless of who it is, would have consequences. Emperor Dinruk is afraid of retaliation. He was protecting himself, not Kinety."

"What about the poison?" he asked, searching for solutions. "We kill the Gaki. The program ends."

"If she opens that vial, she won't make it out of Neontak. You'll all be dead. Like I said, it's a suicide mission. If you kill the Gaki, the remainder of the soldiers Kinety has yet to reach will be simply discarded and left—wherever they are—to die while the Zahrá Che help themselves to a planet that isn't theirs. They aren't going to waste the resources to return them."

Rixton watched Kinety dust herself off and wipe her hands on her jeans. As much as he didn't want to admit it, he believed the alien. "I guess you have a decision to make."

Kek's voice hardened. "Yes, I do."

Rixton reeled inwardly as the magnitude of the situation struck him. "Why did you agree to tell me?"

"You're my bestie."

"*I'm* your bestie?"

"My *best* bestie."

Rixton rolled his eyes in amusement. "That's got Arnie's fingerprints on it," he grumbled to himself, then asked. "Did he tell you what that means?"

"I've got the idea."

"Alright then, bestie, break it down for me."

Kek paused. "Break what down?"

"Why did you agree to tell me this?" he repeated.

And the fun was over.

Kek sobered and sharpened his tone. "Because I don't think you realize how serious this is," he said, surprising himself by how annoyed he actually was. "They're coming. Whether to take her or kill her, I can't say, but they will eventually get her. Obviously, they'll use you to do it. Once they get her, you're dead. I need your cooperation."

Rixton spread his hands in annoyance. "If it's your job to kill us anyway, why do you care?"

Kek stopped. "I don't want *her* dead. *She* doesn't want you dead," he corrected, spelling it out for him. "She's my wife. So, I have a dilemma. I'll leave it to you to stall her next rescue until I figure it out."

Rixton couldn't manage a smile. "Wow, you are a sweetheart," he said in sarcasm.

"You're the first to accuse it," Kek assured, then pointed to Kinety's pocket with the rock in it. "Don't lose that."

"The rock?"

The group rounded the next corner.

"The rock," confirmed Kek, coming to a stop in front of another high wall of dirt blocking the path. He knew exactly what it was. Hands on hips, he turned to face Kinety and played ignorant. "This could go on for miles in either direction."

Kinety's green eyes lingered in his a bit too long before she turned abruptly away and gave her hair a thoughtful fluff. "We need to see how far."

With a running jump, Park tried to scale the side of the broken crust, but the walls were too high, and he slid embarrassingly back down. "I wasn't even close," he muttered in disgust. "Kinety, don't watch."

Smiling, Kinety examined the high wall above them. "Put me up, Arnie."

"Wait ... what?" said Kek, distinctly noticing the height. "That's ten-span high!"

Ignoring him, Arnie cupped his hands, interlocking his fingers, and waited.

Kinety backed up, gaging the distance to both targets, and braced. "Ready?"

Arnie nodded and Kinety took off. At a run, she stepped into the cupped hands, using his upward thrust as a springboard, and launched herself onto the top of the crust in a pretty roll.

The gentlemen below clapped … golf-style.

Kinety bowed to her adoring audience, blew kisses, then crossed the flat top to see what was blocking their path. At the edge just below her, she saw a deep gouge that scraped across the ground, skipped a large stretch, then scraped again far in the distance. It was her pod. The wreck was buried far to her left, and the perpendicular scrape stretched far to her right. She took a moment to marvel, wondering how in the world she'd survived a landing like that. In the distance, clearly visible against the hazy orange sky, was Gimeg Plateau.

"You've been up there long enough," warned Kek. "You need to come back down."

"Kek's right. Is there a way around?" called Arnie.

"No," she called back. "I think you boys need to see this."

"You want us to come up?" Arnie clarified with a tinge of doubt in his voice.

"Yes."

Inside the crack, Arnie scanned the steep wall, wrinkled his forehead in pessimism, then selected Kek to be the first volunteer.

Kek's expression went blank. Did the man intend for him to blow his cover? Because he wasn't going to do that. "Me?"

"Pull the rest of us up?" Arnie suggested, lacing his fingers together.

Oh. That he could do. Kek got a running start and, with Arnie's help, jumped to the top of the ledge. Braced in a squat, he looked over the edge and signaled that he was ready. It was Park's turn to jump. Park, who had absolutely no acrobatic skill in any capacity, yelped at a blue zap from Kek and landed face-down on the hard crust.

Kek laughed aloud, thoroughly amused by the spill, then gestured to Rixton. Mimicking the others, Rixton ran, stepped into Arnie's fingers, and jumped. Kek, being a butthead, helped, catching him halfway, and sent the slender man sprawling. While Park and Rixton sputtered, Kek gestured Arnie forward with a mischievous twinkle in his eye. As Arnie jumped, Kek flicked a finger.

Arnie bumped up the side of the wall like a rag doll *without* screaming and toppled ungracefully onto the ledge, where he flopped to a stop.

Kek laughed aloud.

"Antigravity?" groaned Arnie.

"Telekinetics,"

"You jackass," Arnie grumbled, getting up.

Kek hurried to his feet and jogged away toward Kinety. He found her standing on the far edge. She was looking out into the distance, lost in thought and apparently unaware he'd approached. Without thinking, he reached out to straighten a tangle in her hair but thought better of it and quickly lowered it again. Admonishing himself, he followed her gaze to the plateau in the distance and watched a Zahrá Che patrol craft glint in the sunlight.

Kinety turned her attention back to the gouges cut deep in the ground, the very ones blocking their way. "That was my pod," she said, motioning toward the gouges, easily thirty feet deep.

Kek remembered very well how the gouges had gotten there. "We have to cross that."

Kinety looked forward toward the plateau again, then left toward the crash site. "Ten feet? Piece of cake," she assured and turned to face the others who were just joining them. "Gimeg Plateau. That's where we're going," she told them, then pointed into the deep ravine, "and that's blocking us."

Arnie examined the gouge. "It's too long to go around and too steep to climb out the other side. We'll have to jump across."

Kinety angled her head at the block of crust across the gouge. Chewing her lip, she eyed the gap and then studied the block beside them. "It's narrower over there. Maybe we should jump to that block and then cross the gouge on that side."

Arnie disagreed. "We'll only have the energy to make that jump once. If we go over there, we won't be able to cross the second gap. "We either cross here or walk around."

"Walking around will take too long," she said, backing up. "You coming, Kek?"

Kek backed up beside her. "I'm coming."

The others lined up, bracing for a power run.

Kinety blew out her cheeks—one, two, three—and took off with enough momentum to cross the gap. She leapt, split-legged across the deep gouge, and landed safely on the other side. Laughing, she moved aside, giving Kek room to land beside her, and then waved her arm at the others. "Come on over! It wasn't bad at—aaaah!" she shrieked, flapping her arms.

Without warning, a section of crust disintegrated where she and Kek had landed and crumbled into the deep gorge.

Kek dropped.

Kinety dove for him. She caught his wrist as he slid down and fell, crashing hard onto her chest, but she had him.

Across the divide, Arnie skidded to a stop and dove sideways, knocking Rixton to the ground. As they landed, he snatched for Park, who was airborne, and caught his back foot.

Park shrieked as his jump stalled, and he crashed head down into the side of the crust block with an oof. Dangling by one foot over the deep gouge, he managed a thumbs-up. "Nailed it!" he whimpered.

Rixton reached an arm over the side, grabbed him by the seat of his pants, and hauled him backward. Lying in a pile, they gaped through billowing dust across the now vast expanse. The ground that had been there only moments before was gone, leaving a very wide gap over the deep ravine.

Across the way, Kinety held Kek. "Find a foothold," she gritted down at him.

Kek scraped the toe of his boot along the side until it found something solid, then eased his weight onto it. As he did, the ground beneath Kinety crumbled and sifted away like sand. Slowly, she rode the erosion down until she was standing on the ledge with him. He hooked an arm around her and gripped a random rock in the dirt.

A billow of dust blocked the view between the two groups.

"Arnie!" she called out. "Are you guys okay?"

"No. Rixton's dirty and Park is afraid of heights now," grumbled the disembodied voice. "Do you have Kek?"

"I have him. We're on a ledge," she called, dropping her head against Kek's shoulder in relief. "It's not a good idea to cross the gouge!"

"Yeah, we were just figuring that out!"

Kinety gave a weary laugh. "Meet us at the plateau!"

"Race you there!"

Kek, who'd been a fraction of a second from expanding his armband into a star-fighter, put it away. Frowning, he peered down into her dirty face, stunned she'd actually stopped him from going in. He'd never been saved before and wasn't entirely sure how to process that. "Are you hurt?" he asked softly.

Kinety avoided too much eye contact with him. "My shoulder is a bit unhappy, but I'll live. You?"

Kek tightened his arm around her waist. "I'm ... good," he said truthfully and checked for a place to go besides down. It took effort to reach the top of the crust, where he reluctantly released her.

Kinety moved away and dusted off her bottom. Exhaling loudly, she turned to resume their journey toward the plateau. Five steps later, the ground cracked beneath her, triggering another erosion. "And for my next trick!" she announced, scrambling backward into Kek as the ground disintegrated around her foot.

Kek sputtered at her absurdity and laughed.

In a cloud of dust, the spine of a ridge appeared. He hooked an arm around her for balance, and the two stood still. This time, however, the erosion didn't stop. Instead, it triggered a massive cave-in that spidered around them in a hap-hazardous pattern. When the erosion was finished, Kinety wasn't so quick to let him go.

All around, the gutted remains of a twisted tunnel system lay in tattered ruins. Where they stood was the curved spine of the walls that separated the tubes. "It looks like caves," she said, clutching his forearm and scooting her foot skittishly forward. "What could possibly dig tunnels beneath the water like this?"

Kek hated this planet. He really, really did. "Worms," he said, keeping his arm around her middle and concentrating on maintaining the blue of his eyes, "with tentacles and teeth."

Very carefully, the two made their way together across the narrow ridge to the other side of the tubes.

It was only after they stepped on solid ground that Kinety let him go. With dramatic flair, she fluffed her filthy hair down her back, hoping that might help her appearance, but succeeded only in creating a cloud of dust. "Thank you, Sir, for the lovely adventure," she said in breathless sarcasm, "but from now on, I'd prefer something a bit more … low-key."

Kek laughed, not entirely believing her. "You say so," he said, dusting rocks off her clothes, "but I think this is fun."

"Yeah, if by fun you mean random plunges into the ground, indescribable filth, unbrushed teeth, and an impressive shoulder-ache. I can only imagine what I look like. Now, I'm afraid to put my foot down. I can assure you I've had enough adventure for one day," she said. "Perhaps a relaxing stroll to finish the evening?"

Kek offered an arm, thinking this was a brilliant plan.

Satisfied, she hooked her hand firmly around his elbow, a lady clutching her date, and set a leisurely pace. "Shall we?"

Kek laid his palm over her filthy fingers and smiled, more pleased than he'd ever been in his life. "With happiness."

Chapter 16

After hours of trudging along, Kek slowed. Far against the horizon, the red sun touched the ground, casting a purple haze across the dry ocean bed. The second sun was nowhere to be found, plunging Zahrá Che into a rare sunset. "It'll be dark soon and unsafe to continue," he said, looking around for a place to sit down. "Let's stop here."

Kinety was more than eager to stop. Her feet throbbed, and her mouth was dry. The hunger pangs had long since stopped begging for food, leaving her irritable and tired. After a moment to herself behind a nearby crack, she returned and found Kek sitting against the vertical wall of a block of crust. He rested with his arms draped over spread knees, looking just as tired as she was. Before she could find her own spot, he tapped the inside of his thigh, inviting her to sit between his legs.

"It's warmer over here," he said.

Kinety gave him a once over—attractive, magnetic, interested. His offer was tempting, but ... it wasn't him she wanted. "No. Thank you," she said politely and moved to the wall opposite him. "I'll be fine."

"You'll sleep better against me than in the dirt," he said and patted the ground between his legs.

Kinety looked warily at him.

Kek regarded her with a critical squint and raised his hands. "I won't bother you."

"It's not a good idea."

"Are you worried about what you'll do or what I'll do?"

Kinety faced him sharply, offended that he would say such a thing. Temper flared, she opened her mouth to bite his head off.

Kek laughed softly. "I said that in joke," he assured. "I'm just cold."

Kinety was too. Diffusing, she looked away.

He tapped the ground, inviting her over. "I'll behave."

She glanced at him and tightened her arms against the cold.

"I promise," he swore, opening his hands again.

Somewhat reluctantly, Kinety accepted his offer and sat down between his legs. It felt strange at first, but she forced herself to sit back against his chest. When she did, he scooted his knees against her and wrapped his arms around her shoulders. He was right—it was warmer—and she relaxed against the warm lines of his body. Soon after, the sun lowered, casting the dying world into darkness, allowing the stars to appear.

Kinety gazed up at them and the strange patterns twinkling in the night sky. The stars were foreign and all mixed up, not at all like the constellations at home, and she felt a wave of homesickness.

Kek's deep voice murmured quietly into her ear. "Why the sigh?"

"The constellations look all wrong," she answered softly. "I don't recognize them, and it makes me worry that I'll never see ours again."

His arms tightened around her. "We can make new constellations," he said, looking up and pointing. "That one there, what does that look like?"

Kinety adjusted her head against the crook of his neck. "A fork," she supposed.

Kek chuckled. "Or a trident. If you add those, it looks like someone holding it."

It took imagination, but he was right. "I can see that. There's a square," she said, gesturing to another spot.

"A square stands for unity in all directions," he said, then gestured to a ring of stars around it. "There is a circle around it, which stands for eternity, but the square inside the circle represents the impossible. It reminds us that there is no perfect world, so we shouldn't try to pretend there is. We should love it with its flaws."

Kinety angled her head to see him and smiled. "I like that."

Kek smiled back, then pointed low on the horizon. "Look over there," he said, drawing his finger over the pattern of a low constellation. That one," he gestured to another and traced it, "and that one over there."

Kinety studied both for several minutes, then snuggled into him. "It looks like two people ... holding hands."

"Lovers."

"I hope their story is a good one," she said with a hint of envy.

"It must be," he whispered and slid his hands over the backs of hers. Gently, he eased his fingers between hers, interlacing them. "They're together forever."

Kinety looked at the hands wrapped around hers, then took hers away. Awkwardly, she tucked them between her knees, ruining the moment.

Instead of reacting, Kek pointed to another spot in the sky. "That's a moon."

"How can you tell?"

"It doesn't twinkle, and it's closer than a planet."

"Are those rings?"

Kek furrowed his brow and examined it. "Looks like it."

"It's beautiful, isn't it?" she murmured, her voice soft with fatigue. "I didn't know moons could have rings."

"If there's gravity, it'll hold satellites. If a satellite is destroyed—"

Bzzzt!

Before he could finish his sentence, a band of streaky blue light surrounded them from above. In a reflex, he shoved her hard, throwing her out of the blue light … and vanished.

Kinety spun on her hip and searched for him. "Kek!" she cried, looking around and then up. Directly overhead, the shadow of a silent vessel blacked out the stars. "Kek!"

Mere feet away, two spiky blue flashes of electricity split the darkness. When they faded, there were two demonic creatures with green skin, wings, and goat horns. Their heat signatures radiated off them, brightest at the center. They were naked with large, red eyes that flashed like bicycle reflectors and wide, unfriendly snarls. Their exaggerated musculature was to the point of ridiculousness, but it had the desired intimidating effect.

They were talking.

Kinety saw a flash of blue. Frightened, she drew her blaster.

"Torak's Bride," the larger one said in a low, growly voice. He gestured and the blaster melted in her hand.

She dropped it with a cry.

Jagged teeth appeared in his smile. "Such a delicate throat. Out of my way, Blagins."

The smaller, meaner-looking of the two twisted his head. "If you tear her throat out, Gezhack, I can't hear her scream," he purred, eyeing her. His gesture toward his lower anatomy revealed his intention. "I want to see what Torak likes so much about this little Earthling flower. You can eat her when I'm done."

Kinety backed away in alarm.

With a lurch, both came after her.

Kinety shrieked and whirled to run. Two steps later, Blagins crashed into her back, slamming her violently into the dirt wall. Panicking, she twisted to fight him off but was no match for his strength. She didn't care. She fought anyway. As she struggled, her hands tingled.

He pinned her down, laughing.

With a shout, Kinety slammed her hand into his chest. A blue pulse fired into him like a sledgehammer. In a crunch of ribs, Blagins rocketed backward twenty feet into a mud wall, his chest caved. He was dead.

Kinety blinked at him, startled and unsure what had just happened. Breathing heavily, she faced the second creature but didn't know how to do the blue thing again.

Gezhack snapped enraged eyes at her. Snarling past jagged teeth, he opened a sharp object with projectiles and reared back to throw.

Kinety let out a cry, whirling in fright, and crashed face-first into Torak.

She screamed.

In rabid fury, Gezhack released his weapon.

In a blur, Kinety was tossed to the ground. Torak stepped over her, caught the projectiles, and hurled them back. Gezhack clutched his impaled throat, choking loudly, and sank to the ground with a surprised look on his face.

Kinety scrambled to her feet, still panicking, and tried to run.

Torak caught her. "Kinety!"

With a frustrated shout, she tried to fight him.

He pinned her easily. "Kinety!"

She ducked sharply, bracing for a blow that didn't come.

"Shh, shh, shh," he soothed, pushing her hands down and brushing messy hair from her face. "Look at me."

Kinety pinned wild eyes on him, unsure if it was really him.

"You're safe," he said, gripping her head.

"Tooji?"

Torak nodded.

It was him; Kinety was sure of it. She could feel her natural response to him, a sensation that danced over her skin. Her heart skipped, and her breathing jumped all over the place, just like in the meadow on Earth, just like on Jag Mosrog. Like a magnet, their eyes locked, and she realized her mistake. This was not the man who'd assaulted her on Neontak. The difference was blatant—the magnetism, the powerful presence, the way he spoke to her.

Kinety threw her arms around her enemy's neck. "It wasn't you," she said in a broken whisper. "He looked like you. It wasn't you."

Torak held her against him, hugging her fiercely. "I'll never hurt you," he swore against her head. "Don't ever be afraid of me. If someone who looks like me ever attacks you, kill him."

And the moment was broken.

Kinety opened her eyes. She was hugging the bad guy. Startled by her loss of self-control, she slid her arms away and scanned him with wide eyes.

He was still clutching her.

In a flash of heated cheeks, Kinety regained her wits, and her anger returned. "So, what do I do about the Saphiridians when they try to kill me?"

Torak gnashed his teeth. "They would never hurt you," he insisted.

Kinety pulled away from his hands. "They aren't trying to hurt me, Tooji. They're trying to kill me."

"They know you belong to me," he argued.

Kinety dropped her arms to her sides. She was tired and cold and still shaking from adrenaline. "I don't belong to you," she said warily. "You made that clear."

"The annulment failed," he corrected almost hesitantly. "Our marriage is legal."

Kinety laughed, struck by the ridiculousness of everything. "It doesn't matter," she sighed.

"It does."

"No!" she snapped angrily and turned away from him. As she did, she got a whiff of Kek's flowery scent, which must have lingered on her from before. This didn't help. Still frazzled from the attack, she stared up at the constellations Kek had shown her and tried to regain her composure. First, she peered up at the square in the circle—the impossible—then at the lovers holding hands in the sky. With a heavy heart, she lowered her eyes and let the words happen by themselves. "I don't know you," she said softly. "I don't know who you are."

Torak stepped closer. "I'm your mortal enemy," he reminded, touching her cheek. Gently, he slid his fingers behind her head, peering down at her, and pulled her close. "The one who makes your heart skip."

Kinety's pulse indeed leapt. She could feel his voice on her skin and the thump of his heart against her breasts.

He touched his mouth to hers. "The one you fell in love with," he said against her lips.

Warmth surged through Kinety, and she almost gave in.

It took all her effort, but she turned away, severing the kiss. She did love him—bad—but she couldn't have him. She'd known it for a while now. No matter how much she wanted Torak, to accept him was a betrayal to the men he was sworn to kill, the men she would die to protect. Hating herself, she backed away. Make it good, she thought, priming for the break, and glared at him. "That didn't matter to you on Jag Mosrog," she accused. "Why does it now?"

Torak's shoulders dropped. "It did matter on Jag Mosrog," he said, lowering his hands.

"You left me—alone!" she railed at him. "And you did it in front of everyone."

"I had no choice," he swore. "I knew they'd come after you."

Kinety shook her head and stepped away again.

"I can explain," he rushed, trying to stop her.

Kinety avoided his touch. "I want Kek back. Those aliens took him."

"You're my wife!" he barked angrily. "You can't have Kek."

This time, Kinety was careful to avoid eye contact with him. "Please leave," she said in the flattest voice she could manage.

Torak stared at her, his expression stricken. "Kinety," he said with a crack in his voice.

It was working.

Kinety turned up her jackass meter. "How long until you ditch me again?" she demanded, then quickly continued before he could answer. "You don't want me. You want information."

"No. I don't care about that," he swore. "I care about you. I'm doing everything I can to protect you."

"You can't be protecting *me*, Tooji," she almost choked on his name, "if you're trying to kill my men. We're all together."

Finally, he grew angry. "If I was trying to kill your men, I wouldn't have shown you how to fight the Gaki!" he yelled, then cursed, realizing what he'd just said.

Kinety kept her tone even. "Has your mission changed, then?"

"Kinety."

The catch in his voice nearly undid her. Quickly, she shook her head and added more distance. "Thank you," she said, having trouble speaking now. She needed to hurry. "For what you did, thank you … but I don't trust you. Those soldiers are my friends, my people. They're my brothers and sisters … and I don't want you around them."

"And I'm your companion," he reminded, pointing to himself.

Kinety couldn't look at the hurt on his face. "Not because you want to be."

Torak strode boldly to her and gripped her head. Frowning down at her, he whispered emphatically, "I want to be."

"Tooji—." The blurt was accidental, but Kinety caught herself. Quickly, she closed her eyes, trying to regain her momentum. It was hard, though, and the tears were close. She had to quit talking. "Please stop," she choked.

"Tell me you don't want me."

Kinety couldn't do it. He was breaking her—her enemy. She had to let him go.

Gentle fingers tilted her chin. "Look me in the eye," he whispered, "and tell me you don't want me."

Her chin quivered in his hand, but she met his gaze directly. "I want Kek," she lied.

Torak stiffened. "You're lying."

It was now or never.

With the last of what she had, Kinety added strength to her voice. "I love Kek," she insisted. "Please leave us alone."

Torak released her.

Like an asshole, she turned her back to him, angrily snatched Blagins and Gezhack's weapons from the ground, and walked away.

*****

Kinety moved out of Torak's line of sight and quickly rounded a few corners. Horrified with herself, she clapped a hand hard over her mouth. The weapons landed in a pile at her feet, and she collapsed against the steep wall, trying to be quiet, but there was no stopping the tears. Eyes squeezed, she pressed her shoulder into the dirt, struggling to keep it down, but couldn't hold it back. Her knees buckled beneath her, and she sank into a squat.

And that's how Kek found her. He stood over her for several moments before dropping down on his haunches. "Kinety," he said, touching her shoulder.

Kinety raised her head, saw him, and threw her arms around his neck. Clinging to him, she cried.

Kek folded his arms awkwardly around her, which made her cry harder.

She'd lied.

The faintest sparkle lit in his eyes. She lied. With a hesitant smile, he sank to the ground beside her, placing his back against the dirt wall, and pulled her into his lap. She'd been lying. Closing his eyes, he pressed her head into his shoulder and kissed the top of it, holding her while she cried it out.

A long time passed before she lay quiet against him, sound asleep. She was miserable, but Kek was in a great mood. All he had to do now was figure out how to save her men without actually betraying his people. After some thought, he had the answer.

A portal.

As Kek, he would find the base and help her rescue her soldiers. Then, Kek would die. Torak would reappear, the hero, and open a portal to Earth. When they were across, he would destroy the Zahrá Che base and just go with her.

Simple.

More than pleased with his plan, he kissed her head again, then snuggled his wife close and smiled himself to sleep.

The plan was perfect.

*****

Joboba slapped his hands down, wild-eyed, and glared at Darplano. "What do you mean, 'She got away?'"

Darplano tried to ignore the staring eyes of his subordinates and lowered his head in embarrassment. "The Janosethi operation was a fail."

"A fail!" Joboba couldn't believe what he was hearing. "Get them on the screen. Now!"

Darplano lowered his voice. "There were no survivors."

"No survivors—how? Those assholes are Terran! Are you telling me a bunch of sub-human hominids defeated the Goblasi?"

"Yes, Prime."

"Is everybody so incompetent that we're left with gutter fighters? Is that what this is coming to!" Joboba shouted. "Find me an assassin!"

"Torak's wife is well guarded."

Joboba cracked his knuckles, forcibly calming himself down. "Get the Borzoikans involved," he said calmly. "They can do whatever they like; I don't care. I just want the bitch dead!"

Darplano glanced sideways at his unblinking crew. "I did. They spotted her on Zahrá Che after the Janosethi attack. She'd been separated from all but one of her men. A few hours ago, they tried to separate her from the last one. They beamed him up and attacked her on the ground ... but—"

Joboba pointed. "No!" he warned.

"—it was Torak."

Joboba could barely speak. "Okay. No. Stop!"

"There were no survivors aboard the ship," Darplano continued, "or on the ground."

Joboba's cheeks shook. "Why ... is Torak ... on Zahrá Che!"

Darplano didn't answer.

With a trembling hand, he drew a dagger from his boot and stabbed Darplano. Clutching him close, he followed him down to the ground. "I'll do it myself," he said into the dying man's ear and yanked the blade free, "and I'll find the base."

Standing, Joboba faced the wide-eyed crew and smiled at the next rank in line. "I need forty-eight short troops," he told the woman. "Assemble a team. I want them on my monitor in four hours for mission briefing."

The woman inclined her head and hurried away.

Chapter 17

Kek curled his fingers around his blaster and opened his eyes. There were footsteps to his left near the bodies of the Borzoikan thugs they'd killed last night. Gently, he brushed Kinety's hair from her face, waking her, then put two fingers over her lips. Aiming to the left, he waited.

Moments later, Arnie, Rixton, and Park rocketed around the corner, their blasters raised.

"Dorkymodo!" Rixton hauled Kinety to her feet. "What happened!" he demanded, noticing her swollen eyes.

Kek put his weapon down and stood, watching the group gather around the dead bodies.

Park touched one with the toe of his combat boot. "I feel like we're stuck in a horror spoof. What the fuck are those things?"

"Dead," Kek said, shaking dust from his hair. "We need to get back to Neontak before more show up. It isn't safe here."

Kinety shook her head, blinking down at her tingling hands, and stepped away from her brother. "No," she said, still stuffy-nosed from the night before. "I'm not hiding anymore. It's time."

"Time for what?" asked Rixton.

"It's time to get our soldiers," she said, gathering the weapons she'd collected from the monsters.

Kek looked meaningfully at Rixton.

Rixton, catching the glance, pointed at the plateau. "We're going back to Neontak," he countered.

Kinety straightened her clothes and dusted herself off. "Yes, after I have my ship."

Rixton was shaking his head. "A spaceship? Dorkymodo, you can't—"

Kinety rounded on him. "Did you think I was joking before? You tell me all the time to be a man. Well, I'm being one."

"You aren't trained to—"

"There's no time," she snapped. "We need to get those men before they kill me. I don't have long, Rixton. They know I'm here, so more will come. We don't have time to wait around until the moment is right, until we have magic weapons or a fool-proof plan. I'll be dead long before then. We have to do this now."

Kek and Rixton looked at each other.

"What do you have in mind?" asked Arnie.

Kinety peered up at the sky. "This time, we let them take us. I'll be bait; you boys take their ship."

"The hell you will!" snapped Rixton.

Arnie held up his hand, silencing her brother. "We don't have enough weapons."

Kinety pocketed the horrid devices she'd collected from the winged men. "No, we don't," she said, looking toward the recent crash site. "That alien ship went down over there yesterday. The sun is up now. There should be weapons. We ping a distress signal and see who shows up. Then we wing it," she said, facing them. "We work together, keep each other alive."

"Tag and bag a few aliens? My favorite thing! I'm in," said Park.

Kek, after a pause, indicated he was in.

Rixton raised his hands. "Wait, wait," he said and stopped in front of Kinety. "You need to tell the others. We can't just go on a mission like this without telling them where the hell we are. Zhang is our sharpshooter. We need him."

Kinety faced her brother in annoyance.

"I'm not trying to stop you," he blurted quickly, "but we need Zhang … and the soldiers have a right to know what happened to us in case we don't make it back."

Kinety faced Arnie, leaving the decision to him.

"If we get attacked on the way, the plan stands," he swore. "We tell the others, get Zhang, and come right back out."

Kinety inclined her head, partially diffused, and led the pack back to Neontak.

*****

The group made it back unmolested—not a peep, not a ship in the sky, nothing—and Kek knew why.

They knew he was here.

As the exhausted group stepped through to Neontak, he hung back. "I'll keep watch," he said and hovered near the portal. When he was alone, he vanished. Cloaked in invisibility, he stopped at the edge of the portal and peeked out through the distortion, but there was nobody around. No patrol ships. No stray vessels. That in itself was unusual.

He had an idea.

Cloaking his aircraft invisible took a lot of energy, especially after being Kek for so long, but if he was quick he could pull it off. Behaving normally, he strolled out of Neontak, summoned his fighter, and jumped inside. He made as if to take off, then went invisible, cloaking himself and vanishing the starcraft. The vehicle disappeared from view and he leapt out of it, coiling the heavy band around his finger. Before his invisibility faded, he quickly dashed back into Neontak and reappeared with a winded curse.

*****

The haggard group, filthy from climbing the plateau, staggered wearily back to camp. It was morning on Neontak, and the sky was overcast and colorless. In the village, a guard noticed their approach and stood. "It's Arnie!" he shouted, summoning a crowd. "It's Arnie! He's got the Commander!"

Weapons were drawn, and a welcoming party gathered to inspect them before they could enter, just as a safety precaution. Once cleared, a thousand questions erupted at once.

Arnie laughed, ushering Kinety through. "I'll bring everybody up to speed at the rock. Give us a minute to wash, and we'll meet you there. Is there any food around here?"

Right away, the service team hurried off.

"I'm after the outhouse," said Kinety, dashing away.

As the group reached home, an irate Zhang popped out of the cabin, sleepy-eyed and messy-haired.

Park waved happily. "Hi, Zhang!"

Zhang exploded in a tirade of belligerent Chinese, waving angry arms and shouting indignantly at Arnie.

Arnie paused. "Lemme guess. He's angry because he was left behind," he said to Park.

Park scratched his ear. "That's the gist of it," he said with a grimace, "though probably not so polite."

Arnie gathered his things. "Tell him," he said to Park, "he should run faster."

Park flexed his muscles at the smaller man and relayed the message in a deep voice meant to represent Arnie.

Zhang flailed his arms, gesturing toward the portal and to Kinety's empty bed mat in a tantrum, which increased the octave of his voice.

After a moment of this, Park conveyed the reply to Arnie, using accusatory grunts and indignant pauses. "He couldn't run because he was too busy saving your … ," he paused, then reworded the foul translation, "too busy sniping unfriendly aliens for your safety."

Arnie gave a large nod at the memory. "Good shooting," he complimented, gesturing for Park to convey that. "Very precise."

Zhang plopped angry hands on his hips, undaunted by the flattery, and continued.

Park faced Arnie, hands on hips, and rolled his head in mimic. "Why did you leave the plateau!" he screeched in translation. "I am sworn to protect Kinety. I can't do that when you take off in random spaceships with her!"

"There were too many aliens," defended Arnie. "Did you see how many were inside? You were supposed to shoot those."

Park turned to Zhang and flexed his pecs, again relaying Arnie's defense in a deep voice.

Zhang didn't know whether to laugh or jump up and down, but the amusing argument continued.

Park whirled on Arnie, one eye larger than the other, and trembled his pointed fist. "I couldn't!" he cried in mock insanity. "You left the … plateau … okay, I'm not going to repeat that."

Arnie held up a hand, silencing them both. "We have another mission," he said with a laugh. "We need a sniper."

Zhang went rigid, eyes wide, lips rounded.

"Report to the historians," Arnie ordered. "We leave in thirty minutes."

In a puff of smoke, Zhang was gone.

Arnie sighed at the empty doorway, then motioned to Park. "You're coming too, pilot. Rendezvous at the rock. I'll be right there."

Park vanished.

Minutes later, Arnie stood on the rock, explaining to the soldiers what had happened while he waited for his crew. "We had a throw-down right there in the flight deck, then jumped out. So then, seconds after we hit the ground, the Janosethi ship explodes, killing all inside," he was saying when the others arrived. "There's more, but you get the picture. The moral of the story: We're out of time. They're coming for the Commander and aren't going to stop until she's dead. We must strike now. If we're going to rescue the troops in storage, it has to be done now."

"You're going on this mission?"

Arnie inclined his head. "Neontak was only one stop on this interplanetary rescue. You're stable now, and the Zahrá Che battleground search team is demonstrating remarkable success. There are other humans in this star system waiting to be found. The Commander is leading us there, and it's my job to rescue them. I will be back. You!" he said, pointing to the highest-ranking officer.

The officer stood.

"You will take command of Shit Sandwich Station while I'm away. Gaki are to be exterminated. Human casualties are forbidden. No exceptions. Choose a second-in-command and be ready to report when I get back."

"Yes, Sir!"

The team had gathered. After a brief chat with the historians and a noisy bon voyage, Zhang, Park, Kinety, Rixton, and Arnie headed for the portal, Zhang wearing a brilliant smile on his face.

*****

Torak took a moment to catch his breath, then tried to turn back into Kek. He was too tired, though, so he gave it a few minutes. Before long, he could hear the team coming up the trail. His time was up. It took two tries, but he managed to shift back to Kek just in time and stood, trying not to appear winded. Standing motionless, he joined the passing team.

"Anything?" asked Arnie.

"Not yet," said Kek, "but I made it look like I left."

"Why?"

"Because I'm pretty sure we're walking into a trap. If I'm correct, they were waiting for me to leave."

And he was right.

The group stepped cautiously through the portal ... right into an aggressive offensive. In a blaze of laser shots, three mirrored Zahrá Che fighters raced toward them and opened fire, sending them all to the ground. Arnie shouted, shoving Park and Zhang back through to Neontak, and tackled Kinety sideways onto the plateau. Kek dove forward. Rixton cursed vehemently and scrambled to his feet as the three Zahrá Che ships whipped into formation around the portal.

This time, they would aim.

Kinety's hands tingled as Arnie dragged her toward the portal, gathering energy from the ground as she slid over it. Before they could reach Neontak, she wiggled free, ignoring Arnie's grabbing hands trying to haul her inside, and scrambled back into the orange glow of Zahrá Che. Unsure if the blue would happen again, she thrust angry hands forward toward the blockade.

A blue pulse blinked from her palms, startling her men and knocking the ships out of formation. The vessels toppled end over end, and the line broke.

Arnie stopped tugging and gawked at the upended vehicle. Rixton tripped backward over something and landed on his butt. Kek did a double-take. Kinety lowered her hands, unblinking as two ships collided. The explosion from the two knocked the third ship into a wild spin.

It came right for them.

Kek dove, taking Kinety to the ground. The team leapt out of the way, scattering as the vessel punched through the portal and vanished inside. Kek yanked Kinety to her feet and charged back through after it. In Neontak, the mirrored spaceship skidded across the ground and splashed into a stagnant swamp, snapping trees and throwing a massive spray of water. It sloshed to a tilted stop, speckled with leaves and stringy mud.

Hauling ass, Kek threw Kinety at Arnie. "Get her out of here!"

Arnie grabbed her.

Soldiers from the camp rushed forward to help, their blasters drawn.

From its position in the water, there was a hum and the spaceship's weapon appeared, firing lasers at the soldiers and scaring bizarre-looking birds from the trees. Soldiers ducked out of the way, encircling the ship, and returned fire, but their blasters wouldn't penetrate the skin of the vessel. Using the Gaki technique, the soldiers surrounded it and closed in, intending to breach the craft.

Then a door swirled open on the side and a ramp appeared. In a crash of booted feet, Zahrá Che soldiers charged out and splashed into the swamp, firing indiscriminately as they came. Using superior weapons, they held the Neontak defenders back, striking trees and sizzling water.

"Find her!" one barked.

"There's her guard," another answered, identifying Arnie and firing.

Zahrá Che soldiers took off after him.

Arnie ducked back and hauled Kinety across a gap in the reeds toward a thick patch of grass, moving her away from the ship. "Park!" he called, pushing her to him and dashing the other direction to lead the chasers away.

Kinety sloshed into the muddy water.

Park eased her quietly behind a clump of broken trees, motioning her down and putting his finger to his lips for silence. Using hand signals, he guided her around a patch of folded tree trunks toward the back of the ship, moving her away from the fight.

The aliens followed Arnie.

"Let's take it," Park whispered, turning his gaze to the ship.

Kinety gave him a curt nod, wiping muddy water from her face, and righted herself in the muck. "Let's go."

At the center of the chaos, Kek stepped into the disturbed swamp, placing himself between the aliens and their target Arnie. With a ripple, his watery reflection shimmered against the wavy image of the sky.

Enraged Zahrá Che charged into the water with a splash, firing angrily at him. Laser blasts struck him in the chest but the shots went through, exposing scaly holes that instantly filled in.

Kek snapped a hand toward a shooter. The alien's white chest caved with a crunch, and he rocketed backward into a patch of grass.

Onlookers lowered their blasters. The other shooters watched in surprise.

Kek grabbed the end of the next alien's weapon, ripped it sideways out of the attacker's hands, kicked the second one in line backward into the third, killing number two, and used his weapon like a bat on the fourth. With barely a glance, he slashed his knife backward across first's throat, killing him, stabbed the fifth, elbowed the sixth out of the way, then caught him by the head and snapped his neck. Kek spun, taking the seventh's feet out from beneath him. The knife flipped in his hand and he threw it, impaling the third, who'd moved. With a wave of his hand, he sent the last two invaders flying backward into a grove of trees fifteen feet away, killing them.

Unblinking troops gaped in silence as Kek stepped into the ship. "Was that Kek?" someone asked.

There were three aliens inside the sleek spaceship.

Kek snapped his hand toward two, magnetically pinning them to the wall, and snatched the pilot by the throat. With a roar, he slammed the little bastard hard into the panel, breaking the helmet. It fell away, revealing not a Zahrá Che but a small-framed, snub-nosed Saphiridian. Horrified, he stared into the familiar face, stunned to see one of his own. "What are you doing here?" he whispered.

The grimacing pilot clawed at the hand around his throat but didn't answer. Dragging the pilot with him, Kek crossed to the Zahrá Che pinned against the wall and snatched the helmet off a second one. Saphiridian.

Kek yanked the helmet off the third Saphiridian, and his eyes went white. "What are you doing here?" he asked again.

None would answer.

Kek melted away, revealing Torak in a ponytail. With a shout, he severed the leg of the third Saphiridian. "What is your objective!" he roared.

The man screamed in pain and went down. "Eliminate the Savage Bride," he cried in a spray of spittle.

Standing in pooling blood, Torak crushed the pilot's throat and rammed the body backward into the panel. "Why would you do that?" he cried, rounding on the second man in a rage.

"She's a distraction," the terrified Saphiridian squeaked.

"Aaaah!" Torak caved the man's chest with a crunch, then staggered backward in disbelief as the carcass fell. They'd betrayed him. He gripped his head, struggling to wrap his mind around this. Kinety was right. The Saphiridians had betrayed him. Breathing loudly, he vanished into thin air and ran out of the ship.

*****

Park peeked around the silver vessel. While Earthlings and Zahrá Che splashed in the swamp, he motioned for Kinety to follow him into the spaceship. She gripped her blaster and dashed up the ramp. Together, they hurried inside, braced to fight, but the ship was unmanned. There were no Zahrá Che inside, only three dead Saphiridians and an impressive collection of blood spatters.

"Let's throw them out," Park said, tucking his weapon in his waistline.

After the dead bodies were evicted, Kinety hurried to a hover-seat in front of the panel and tried to figure out the controls. "Park!" she

221

called, gesturing the young pilot to the seat beside her. "Sit down. I'll show you how it works. Are you familiar with electromagnetics and antigravity … ?"

Outside, defenders scoured the swamp, gathering the fallen weapons near the bodies. Arnie whirled this way and that, looking for Kinety and Park. "Where is she!" he shouted.

Rixton, barking orders near the water's edge, pointed Arnie toward the back of the ship. "They went around back."

Arnie charged around the back of the ship, knee-deep in the water, and nearly crashed into Torak, who was taking a moment to collect himself. With a growl, Arnie slammed him backward against the vessel. "Who are you!" he snapped, shoving his blaster beneath Torak's jaw. "Who the fuck are you!"

Torak glanced at him, unintimidated. "A sweetheart," he answered through his teeth. "Your mortal enemy."

Rixton appeared beside Arnie and lowered the larger man's blaster. "It's him," he said, sloshing to a stop.

Arnie glared. "Are you sure?"

Rixton took the blaster from Arnie and shot Torak in the chest. In a shimmer of reptilian scales, it healed. "Yep," he said, handing the weapon back. "That blaster won't kill him."

Arnie blinked at Rixton, then down at the useless blaster.

Torak gripped his head, grimacing hard in disbelief. "Why would they do this?"

"The Saphiridians?" Arnie stepped further behind the ship so nobody would see them talking and poked Torak's shoulder. "You are a weapon. You told the Zahrá Che if anything happened to Kinety, there would be nothing left but an asteroid belt when you were done. This," he jabbed a finger toward the swamp, "is an attempt to annihilate the Zahrá Che and keep you focused. Since she arrived, you haven't fought for them. The *only* ones who benefit from Kinety's death," Arnie said heavily, "are the Saphiridians."

Torak looked stricken.

"They're trying to regain control of you," said Arnie. "She's been telling you this."

Torak's eyes fell out of focus and black curls slid onto his blood-spattered forehead.

Rixton stepped away from the men and peered around the spacecraft, then back-smacked Arnie's shoulder. "Secret's out. Everybody knows now," he whispered, motioning to Torak.

Torak paled. "Everybody?"

"Where is Kinety?" asked Arnie.

"I think she's inside," said Rixton.

Arnie angled past Torak to see the soldiers. "Keep her in there, Rixton. Have her prepare the ship for departure. Don't let her come out."

Rixton hurried away to follow the order, and Arnie stepped back to Torak. "Give me Kek."

Torak blinked at him. "Why?"

Arnie sniffed the air. "My soldiers don't know Torak. Is there a way to fight the Gaki alone?"

"Carefully," said Torak, "but yes."

"Good, because they're coming." Arnie indicated the wary soldiers detecting Gaki stink on the air and calling an alert. "Will you teach them?"

Torak shouldered the filth from his face, then nodded.

With skilled precision, the fighters began pairing up, bracing for the oncoming Gaki encounter.

Kek stepped out, composed now. After an embarrassed glance around, he moved into a bare clearing beside the stagnant water and waved the soldiers into a group in the swamp. Puzzled by the order, they gathered. When he stood alone, Kek clapped his hands, calling the approaching creatures to him. The air began to buzz. It took a minute for the Gaki to organize. Kek waited, allowing the Gaki to line up, and held his hands open to show the soldiers he was unarmed.

The buzz was deafening.

"They're communicating," he called out. "They attack in order, front and back, allowing the alphas to eat first. Listen for the pitch. This is how they communicate."

As a circle formed, he eyed the ring, then pointed rhythmically at it like a conductor speaking to his orchestra. This motion revealed the top of the blur as the tallest Gaki. The buzz pitched. Right on cue, that's where the dust broke, and the biggest Gaki attacked first.

Kek jerked his head sideways away from the chomping mouth. He caught the beast by the neck, spun, and hurled it into the face of the one charging behind him. Instantly, the first two clawed and tore into each other, both erroneously believing it had struck its target. Kek spun in time to catch the third attack. This one, he threw into the pile, spun again, caught the fourth, and added it. The circle soon broke, and the Gaki dog-piled into the center, biting each other.

Kek stepped out of the confusion and moved to a different spot, this time over wet ground. Standing alone, he began clapping his hands, attracting the attention of the blood-thirsty animals. Oblivious to what had just happened, the remaining Gaki crawled off the pile of carcasses and buzzed back into motion. Right away, a ring began to form in the mud. A blur of distortion closed around

Kek and, as it shrank, he lifted his impaler to demonstrate it as his only weapon.

His audience watched in unblinking silence.

The knife he held backward in his right hand so the blade exited pinky-side and the spine rested against his forearm. Again, he rhythmically bounced his left fingers, picking up the tallest Gaki in the ring. On the wet ground, there was no dust, but a gouge formed around him in the semi-wet mud. Holding the blur tempo with his left hand, he waited for a footprint to break the smooth trench and punched, slicing the Gaki with his blade. On the backswing, he twisted sharply, impaling the rear-attacking Gaki on the point, twisted, and struck forward again. His left hand, he held out to the side, fingers wide. The group didn't know why until a random Gaki charged out of turn, altering the pattern. The moment it struck his arm, he sidestepped into it, switching places, and threw it into the oncoming attack opposite where the snarling creatures again dog-piled each other.

While they fought, he stepped away, found a thick stick, then moved into a new position. Ready, he clapped his hands. When Kek was encircled again, this time by a smaller ring, he did not wait for the predators to strike first. Holding the stick like a bat, he swung into the ring as if striking a home-run and cracked the spinning Gaki against his club. They crashed violently into each other and, while they dog-piled in frenzied confusion, he walked away.

His audience cheered.

After that, the remaining Gaki had no more interest in playing and scurried off, ending the impressive demonstration.

Kek stood, watching them go, then faced the soldiers. His eyes were white with Torak's characteristic electric current running through them. "Going solo against Gaki is dangerous and should only be used in an emergency. Boil river water to drink. Rainwater is clean." He tossed the club aside and lifted one of the dead animals. "You can eat Gaki," he said, tossing the carcass to a soldier to clean, then motioned a few people toward the woods to find more edible plants.

Zhang stared after him, muddy hands on hips, tongue in cheek. While they were gone, he collected blasters, compression suits, and anything else that could be used in the ship. Around him, muddy soldiers followed suit, collecting anything they could use, including bones of the fallen to shape into weapons, and all were brought back to camp. The river dams were broken, and the village was surrounded by a brand new moat of water too deep for the Gaki to cross.

Chapter 18

Inside the ship, Kinety was able to find the correct constellation and retrace the path to the galaxy and solar system with the moon Gelphii in it but was careful not to select it just yet. She explored other regions out of curiosity, goofing off and playing with the mapping system until she understood it, then began searching for Zahrá Che, Saphiridia, and Neontak.

Kek, somewhat recovered from his initial shock, paused guiltily outside the spaceship entrance, fussing over his appearance. His dark hair was neat again and fastened in a ponytail. The blood was gone from his face and the worst of the mud rinsed from his faded camouflage fatigues. The secret was out. He'd lied to her. This was going to hurt, and he knew it. One more time, he practiced his apology in his head.

I deceived you as Kek and didn't listen when you said the Saphiridians were attacking you. They have now betrayed me entirely. I feel shame for not heeding your warning. Your anger is valid for these failures. Please don't hate me.

That was the gist of it. He'd rehearsed it at least four times. There was no making it better. Clamping his teeth, he braced himself, waited as Park hurried out of the craft, and went inside.

Kinety was at the control panel.

Ready to face her, he wiped his sweaty palms on his pants and cleared his expression. "You said you wanted a spaceship," he said in a deceptively casual tone. "This is definitely a spaceship."

"Kek!" Kinety turned to face him and stood. For several seconds, she didn't speak.

His heart hammered loudly. "Kinety—," he began softly, ready to let it fly.

Kinety beamed at him. "Rixton said you fought like a lion," she bounced, breaking into a wide smile.

There was no anger in her manner.

Kek blinked in confusion. She wasn't mad? Had ... she not seen the fight? "Did he?" he squeaked, glancing at Rixton, who stood by the exit with a knowing squint in his green eyes.

Kek's silent gaze asked the question. Didn't she know? Everyone else did.

Rixton gave him a mock salute and left.

"I'm so proud of you!" Kinety went on, giving his shoulder a squeeze.

Kek quickly deleted his look of confusion. "Now … we-we-we can go get the soldiers," he said with a toothy smile. "Who is Romeo?"

Kinety was caught off guard by the question and gave him a funny look. "Romeo? From Romeo and Juliet? It's … the greatest love story in history. They died for each other. It's Shakespeare, silly," she said, amused by his lack of literary knowledge. Chuckling, she returned to the flight panel. "Do you think it still works? After the crash, I mean," she asked, looking at the buttons. She was kicking herself now for not watching how Deek and Jael flew the larger craft, but she did remember where they held their hands and some of the things they did. "I've been trying to turn it on."

Kek examined the panel in front of the pilot seat. "This all looks like some sort of flight control," he bluffed, "aaaand … that's probably weapon stuff since this is a fighter. Try over there," he suggested with a nonchalant point. While she scanned the area he recommended, he fooled with a few controls beside him to keep the craft from sending a signal. "Why did they have to die?"

Kinety placed her hand on a spot and rotated her palm. "Hmm? Oh. Because they were in love. All they wanted was each other, but the world refused to leave them be. Rather than live apart, they chose to die together." The panel lit up. "I did it!" she cried and spun to face him.

Kek snatched his hand down and leaned forward to see. "Show me what you did," he said eagerly.

As she stretched left to show him where she touched the panel, he leaned across to see and 'inadvertently' activated a few more controls. "What if you twisted it a bit further?" he asked, priming the power core by his thigh. "That's a horrible story."

Kinety put her palm on the starter and twisted it further, then shook her head. "No, it won't go," she said, checking around for another place to try. "The story is horrible, yes. That isn't the part that matters. Their tragedy demonstrates the power of love."

Kek angled his head to get a better look at what she was doing. "Does it do anything besides twist?" he asked, glancing behind himself, then slid his finger up the side of the panel. A screen appeared. He called up a diagnostic of the craft and rerouted power around a critical fracture in the crystal housing chamber.

Kinety twisted the light the other way, and the panel went out. "Whoops, not that way," she said, correcting it, then pressed. Pressing did nothing, but when she slid her hand down, the craft shuddered. "Oh! I almost had it!" she cried.

Kek reset two switches and covertly adjusted another. "Try that again."

Kinety rotated her palm and slid the light down. The craft shuddered and … a fine purr vibrated through the system, bringing it to life. "It's working!" With a cry, she leapt up from her seat and threw her arms around his neck. "We did it!"

Kek caught her in surprise, inches away and beaming in unexpected delight. Without meaning to, he looked at her lips.

Kinety's breath caught. "I'm sorry," she said, untangling herself from him, and awkwardly backed toward the exit. Fidgeting, she pointed toward the door. "I'm going to see if Arnie and the others are ready to go."

Kek braced his hand on the blinking panel and slumped in frustration. That was close, he thought, angry with himself. He'd nearly blown it because he couldn't keep his hands off her. The last thing he needed was for her to fall for Kek now. Keeping up the fake identity was exhausting and took entirely too much energy, which meant Kek had to go. The question now was how to kill him off and bring Torak back into her focus.

In the meantime, while she was gone, he finished booting the system.

*****

After a short goodbye, Arnie, Rixton, Park, Zhang, and Kek boarded, and Kinety sealed the ship. Each was given a stretchy white compression suit to put on beneath their clothes, which earned a generous amount of male giggles. With Kek covertly helping, the eager flight crew strapped in and 'figured out' the complicated controls. They would not use the portal but would travel out of Neontak's atmosphere, which was actually closer. Soon, the ship lifted off, and the journey to find Kinety's soldiers began. When the spaceship was safely in space, the pilots took it through a series of random flips, turns, zips to the side, lurches, and rolls, allowing the fliers to become comfortable with the controls beneath their fingers.

Park, after designating himself as lead pilot, added plenty of sound effects and worked hard to make his passengers dizzy. While he practiced maneuvers and procedures, Zhang figured out how to use the weapons systems. His shout of delight and rapid burst of Chinese signaled his enthusiastic eureka as the controls began to make sense. Fortunately, there were no Saphiridian ships in the vicinity to obliterate while he became intimate with the system, but there was plenty of meteorite debris to hone his accuracy skills on.

Arnie and Rixton occupied themselves with a boisterous game of catch-the-water-droplet, but Kinety didn't care to watch. Instead, she perched at the navigation panel with her hair floating around her and stared out at the stars with her chin in her hand. Torak was on her mind. It had occurred to her, regardless of how much she hated to admit it, that she would have gotten nowhere without him and hated herself again for the way she'd behaved during their last meeting. Though she'd somehow managed to receive all the credit, it was because of him and him alone that she had survived the Zahrá Che kidnapping, the Gaki encounter, and the demon-monster attack. Kinety didn't fool herself for a moment; she'd been completely helpless without him, a notion that didn't sit well with her. Of course, he would never believe her now, but she appreciated all of it.

Her elbow slipped on the control panel and, without warning, the ship lurched to the left and tilted, enhancing the fun going on behind her.

Someone moaned.

Kinety raised her head, blinking back to the present, and watched the two floating idiots pretend to walk. Neither Arnie nor Rixton were strapped in, and both were soaked. She might have thought their antics were funny, but Torak weighed too heavily on her mind. Everyone else here knew how to defend himself, survive in the wild, and use weapons, she thought with a twinge of envy. Well, they had four days aboard the ship, she decided and pressed the gravity button.

Arnie and Rixton crashed to the floor in a pair of shrieks.

Gripping the walls carefully while her legs adjusted to the artificial gravity, Kinety made her way toward the spaceship cargo bay, her brow furrowed in concentration. She entered the hallway at the same time as Kek, who was wearing a skin-tight compression suit.

Both stopped.

Kinety paused, holding the entryway, and watched him approach with a pitter-patter of her pulse. Apparently, he'd been doing laundry. She couldn't help taking a moment to appreciate his outlined physique and felt a touch of shame for enjoying it. She was still married to Torak. He was the one she loved, yet here she was having hot flashes for another man. It wasn't entirely her fault, though. Kek was absolutely gorgeous and made no secret of how he felt about her.

His sun-bleached hair was pulled back into a finger-brushed half-ponytail with tendrils that hung into pretty eyes, giving him a wild, boyish look. He appeared relaxed with a slightly scruffy chin and the long sleeves of his compression suit pulled casually up his forearms. His long legs, outlined against the white compression suit, were muscular and steady—a testament to his impressive build. Everything about Kek drove her mad, but she could do nothing about it. Despite her attraction to him, she couldn't help hoping that, by some miracle, this whole Wife of Torak thing actually ended up working out. She'd lied to Tooji, a fact that hung heavily on her heart. It was him she wanted.

"Kek," she said, remembering to smile.

"You should be strapped in," he said, stopping inches from her.

Kinety dropped her head back to look at him. "I wanted to see you," she said, then, with rounded eyes, quickly corrected herself, "sp-speak to you."

His arm slid around her back. "It sounds important," he said, hooking his fingers around a contour in the wall.

Kinety hesitated. "It is."

The ship spun.

Now, she was against him.

As the ship stabilized, Kek loosened his grip but lowered his head ever so slightly, watching her.

Kinety's heart stopped. For a moment, she thought he would try and kiss her again. She didn't know whether to skitter away to safety or go for it—but he didn't. He merely leaned in close and spoke softly, much to her dismay.

"What's on your mind?"

In relief, Kinety released the breath she'd been holding and scooped hair behind her ear in disappointment. "I don't remember," she murmured like an idiot.

He cocked his head and studied her upturned face.

Kinety paused to recall her thoughts at the panel, then remembered what she'd wanted in the first place. "I want to learn to defend myself," she recalled. "Rixton's taught me some, but ... will you teach me?"

Kek's eyes squinted into a smile. "Now?"

"Now."

*****

Kek began by explaining the basics of weight control, balance, and posture. Of course, the lesson quickly attracted Rixton and Arnie, who both enjoyed starting at the beginning with Kinety. Once the basics were out of the way, Kek began demonstrating simple attacks and defenses but tailored each to end in a kill strike. When barehand was perfected, the same techniques were performed with different weapons with focus on critical targets and weaknesses during each strike.

When Kinety had enough, she left the men and staggered back to the flight deck where the food was kept. Taking a bite, she plopped down between Park, who was enunciating words in English, and Zhang, who was struggling to pronounce them. After a good laugh at Zhang, Kinety sighed at the unappetizing blob in her hand and got up to take a shower.

It was a quick one.

The aliens used soap, but it just wasn't the same. There was no lather, no perfume, no happiness. Kinety missed flowery soap and shampoo and conditioner, but there was nobody to complain to. Glad to be clean, she dried herself off and stepped into the supply storage closet to get dressed. Halfway into a clean white compression suit, she heard another moan and froze.

Someone was in the washroom with her!

Startled, she yanked the suit on and peered beneath the lowest shelf. A pale heat signature glowed up. On her knees, she carefully slid the stacked supplies aside and saw the pale pink head of a Zahrá Che!

And it was alive.

She pulled the little alien out and turned the unmoving body to take a look. With a jolt of surprise, she recognized the beaten face. "Deek!" she cried, laying him flat. He was wounded. "Deek!"

Deek breathed heavily, struggling to wake.

Kinety got a clean washcloth and wet it, then hurried back. "Deek," she said, tossing wet hair over her shoulder and wiping his face clean.

The cool water brought him around, and a swollen eye cracked open. "Eeeee!"

"It's okay! It's okay," she rushed, quieting his panic. "Oh, you poor thing. Are you alright?"

The eye paused on her, then closed. *"Ugh,"* he groaned irritably.

"What happened?" she asked, wiping dried blood from his skinny neck.

"Saphiridians stole the ship," he snapped, jerking away from the rag. *"Why do you have it, foul Earthling?"*

Kinety puckered a sly dimple. "I stole it from the Saphiridians," she bragged and sat back on her heels. "Do you want some blob?"

The alien nodded and sat up. *"Where's Jael?"*

Kinety handed him a chunk. "Unless he's found a cubby to hide in, he's not aboard. Do you remember me?"

"Unfortunately."

Kinety noticed the faintest glance toward the commode and realized he needed to be alone. "Why don't you freshen up," she said, standing, "and when you're ready, you can come out and meet the others."

He took an annoyed bite, not at all caring for the idea of meeting anyone but said nothing.

Kinety cleaned her belongings and slipped out the door. On the other side, she found herself face-to-face with Kek, Rixton, and Arnie.

"Who were you talking to?" demanded Rixton.

Arnie touched his ear and frowned. "Was that Deek? I heard Deek."

Kinety shut the door. "I found him unconscious in the storage closet."

Arnie made a face and glowered at the door in disgust. "Are you serious?" he grumbled, then crossed his eyes.

"He's worried about his little friend Jael," she said. "Do you think he could still be on the ship?"

A scowl twisted Kek's handsome face. "If he's hidden on the ship, I'd prefer he remain hidden."

"Be nice, you guys," Kinety scolded.

Before either of them could inform her she'd lost her mind, the bathroom door slid open.

Deek, looking wobbly and pale, stepped out, took one look at Kek, and whirled. "Eeeee!" he screeched and ran back to the cubby. *"Aaaah! Aaaah! Aaaah!"*

Kinety caught him by the legs and tried to pull him back out. "Deek, let go! They're not going to hurt you," she grunted, tugging at his skinny legs.

"Are you sure?" asked Kek.

"Eeeee!"

"Kek!" she snapped over her shoulder. "You're not helping."

"Leave him in there."

"Let. Go. Deek!" she gritted, giving him a yank. With a yelp, she and the alien landed in a heap on the floor. Kinety held him, stopping his pitiful attempt to escape. "Deek!" she snapped, making him sit down. "They're not going to hurt you. Be still."

Deek glared at the men. *"Where's Jael?"*

Kinety, the only one besides Arnie who could hear him, answered. "If you'd like to search for Jael, you can, but I don't think he's here."

With an unfriendly scowl, the alien accepted her invitation and stomped toward the flight deck.

Rixton stared, watching him pass in wide-eyed silence.

Kek spoke over his shoulder to Kinety. "Tell him, if he goes near a flight panel or tries to get a message out, I'll break his arms," he warned.

Deek slowed to an irritable stop, receiving the message, then continued toward the flight deck.

Kinety got up and set her hands on her hips. "That wasn't nice," she scolded.

Kek's blue eyes shifted to her. "I'm not a fan of the Zahrá Che," he grumbled.

Groaning, she turned to go. "I should go introduce Deek to Park and Zhang."

Just then, chaos—a shrieking barrage of Korean Hangul, sputtered Chinese obscenities, and high-pitched 'Eeeee' cries—erupted from the flight deck.

Kek paused to listen. "No need. They've met," he said in amusement and motioned the men back to the sparring room.

*****

They would arrive in eight hours. While Park and Zhang slept on bunks in the flight deck, an easy feat now that Deek was able to demonstrate how the spacecraft worked, Kinety set the course to Gelphii. When she was done, she returned to find Arnie sleeping where he'd fallen after sparring with Kek. Rixton curled up on his tiny bunk in exhaustion, with his arm spilling onto the floor. Deek, who was now mourning Jael, had long since turned off the lights and helped himself to Kinety's bunk, leaving her to find a spot on the floor. She didn't mind. A couple of flattened compression suits later, she was well on her way to falling asleep. That is, until a strong arm curled around her from behind. Startled, Kinety twisted her neck and found Kek snuggled against her.

He blinked his eyes open as if only just woken and found her watching him. "You touch me and I'll scream," he warned and relaxed into her rolled-suit pillow.

Kinety chuckled quietly and tried again to go to sleep.

A few minutes later, Kek brushed her hair back, exposing her ear, and propped himself up on one elbow. Careful not to wake the others, he whispered softly into it. "How did you knock this ship down?"

Kinety blinked her eyes open and let the question register. She'd wondered how long it would be before someone asked. Frowning, she rolled onto her back and peered up at him. "I didn't think you saw that."

"I saw it."

She shook her head and moved out of his arms. "I don't know. I think it's static electricity."

He stared at her. "Static electricity or electrostatics?"

"Is there a difference?"

Kek hesitated, thinking it unwise to answer that. "How did you learn to … ?"

"I didn't. It just," Kinety examined her hands, "happens. My fingers tingle and collect energy, like a ball. I can make it big or keep it little, and I can throw it, just … not all the time."

Kek raised higher on his elbow. "I don't understand."

"I think Torak," she paused at his name, "gave it to me—as a gift, maybe. He does it," she explained thoughtfully. "It looked like

232

magic before. It scared me when it started, and it comes and goes. When it happened the other night, it killed that demon thing."

A look of concern settled on Kek's features. "It looks dangerous," he warned. "Next time you see Torak, you should ask him to show you how to control it."

At the mention of Torak, Kinety lowered her hands, and her voice went flat. "Torak won't be coming back. I made sure of it."

Kek's fingers rubbed a lock of hair. "Why would you do that?"

She moved away again. "To protect you," she said, gesturing to the others.

"I don't think you need to protect us from Torak anymore."

Kinety sat up and curled her ankles together. "Yes, I do." When he didn't answer, she smiled sadly. "Everything that's happened has been because of Torak. We're alive because of him. And you're right," she admitted quietly, "he's not my enemy. He's my companion."

"Then, why send him away?"

Kinety gestured to Arnie and Rixton. "To protect you," she said again, this time holding his gaze so he would listen. "Torak is bound by honor to complete his mission. I can't ask him to just change his loyalty, to become a traitor."

"The Saphiridians betrayed him. That doesn't make him the traitor."

"We know that," she assured with a nod, "but he doesn't know that. They've manipulated him and used him his whole life. They've convinced him he's a monster. I can't just," she searched for the words, "bat my eyes and expect him to turn that kind of loyalty off. If he finds that base, Kek, he'll have to choose."

Kek bumped her foot with his finger. "I think he'd choose you."

Kinety shook her head. "I can't risk it."

A long pause danced between them, giving their close positions a touch of awkwardness.

"Maybe … you should trust him," Kek said with a bit of a stammer.

Kinety fidgeted with the corner of her rolled compression suit pillow. "I want to, but every time I try, I remember watching him walk away on Jag Mosrog. He says he wants me, but I can't gamble your lives only to find out I've been fooled again."

Kek's blue eyes held hers.

Warning bells went off in Kinety's head. She felt her core warm and quickly redirected her gaze. A deep breath and a firm self-admonishment helped clear the worst of the sensation, but her heart was really banging. Was she falling in love with Kek too? A frown darkened her brow at the thought, and she turned away.

"Why do you frown when you look at me?"

"You remind me of him," she said with a grimace and tried to stand. "I'm sorry. I should go."

Kek stopped her. "Is that so bad?"

A sting began behind her eyes. "It is," she said, trying to ease from his grip. "You deserve better than that."

"Kinety … ," he said, gathering courage, "there's something I should tell you."

Kinety stood up. "Don't," she whispered.

He caught her hand. "If you'll just—"

"Don't say what you're about to say," she pleaded, trying again to pull her hand away from his.

Kek stood up and slipped his hand behind her head, trying to calm her. "I won't," he promised quietly. "I won't."

Arnie stirred and exhaled.

Kinety glanced at Arnie's sleeping form, embarrassed that she'd disturbed him, and pushed her hair from her face. Being this near Kek was dangerous, but the panic was ebbing. "Sorry," she whispered, avoiding Kek's eye.

Instead of responding, Kek lowered his head to kiss her. If he couldn't tell her, he'd show her who he was.

Kinety recoiled from the advance in anger. "No! I can't be in love with two men, Kek. I refuse," she whispered hotly and twisted out of his reach. Scowling, she crossed the room to where Rixton was sleeping and yanked her brother off the bunk. He rolled onto the floor, blinking in confusion as she stepped over his sprawled body. From now on, this is where she would sleep.

Chapter 19

When Kinety woke, it was with a burst of adrenaline. She still didn't know what to do with all the soldiers when she got them because the ship didn't have supplies to see them home, but today she would take custody of them.

One bridge at a time.

After a delicious breakfast of water-flavored blob, she pulled her hair back into a tight ponytail and pulled on a clean white Zahrá Che space suit. Eager to reach the flight deck, she rushed out of the restroom and smacked right into Kek.

Kinety staggered back in surprise, then awkwardly averted her eyes and tried to pass.

Kek caught her arm, stopping her.

Kinety wasn't ready to look at him yet, especially not with her heart doing backflips. Her cheeks heated, flushing pink. Even though she couldn't have him, she still wanted Torak. Legally, at least in this galaxy, she was his wife. Kinety hadn't sorted out how to feel about that. Kek, on the other hand, was becoming a real problem because she was falling in love with him too. And who could blame her? He wanted her and made no attempt to hide it, the opposite of Torak, who couldn't seem to make up his mind. The problem was, now was not the time to be worrying about romance—from either. She had more urgent issues to worry about, yet here she was.

After several seconds of silence, Kek got the message and released her.

Kinety hesitated another moment, then passed without speaking.

On the flight deck, she found Deek sitting on a bunk with his skinny arms folded in a pout because Zhang wouldn't let him near the navigation system. Just to be irritating, Kinety walked by the little creature and ran her hand over his head, earning a hiss and a bristle. It was quite satisfying. Park, on the other hand, was all focus. He sat at the flight panel, peering out at a small, blue moon growing in the window. "Is this it?" he asked when she stepped up beside him.

"Gelphii."

Park squinted at it.

"Its atmospheric pressure is a bit low," Kinety warned, "so we can't stay there long." She gave his shoulder a squeeze and hurried to the navigation panel Zhang was guarding.

Kek, Arnie, and Rixton entered the flight deck and watched as Kinety pulled the moon into focus and spun it until she found the peninsula she wanted, then added it to their course as an endpoint.

"It's a moon," she said with a glance at the beautiful sight. "Gelphii. I programmed our course last night."

Deek threw his little hands up and shook his head in disgust, then folded his arms again, only better this time. He just … couldn't look, unless it was to peek in objection. Fuming, he re-refolded his arms.

"Link successful. One well-hidden Zahrá Che base coming up. Destination in thirty minutes … if I don't wreck," Park announced, easing the power back and whistling to himself.

While the moon grew in the window, Arnie passed out instructions. "Park, you'll stay and fly the ship. Be ready—whether to land or get us the hell out of here, I need you on your toes. Zhang," he spoke slowly so Kinety could translate, "you are our defense. Keep a lookout. I'm pretty sure this will piss the Zahrá Che off. Be ready to shoot. Deek, you stay here on the ship," he told the unfriendly alien. "I don't want your people thinking you were a part of this. *Don't* go near the control panels or *I'll* break your arms. You sit there on that bunk until the rest of us get back."

Deek gave the large man a sidelong glare and crossed his tiny ankles.

"Everyone else—full battle rattle," Arnie teased, then tucked his one extra blaster into his waistband.

Rixton held up his sole blaster, which comprised his entire arsenal. "Itty bitty battle rattle," he informed Kinety, eyebrows high.

Kek blinked, missing the joke.

"Fifteen minutes," warned Park.

As Arnie passed out weapons and briefed the rescue team, Kinety's imagination kicked in, offering horrible scenarios, and her already elevated temperature increased. With white knuckles, she gripped the navigation panel, watching the smooth skin of the moon contour into an identifiable landscape. It was lopsided and had patchy landmasses surrounded by and containing water. Where there was water, there was sure to be life. Kinety thought of the Gaki, and her breathing shallowed.

Arnie double-checked her blaster settings and handed it to her. "You got this?" he asked quietly.

Kinety blew out her cheeks and smothered a groan.

"You know we aren't going to let anything happen to you," he swore.

She shook her head. "It's not that," she said breathlessly. "I just have a bad feeling."

"About what?"

"I don't know. Something is gnawing at me, like I've missed something or made a mistake," she confided.

Rixton brushed by and turned her so she faced him. "Whatever it is, Dorkymodo, it's too late. Nothing matters now but the mission. Ignore everything else and focus. Only they matter," he said firmly, pointing to Gelphii. "Nothing else. Whatever is down there, we deal with it. You do what you have to do."

Kinety took a deep breath, nodding at her instructions, and watched the surface of the moon blur past the window. As Park slowed their approach, she stepped closer, scanning for the peninsula.

Kek joined her.

Kinety took his hand and gave it a quick squeeze. "There it is," she said quietly when the peninsula rolled into view.

"I see the peninsula," said Park, "but the landing zone isn't there. It's been deleted."

The others—minus Deek—joined her at the window, searching for anything that resembled a base.

Kek was tempted to push a few buttons and help out but resisted the urge. Intentionally not watching, he angled away and waited for his companions to figure it out.

Park lowered the wobbly ship and moved slowly over the region, looking for anything that suggested activity. "I don't see anything," he said, switching screens. "No aliens on the ground, no aliens in the sky—besides us. For such an important location, there's an impressive lack of security here."

He was right.

Kinety frowned, more determined than ever now. She needed to find those soldiers. "Deek," she said with a glance at the little alien. "Why are there no ships?"

Deek shook his large head. *"Sorry,"* he said with an annoying stretch and leaned back, fitting his fingers together. *"I've never been here."*

Kinety faced him. "Please help us."

Deek gave her a you've-got-to-be-kidding look and crossed his ankles the other way.

Kinety's halo landed on the floor with a clank. "Get over here and look," she snarled, "or you'll sleep on the floor from now on!"

The alien glared at her, then deliberately uncrossed his ankles and stomped to the window. With a shove, he brazenly pushed Kek out of the way and pressed his broad forehead to it. It only took a moment for him to find what he sought. *"Radiation,"* he said simply, indicating an area to their left. *"It's over there somewhere."*

"It's there *some*where?" Arnie echoed, spreading his hands in annoyance. "That's the best you can do?"

Deek blinked at him. *"Why is that hairy beast growling at me?"* he demanded at Kinety.

"The hairy beast can hear you," Arnie informed the creature, giving the tiny communicator in his ear a tap. "Just tell us where it is."

"I can't. I've never been here. Ask the female," he grumbled, gesturing Arnie's attention back to Kinety.

"But I don't know," she argued.

Deek made a dismissive gesture. *"You do know,"* he countered with a wave.

Kinety shook her head. Puzzled, she looked out again, searching for anything familiar, but there was nothing. Even the jagged landscape was odd and bizarre-looking to her. "I've never been here either, Deek," she insisted. "I don't know what I'm looking for."

Deek was peering out the window. *"Yes, you do, foolish Earthling,"* he said in a distracted tone. *"You keep dreaming about it."*

Kinety whirled on him. "You've been eavesdropping on my dreams?"

"Eavesdropping!" Deek gasped, horrified by the accusation. *"You practically shout them. Just tell the man,"* he jabbed a skinny finger at Kek, *"and be done with it. I'm tired of you telling me."*

Kinety curled her fingers and went after him. "You little roach!"

Before she could kill the alien, Arnie caught her and yanked her to face him. "He says you know."

"But I don't!"

Arnie didn't believe her. "What dream? Can you remember it?"

Kinety turned her palms up. "No, Arnie, I can't—," she stopped and her expression faded. Suddenly, a string of bizarre memories flickered in her head. These weren't dreams; they were nightmares and were always about—she looked at Kek—the day they met. She remembered the way he'd watched her, his charming smile, the soothing sound of his voice. He'd risked his life to save hers. She remembered that moment so well—the raw fear. She'd never been so frightened, knowing she was moments from being slaughtered, eaten alive … and there he was. Every night, she relived that attack, watching his amazing jump into the Gaki ring, her hero, arriving to help her out when she needed him most … but that told her nothing about the base.

Kinety delved deeper, recalling the more broken fragments of her nightmares—the faceless aliens trying to kill her, running blood-soaked through the field of human bones, and Orlando.

Orlando.

She paused, zeroing in on him.

Orlando had taken the shot meant for her. Mere seconds before they'd killed him, he'd told her where the men were.

"They're floating … ," she recalled and spun to look out, "… in water!"

Arnie scanned the ground. "There's a river."

Kinety shook her head. "It was cold."

"They're underground," said Kek, looking at the spot where the radiation was the densest.

Rixton pointed. "There's a waterfall," he said, squinting, "and the river at the bottom is smaller than the one on top. Park!"

"I'm on it," Park said, angling the ship toward the fall. "Zhang, are you ready?"

Zhang, perched at the weapon station, gave him a thumbs-up. "I am relly," he answered, showing off his newly learned words.

Deek looked constipated.

Kinety dropped a noisy kiss onto his big head, earning a squeal of disgust and a glower. Shuddering, the cross alien marched back to his bunk and flopped angrily onto it. Absolutely disgusted, he re-re-refolded his arms.

*****

Minutes later, Kinety, Kek, Arnie, and Rixton stepped off the ship onto a bank near the splashing waterfall. Behind them, the door liquified shut, and the spacecraft lifted away. The band around Kinety's wrist stung sharply, rendering her hand temporarily unusable and earning a hiss of pain. She cursed, forgetting about the mission for several unpleasant moments while the bracelet oozed something spicy into her veins. Her heart jolted when it arrived, jumped hard, then calmed. A full minute passed before the sting subsided. When it finally did, she released her jagged breath and her breathing smoothed out, easing the dizzy. With a curse, she relaxed, then found the others recovering too.

"That sucked," Arnie said, controlling his own breathing, and motioned the team forward toward the waterfall.

Kek took the lead with one hand angled back toward Kinety, who was guarding his left. Rixton kept his hand on her back, watching the team's right. Arnie covered the rear. Within seconds, they were soaked. Together, they moved behind the fall onto a metal bridge that led them over the raging water. The roar was deafening.

On the other side was a wide door.

Kek paused the team using hand signals, fired at the door latch, and then motioned them forward. The whole group burst inside into a massive cavern lit with pale light. In the cavern was a lake. A narrow walkway made a ring around the outer edges of the swirling water.

The lake was empty.

The group went still, watching the water roll and slap around the only two canisters left. One had no visible human inside the window at the top; the other was partially submerged. Debris and scattered tiny footprints everywhere else suggested the cavern had been emptied in a hurry.

Kinety's stomach dropped. "No. No!" she choked and took off running along the narrow edge toward the canisters.

"Dorkymodo, no!" Rixton shouted. "You don't know what's in there!"

Kek took off after her. Rixton cursed sharply and followed, covering them. Arnie ran around the other side, his blaster ready.

Without stopping, Kinety tucked her blaster and dove toward the nearest canister. Growling in frustration, she surfaced and swam to it. Using it as a buoy, she crawled up until she could see in the window. Kek splashed in beside her. The soldier inside was dead; his decaying body crumpled and distorted.

Kinety slapped the glass. "No!" she cried and sloshed back into the water toward the partially submerged canister lying almost sideways nearby.

Kek caught up and grabbed the bobbing tube.

A jagged split coursed down the side beneath a buckle in the shell, evidence of a hard strike.

Kinety rotated it until she could see inside and saw a pale glow of heat. "She's alive!"

Working together, Kinety and Kek sloshed the canister to the bank. Rixton tucked his blaster away and dragged it out of the water. Using a rock, he shattered the glass, draining the water in a splash, and scratched the chip off her neck.

Instantly, the soldier's eyes opened and she gasped sharply. She had short brown hair and thin eyebrows over astute brown eyes, widened in panic.

Rixton grabbed a fistful of her shirt and heaved the wet soldier out. A blaster fell out beside her. Startled, she reflexed sharply, throwing her arms wide and crying out in alarm, inadvertently knocking a spot on the canister. With a hiss, the broken lid opened.

Rixton clamped an arm around her, pinning hers down. "Settle! Settle," he coached, calming the freezing cold woman and pressing the bleeding wound on her neck.

Kinety and Kek crawled onto the shore.

Shivering violently, the woman focused her eyes on them, then at the lake. Fear and confusion twisted her expression. "Where am I?" she asked in a broken voice.

"On a moon called Gelphii. You were taken by aliens," Rixton answered. "What is your name, soldier?"

"Sh-Shiva. Sergeant … Tess Shiva," she managed. "I remember the aliens."

Kinety pointed to a small opening in the rock. It was glowing, the way all computers did to her now. "Is that another room?" she asked, shivering.

Kek hurried to check, then waved for Kinety to join him. "It's a control room."

Arnie moved back toward the entrance. "Rixton, let's get Shiva to the ship," he ordered. "She's hypothermic. Kek?"

Kek waved them on. "Five minutes," he called to Arnie. "We want to look around."

Arnie gestured Rixton out. "I'm waiting," he called to Kek.

Kek gave a short nod and followed Kinety inside the computer room. Rixton hooked his arm around Shiva's ribs and heaved the unsteady woman to her feet, grabbing her blaster as he stood. Clutching a wad of fatigue at her shoulder, he led her slowly around the lake toward the waterfall.

The computer room was small inside, designed for one, maybe two little Zahrá Che aliens. Panels, similar to the ones on the spaceship, lined the walls. Kinety hurried to the closest station and started hacking. It was the archives she was interested in. Without being told, she knew their destination would be there.

Kek moved to the other. "There were 273 canisters here minus the two left behind," he said over his shoulder. "All listed as alive."

Kinety dug back far into the archives. "Jakkard Reth," she said softly.

"Jakkard Reth … the solar system?" Kek blurted, then winced, hoping she hadn't noticed he was familiar with the name.

Kinety didn't notice. "I just found an encrypted signal that links somewhere in there," she answered, trying to zero in on a location. "There are four planets and a broken moon."

Kek wasn't impressed. "There's nothing there," he assured, quietly connecting with the database. "The sun is too big. The planets are all either dead or volcanic."

"Volcanic?" she asked, selecting a planet just beyond a zone marked Potential-For-Life called Fl'drowdo. "Floop…flowo…do—I can't even pronounce it. Is there an atmosphere on planet Floopin Floppin?"

Amusement flickered on Kek's face. "Orbiting that close to its sun would make the planet toxic," he said, joining her at her station. "Full of diamond dust and radiation. Why are you looking there?"

"The encrypted signal ended not far from this planet's orbit."

"Impossible. Can you retrieve the transmission?"

"No. Only remnants of the signal."

"Must have been a decoy."

241

Kinety shook her head. "I don't think so. Remember when I spoke to the emperor?"

"I remember you said that. Yes."

"The air was sparkling around him. He was coughing, and his skin was burned."

Kek took a moment to absorb this new information, then moved to a different screen. A shift in the air startled Kinety silent. Warily, she walked toward the exit, wondering what it was. Kek saw her walk out but let her go. When she was completely out of view, he dug into the computer, working quickly.

Kinety paused to look again at the empty lake, then hurried out of the cavern and emerged on the other side of the waterfall, soaked yet again by the splash. As she exited, she looked up and jolted in horror at a Saphiridian ship darkening the sky. Her heart stopped. In a panic, she rushed around an outcropping of rocks, heading for the insertion point to find the others, and skidded to a stop.

Saphiridian soldiers were everywhere.

What she didn't see was her ship. Backpedaling, she pulled her blaster and, in the thickest of the uniformed aliens, spotted Arnie and Shiva on their knees on the ground.

"Don't! Move!" shouted a deep voice in Saphiridian military speak.

Kinety turned and went rigid.

A Saphiridian soldier pushed Rixton into view, holding a blaster to his head. Her brother, messy-haired and bleeding slightly from a fight, stared at her with his hands visible. The bulky ship landed nearby, blowing a billow of dust, and lowered a ramp with a clank. A high-ranking soldier standing in the doorway stepped forward, his snub nose visible behind the visor of his brown helmet. "Wife of Torak," he taunted slowly, glaring an evil smile at her and extending his gloved hand invitingly toward the open door of his ship, "are you coming quietly, or should we be more persuasive?"

"No!" Rixton growled, earning a silencing shove against the temple.

Kinety grimaced at the clunker-junker, knowing if she boarded, she was dead. Very carefully, she spread her arms wide and bent to place the blaster on the ground. "Rixton," she whimpered.

"They'll kill us anyway!"

Unarmed, Kinety spread her hands, ready to be apprehended.

Two Saphiridian soldiers rushed to collect her.

Kek appeared, his palm extended. "You touch my wife, you die," he warned, his voice calm, dangerous.

Kinety turned in surprise.

A soldier in brown gripped her upper arm roughly and yanked her toward the ship. A blue flash struck the man, caving his chest with a crunch and knocking him backward twenty feet.

Kinety stumbled and fell with a yelp near the feet of the second soldier. Stunned, she blinked at Kek.

"Arrest him!" shouted the leader.

Kek opened his hand again, palm out, and made a circle.

The gun against Rixton's head melted, and the man holding it began to choke. Wide-eyed, he clawed at his throat hidden beneath his helmet.

Kek opened a circular blade with a hinge, his gaze locked on the soldier reaching for Kinety. "Your death will be slower," he warned, advancing.

The man froze, open-mouthed.

In that instant, everything made sense to Kinety. "Tooji?"

The Saphiridians went still, gaping at the blue-eyed aggressor.

"Torak?" the leader whispered in confusion.

Kek's face faded and his blond streaks dissolved, leaving Torak in his place. The form-fitting white compression suit turned black. "Arnie," he barked without looking, "take the ship."

Instantly, Arnie was on his feet, dragging Shiva up. Nobody noticed, though. They were all staring at Torak.

"Traitor!" the leader spat.

Torak charged the man and snatched him up by his uniform, yanking him off his feet. "M'ran portak, you just attacked my wife," he hissed, using an insult similar to motherfucker. "Who betrayed who?"

The leader, whatever he might have wanted to say, wisely kept his mouth shut, and the soldiers didn't move.

Three Saphiridians tumbled out of the ship.

"Clear!" called Arnie.

"Rixton!" Torak shouted.

Rixton didn't have to be told twice. Scrambling, he darted for Kinety and hauled her past Arnie onto the Saphiridian craft.

"There's a fleet coming," Torak warned. "Get the fuck out of here."

"Where are the others?" shouted Arnie.

Torak waved. "I'll find them."

Arnie pulled the door shut and shoved Kinety toward the flight panel. "Fly!"

"I don't know how to fly this piece of shit!" she argued, rushing to the controls and frantically trying to figure them out.

Arnie activated one of the weapons. "Ask me how many ways I don't care," he argued back.

"They worked it like a video game," she said, trying to understand the buttons. "I don't play video games."

Rixton, who had just reached the second weapon across the fuselage, whirled. "I do!" he said, hurrying over.

"We've got incoming!" Shiva warned from the navigation screen.

"Get us off the ground now!" ordered Arnie, not caring which one obeyed.

Eyeing the controls, Kinety pointed to a button beside a lever. "That means elevate."

Rixton slapped it, launching the ship straight up and dropping Kinety to the floor. "Got it," he said, wiping a trail of blood from his nose. Using a knob near the left side of the controls, he wobbled the ship left and then right—much too sharply at first.

Kinety rolled into a wall full of pipes.

Arnie snatched her up and thrust her toward the station he'd been working. "Kill anything not Zahrá Che," he ordered, crossing to a different panel, "and don't shoot Kek … Torak!"

Kinety jerked her levers back and forth, figuring out how to use the rickety system. "Does anyone want to tell me why I was the only one who looked surprised back there?" she demanded angrily, selecting a target and firing the lasers. The Saphiridian fighter dodged her and fired back, grazing the ship. A section of wall sparked beside her. Kinety shrieked and ducked, then quickly fired back.

"Surprised about what?" Rixton asked, giving the ship full power and changing course.

"Bullshit!" she railed at her lying brother.

Arnie spun from his panel. "Eyes on your target!" he scolded sharply.

Kinety jerked her weapon around and fired. "Neither of you jackasses were the least bit surprised. How long have you known?"

"I knew the day he arrived," said Arnie.

Kinety's mouth fell open. Horrified, she glowered at her brother.

Rixton glanced at her. "Every time he gets mad, his eyes turn white and crackle with electricity," he said, focusing on flying. "It wasn't hard to figure out."

"Why, Kinety, you look surprised again," Arnie said sweetly.

She glared at him. "A bit," she agreed, firing daggers.

"Which means you aren't shooting," he scolded. "Get your ass to the navigation panel and figure out where the hell we're going. Shiva, take over!"

"If there's anyone here racking up surprise points," Shiva said, hurrying to Kinety's laser gun, "that would be me. Tell me what to do."

Kinety pulled her in front of the panel. "This is how you aim," she said, maneuvering her hands, "and this button is fire. You see that piece of shit that looks like the tin can we're in? Kill it! Don't shoot at silver ships, don't shoot tiny black fighters."

"They're flanking us!" called Rixton.

Kinety hurried to the navigation panel and pulled up planet Fl'drowdo. The computer wasn't as advanced as the Zahrá Che system but was similar enough that she could maneuver through it. Working quickly, she set a course for the volcanic planet.

"Since we're all sitting here doing nothing," Shiva said, firing, "would someone like to tell me what the hell is going on?"

Over his shoulder, Arnie explained in a tiny nutshell. "… and we are the rescue team," he finished.

"Hold on!" warned Rixton.

Kinety grabbed a lip beneath her panel a split second before the ship rolled, nearly launching her into the ceiling.

"They're blocking us in," Rixton said with a note of worry in his voice.

"Get us out of here, or you do not get a Christmas bonus!" threatened Arnie.

"Hey! I've been piloting spaceships for eleven-and-a-half minutes," Rixton shouted back. "I'm doing a good job! I'm getting a Christmas bonus."

"Find someplace to hide!"

Rixton made a face. "We are in space!" he informed his pinheaded superior. "If you see a tree, you let me know."

"So, is that Torak in the little black fighter?" asked Shiva between shots.

Kinety rushed to a window that appeared to have been installed with silicone caulking and aluminum foil and gripped a handle welded into the frame. Outside, Saphiridian ships of varying sizes darted this way and that, trying to surround the stolen ship. "Tooji!" she whispered, watching in horror as the Saphiridians opened fire on him.

Suddenly, a blue flash blasted by them, striking two blocking ships. Both lurched backward out of the way.

"Go, go, go!" shouted Kinety.

Rixton jerked the ship toward the opening and shot forward.

A Saphiridian fighter with disabled blasters rocketed toward them. "Kamikaze, right wing!" called Arnie.

Torak went after him.

Rixton searched the sky to find the fighters. "How do you know he's Kamikaze?"

"Because he's not shooting and he's not afraid of Torak! Move!"

Rixton rolled the ship.

Shiva picked him up in her window. "Kamikaze coming back. Ten o'clock low!"

Kinety clutched her handle with both hands, searching the sky for Torak as Rixton jerked right.

"I can't shake him!" Rixton growled.

Rockets full power, the Kamikaze dove.

"It's too late," Arnie warned calmly. "Brace for impact."

As the fighter screamed toward them, Torak came up from below, intercepting the rogue aircraft.

They collided.

The explosion, mere feet from Kinety's window, sent shockwaves through the steampunk vessel, throwing her hard to the floor. Horrified, she raised her head and gaped at the sparks outside. Her voice failed. "Tooji," she whispered, then shot to the window, slapping both hands against it with a wild sob.

Outside, the sparks faded.

"Toraaak!"

It was gone.

She screamed. Blood-curdling. Intense. Deep.

Kinety went dizzy. Slowly, she began to sink.

Through the fog, a warm hand slid over the back of hers, pinning it to the window.

She went still.

"You are the worst coward I have ever met," said the sweetest voice in the universe.

At the sound of it, Kinety's knees gave out entirely and she cried.

Before she could crumple to the floor. His strong arm snaked around her waist, holding her up.

Kinety turned in his arms and peered at him through wet lashes. Breathless, she looked outside at the debris, then at him again. "Tooji?" she whispered in confusion.

Torak followed her glance. "I destroyed the assassin fighter. The debris struck the ship as I came in," he explained.

Tears streaked down her cheeks. "I thought you died," she managed.

He brushed hair from her eyes with a gloved hand. "I heard that," he whispered softly.

Kinety peered at him, her face drawn in bewilderment. "Kek?"

Instead of answering, Torak switched, fading the black of his hair until only the highlights were left, then blued his eyes. "I have shapeshifter DNA."

"You asshole," Kinety murmured, sliding her arms around his neck in disgust.

Torak smiled. "You fell in love with me twice," he teased.

"Last night," she began thoughtfully. "Is this what you were going to tell me?"

"It was. What did you think I was going to say?"

Kinety snuggled against his neck. "That you loved me."

Torak's arms tightened. "That was next."

Arnie tapped Torak's arm. "This is very romantic and all," he said, pulling them apart, "but we have a tail—a real damn big one."

Torak released Kinety and turned to look. "Yeah, I pissed them off," he said, brushing Rixton away from the controls. "Kinety, did you program Fl'drowdo into the navigation system?"

"Yes."

"Then they already know where we're going. I can buy us a few minutes. All of you, buckle in for a wormhole," he warned, rerouting power for speed while they scrambled for seats. "Ready? Squeeze your legs hard in three ... two ... one!"

The ship rocketed forward.

Kinety pinched her knees together hard and tightened her stomach, fighting the incredible G-force. When they came out of hyper-jump moments later, only she and Torak were awake. The others had passed out. Realizing this, a hesitant smile broke across her face.

Torak laughed, sounding remarkably like Kek. "You're a badass," he confirmed, borrowing Arnie's phrase and angling the ship. "That's why I married you."

"You married me by accident," she corrected, squinting at the bright light of a massive sun.

He zeroed in on a lopsided planet. "Probably not as accident as you think. I never imagined a scenario where I would say such words, so the moment caught me off-guard. I wanted to say you were my wife ... to see how it felt. I just ... grew chicken after I did," he admitted. "Don't look at the sun or its light."

Kinety turned away from it. "What do you mean by that?"

Torak smiled again. "I opened a language link, taking your language, but you and I started talking. I ... got distracted and didn't withdraw the pulse as I should have done. The link appears to have become bidirectional at some point, probably when I kissed you, which transferred my languages the other way. I didn't take it back when I left you, either, because I ... hoped it would help me track you down after the mission. It wasn't until later I realized the consequences," he admitted and glanced at her. "The court garbage was for show. You know that, right?"

"I do ... because of Kek," she said, watching the planet grow in the window. "Always there when I needed him. Genuine. Devastatingly handsome. He never hid how he felt. It was nice ... and it was impossible not to fall in love with him. I'm really relieved that was you."

247

Torak beamed at her. "Wow! I can't get enough of the compliments. I'm not used to hearing this," he giggled, glancing at another screen. "Shit. That bought us no time at all. The whole fleet just followed us in."

She laughed at his giggle. "What does that mean?"

"That means you should wake Arnie," Torak said, getting busy.

Kinety unbuckled quickly and hurried to Arnie, who woke with a start. It took a moment for him to orient, but when he did he noticed the screen. With a curse, he hurried to wake Shiva. Kinety woke Rixton.

"All of you, in spacesuits, now," said Torak. "Lock the helmets."

Kinety wrinkled her nose. "But they're Saphiridian suits," she complained with a grimace.

Torak pointed. "Move it!"

"Get to your guns, Shiva," Arnie ordered, taking position at his own station.

Torak spoke over his shoulder. "Rixton, take over. I programmed it to reach the Zahrá Che base. You'll have to put it down and get the hell out of this ship. Both Zahrá Che and Saphiridian will attack it. Get to the sun side of the base and wait for me," he said, sliding out of the pilot seat, then pointed at Kinety. "*Don't* lose her."

"Aye, aye, Captain," Rixton said. "One Dorkymodo, grounded."

Torak double-checked Kinety's suit and snapped her helmet into place. "Don't do anything stupid!" he warned, turning to leave, then stopped. Abruptly, he turned around and pulled a tiny black dot from his pocket. "It's a tracker. Open your mouth," he said, reaching for her.

Kinety backed up, looking at it. "What?"

"Open your mouth."

"Oh, hell, no!"

Torak grabbed her and the helmet was off.

"No! Aah! Get your—you are not about to—mmrph ffr grrph!" She was on the floor by the time he was finished.

"I'm not losing you again," he said simply, stuffing her hair into her suit and yanking the ugly brown helmet back down into place. Like an ass, he kissed her helmet in front of her mouth and released her.

Kinety growled in outrage, furious, and kicked at him. He dodged it easily, showing even white teeth, then jumped … through the freaking window! She gaped at him.

On the other side, his fighter materialized with a pop and he took off.

Blinking stupidly, she pointed at her amused brother. "Shut up!" she snapped, crawling angrily to her feet, then glared at the smiling Arnie and confused Shiva. "All of you, just shut up!"

*****

Torak picked a ship at random and holographed into the electronics. On the other side, he appeared on the main screen, startling the Saphiridian crew, and climbed aboard. Almost instantly, one tried to shoot him. Torak ignored him. Eyes blazing, he scanned their familiar faces, each now wearing a blatant look of betrayal, each knowing exactly why he was there. Singling out the ship's Superior, Torak spoke in a deadly voice. "Get Joboba in here now," he said in a low growl.

The Superior moved quickly.

Moments later, a holograph of Joboba flickered to life, placing the Prime in the center of the ship mere feet from Torak. Instantly, the older man adopted an arrogant expression. "Well, well, well. Look who it is," he marveled.

Torak paced a few slow steps past his former commander, glaring in unbridled hatred. "If you touch my wife," his brows lifted, "I'll kill you."

The Prime's eyes glittered in anger. "You!" he roared. "You dare threaten me. Traitor!"

Torak stopped. "Who's the traitor, Joboba? My own people," he indicated the crew around him, "dressed up like Zahrá Che and carried out an attack, like cowards."

Joboba flashed a mocking smile. "Your little darling needed a ship," he said, spreading his hands. "I simply provided one. The Zahrá Che vehicles are so much easier for a novice to fly."

Torak paced a few steps the other way, watching the see-through holograph. "Has everything been a lie?"

Joboba gave the question some thought. "Not … *every*thing," he supposed.

Torak wanted to squeeze the man's neck. "And the Gaki," he said, angling his head at the smaller man. "You ordered the slaughter of innocent people … for what? A planet that doesn't belong to you?"

"This is war," Joboba said smoothly, wearing no expression on his face.

Torak huffed in amusement. "Then perhaps you should fight it yourself and do some of the dying," he said calmly, pinning the Prime with a meaningful stare. "But, no. That's impossible for a little man with such big importance. You cheat so easily … and lie —the toys of a weakling."

Joboba glared.

"How many innocent people have the Saphiridians killed because of your lies?"

The phony confidence vanished from the Prime, leaving him shaking in anger. "I can see this woman has turned you against us," he seethed with mounting rage.

249

"No," Torak corrected politely, "*you* turned me against you. If you had simply accepted her, I never would have known. But I do now."

Joboba thrust a finger at Torak. "This is why we wanted her dead," he spat, raising his voice. "Right here. She did this. She'll pay for what she's done. I'll kill *all* her men."

"I won't let you."

"You're too late," sneered Joboba. "My fleet should be arriving about now."

Torak's steel gaze remained steady. "Where do you think I'm projecting from?"

"You're too late!" Joboba screamed. "Their orders are to kill the bitch!"

Torak waved his hand toward a screen, setting a fifteen-second countdown, and cut his gaze to the Superior. "You have fifteen seconds to break formation."

The Superior cried out and ran to the panel, trying desperately to stop the countdown, then spun in outrage. "I'll see you in Hell first, freak!"

Torak inclined his head politely, accepting that as his answer, and disappeared, leaving the shrieking crew to their fate.

Chapter 20

The navigation system guided the stolen Saphiridian ship to the volcanic Zahrá Che base and slowed, reaching the end of its instructions. Diamond dust sparkled beautifully in the atmosphere. Visible heat waves distorted the view, and hot air warmed the ship as it rumbled toward the planet.

Right away, their clunky vessel was surrounded by sleek silver Zahrá Che ships with weapons primed.

Kinety hurried to communicate. "Emperor Dinruk, it's Kinety," she said, identifying herself quickly. "There's a Saphiridian fleet hot on my tail, and they're mad!"

In unison, the fighters backed away and allowed the craft to pass. Carefully, Rixton wobbled the controls downward, trying to land the heap of junk. As her brother maneuvered the ship to the ground, Kinety hurried to the window, palm to glass, and looked past the intimidating Zahrá Che vessels. There, resting side by side on the burnt tarmac, were three massive transport vehicles, no doubt loaded with 271 loaded canisters.

"There they are!" she whispered.

"Easy does it," Rixton coached himself, trying to guess where the ground was by the gauges. "Easy does it."

Wham!

The ship slammed hard into the planet, knocking a cloud of burnt orange dust high into the shimmering air and dropping Kinety to the metal floor.

"Whoops! I was watching the wrong screen," Rixton said apologetically and turned to be sure the others were okay. "We're down."

"Good job. My back is only slightly broken," Arnie groaned, giving him a wobbly thumbs-up.

"You are fired," Shiva informed him from the base of her seat. "If I outrank you, your aviation career is over."

Kinety, however, wasn't interested in playing. Outside, the Zahrá Che fighters spread out above the tarmac to guard the soldiers; others primed their weapons to fight. In alarm, she pressed her face to the window. Just visible, high in the orange atmosphere, Saphiridian fighters by the hundreds swarmed the sky, firing at the transport ships. The Zahrá Che fired back, but there were far too many arriving for the guarding Zahrá Che to remain where they were. Left with no choice, the silver ships engaged, leaving nobody to protect the transporters.

"Rixton!" In a panic, Kinety slapped the door panel and took off down the ramp.

Rixton charged after her.

Arnie swore loudly. "Shiva!" he shouted, running to his guns.

"I'm on it," she called back, swinging her weapon toward the massive invasion.

Beside Rixton, Kinety raced like a wild woman toward the transport ships, ignoring the violent fight swirling above. A Saphiridian fighter diving low saw them and fired, peppering the ground around them with laser blasts. Rixton tackled Kinety sideways, taking her into a ditch as a Zahrá Che ship screamed toward them. Barely visible, they spotted Deek at the controls, which meant Zhang and Park were working the guns on either side of the craft. Lasers blazing, the friendly fire took the fighter out.

It crashed with a rumble, sending debris and body parts splattering over the ground.

When the spray ended, Rixton raised his head and pulled Kinety to her feet. "Go!" he shouted, shoving her into a run toward the first transport ship.

*****

Shiva took out another fighter. "Fifteen!"

"I'm on twenty-two," Arnie informed her. "Shoot faster."

Just then, Torak's black fighter came around, guns blazing.

"Oh, look. There's Torak," she said, firing at a craft below him, then recoiled as a shot struck the side of the ship. "Ow! What the— Arnie! Torak is firing at us."

"If Torak is firing at us, that means—," Arnie spun from his station, wide-eyed, and grabbed her, "—get out! Get out!" he shouted, hauling her down the ramp.

Directly overhead, a large Saphiridian ship darkened the sky. Seconds later, the stolen ship was struck.

The explosion was massive.

Arnie and Shiva flew forward from the concussion and crashed hard into the ground. They rolled, sliding across the dirt in a shower of metal and sparks.

Arnie landed on his stomach, stunned by the blast, then loudly caught his breath. Slightly unsteady, he found Shiva a few feet away and grabbed her by the front of her suit. "Are you alive!" he shouted, breathless from the heat.

"Barely," she gasped, trying to sit up.

"Good. Break time's over," he panted, pulling his blaster and climbing to wobbly legs. "Let's go."

*****

Overhead, the Saphiridian fighters kept coming, casting a deep rumble into the atmosphere.

Kinety and Rixton tore into the first transporter. Rows and rows of canisters, about ninety in total, lined the walls, but this time the soldiers were awake and frightened. When they saw Kinety and Rixton—humans—they began shouting and pounding on the glass.

"The latch is on the lowest point of the glass," Rixton instructed, recalling how Shiva had accidentally opened her own canister. "Slide your finger from right to left. Get those chips off them."

Kinety grabbed the nearest canister and opened it but couldn't get the soldier out. "Cover your head!" she ordered and pulled the canister down. "There's a chip on your neck. Pull it off!"

It crashed loudly to the floor.

Without the slightest hint of gentle, Kinety grabbed the man by the shoulders and heaved him out. "Get your blaster!" she barked, shoving the confused man toward the open canister on the floor.

The man cried out, grabbing his wrist in surprise as it began working, and tried to pull the breathing bracelet off.

Kinety stopped him. "It's a blood regulator. Without it, you don't breathe," she said, moving to the next canister and hauling the next man out.

Rixton grabbed Kinety, shaking his head inside his helmet. "It'll take too long this way," he muffled. "You open the canisters and pull them down! I'll drag the soldiers out. Go!"

Canisters thudded loudly to the floor, littering it, as more and more soldiers helped to free their pinned comrades. Another group removed the chips.

"I can't breathe," one man wheezed when he slid free and gripped his throat. "I can't breathe."

Kinety grabbed his wrist and found his band malfunctioning. With a yank, she pulled her helmet off and dropped it down on his head. Clawing at her suit, she stripped it off and pulled it quickly over his feet with the help of several others. Seconds later, she'd snapped the helmet shut at his neck, sealing it.

The man calmed, and she hurried to the next one in line.

When they were free, Kinety faced the large group and shouted. "Little body, big head are the good guys," she said, winded from the toxic air, and pushed the tip of her nose up. "Snub-nose are bad!"

Rixton shoved his way to the exit. "Everyone grab a blaster," he bellowed and jumped to the ground. "Get to the sun side of the base."

Just then, Arnie rushed up, intercepting the crowd. With one arm extended in the correct direction, he took over, moving the armed soldiers toward the massive sun. "Move! Move!" his powerful voice bellowed, leading the mass away from the transport ships.

Violent dogfights zigzagged through the air, dodging laser fire and pulse cannons. Zarah Che zipped silently by, breaking sound barriers and throwing concussions across the planet's surface. Saphiridians thundered after, rattling the ground and firing deafening explosives. All around them, space fighters crashed to the ground and debris fell from the sky, sparking fires and igniting the orange dirt.

Shiva darted to the front of the group with her arms high and shouted over the chaos. "This way!" she waved through the smoke. "Follow me!"

Rixton and Kinety let Arnie and Shiva take the soldiers and darted into the second transport ship, which was being pelted from above. Several soldiers from the first transporter hurried in after them to help by offering instructions on armbands, details on bad guys, and pointing confused abductees out toward Arnie, who was waiting.

*****

Torak zipped his black fighter around the top of a massive mothership, taking her weapons out one by one. The enemy swarmed him, trying to stop the assault, but he was focused. Simultaneously, two Zahrá Che ships worked together, blasting the fighters that threatened him.

With half an ear, he monitored the communication channels from both sides until he heard a Saphiridian order to take out his Zahrá Che defenders. Instantly, he whirled on one of the Zahrá Che fighters and fired warning shots at it, barely missing the shiny silver skin.

It spun away, likely startled by the unexpected attack, just as the mothership released a warhead. The projectile slid past, missing the mirrored ship by inches. Its silver partner twisted over, lining itself up with the cannon, and fired, destroying the weapon before it could rearm. The explosion tore a hole into the side of the mother ship, destabilizing it.

Torak and the two Zahrá Che defenders backed away.

As the Saphiridians fought to seal the leak, the wounded mother ship went down and scraped across the ground with a deafening rumble. The moment it lurched to a stop, foot soldiers came pouring out, heading for the transport ships at a run.

Torak cursed sharply. Teeth clamped, he spread his hands, gathering energy, and opened fire.

*****

Through a thick fog of smoke and dust, Kinety and Rixton charged out of the second ship and raced toward the third, unaware of the horde of Saphiridian soldiers in brown uniforms descending on them.

One landed on Kinety's back, taking her down.

Rixton was on him in a flurry of violent punches. The alien released her to fight, and Rixton shot him. Roughly, he jerked Kinety to her feet and tried again to get to the next transport ship. To their left, there was a flash and the first transport ship exploded, knocking everyone airborne.

Rixton and Kinety toppled together and slid to a stop just as three more brownies reached them, each trying to get to Kinety. With a shout, Rixton grabbed the head of the first one, swinging himself up and around, kicked the second in the head, snapping the first one's neck as he landed, twisted, and shot the third.

Kinety blinked at her brother. "Oh, my God! You're a badass!" she marveled.

Rixton hauled her into a run, uninterested in compliments. "They're taking out the transports," he said, shoving her toward the canisters. "Hurry!"

Kinety didn't have to be told twice. Moving faster than before, she ran through, opening and knocking the canisters down. At the entrance, her helpers appeared, giving the escapees rapid instructions. Outside, human soldiers joined the fight, firing their blasters at anyone in brown, guarding the men and women coming off the last transport. As the transporter emptied, the wounded mothership, sitting cockeyed on the ground, primed her weapon and turned it toward the soldiers fleeing from the craft.

Rixton and Kinety whirled at the sound and ran to the clear panel above the flight controls.

"Block her!" Rixton shouted, pointing Kinety toward the pilot station.

She landed on the power screen, slapping as she fell, and powered the empty ship. At a run, Rixton crashed into the weapon system and was shooting before the gun was pointed. "Go left!"

Kinety, unfamiliar with the transport's flight system, jerked the vehicle forward.

"That's not left!"

"The controls are backward," she argued, scraping the hull loudly across the ground and placing the transport between the mother ship and her men.

Shouting, Rixton fired, trying to take out the large cannon, barely visible through the haze.

Overhead in the sky, Torak roared up into a barrel roll, firing as he came down. As he dove, his deep voice crackled from the transport panel, startling Kinety. "Get out! Get out!"

The smoke thinned around the mother ship just long enough for Rixton to spot a second cannon, already primed, turning toward them. Cursing vehemently, he charged at Kinety. "Run!" he shouted, grabbing her shirt and a handful of hair as he passed.

They jumped.

The transport exploded before they hit the ground, launching them both.

Rixton hit hard, and Kinety rolled over him.

Instantly, bootstomps sounded through the haze and guttural voices shouted, "Get her!"

Torak's star-fighter whirled on the wounded Saphiridian mother ship and launched a massive blue pulse at the bitch. The front of the vessel caved, crushing a cannon, and several fighters tumbled from the sky.

Breathless, Kinety flinched, ducking the debris, and saw the foot-soldiers coming. Frantically, she searched for her blaster, but it was gone. "Rixton, they're coming," she wheezed, climbing to her feet to run, but Rixton wasn't getting up. "Rixton!"

Rixton blinked glazed eyes at her. "Go," he whispered, trying to push her.

The next wave of Saphiridians was almost there.

Kinety snatched the Borzoikan projectiles from her pocket and put a knee down. One at a time, she fired the ugly things, killing one soldier and knocking another back. Empty-handed again, she took her brother by the collar and yanked. Dragging him with her, she backed toward her men. "Marco!" she cried in panic.

Arnie's voice cut through the fog. "Polo!"

"Marco!"

"Polo!"

"Marco!"

Arnie came in firing and pulled her down.

"Rixton's hurt!"

Arnie gave him a quick check. "He's okay. They just rang his bell," he said, heaving Rixton over his shoulder and handing his blaster to her. "Cover us," he said, climbing to his feet. "Let's go."

Before Kinety could fire off a shot, her own soldiers rushed past them, firing, holding the advancing Saphiridians back.

Overhead, Torak's blue energy pulsed again, knocking more fighters down and throwing Saphiridian soldiers backward to their deaths. In a sea of white suits, Zahrá Che soldiers on foot joined the Earthlings. Deek eased his ship above them, weapons forward. In a wave, the other Zahrá Che ships joined them and spread out in formation, ready to launch again.

The Saphiridians called a retreat.

In unison, the brownies on foot, all receiving the same order, lowered their weapons and began backing up. The Earthlings and Zahrá Che held their fire, allowing them to return to the large ship. Moments later, the mother ship whined loudly, lifting its wounded bulk off the ground. The remaining space fighters darted inside, and the Saphiridian fleet limped away.

*****

Torak remained where he was until the Saphiridian vehicle was gone. Then, furious, he thudded his boots onto the ground and whirled, his electric eyes flashing in raw anger. "Kinety!" he roared.

Terrified Zahrá Che soldiers scattered.

Kinety stumbled to her feet, breathing heavily as she passed her men, and headed for him.

When he saw her, Torak stomped across the vast field, screaming in anger. "Are you serious! You've lost your dammit mind," he shouted, using the foulest words he could find from her language. "You can't put a transport against a fucking cannon," he raged with a point. "You're gonna get yourself killed, and I'll have to ..."

The Zahrá Che watched in wide-eyed silence, certain he was about to kill her.

Kinety didn't care. She just wanted his arms around her. Unintimidated, she crossed to him, not at all bothered by his temper.

Torak snatched her up, earning a collective gasp from the small aliens, and hooked his arms around her back in a full-body hug. "Don't you *ever* do that again," he gritted through his teeth.

The Zahrá Che looked at each other.

Kinety placed her hands on the sides of Torak's handsome face. "Tooji," she whispered, smiling. "I love you."

Completely diffused, Torak slid his hand behind her head, frowning down at her filthy face, and pucker-kissed her as angrily as he could. "Dammit, woman! You scared me."

Kinety laughed at him.

When Torak raised his head, Emperor Dinruk was standing twenty feet away. Breathing heavily, the warrior looked at the monarch. "Shit," he said, kissing her dirty head and closing his eyes in irritation.

Kinety stepped out of his arms and faced the emperor.

Torak and the emperor eyed each other awkwardly for several long moments before Kinety broke the silence. "Emperor Dinruk," she said, bowing her head respectfully, "meet my companion Torak."

Dinruk inclined his bulbous head, accepting the introduction. *"The pleasure, I am surprised to say, is mine."*

Torak gave a short nod. "Emperor."

"I'm here to pick up my men," Kinety said, curling her fingers around Torak's large hand.

"Then we have much to discuss. Please," the Zahrá Che leader gestured to the large building, *"gather your men inside where the air is sterile."*

Kinety waved to Arnie. "Bring 'em in!" she called and pulled Torak with her behind the emperor.

The building was a hangar, easily large enough to house several gliders.

Inside the large hall, the wounded were tended to, while the Zahrá Che aliens passed out blob. Torak and Kinety walked through the crowds of anxious men and women, searching for her brother. As she passed, scattered soldiers eager to get home flagged her down with questions and concerns. After nearly an hour of answering what she could and translating between the confused abductees and swarming aliens, Kinety found Rixton sitting against a wall, exhausted but alive. "Are you okay?"

Rixton wagged his head, negating a yes or no answer. "Arnie says they rang my bell, past tense. My ears are still ringing, though," he confirmed with a yank on his earlobe.

"You scared me."

"I scared me," he agreed.

Kinety kicked his foot. "You're still a badass. That fight was awesome."

Arnie perked up. "What fight?"

"Rixton can tell you all about it," she said to Arnie, then lowered her voice. "The soldiers are all asking what the hell we're doing here, but now is not a good time to explain—not while we're with the Zahrá Che. I've been stalling about the details, saying Torak and I are meeting with the emperor, but that's not the real reason why. If they find out—"

Arnie gave her a push, catching on. "They won't, not yet," he promised. "Go—talk to the emperor. Get us out of here. I want to go home too."

Kinety slapped Arnie's hand and gave him a fist bump, then squeezed Rixton's knee. Satisfied, she signaled to Torak, who was *not* enjoying himself, that she was ready to see the emperor.

Torak scowled. "For as long as I can remember, the Zahrá Che have been my enemy," he confided, watching the little aliens mingle with the soldiers. "It feels awkward sitting among them now, expecting to share food and chat like old friends. They're conniving and manipulative, and I don't want to be here."

Kinety brushed wild curls from his eyes. "We're not here to make friends. We talk with the emperor, get him to release my men, and we go."

"I can take your men without his permission."

"We negotiate, Tooji," she insisted. "It's long overdue."

Torak kissed her fingertips just as an alien approached. He stiffened, irritated by the interruption.

"Hello, Zodoo," Kinety said, giving Torak a stern look to behave himself.

"Greetings," the creature thought back politely and handed them some blob.

Torak refused the food, but Kinety accepted it graciously.

If Zodoo was offended, he didn't show it. Instead, he extended his skinny arm. *"Torak and his bride are welcome to clean up before meeting with His Excellency. If you please, you may follow me."*

Kinety's eyes lit up at the thought of a shower.

Torak stood, gesturing her forward. He didn't want a Zahrá Che shower; however, he was indescribably filthy after his Neontak vacation. Reluctantly, he escorted her to a water room and swallowed his pride. Fifteen minutes later, clean and wearing wet hair, they were brought to the emperor. Deek stood beside the leader, his face stoic, his posture rigid.

Kinety squealed when she saw him. "Deek!" she beamed. "You are such a little badass!"

The emperor looked at his pilot, surprised by the blunt compliment.

Deek's little eyes flicked her direction and then forward again in embarrassment. Other than a sharp pinking of his head, he gave no response.

Emperor Dinruk, however, appeared pleased. *"There was concern that Deek had met the same fate as Jael. It was a relief to find him alive and well. In fact, Deek has shared the details of his unfortunate experience at the hands of the Saphiridians, their organized deception, as well as your courteous treatment of him upon finding him alive. My thanks, Savage Bride."*

Kinety held up her hand. "It's … just Kinety."

He gave her a regal wave, assuring that her complaint had fallen on deaf ears.

Kinety gave up. "I think very highly of Deek. He is a complement to your fleet and to your race."

The emperor accepted the compliment graciously and faced Torak. *"Deek also describes a side of you—the Kek side—that I greatly hope to become acquainted with."*

Kinety blinked at Deek. "You knew?"

Torak, who was ready to go, glanced down at her. "He's telepathic," he reminded her in a tone suggesting he'd had enough of the small talk.

Realizing her time was short, Kinety got to business. "Emperor Dinruk," she said, adjusting her tone to diplomacy, "you and I made an agreement before, which I believe now has been satisfied. In exchange for pleading your case to Torak, you generously offered to release custody of my men to me. Are we still in agreement?"

Emperor Dinruk acknowledged her question. *"We are, but before that, I hope to understand better who I am dealing with. The description Deek has provided of Torak does not match the Torak my people believe they know. You don't trust me,"* he said outright to the assassin, *"and I don't trust you. Yet, I wonder how much of our uncertainties are based on misinformation, propaganda, and outright lies."*

"I have no reason to lie," Torak said a bit sharply.

"Indeed," the emperor said and chose his next move carefully. *"Then, perhaps you would put to rest a matter that has caused me great anguish, Torak."*

A bit impatiently, Torak waited.

The emperor held the destroyer's gaze with a hard one of his own. *"Did you kill all those people in the video?"*

Torak hesitated, reigning in his annoyance. "You only received part of the story," he said in a flat tone.

"Did you kill them?"

Torak was slow to answer but didn't look away. After a moment, he inclined his head. "I did."

"Why?"

"If Your Highness is truly interested in knowing why, I recommend retrieving and viewing the actual, unedited footage … with audio. The original is in the Jag Mosrog Redaction Archives in a file titled R4W 53RV3R," Torak answered, refusing to defend himself. "Your experts should have no trouble recovering this."

The emperor lowered his gaze, appreciating the suggestion. *"I will,"* he assured, gesturing toward a random soldier to begin the task immediately, then returned his attention to his guests. *"Considering the incredible deception toward you by your own people, I intend to launch a full investigation of other incidents involving you as well. In the future, Torak, please know this: The Zahrá Che are not your enemies. In time, it is our hope that you will come to realize this and allow our past wrongs to move behind us. In the meantime, the Zahrá Che consider your companion Kinety to be an ally and a friend,"* he said, turning to her. *"Regarding our agreement, you kept your word, Kinety, and I will keep mine. I hereby release all remaining Earthling soldiers into your custody and humbly beg your pardon for the illegal manner in which we obtained them and the unethical use thereafter."*

"Thank you." Kinety wanted to whoop and clack her heels but controlled her emotion and spoke in a steady voice. "I am without a vessel and would like to borrow the transporter and Deek to take them home. Without the canisters, my men should all fit in the one still remaining."

The emperor waved imperial fingers. *"They won't fit."*

"I have just under three hundred soldiers. It would be tight, but—"

"There are seven hundred more at a different base, still deactivated," he corrected.

Kinety glanced at Torak.

"I will transport them all for you, but only within this galaxy quadrant," the emperor offered. *"Unfortunately, I no longer have the resources nor the time to return that many to your star system. Pod transports would take too long, at least eight of your days. Gliders can reach Earth within hours via smaller wormholes, but we can't spare the vessels or the time it would take, which would equal about the same. Our sun has become unstable, our hour desperate. We must leave our planet now."*

Torak squeezed her hand, signaling it was time to go. "Send the Earthlings to Neontak, Highness," he said, angling to leave. "I'll get them home and close the portal."

Emperor Dinruk stood. *"Thank you, Torak, for coming. It was a pleasure to finally meet you. I will find the footage."*

Unsure how to respond, Torak gave the emperor an awkward nod and practically ran Kinety out.

Chapter 21

A formation of silver transport ships loaded full of human soldiers, most still sleeping in their canisters, traveled toward Gimeg Plateau on planet Zahrá Che. Deek led the pack, carrying Kinety, Rixton, Arnie, Park, Zhang, Shiva, and Torak. Real-time monitoring screens were activated to connect the long convoy, allowing Kinety and Arnie to communicate freely with the awake soldiers in the transports behind them.

With days left to travel, the team had no choice but to amuse themselves. While Deek taught Park to properly pilot a ship, Zhang practiced his English and monitored the weapons systems for security.

In the back, the activities were much more interesting. The team was working on self-defense again, but this time with a twist. Torak used the onboard computer to pull up images of different alien species, then systematically noted the associated threats and weaknesses. As each was explained, he instructed Arnie, Rixton, and Kinety in fighting techniques against them, concentrating on death strikes. Shiva watched, laughing in amusement, but was more interested in studying the aliens than fighting them.

When the fighters were ready, Torak would morph himself into the creature described and allow his students to attack him using weapons he'd retrieved from his star-fighter, which was compressed again into the ring around his finger.

Rixton launched hard at Arnie. "Do you have family, Torak?"

"No. Yes. A wife."

"Friends?"

Torak chuckled. "No."

Kinety, who had pulled her hair into a sweaty ponytail and knotted her clothes behind her back, raised her telescoping stick. She didn't remember the names of the bizarre creatures but was retaining the technique to fight each one. This time, Torak resembled a dinosaur with a scrambled face. With a war cry, she attacked, striking the creature on his neck to stun him, then spun in for the kill. Beside them, Arnie went through the same motions, using Rixton as his target.

The Torak monster caught Kinety's stick and tugged her into his arms. "Your strike was too high," he murmured and placed his teeth over her neck. "You're dead."

Rixton ducked a strike from Arnie and spun behind him. "Weren't there any Saphiridians you liked to spend time with?"

"Between missions?" Torak specified, catching Kinety again and biting her throat. "Your stun strike was too slow. Strike fast, kill quick. And no resting. When you rest, you die."

Kinety leapt back, red-faced and panting.

Arnie yanked Rixton over his shoulder and dropped him on the floor at his feet. "So you never went drinking with the boys?" he grunted, bracing to start again.

"Drinking what?

"I mean … played games? Sparred with friends?"

"No. I'm an assassin. I kill people. I don't make friends with them." Torak wrapped Kinety with his tail and yanked her backward against him. "That was better, but you forgot about my tail. You're dead."

With a snarl, she roared in anger and attacked again.

"Do you enjoy killing?" came another grunted question.

"No." Torak grabbed Kinety, but this time before he could bite her, she placed the tip of her knife against his throat. He caught her hand and set the blade a bit lower. "Too high and you'll simply open a second breathing hole. It may kill him, but not before he tears your throat out. See this indention?" he said, indicating the spot he meant. "Tip goes there, slice straight across. Again. Different species."

Kinety stumbled back, grimacing in fatigue. "Why did you kill all those people in the video?" she panted.

Torak shifted into an unfriendly-looking insectoid. "It was a setup," he said, reminding Kinety of her targets and motioning her into an attack. "The video only told part of the story, that I slaughtered innocents, but their fate was not my doing."

Kinety attacked. "There was green stuff on their skin," she wheezed, struggling to keep her weapon away from his six claws.

"You saw that?" Torak asked, catching it anyway and snatching it from her. With the whip of a poisonous tail, he caught her, yanked her in, and pierced her with his stinger. "Most people can't see it. You're dead."

Kinety stumbled back. "Why can I?"

Torak wagged his antennae, beckoning her forward. "Because I can," he said, disarming her. In a blur, the stick landed at the base of her neck. He yanked her in and clicked his mandible around her throat. "Watch out for the antennae. You're dead."

Kinety shrieked in disgust and shimmied away from his insectoid appendages with a shudder.

Torak demonstrated the strikes on her, then handed the stick back. "The Zahrá Che set up a meeting to hold negotiations. When I arrived, everyone in that room was contaminated with a neurotoxin, one of the few toxins the Zahrá Che are susceptible to. It kills all but their survival instinct," he said, signaling for her to attack. "I always believed the Zahrá Che poisoned their own people. Now … I don't know. I guess the Saphiridians must have stolen samples of the neurotoxin from a Zahrá Che lab and used it for the setup."

"Like zombies?" Rixton asked.

"Zombies?"

"Walking dead. Rotting people that kill and eat until they disintegrate."

Kinety spun the stick, striking each vulnerable target.

Torak blocked the strikes. "Yes," he said, catching the last one and yanking her forward. He messed up her hair with his antennae. "You're dead. Faster."

Kinety roared in anger, spun her weapon, and engaged again.

Arnie mimicked the fight against Rixton.

Torak caught and reversed each strike so she could complete the pattern. "That part was edited from the public images. It's a slow, painful death and violent when it kicks in. I was brought there to be exposed—faster and hit higher on the third strike—and walked into a trap. There were cameras everywhere."

Torak caught the stick on the kill strike. "Same thing, but do it moving forward. Back me up," he said, tossing it back to her.

"I'm tired," she complained.

"That's when the fight matters. Attack me," he said, clacking his mandibles at her. "The contaminated people saw me and panicked," he shoved Kinety back, restarting the attack, "and, right away, the neurotoxin kicked in. They had seizures and convulsed. Made for excellent footage—strike harder. Push me backward. Again."

"Why didn't you expose them?" Rixton asked, growing winded from defending himself against Arnie's strikes. "Even dead, there would have been evidence."

"I was accused of that part too. Harder," Torak said, knocking Kinety's stick away and spinning so they faced the opposite direction. "The population saw the edited slaughter with their own eyes and believed it. The universe needed an enemy, and I was chosen," he said, then caught the stick and disarmed her. "Same thing. Use the impaler."

Kinety, sweaty and purple-faced, lurched forward with the blade tucked safely inside its sheath.

"I walked into another trap soon after that. Similar scenario," he caught Kinety by the wrist, yanked her in, and clamped his mandible around her throat, "similar result. Different species—silence your breathing. After that, I was finished with negotiations. This scenario wasn't the last. The Zahrá Che were cruel in their desperation, or so I thought. At the time, I honestly believed they tricked the Saphiridians into war. Now, I don't know who did what."

"It looked like you attacked them," panted Arnie.

265

Torak caught Kinety and grappled with her. "That was the point. The Zahrá Che goaded and antagonized the Saphiridians until they became the victims. Claiming self-defense, the Zahrá Che began a series of bio-attacks," he brought Kinety to the floor and made her fight on her back, "which decimated the Saphiridians. They were winning with the viruses and almost got Neontak until I summoned the Gaki. It was a horrible retaliation but effective," he said, piercing Kinety in the side with his stinger. "They couldn't fight the beasts. Defending their own world took all their resources, redirecting their attention away from the war. Everything they had was put on that portal and, still, the Gaki got through, so the Zahrá Che began stealing soldiers stronger than themselves to help thin the swarms. Kinety's men," he clarified. "It wasn't fair, but they were out of options."

Kinety hooked a leg around his from the floor and heaved him backward to the ground. In a flash, she was on him. From this new position, Torak quickly pointed out his vulnerable areas for her to attack, then promptly began defending them.

"Sounds like you're both assholes," said Arnie from his back on the floor.

"Both sides have much blood on their hands," Torak said, ruffling Kinety's hair with a claw she'd missed. "You're dead."

Arnie flipped Rixton. "So, because of those videos, you were branded as an assassin? The Saphiridian's celebrated killer, the Zahrá Che's worst nightmare."

Torak tickled Kinety's side with another free claw. "Not celebrated," he corrected, rolling her to her back. "I was always an assassin, known throughout the galaxy. The video just made a monster out of me. Even with my own people, I see … saw … fear in their eyes when they looked at me. Mistrust. Repulsion. I guess, eventually, I became the monster they'd created. It's what I was designed to do. That's *why* I was born. I was a tool to them," he said, finally receiving a death blow. He fell sideways and lay there pensively for a moment. "I always knew it, but I didn't realize the depth of manipulation. I don't know who my enemies are anymore."

Kinety put her knife to his throat again. "Me," she wheezed.

Torak stopped fighting.

"You look disgusting," she grimaced.

He shifted back to himself. "Do not engage an insect, wife. Have Arnie shoot it," he warned helpfully, then pulled her to her feet. "Next species."

Torak shifted to Zahrá Che and pointed a blaster at her.

Kinety spun a kick, knocking him easily into a wall. "So, what now?"

Torak stood, holding his hand out, and energetically lifted the exhausted Kinety from the ground, demonstrating the Zahrá Che antigravity technique.

She yelped and flapped her arms.

"My face is the most hated in the galaxy, and you're married to it —stop struggling and roll sideways until you fall. It shifts the balance," he coached, teaching her how to get out of Zahrá Che levitation. "Now that they know we're together, they'll still come after you, but the tactics will change. I can't trust anyone anymore."

When Kinety hit the floor, Torak levitated her up again. "Everyone is a threat—especially the Saphiridians."

"What will they do?" asked Arnie.

Torak stopped and inhaled a deep breath before answering. "Try to kill her or badly harm her. If they can't make the Zahrá Che look guilty, I imagine they'll make it look like I did it."

Arnie paused. "Why?"

"Because then I would truly have nowhere to go," he answered, lifting Arnie with his other hand. "Harming a companion is unforgivable. It means one cannot be trusted even by his own."

Arnie rolled out of the anti-gravitational hold and landed beside Kinety, who clearly was finished with the lesson. "I wish that was the understanding on Earth. That was easy," he bragged. "So, it's all about outsmarting the Zahrá Che, right?"

Torak faced him as Kinety slumped into a hover-chair. "Exactly," he smiled, tossing Rixton a weapon and morphing into a tall thin spider-looking creature. "Tutorial's over, gentlemen. Let's see how you do against a few random species. Both of you … attack me."

*****

Worn out from her lesson, Kinety sat at the computer panel staring at Neontak. It wasn't too close to Saphiridia. Why couldn't the Zahrá Che have it? In frustration, she rubbed her eyes, dragged her hands down her face, then replaced them on the panel. With no warning, warm hands slid over the backs of hers.

Kinety leaned her head backward against Torak.

"They can't have it," a whisper told her ear, "because it *is* too close to Saphiridia. The two races don't get along well enough to share a system."

A warm shiver danced through Kinety's body at the sound of his voice, deep and intimate and meant only for her. Closing her eyes, she snuggled into him, enjoying the sensation of his nearness.

A faint spark of blue danced over their hands.

"I can feel that."

"Take it," he whispered.

"How?"

"Your fingertips. Draw in through your left hand, gather it in the middle, discharge through your right."

Kinety felt the charge tingle over her hand. With a frown, she concentrated on drawing the energy in. Holding it wasn't as easy. Before she could lose it, she pushed it out her right hand. A very tiny blue light sparked against his waiting hand.

Torak laughed, but Kinety was proud.

"Practice holding it," he warned. "It's powerful stuff. It allows you to do amazing things, but the opposite is true as well. If you discharge incorrectly, you'll fry electronics or could kill someone. Be careful."

Kinety nodded and relaxed toward him. "I will."

His long fingers interlaced gently with hers, and he crossed her arms in front, hugging her from the back. "I'm sorry about Kek," he said, nuzzling her ear.

Kinety could just see his lips. "Will you always do that?" she asked, closing her eyes and leaning into him. "Become someone else?"

"If it serves my purpose, yes."

"How do I know what you really look like?"

The lips smiled.

Kinety drew away slightly. "You aren't really an insect, are you?" she asked with a dry grimace.

Torak's laugh was contagious. "I can be—if you like antennae," he teased and clicked his tongue.

Kinety let out a squeal of laughter and cringed from him. "No. I don't!"

"This is me."

"Good."

"You approve?"

"I do.

He smelled her hair. "You're clean."

"I showered."

"I'm getting you dirty," he said, releasing her hands and backing away.

Kinety turned her head to look at him, sweat-soaked and messy. "I don't mind," she said, but it was too late. He'd backed off. "Are your days different from mine?" she asked, changing the topic.

"I don't sleep as much as you do, but I'm not designed to," he said with a quick smile. "I can usually recharge without losing consciousness."

"How old are you?"

Torak hesitated thoughtfully at the strange question, then pulled the map forward until he reached Earth. There, he selected the planet's information chart. He stared at it for a full minute, calculating the numbers in his head. "I am almost eighty of your Earth years—seventy-nine years, five months, and four of your days. Do you want hours?"

Kinety lifted her brows, impressed by his IQ, and shook her head to decline the offer. "Seventy-nine! I'm ... twenty-three," she muttered, even though he hadn't asked. "Rixton's almost twenty-six."

Torak wasn't sure what to do with this information. "Why are you counting?"

She paused, caught off-guard by the question. "We just keep track."

"Is there a reason?"

Having to explain this made her feel a bit weird, but she gave it a whirl. "Humans ... concentrate on different things depending on their age. When we're young, we learn. As adults, we get married and have kids. After we mature, we teach our young. Then, we get old and die," she said with a celebratory chuckle. "Are you not aging?"

"I assume I am." Torak's eyes went wide. "Which phase of life are you in?"

"The adult phase."

They grew wider. "Oh."

Just then, Rixton walked in. "What are you two doing?"

Torak straightened, slightly red in the cheeks, and wiped his palms on his thighs. "We-we-we're discussing reproduction."

Rixton blinked at his sister.

"She's in her reproductive phase now, but I'm a bit caught off-guard. I've never trained to reproduce," Torak said, giving his head an awkward scratch. "Wait ... where would we do this?" he asked, looking around for someplace appropriate. "Copulation? I've read about that."

Kinety's mouth popped open in surprise, floored by the misunderstanding.

Torak faced Rixton abruptly. "Can you train me?"

Rixton did a fish-out-of-water thing with his mouth. "You want me to teach you to have sex?" he sputtered. "With my sister! Hell, no!"

Arnie walked in.

Torak spun to face him. "Will you train me to have sex? Rixton won't do it."

Arnie walked out.

Kinety started laughing. "I told him my age," she explained to a horrified Rixton, then gestured in amusement at Torak. "He's jumping to conclusions."

"No! I know what it is. I've seen animals do it," Torak assured anxiously. "I can figure it out."

Rixton spread his hand. "How do the other aliens breed?" he asked, thinking this was an obvious question.

"The Zahrá Che cloned themselves out of the breeding process. Dragonians use internal fertilization and lay eggs, mostly. The Trychul insectoids lay eggs and use external fertilization. Some species pollinate. I'm not equipped for that."

Rixton had to process this. "The Saphiridians are half-human. If they're not cloning, they're copulating, right?"

Torak didn't have a clue. "I am not Saphiridian. Interracial breeding, especially with a chimera, is forbidden to protect the bloodline. Wait. Are you not concerned about this?" he asked Kinety.

Kinety frowned at him, no longer amused. "Should I be?"

Torak cocked his head at her in amusement, baffled she was unaware of this common knowledge. "Well, yeah. I have mixed blood."

"So?"

"So, I'm a motley. You're an Earthling. I'll ruin your bloodline."

Kinety stood, scowling, and set her hands on her hips. "Is this the crap they've been telling you?" she asked angrily. "That your blood is dirty?"

Torak blinked at Rixton, not quite sure how to answer.

"I'm really beginning to not like the Saphiridians," she grumbled, then faced Rixton. As hard as she tried, she was unable to hide her irritation. "I was just telling him how old I am," she said in exasperation. "I wasn't talking about reproducing. Apparently, he stopped aging. He's in his eighties. Excuse me."

Torak watched her leave. "I said something wrong."

*****

Shiva called back. "Eight hours to the wormhole. I'm taking a nap," she said, then tried to convey that to Zhang. "Chóngdòng, bā xiâoshí," she said in horrid, broken Chinese.

Zhang laughed at her disgraceful attempt, corrected her, then summoned his own bunk for a nap. "Sheeba Chinese terribre. Rearn more tark tomorrow, prease."

The other occupants moved to the back room and, soon, it was lights out.

Sometime later, a strong arm snaked around Kinety from behind, waking her. She rolled sleepily onto her back and peered into Torak's handsome face, just visible in the pale blue light coming from the computer panel above them. "You smell like Kek."

He made a sound. "I can't get the flower oil off."

Kinety yawned. "What are you doing here?" she asked quietly.

"You were all the way across the ship," he said, propping on an elbow, "and I didn't like it."

Kinety laughed softly. "You're silly," she said, brushing a curl from his eye and knocking it into the other one. "What could the big strong Torak possibly be afraid of?"

"Besides your piloting skills? Many things lately."

"Like what?"

Long fingers trailed along the side of her face. "That I'll mess this up."

"Mess what up?"

"You."

"Me?" she asked, adjusting the thin suit-bed beneath her head. "How would you do that?"

"I don't know," he said awkwardly. "I'm a destroyer. I destroy things. It makes me worry."

Kinety slid her hand down his arm until she reached his fingers and kissed them. "You'd have to work pretty hard to run me off," she said, curling her hand around his.

"Why do you not fear me?"

"Should I?"

"Everyone else does. There's enough video footage of my sins that nobody in this universe will ever look at me like you did—like you do. Something is wrong with you."

Kinety pushed her fingers into his unruly hair and attempted in vain to brush it back. "It makes my heart hurt that you believe their nonsense. They've treated you like a monster and told you horrible, ugly things about yourself, but they aren't true. You aren't a monster, Tooji. If they refuse to see you as anything else and choose to cast you aside, then it's their loss. They don't deserve you. Let them fight their own battles."

Torak ran his hand over his jaw. "I'm gonna mess this up," he said more to himself than her.

"What if you don't?" she asked.

He braved a peek through his pained expression. "What do you mean?"

"I was kinda hoping you'd keep me," she said.

Torak chortled and leaned over her. "I'll keep you," he said, lowering hesitant lips.

Kinety slid her arm around him and eased him closer. "This is long overdue," she said, pressing her lips lightly against his, barely touching them. Once, twice, three times, she teased him in an open-mouth feather kiss, then changed her angle.

Torak's heart sang with delight. "Oh, I'm liking this," he whispered, moving in for a better position.

271

Enjoying herself immensely, Kinety touched her tongue lightly to his. He paused in surprise, unused to such intimacy, and came back for more.

Gripping her hip, Torak deepened the kiss. Unfamiliar feelings swirled in his belly, making him want to experience more and, before long, the two were getting steamy.

Kinety was just reaching for his hand to get it involved when, out of nowhere, her horrible, awful, terrible brother stood sleepily from his bunk, grabbed her by the ankle, and *yanked* her away from Torak. Grumbling incoherently, he dropped onto the floor beside her and tossed his arm over her, ending the romantic tryst.

Torak rolled onto his back, his quiet breaths coming in heavy lungfuls, and stared at the dark ceiling with wide eyes.

Smiling, Kinety stretched her arm across Rixton's waist and took Torak's hand. Close to purring, she interlaced her slender fingers through his, snuggled into her makeshift bed, and went to sleep beside her brother.

*****

The next day, Kinety clapped her hands together optimistically and scanned the room. "Two hours to the next point, and we have nothing to do. We should play. Anyone got any ideas?"

Arnie sniffed and gave a macho scowl. "Men don't play."

"They do when they're told to," Kinety corrected and pointed at the floor. "What games do you know?"

"Dominoes. Cards. Board games," he offered, finding a spot to sit. "Shiva, wanna play?"

"I can't. I'm flying the spaceship," she called from the flight deck.

Rixton lounged against a wall. "We could play charades," he suggested, "or we can make music."

Kinety's green eyes lit up. "Ooh! That would be fun," she said and got down, forming a ring with the others.

"What is this?" asked Torak.

"Games," she smiled and tapped the floor beside her. "To pass the time."

Torak was completely confused. "Why?"

"Because it's fun!"

Rixton kicked the side of Torak's boot. "Have you never played before?"

"No."

"What did you do between missions?" Rixton asked and pointed to a spot beside Kinety.

Torak gave it some thought. "Studied the enemy. Weapons systems. Fighting techniques," he said, sitting awkwardly down. "Weapons maintenance. Evasive maneuvers."

Kinety scowled, then realized Deek wasn't with them. She caught the alien's eye and tapped the vacant spot on her other side. "That's it? Weren't you ever lonely?"

Torak shrugged, then gave a slight nod. "A bit, I guess. I asked my creator Glarnt for a companion once. It was a long time ago."

Deek approached hesitantly, then sat down.

"What did he say?"

"He … laughed," Torak admitted with some embarrassment.

Scowls passed between the others.

"But I was serious," Torak continued. "Finally, he agreed and began collecting DNA to create a female for me—non-reproducible, of course."

"Where is she?" asked Rixton.

"Before he had all the DNA he needed, Glarnt was killed," he said and gestured to Deek. "The Zahrá Che blew up the lab with him inside. He'd made me look human to ensure that nobody in this galaxy would be interested, so building from scratch was the only way to get one. Glarnt was the only one who knew how. I've been alone ever since."

Deek's big eyes shifted to the assassin and back. *"It was not Zahrá Che,"* he said flatly.

Torak glared at him. "It *was* them. You killed the only person who ever cared about me," he said, breeching the tender subject. "The only family I ever had."

Deek shook his head.

"You lie!" snapped Torak.

Rixton, stuck on the other side of the language barrier, looked back and forth between the two.

Deek turned his head just enough to give Torak a heated glance. *"The Zahrá Che emperor supports a companion for the assassin Torak. You are too focused on war. Your psychological profile suggests a severe imbalance without a counterpart. Many times, you have demonstrated this to be true. No harm would come to your companion or creator through Zahrá Che."*

Torak's disbelief was evident in his features. "Liar! You killed Glarnt!"

"No! We didn't!" argued Deek. *"You should question the Saphiridians."*

Torak reigned in his natural instinct to defend the Saphiridians and, unable to argue, stared hard at the alien instead.

Deek withdrew his posture slightly but continued. Blatantly, he no longer looked at the assassin. *"Zahrá Che have strict orders to defend any companion of Torak. We didn't kill Glarnt. We will not harm Kinety."*

Torak was getting angry. "Why would they lie about that?"

Deek didn't answer.

"Why would they lie!" he demanded.

Deek drew away from Torak's temper but didn't leave the group. After another moment of silence, he answered carefully. *"Certain social structures have been prohibited from you to keep you easy to manipulate. Your focus is permitted to be on war and war only. Any attempt to broaden your focus or attract your attention results in immediate extermination of the distracter, regardless of race."*

Torak gaped at him in disbelief. "You've known this?"

Deek paused uncomfortably. *"This is common knowledge."*

Anger darkened the ring around Torak's electric irises, which snapped sharply from Deek to Kinety and back. His breathing increased. "Did you ... ," he began suspiciously, pointing at her.

Deek quickly denied any involvement in setting the two up.

"Do the other species know of this isolation campaign?" Torak wanted to know.

"Yes," answered Deek. *"Communication with you is strictly forbidden. You are heavily guarded for this reason. If it got out that you requested a companion, then I suspect this is why Glarnt was killed."*

Torak gaped at him, stunned.

Deek braved a peek at the assassin, then stared ahead at nothing.

Torak, however, struggled to wrap his mind around this new revelation and, yet, another betrayal. Visibly struggling to control his temper, he got up and left the room, separating himself from the others.

Quite uncomfortable now, Deek remained where he was, unmoving and avoiding all eye contact.

"I missed, like, half of that," Rixton mumbled.

Arnie explained Deek's side of the conversation in a nutshell, his voice low.

Rixton frowned, then gestured silently for Kinety to go after Torak and talk to him.

Before she did, Kinety reached and took Deek's hand, startling the little guy. When he glanced at her, she squeezed his abnormally long fingers in a friendly gesture and, then followed him out. She found Torak at the end of the hallway, peering out at the stars through a random window in the wall. How it had gotten there, she had no clue, but the view was magnificent. Gently, she slid her hands around his arms from behind. When he didn't acknowledge her, she lowered her hands and stepped slightly to his side so she could see out too.

"It's a hard blow learning you've been betrayed, but you already knew this. I know hearing it again hurts, but you discovered this on Neontak," she reminded softly.

"It's not just the betrayal," he said, speaking just above a whisper. "I feel like such a fool."

Kinety shook her head. "This was a well-orchestrated campaign. The way they spoke during that first attack on Zahrá Che, saying one thing over the radio while doing exactly the opposite—these people were well-trained in deception. One or two deceivers you might have caught, but when it's all of them working together as a well-oiled machine … that wasn't your fault."

He exhaled and turned away.

Kinety touched him again. "You're a good man, Tooji. They knew it. That's why they had to trick you."

"They took Glarnt from me. If they harm you … ," he warned in a breath.

Kinety slid her hand down his forearm, stopping him. "Those are dark thoughts, Tooji. Don't dwell in them," she said and took his hand. "Come on. Your friends are waiting."

Torak remained where he was. "Friends."

"Yes, friends," she said firmly. "You have a room full of them right in there."

Torak glanced toward Deek with a sour huff and looked out again.

This time, Kinety sharpened her tone, scolding him for his intolerance. "It took a lot of guts for Deek to say those things because he knew it would hurt you. He defended himself against false accusations without knowing how you would react and told you the truth because you have a right to know. He knew you wouldn't like hearing it. It's been a long time since someone has been honest with you. That's a friend."

Torak continued staring out.

"Arnie admires everything about you," she said, looking out at a distant star, "and wants to know all your techniques. He wants to be just as fearless and just as confident as you. He's even been sitting like you and standing the same way, even though he doesn't realize it. He'd be there in a moment if you ever needed him but would still tell you if you're being a butthead. That's a friend."

Torak huffed, this time with a hint of amusement. She was right. Arnie would.

So, Kinety went on. "Rixton knows how I feel about you. He accepts you just as you are, and he's beginning to see you as family. That's a brother. To Zhang, you're a respectable leader. To Park, a brilliant mentor."

Torak's gaze shifted in the glass to the reflection of her face. "And you?"

"Head over heels in love," she said.

Finally, he faced her. "Is that the truth?"

"Every word," she said, touching his curls.

Torak caught her hand and kissed the inside of her wrist.

"Come with me," she said, giving him another tug. "I'll show you how to play with friends."

When the two returned, Arnie and Rixton were on their feet sparring, and Deek was sitting quietly on his bunk. The two stopped, waiting to assess the mood, so Kinety smiled.

"We're going to make music," she said, reclaiming her spot on the floor and waving the others back down. Specifically, she motioned Deek to come sit by her.

Deek glanced uneasily at Torak, then joined the group sitting cross-legged and knee to knee.

"Park! Zhang! We're about to make music," called Arnie.

Park skidded into the room. "I can sing!"

Kinety divvied out sounds. "Arnie, you clap. Don't lose the beat," she said. "Rixton, rub your hands together. Torak, you say 'Bum' every other time Arnie claps. Zhang, you double-snap opposite Torak. Deek, you say 'Eeeee' aloud every four claps."

Deek demonstrated quietly and blushed.

"I'll hum and, Park, you sing a vocal. Ready? Go!"

Arnie clapped.

Rixton rubbed.

Torak bummed.

Zhang snapped.

Deek eeeeeed.

Kinety hummed.

And Park screeched like a wet cat.

*****

Long after the crew had retired to bed, Torak opened the water room door, still wet from his shower, and was about to step out when Kinety tiptoed past. He ducked back, wondering what she was doing, then peeked around the door. She was carrying food. Zhang was piloting, so he assumed at first that she was taking him something to eat, but she didn't head for the flight deck. Instead, she turned toward the perimeter hall and vanished inside.

Hesitantly, Torak followed her.

*

Kinety slowed as she entered the hall and softly cleared her throat.

Deek shifted his bulbous head ever so slightly but didn't acknowledge her. He was sitting before a transparent panel, his pink eyes peering out at the blackness of space.

Kinety gave his large head a tickle. "How you doing, little man?"

Deek spazzed and scratched the sensation off his head. *"Aaah! Don't touch me,"* he grumbled, scowling.

Amused, Kinety summoned a hover-stool and sat down beside him. "Wow," she marveled, scanning the universe. "Look at the view."

Deek gave her a dry look, then pointed at the window. *"I am,"* he told the idiot.

"It's beautiful, isn't it?"

His little eyes fixed on a distant star. *"Why are you bothering me, primitive hominid?"*

Kinety glanced at him, then pushed her hair to one side and leaned her shoulder against the clear wall. "Actually, I had some questions. Here," she said, handing him some food, "I brought you something to eat."

"Go away," he muttered, taking it.

"Answer my questions, and I'll leave you be."

"What questions?"

"What happened?" she asked, taking a bite of water-food.

The alien glared at her for being vague.

"Zahrá Che and the Saphiridians. Why the hatred? Where does it come from?"

"We made a mistake," Deek thought, watching a distant asteroid tumble slowly by.

"The Zahrá Che?"

He nodded irritably.

"You mean when you created the Saphiridians?"

"They were going to be our future," he said sourly. *"We spliced our DNA with humans and isolated what we believed would be positive attributes. We wanted strength where the Zahrá Che was weak, courage where the Zahrá Che was passive. But ... something went wrong."*

Kinety took another bite, waiting for him to continue. He didn't. "What went wrong?"

"Attached to those desirable attributes were greed, narcissism, and aggression. We isolated IQ, but when blended with high concentrations of the other characteristics, it became calculation and deceit. We were always sick and weak, so we increased their health. That became superiority. It seemed," his gaze shifted to a tiny star far in the distance, *"like such a good idea. They were to be all that we were not. Unfortunately, we succeeded in creating exactly that. Saphiridians evolved to favor their aggressive sides. What we failed to add was tolerance, decency, or honor in any capacity. They have no humility, no love, no satisfaction. In time,"* he thought softly, *"I think the Zahrá Che lost those things too."*

"Were things always that way?" she asked, crossing her ankles.

"It happened quickly," thought Deek. *"Like rebellious children, the early Saphiridians fought for their emancipation. They wanted*

to be their own people, not a hybrid. Being more evolved, the Zahrá Che felt that guidance would win them favor with the Saphiridians, but politically they refused to get along. It was not that they couldn't," he clarified. *"They just didn't want to. Fights broke out. This war is the bloody end of a long era of squabbling between our species. In everything, they would disagree simply to be contrary. Eventually, the Saphiridians wanted to eliminate their history altogether because the Zahrá Che, in their eyes, were weak. When our planet began to die, Saphiridians viewed it as their opportunity to rid the world of a subclass species that considered itself superior. Their goal is to ultimately annihilate anyone not worthy of their genetic standards—anyone they deem beneath them—which includes anyone not Saphiridian. The idea shows no signs of slowing down, either,"* he added, turning his attention to a cloud just visible orbiting a distant sun. *"Their recent behavior suggests they plan to expand into other solar systems."*

"What is that?" she asked, following his gaze.

Deek blinked at the stupid question. *"Icy planetesimals,"* he told the moron, then shook his head in disgust.

"Why can't you just move?" she argued. "Why ask their permission for anything?"

"The Zahrá Che used all available resources to create the Saphiridian. We considered them a legacy and our salvation, and no materials were spared. We terraformed a planet using our supplies until there was nothing of value left on our own planet. We tried to repair the damage, but our sun gave out, leaving us with nothing to save. Once our primary sun began to die, we searched the galaxy but couldn't find an unclaimed planet to terraform for ourselves."

"Why not look in another galaxy besides the Milky Way? Where is Andromeda?" she muttered, looking for it.

Deek's head sagged at her ignorance, and he shook it. After a patient sigh, he looked at her with a twisted, sidelong expression, unusual for his stoic species. *"We couldn't get to Andromeda if we wanted to. We can't leave our galaxy,"* he annunciated, impressed she lacked such common knowledge. *"Intergalactic space is too empty to cross. Doing so is rare."*

"Oh. So, we're all from the Milky Way?"

Deek tossed his skinny arms toward the window. *"Of course, we are, primitive sub-species! And we don't call it the Milky Way. That's a stupid name. Did you not receive basic space education?"*

"Not really. Our schools focus more on morality politics and underhanded social structures."

"Earthlings will not become a Class I civilization until you learn how to prioritize the things that matter and discard the things that don't. This is basic science."

Kinety laughed. "Humans are still bickering about whether or not aliens exist or we're alone in the universe."

"Alone?"

"I didn't know for sure, myself, until you arrived."

Deek banged on his temples and giggled aloud. *"It is so hard to talk to you,"* he complained in amusement.

The sound reminded her of a chirping cat.

Kinety puckered dimples into her cheeks, enjoying his meltdown. She'd never heard him express humor before. In fact, she'd believed he was incapable of it. Once again, she'd been wrong. "Speaking of other species, how is it that we meet all these creatures and visit all these planets, yet we're not affected by the diseases and germs there?"

Deek pointed to his bracelet, then looked at her like she was a moron … again.

"The armlet?" She touched hers.

"Yes, ignorant sub-human, the bracelet. All soldiers are vaccinated for immunity through the bracelet. It regulates blood gasses and provides gene-specific antibodies. Zahrá Che wear them as well," he said, raising his arm to display the sleek one on his own wrist.

It was so thin Kinety had never really noticed his before. "I didn't realize you wore one too."

Deek gripped his head in mock agony. *"You make my brain hurt,"* he informed her, then explained slowly. *"The Zahrá Che are structurally more susceptible, whereas the Saphiridians are more adaptable and can survive in numerous atmospheric combinations. Now that our sun is dying, Zahrá Che must wear breathers,"* he said, examining his. *"We invented the breathing technology as a temporary fix, but it's become ages—long enough that they have also now been programmed to auto-vaccinate as well."*

"That's why you wanted Neontak so bad."

"Neontak matches the Zahrá Che needs exactly. We asked. They said no. We tried to take it. That was all the excuse the Saphiridians needed. They intend to annihilate us, though they can offer no plausible reason for this."

"So, ultimately, the Zahrá Che created their own destruction?" she said, watching his reflection through the clear wall.

Deek leaned his shoulder against the wall, mimicking her relaxed posture, and folded his arms. *"Yes. The Saphiridians were not grateful for the things they were given. Rather, they had only animosity and disgust for the Zahrá Che compassion, which they considered a weakness. All we wanted was for them to thrive,"* he thought softly.

"What started this war?"

Deek finished the last of his water-food. *"After so long enduring their belligerent hostility, the Zahrá Che used bioweapons on the Saphiridians in an attempt to eliminate our mistake. The Saphiridians discovered this and responded with violent aggression."*

Kinety had heard that before and didn't respond.

"The Zahrá Che are not the most honorable species—we never claimed to be—but we created true monsters. We've paid dearly for that since."

Kinety sat up straight and stretched her arms on her knees. "Classic brain versus brawn," she chuckled, "with a xenophobic twist."

Deek considered the comparison, then nodded reluctantly.

"It's unfair, isn't it?"

He nodded again. *"The Saphiridians are a trash species."*

Their eyes met in the reflection.

"Isn't that the same reason you don't like Earthlings?" asked Kinety.

Deek's guilty focus shifted out into space, and his eyes froze into an unseeing stare. This time, he didn't answer.

Kinety lowered her lashes and got up. "I'm gonna turn in. Good night, Deek," she said, sending the hover-chair away.

*

Torak shifted himself invisible, letting her pass, then exhaled a heavy breath. He'd never heard the Saphiridian history from the Zahrá Che perspective before, and another pang of betrayal soured his stomach. Nothing he'd been told matched any of what Deek had said. Yet, Deek's telling explained many of the questions that had lingered unanswered in his mind throughout his life.

The amount and depth of the propaganda he'd been fed blew him away. Everything he'd ever believed was a lie. As puzzle pieces slammed together with thunderous clarity, he stared out at the icy planetesimals, staggering beneath the weight of the reality.

Chapter 22

The last of Kinety's men, nearly one thousand of them, crossed from Gimeg Plateau on Zahrá Che to Neontak and gathered in a group, well-guarded by the Neontak veterans. Kinety and Torak were the last to go.

Heavy-hearted, Kinety turned before crossing, brushing her hair into the breeze, and faced Deek. "I wish you and your people the best. May you experience peace and happiness," she said, giving his little hand a squeeze. "I hope you find a home quickly."

"Me too," he thought, taking his hand away and wiping it clean. Reluctantly and without making eye contact, he handed her a link to his communicator. *"Don't use that."*

"I wouldn't dream of it." Ready to go, Kinety turned to face Torak, who was waiting. Before stepping through, he turned her toward the portal, then pointed to a small stone on the ground just to the left of the opening.

Kinety followed his point.

"Get that."

Kinety picked it up. "It's a rock."

Torak put his hand on the small of her back. "Bring it with us," he said and guided her through. "It belongs in Neontak."

This time, when they stepped through, the portal darkened behind them.

On the other side, Torak turned her to face the darkened portal and pointed to a rock on the ground just to the left of the opening. "Pick that up," he said and waited. "It takes time for the wormhole to destabilize. When it does, the portal turns black."

Kinety retrieved the rock, very similar in size to the one she held in her other hand, and waited.

It turned black.

Torak gestured toward the dark portal. "That rock belongs in Zahrá Che. Toss it through."

Kinety examined the rock, then threw it across.

With a pop, the portal from Neontak to Zahrá Che collapsed.

"If that's how you close it, how do you open it?"

Torak surveyed the soldiers standing nearby in a tight crowd and took a deep breath. "Do you still have the rock I gave you on Earth?"

Kinety pulled it from her pocket. Oddly enough, it almost exactly resembled the Zahrá Che rock she'd just thrown and the Neontak rock she held in her hand. "Why did you collect this—on Earth, I mean?"

"To … open a Gaki portal," he muttered sheepishly. "You're sure this is it?"

She made a face at him, then glanced uneasily at the stone. "Yes."

"Positive?"

"That's it," she assured.

Torak motioned for her to stand out of the way, then gathered two handfuls of energy. It took several minutes to gather enough. Eventually, his hands crackled blue, and energy danced over him. As he absorbed, he held the two rocks, one in each hand, wide apart. Still collecting, he slammed the two small stones together, creating a deafening explosion, and backed up, leaving a swirling, ten-foot disturbance in the air at the position of the strike. It shimmered and waved like a thin layer of water standing vertically in the middle of nothing.

Wide-eyed, Kinety watched.

Torak held the two stones out. "Earth," he said, indicating the rock he'd given to her, then motioned to the other, "and Neontak."

Kinety was paying attention.

Very carefully, he placed the Earth stone on the ground just to the left of the opening and then took her hand. "If this is a meteorite, we're in for a nasty surprise. Ready?"

Kinety's heart pounded. With a broad smile, she clamped her fingers tight around his and bounced with excitement. "I am."

Clutching the rock, he stepped through, pulling her with him.

There was an unwet watery sensation that added resistance. On the other side, they both stepped out, right into the meadow where Torak had found the rock.

Kinety scanned the field and exhaled in high emotion. "This is where we met," she said, biting her lip.

Torak looked wistfully at the grove of trees, remembering that fateful night. "If this is where they belong, they can come home now," he whispered.

Kinety gave him a laughing sob. "It is."

With a gesture of his head, he led her back through.

Kinety found Arnie standing on the other side, waiting breathlessly for her to return. Through a blur of tears, she beamed at him. "Home," she pointed at the portal, "is that way."

Barely daring to believe her, he hurried through to see for himself. When he reemerged a few minutes later, he had his cell phone in his hand and tears in his own eyes. Struggling to speak, he stood in front of the portal and faced the dead-silent crowd of soldiers. "Troublemakers!"

All four stepped forward.

"You're escorting. I want two of you Earth-side and two in Neontak. Move 'em through. Move 'em fast. Don't let that bottleneck clog up."

"Yes, Sir!"

"Shiva!"

"Here, Sir!"

"Organize the crowd from the back. No stragglers. Nobody gets left behind."

"Yes, Sir!" she called back and was gone.

While the Troublemakers organized, Arnie called the rest of the soldiers to attention. "Colonel Nelson is waiting for us on the other side, girls and boys. Get through the portal and get out of the way. Move it! Let's go home," he shouted, stepping aside and gesturing them through. "Go. Go!"

As her soldiers filed into the portal, Kinety turned to Torak, almost giddy in her excitement. "Come on," she said, taking his hand and trying to pull him to the portal.

Torak watched some soldiers pass through and squeezed her fingers. "I can't."

Kinety blinked at him, certain she'd misunderstood. "What do you mean you can't? There's nothing left for you here."

Torak noted the mass of Earthlings still waiting to cross. He watched Shiva organizing the troops into two running lines as he spoke. "The Saphiridians are on their way. The gate has to be closed from the same side it opens from, so someone has to stay here and close it. I'll close it and meet you later."

"No!"

"If it isn't closed properly, the Gaki will invade your world … or worse—the Saphiridians. We can't risk—oof!"

A blinding beam of light struck them.

With a violent shove, Torak knocked Kinety airborne and bowed sharply. She sprawled hard and skidded to a stop. Stunned and breathless, she rolled to a hip, struggling to catch her breath.

Torak slammed hard to his knees, grimacing in pain.

"Tooji?"

Growling a cry, he folded forward, writhing. Struggling to breathe, he forced shaking hands together and pulled his ring free. "Go!" he grunted and slung it at her.

Kinety shook her head and tried to argue. A rumble shook the air. She looked up and watched the sky overhead darken as a massive Saphiridian fleet screamed toward them. In alarm, she hurried to the soldiers and waved them toward the portal. "Run!" she shouted, urging them faster and looking up at the invasion. "Move! Move! Move!"

"Three lines!" Shiva yelled. "Go!"

The soldiers picked up speed.

Kinety watched them for a moment, then spun back to Torak, blurry now through fresh tears. "I'm not leaving you."

"Protect that," he gasped, then panted with difficulty.

Kinety shook her head in horror. "Tooji, no. Use it to get away."

"They can't … get it!" he managed.

Another beam blazed beside her and zipped closer.

Kinety dodged it and picked the ring up. "Tooji!" she cried, reaching for him. "Tell me what to do!"

Shiva reached the portal. "Kinety!" she called, motioning for her.

Torak waved an unsteady arm, motioning her toward the portal, and collapsed to an elbow. He couldn't talk anymore.

A fat tear rolled down her cheek. "Tooji, please don't send me away," she managed.

Behind them, a troop transporter lowered toward the ground, preparing to unload its armed cargo.

Torak's elbow collapsed, dropping his face into the dirt. With the last of his strength, he grabbed a handful of dirt and threw it at her.

Saphiridian soldiers thundered over the ground, running for them.

Torak struggled to pick up the Earth rock. "Thr—," he managed over the cacophony of footsteps.

The Saphiridians charged, snarling.

Shiva grabbed her and yanked.

Kinety staggered backward through the portal, crying, and both women fell on the other side. Kinety grabbed the stone on the ground to the left. "I love you," she sobbed and threw it.

The portal darkened behind the rock, but there was no time to wait for it to destabilize.

A split second later, Torak's Earth rock sailed through and landed beside her leg. The portal slammed shut with a *Crack!* The shockwave sent Kinety and Shiva tumbling. Soldiers went flying, trees jolted sharply away, and a military truck rolled. Birds flapped their wings in panic as the dust swirled into the empty space.

The portal from Neontak to planet Earth was gone.

*****

Kinety pulled herself up, broken-hearted, and clung to the tree where she'd met her Tooji. As she stood, a deafening cheer went up. They'd made it. In disbelief, she watched the military swarm the sprawled soldiers and set up a perimeter. A camp came to life right where they were with medical teams and extraterrestrial experts flown in by helicopter. Seven hundred confused soldiers had no idea what the hell had just happened, but the rest knew and were eager to tell the story to anyone who would listen. The Neontak soldiers were easily differentiated by the puckered scars marring their necks and quickly separated from the masses. The Troublemakers, an elite team now, stood proudly together. They'd rescued twenty-one total and collected the effects of many of the deceased before being summoned back. Their reward was happening around them.

There were many fingers pointed at Kinety, but she didn't care. She wasn't in the mood to talk.

After a firm order from Arnie that she be left alone, Kinety separated herself from the noisy group and stood watching. Since she wouldn't join the others, guards moved in to block her from escaping, but she paid no attention to them. Her mind was elsewhere. Commanders and generals and VIPs from every relevant department eyed her from afar like sharks, waiting, watching, wondering, but Arnie was insistent. He had not been officially debriefed; therefore, his mission was ongoing. Like a boss, he stood nearby with his arms folded, waiting for her to be ready before allowing anyone near.

Except Rixton, of course.

When Rixton made his way across the meadow, Arnie joined him.

Rixton stopped in front of his sister. "I'm proud of you," he said, messing up her hair like an irritating ass.

Kinety shook it back into place and watched the bustling camp. "I didn't know I'd have to leave him," she said with a catch in her voice. "I thought he would come."

"Why didn't he?" asked Arnie.

"The gate had to be closed from there," she said, wiping her eyes, "to keep the Gaki and the Saphiridians from following."

Rixton's green eyes lowered, and he spotted the ring on her finger. "Is that—that's Torak's star-fighter!"

Kinety spun the heavy ring around her knuckle. "He gave it to me and pushed me through. The Saphiridians were coming—all of them. They're going to charge him with treason, and he didn't want them to get it."

"He wouldn't give that to you unless … ," Rixton trailed off.

Kinety leaned against the tree. "They're gonna kill him," she said, giving Arnie a hard stare.

Arnie stared back. "What are we going to do about that?"

Rixton went still, looking back and forth between them. "Did he teach you how to open a portal?" he asked his sister.

"I'm not strong enough to open a portal."

"By the way, we've been gone for two years."

"What? We've been gone a month."

"Two years," Rixton said again. "Time moves faster here than in space, which explains why Tooji is seventy-nine years old in Earth years."

"We're faster?" Kinety brightened with a jolt and grabbed wildly for her phone. "Hopefully, that buys us some time," she said, thumb-typing frantically into it. "Arnie, I want the commander—the one we talked to from the ship—and a truck ... and tell him to get Neil deGrasse Tyson on the phone."

Arnie drew his phone.

Using Deek's link, she typed out a message:

Deek, come get me!

Why are you bothering me, primitive hominid?

How soon can you get here?

Twelve Earth hours.

LOL! You were already coming, weren't you?

I'm Deek! Who is Lol?

A smile broke across Arnie's mouth. "Colonel Nelson," he said, holding his phone to his ear. "She's ready to see you, Sir ... Yes, Sir ... You may want to gather your need-to-know buddies ... Well, because we're going on a mission ... That'll be classified ... Very classified."

"Wait, wait, wait, wait, wait," Rixton said, spreading his hands. "Before we do anything stupid, I just ... want a cheeseburger."

*****

In an onsite tent, Kinety, Arnie, and Rixton, dressed in SWAT fatigues loaded to the nines with sensors, trackers, and recording devices, busily tucked weapons into their pockets while they waited. Around them bustled twenty or so of Colonel Nelson's friends, each busy with a specific task relevant to alien information, space defense, and technology.

"And it's called Jag Mosrog?" asked Colonel Nelson.

Kinety stood in a ring of officials, pointing to a spot on a 3D map of the stars. "Yes. It's a spaceport, about here," she said, showing the Colonel and seven other officials the location on a 3D map of the stars. "It looks like our moon, but it's hollow—kinda Death Star-ish. There's a council there, composed mostly of hybrids."

"So, it's hybrids against full-blooded?"

"Pretty much. We were originally hybrids ourselves—pure humans from Tiamat and hominids like Neanderthal—but we're still

286

classified as human, so the distinction is subjective. Many of the alien hybrids are composed using human DNA as a base. They consider ours tainted, but it's easy to remove the impurities. Shiva won't know much about their civilizations, but she can describe several species in detail and give you a first-hand account of the rescue. Actually, you know what?" she said, pulling her phone from her pocket. "This cell phone is linked to the Universal Internet. It'll explain that better than I can. Get me another one, and you can have this phone."

The commander's eyes went wide, and he tried three times to pull his cell phone out. "This is my work phone," he said, juggling it. "The Universal Internet would be written in a different language, right?"

"There are many languages. It's still in the original dialects and symbols. Some languages don't translate well to our language or writing style because the numbers and symbols have embedded frequencies, but you'll get the idea. Arnie's phone is also connected. I converted his to English, but he still struggles to decipher some of the translations. Do you want it too?"

Colonel Nelson's voice increased an octave. "Yes," he squeaked, grabbing an eavesdropping scientist and snatching the woman's work phone from her. "How did you get into their system?"

"I'm a hacker."

Colonel Nelson looked ready to swoon. Through a chorus of singing angels, he made the sign of the cross and murmured a heavenward prayer of thanks.

A young soldier at a monitor called out over her shoulder. "Sir! We're picking up an anomaly on radar."

Colonel Nelson took Arnie's phone and handed him the new one. "You'll answer all my questions when you get back?" he asked Kinety.

"Every last one of them ... if you'll help me find a job."

Colonel Nelson laughed. "That was easy. You're hired. I'll find something to keep you busy. How does top-secret sound?"

She gave him a thumbs-up.

"You can work with me," Arnie said, giving her a whack on the shoulder.

"And me," Shiva corrected, giving Arnie a sharp elbow to the ribs. "You're not leaving me out."

"And Shiva," he grunted obediently.

Kinety faced the commander and held out her hand. "Sir, it's been a pleasure meeting you."

Colonel Nelson cradled his priceless phones. "Stay in touch."

Suddenly, from the dirt road into the camp, a truck squalled its tires, slinging rocks and dirt and fishtailing into the small parking lot.

Camp guards continued their conversations as Zhang and Park, dressed in matching black fatigues, spilled from the doors, which neither bothered to shut, and charged up the hill.

"You aren't leaving without us, you bunch of assholes!" Park railed, marching furiously toward them. "Who the hell do you think is going to cover your ass!"

Zhang wasn't so composed. In a spew of vulgar, musical Chinese curses, he informed Kinety he was coming too and that she was fat.

She laughed and slapped their hands. "Security knew you were in route ten miles away," she answered, gesturing to the guards. "Are you armed?"

In answer, Zhang snapped his backpack forward, revealing a sniper rifle case. "Heaviry armed."

Above them, a sleek, mirrored spaceship shimmered into view, barely distinguishable from the sky, and landed in the field exactly where it had before.

As the door liquified open, Kinety waved her team forward. "That's us, boys. Load up!"

Chapter 23

Deek folded his arms and glared at Kinety when she told him her plan. *"We're gonna die."*

"Perhaps," she acknowledged, "but Torak won't—not as a traitor."

The alien's eyes shifted to the rest of the eager team. *"Earthlings are insane,"* he grumbled in disgust and turned back to the flight panel.

Arnie relayed the conversation, bridging the communication gap.

"How will they kill him?" asked Rixton.

"Toojidium energy is what powers our craft, but whereas we store it in the crystals, Torak can manipulate it because he's made of torakonium. He has harnessed this power and uses it freely."

"Right. The blue stuff," said Arnie.

"Yes. Theoretically, it can be neutralized in a vacuum force," Deek explained.

"Zero-point energy!" said Arnie.

"Whatever you call it. We use that to store our power. If exposed to that field, toojidium will neutralize, as well. It is part of him. Without it, he is weak. The Saphiridians will utilize this field so that he cannot draw on this power and then kill him in any manner they choose."

Kinety paled and gripped a panel. "How do they neutralize it?"

"In the skypods. Each power capacitor has a chamber between two plates, a neutral zone. The easiest way would be to put him in one."

"Won't they bring him to trial?"

"No. They'll holograph him into the courtroom."

"So, we check the skypods."

Deek made a negative gesture. *"There are hundreds scattered all over Saphiridia. If they find out you're attempting a rescue, you won't make it in time."*

Kinety's stomach twisted. "How do we find him, Deek," she asked in desperation. "What do we do?"

Deek turned in his seat and kicked a tiny foot. With a heavy shrug, he shook his large head. *"I don't know."*

Arnie squeezed her shoulder and handed over the reconfigured cell phones. "No worries. We have time to figure it out."

Deek turned back to the window. *"You have much less time than you think. We are almost there."*

"Almost there!" Kinety cried.

Rixton stepped forward. "I have an idea."

"It'll have to wait," said Deek. *"Buckle up for the first wormhole."*

"Wormhole—already? It took us days to reach our destination before," said Kinety, pushing the others toward their seats.

"Three just to get to the wormhole!" said Arnie.

Deek buckled himself in. *"The first wormhole closed. We had to wait for it to open again, but we aren't using that one. Before, we had to line up with Gelphii, then go to Zahrá Che through a larger wormhole. This is a glider, not a pod transport. Gliders can use smaller wormholes. That's how I reached Earth so fast. Besides,"* he said, working the computer, *"Saphiridia is on this side of the galaxy. It's almost a straight shot."*

"Saphiridia?" Kinety sputtered. "I thought we were going to Jag Mosrog. That's where the council is."

"Nope. The council would have far too many questions, and the answers would expose the Saphiridian's long list of crimes. We'll pass Jag Mosrog, but Torak's trial will be on Saphiridia,"

"How much time do we have?"

"We don't. The trial will start at Saphiridian high noon. That's in about," Deek checked a screen, *"three of your Earth hours, and we are four hours away. Wormhole in three, two, one …"*

*****

Kinety brushed her hair and fluffed it around her shoulders to hide the tiny radio in her ear. She was dressed to the nines in black battle fatigues and genuine combat boots, just in case she needed to look terrific during a fight. She also matched her team exactly, which was totally fashionable. "You're sure they won't pick up these transmissions?"

Deek gave her a sidelong look, certain she was making fun of him. *"We don't use those anymore,"* he informed her haughtily. *"Our technology is far superior. I assure you, nobody will pick up your very obsolete conversation."*

Kinety smiled at him and straightened her clothes, not at all bothered by his snippy attitude. She was used to it by now. "Good," she said lightly. "How long until we get there?"

Deek glanced at a panel. *"We're locking into orbit now."*

"You're sure the trial is at Ohizigi? You confirmed the address?"

"Strap in for entry," he said, ignoring the question.

Deek entered on the back side of the planet to avoid detection and snuck around from a direction opposite of where the Zahrá Che usually approached to engage in battle. Stealth was the name of the game today. If the team got caught, they'd be killed and all would be lost. Only Kinety would be exposed to the Saphiridians, and it had to appear that she was alone.

In their seats, Arnie and Rixton checked and double-checked their harnesses and assorted tools. Zhang snapped his rifle together and screwed a silencer onto the end of the barrel. Park primed the onboard weapons, humming off-key K-pop songs while he worked. This time, he'd brought his music with him. Kinety went over the specifics of the clicker in her left hand. She wore it like a ring and could click it with her thumb simply tucked into her palm. One beep meant no, two meant yes.

With a click, Deek switched the craft's skin to mirror, essentially making the vehicle invisible, and dove straight down toward an ocean to distort their flight signature. The only reason this was even feasible is because he knew the Saphiridians were not watching for Zahrá Che spacecraft. None would be stupid enough to come here. Near the waves, he leveled out and gave the ship full power, bringing them toward their destination, the Saphiridian city of Ohizigi, at dizzying speeds.

The walls of the craft faded from solid to see-through, offering a complete view of the outside. Through the windows, the city of Ohizigi came into view. It was enormous and ridiculously futuristic with a clunky, steampunk feel to the place, which explained their spacecraft. The buildings were tall and cramped, the ground cluttered with grungy metal buildings patch-worked together without regard for a color scheme.

Scattered here and there throughout the massive city were skypod capacitors similar to the Zahrá Che energy recharge pods. Though more rudimentary, they almost appeared to be the most advanced piece of technology the species had on display. In fact, they could have been stolen directly from the Zahrá Che and scuffed to fit in.

The only problem—there were bazillions of them.

"Kinety," Deek warned, using her name for the first time. *"You're building is coming up. This is a high-profile case; the trial will be on the top floor. Check your radio connections."*

A radio check and the clicker were tested, resulting in unanimous thumbs-up.

"Get ready."

Kinety unbuckled. "Will y'all be able to understand Saphiridian?"

Deek tapped his panel. *"I'll run the audio through the translator."*

Rixton gripped her shoulders. "Don't show weakness, Dorkymodo. Torak's wife doesn't take shit—not from anyone. She's cool and collected, always, but she can be a bitch."

She nodded.

"And don't fidget."

"No fidgeting. Got it."

"I don't know how long it'll take us to find him and then to get him out. Just keep it going. Don't let them stop you."

Kinety blew out her cheeks and breathed deep, preparing to exit. "What if I faint?" she worried suddenly.

Arnie gave her shoulders a quick squeeze, psyching her up. "If you faint, you'll wet yourself and look stupid."

"Okay, scratch that," she said with a shudder.

"Use your compass," he warned. "Establish north immediately. We're looking for body language."

Kinety glanced down at the compass bubble ring she wore on her finger, right beside Torak's star-fighter ring. "Be careful," she told her team, giving Zhang's hand a squeeze, "and Park, no singing over the radio."

*****

Joboba templed square hands and pressed his fingertips together, sweeping brown eyes around the elegant maroon and brown courtroom. "The verdict is in," he said, prolonging their agony and savoring the moment. Almost smiling, he sneered at the holographic image standing before him and slid his fingers together, intertwining them. "Torak, Master of War: For the crime of treason against the Saphiridian people, the jury hereby sentences you to death. Do you have anything to say before your sentence is carried out?"

Torak stared at the Prime, wondering how in the world he'd ever admired him. The man was a gleshmog, dramatic and phony. Now that the blinders were off, he wondered how he'd missed that. If Joboba was hoping for a plea or an excuse or a whimper of fear, he wasn't going to get it from Torak. Unshaken, he maintained his blank expression, refusing to give him any satisfaction.

Joboba tried to hide his disappointment behind an amused expression, but it was there. "I know you thought you couldn't be stopped," he taunted, "but we've always had the Torak Beam standing by just in case you got out of line—programmed and ready to send you to your little chamber where your nasty blue energy can't help you. Anyway," he rubbed his hands together casually, "if you have nothing to say," he shrugged and faced a gray-haired man at the execution panel. "Duluth, on my signal …"

Torak looked away from Prime and placed his gaze on a bare section of wall. He didn't want the last thing he saw in this world to be Joboba's ugly nose. Drawing a deep breath, he pictured his wife's beautiful face.

Crash!

Without warning, Kinety threw the doors wide, slamming them open and scaring the shit out of everyone inside. "Okay—pause!"

Torak's holograph jolted sharply, and he blinked at her in surprise. Instantly furious, he threw his hands up and huffed in outrage. He'd given up everything to save her! What was she doing here?

Eyebrows high, she marched haughtily into the courtroom and peeked quickly at her compass. Immediately, she noted which direction was north. "North! I have something to say," she said, scanning the room. There were differences from Earth trials, such as the general setup and placement, but there was a judge, jury, an audience, and security guards. There were no lawyers. The jury asked the questions while the judge, Prime Joboba, made the decisions.

Joboba slammed his hands down on the table before him. "How dare you interrupt this court, Earthling!" he roared.

"Kinety, do you copy?" Park's voice buzzed in her ear.

Two beeps. "Shut up, Jaboobee," she said, approaching Torak's hologram. "Where are you?"

Torak, clearly caught off-guard, scanned his prison in jerky agitation. "I don't know," he said, frustrated that he couldn't reach her.

It was time for the theater.

Kinety slid angry eyes to Joboba and set her hands on her hips to hide how badly they were shaking. With dramatic flair, she tossed hair over her shoulder and faced him. "Where have you hidden my husband?" she asked slowly.

A guard glanced toward the window.

Joboba's eyes moved ever-so-slightly to the same window, and he smiled. "I'm not sure it matters anymore, Bride," he said, finally beginning to enjoy the trial. "Torak has just been sentenced to death for treason."

"What in the *west* are you talking about!"

*****

Park pressed his radio to his ear, catching her message. "West side!" he called, pointing Deek in the correct direction.

With one hand, Deek shifted the craft to the west side of the building and moved from one skypod to the next. With the other hand, he secured Kinety's radio signal so it couldn't be tampered with and, after a quick hack, threaded it into a public broadcast.

That done, Deek moved quickly toward the skypods. Bringing the ship as close as he dared, he moved in, attracting the magnets just enough to make them sway before moving on. He moved carefully, watching Park for more hand signals. Across the flight deck, Arnie, Rixton, and Zhang waited, listening intently for signals from Kinety.

*****

Torak, no longer calm and collected, now paced inside his prison like a caged animal.

Joboba grinned like a cat, enjoying the war god's agitation. "I realize you all were eager to witness Torak's execution," he told the murmuring audience, "however, since his *lovely* bride is here," he

293

paused while the audience laughed, "we may as well charge and convict her, too, just to make it easier on ourselves later. We've got an executioner standing by. What do you say, jury?"

The jury clapped.

Torak hissed at the brave fools, his unique eyes glittering dangerously.

Kinety drew up in outrage. "Convict *me*?" she specified, pointing to herself. Quite strategically, she stepped slightly behind the hologram and faced the 'judge' so she could see Torak when she looked at Joboba. "Perhaps your breathless audience would be more interested in *your* crimes, Jaboobee. How about we start with the slaughter of innocent people, the massacres you ordered without provocation, the lies you created?"

Joboba gave his head an amused shake. "I'm sorry. You'll have to be more specific than that."

The watchers were indeed amused.

"Anything?" Park asked in her ear.

Kinety clicked the buzzer in her hand once, telling him no. Torak was pacing, solid as a rock. Part of her began to worry that perhaps he wasn't inside one of the skypods. "I am referring to the video where Torak walks into a room full of Zahrá Che and starts killing them. Would you like to tell your faithful followers what really happened that day, or should I?"

Joboba leaned forward with a wave, inviting her to do the honors, and folded his hands together in rapt attention. "Please."

Highbrow snickers passed between the people watching.

"The Saphiridians set that up," she blurted and gave a smug nod, effectively ending any trial lawyer career ideas she may have humored. Sounding quite like an amateur, she took a moment to scan the people gaping at her for her audacity.

"The Zahrá Che in that video were covered in green zombie toxin," she didn't know the name of the bacteria, "but the video was edited to filter that part out. Everyone in that room was already going to die. The death from that toxin is a horrible one," she paused to emphasize, "and Torak is not immune. Out of self-defense," she thrust a point into the air, "and as a mercy to the victims, he did what he had to do—not because he's a monster, but because he's a good man."

The audience actually laughed.

Torak stopped pacing and cocked his head at her, absolutely baffled.

Kinety pretended not to notice and, avoiding Torak's gaze, jabbed a finger at Joboba. "That toxin is controlled by the Zahrá Che government, and *you* stole it."

"What about any of these?" asked Park.

Ding.

Kinety paused, looking for some reaction from anybody, but there was none. It was almost as if they already knew this, she marveled. She kept going, guessing now. "You, Jaboobee, are the *only* one who would have ordered the use of that toxin. The Zahrá Che would not have done that to themselves. And the Saphiridians were the *only* ones who benefited from the fake attack. You created a terrorist by blaming Torak, and you've used him as a weapon to hold the galaxy hostage ever since. Explain that!" she demanded.

Joboba squared his shoulders and sat taller, absolutely recalling that. "I ... used the toxin to create a propaganda video on a species with no value. My experts edited the footage, and the universe ate it up," he conceded, entirely admitting to the accusation.

All eyes shifted back to her.

Shit.

Kinety had expected him to deny the charge and was prepared to argue. His blatant confession completely caught her off-guard, and she blinked around the courtroom, speechless. He was definitely a politician, the little bastard. With all eyes on her, she scrambled for more time-consuming accusations. "You also ... set up all the assassination attempts on me, an innocent abduction victim," she added, looking through Torak's holograph. He was pacing again, but this time his focus was on Kinety, and he wore a worried expression on his face.

Dammit! Why hadn't they found him yet?

Joboba sat back in his seat, entirely enjoying himself now. "Well," he said, feigning trouble with this answer, "I don't consider you innocent in any capacity, but ... yes. I mean, the attempts were from me. Unfortunately, all have failed ... so far. I'm not one to give up, though."

Snickers from the audience.

Kinety almost folded here. He was making an ass of her ... rather easily, in fact. She'd never had training as a trial lawyer before, and it was quite obvious. She'd also never gone toe-to-toe with a forked-tongued politician. What else? What else had he done? "Y-you murdered Torak's creator Glarnt and blamed that on the Zahrá Che. Why don't you tell them about that!"

She set her hands on her hips and waited for him to get out of that one.

Joboba made a face, implying he'd forgotten about that, and got comfortable in his seat. "You seem to know plenty about that," he said, resting on an elbow. "Why don't you tell them?"

Kinety felt like an untied balloon must when it slips from slobbery fingers and flops wildly about the room while the mass of air deflates in an embarrassing splutter. He wasn't denying any of the charges. Didn't these aliens have laws against crooked politicians? Humans didn't—their politicians got away with murder and plenty more—but she'd always assumed aliens were higher beings. To discover how similar the two species actually were was disheartening. Her grimace preceded the stammer. "So, you … don't deny that?" she half-countered, half-whimpered.

"Nnnope," he assured and grinned, waiting for more.

Torak blinked at Joboba, astonished by the blatant admission, then frowned at the giggling spectators.

Kinety began to sweat. "Uh … well," she managed, pausing to peek at Torak, who looked like he wanted to put his arms around her and whisper for her to shut up. "Perhaps your audience would be interested in your poorly veiled attempts to annihilate a species that actively approached you for help. It's time they know about the dirty tricks you've—," she paused as Torak shifted his weight, "—played obstructing the Zahrá Che's hunt for a new home," she finished with a damning point.

Torak finally caught her eye, his expression quizzical.

Quickly, she turned back to Joboba and worked to regain her momentum. Adding outrage to her voice, she scolded the leader. "I think your citizens will find those … tidbits—," dammit, she should have used a stronger word, "—far more interesting than whatever bullshit you pull out of your ass to blame on me."

"*Anything?*" asked Park.

Ding.

Joboba gave her comments a moment to sink in, expertly using the silence that followed and a few well-timed facial expressions to make her look like an ass. Then, as if realizing it was his turn to speak, he snapped upright, blatantly surprised she was already finished.

More laughter.

Using comedic theatrics, he rubbed his hands together, wondering how best to put this. "I don't like the Zahrá Che," he said, gaining momentum, "and I don't have to give them anything. It is not my job to babysit a whiney race so stupid they cloned themselves out of the breeding process. Their unfortunate circumstances do not permit them to take a planet that does not belong to them, nor does it permit them to use bioweapons, which essentially started this war. They made bad choices. If their race dies as a result," he shrugged, palms up, "then that's their problem. The universe will be a better place without them."

Beneath the humor, Kinety saw a cold, hateful man. She had never heard someone speak so ugly before and stared at the snub-nose alien, stricken by the ease at which he would condemn an entire species. Speechless again, she struggled to think of a response.

Torak was pacing again.

Park's blessed voice startled her from her surprise. *"Anything?"*

Ding.

Joboba's smile shifted, implying he had listened fairly to her complaints and was ready to share his own thoughts on the matter. "Now, let's discuss you," he countered sweetly, speaking in fluent politician. "You have a fascinating list of crimes to answer for. Why, there's theft of a weapon of mass destruction ..."

*****

Deek flew to the next sky-pod and glanced back at Park, who was growing more and more frustrated with every no-go. Pressing the radio hard into his ear, he held his head, causing his hair to stick comically from his fingers. "Come on, dammit!" he hissed, waiting for the word.

Kinety had said the pod was to her left while facing north, but now Arnie and Rixton were beginning to worry that she'd gotten the direction wrong. Both were following the interruption of the trial closely and passing worried looks. They'd long since grown tired of face-palming, however, and now merely passed random grimaces back and forth.

Zhang kept his head down and his lips pinched, and obsessively wiped a soft rag over the silencer at the end of his rifle ... waiting for something. He, too, was following what he could of the conversation. Judging mostly by tone, it was clear even to him that the hunt was taking way too long.

*****

"... and then there's your blatant disregard for the volatile nature of the creature Torak—"

"Creature!"

"—your careless mishandling of the Torak, as well as unauthorized reprogramming of the weaponized war anomaly. As a diplomat for the Earthling race, it is shockingly evident that your values are at odds with the Saphiridian methods and way of life."

"Diplomat?"

"Because of you, Torak no longer cooperates or finishes his missions as instructed. As a representative of your species, I have no choice but to place the blame ... ."

Torak blinked at him, then at Kinety, and back. He looked worried.

Kinety wished Deek would hurry the hell up. She was out of accusations, and the odds of stalling the trial much longer were dwindling fast. Right now, Joboba was playing games with her, but she could tell he was reaching the end of his tolerance. His smiles were getting shorter, and he was countering faster now. Clearly, he was ready to deflect the court's attention away from himself and onto her, and it was much too soon to do that. She had to redirect it. "I wasn't finished!" Kinety interrupted hotly.

Joboba snapped backward with a phony start, earning another healthy laugh, and apologetically gestured for her to continue. "By all means."

Kinety was careful not to stammer. She actually had nothing to say, but that was irrelevant. Desperate, she summoned the theatrics. Joboba was using them, so why couldn't she? She strolled importantly across the floor, attempting to look suspenseful and in command, while she tried to think of something interesting to accuse him of.

Torak set his hands on his hips and spun to a stop, watching her make a fool of herself. Shifting his eyes away, he exhaled in embarrassment.

At the end of her ten-foot pace-space, Kinety drew herself up importantly. "I intend to make the council on Jag Mosrog aware of these accusations," she threatened, "and request a formal investigation into the aggression and provocation by the Saphiridians that has resulted in the deaths of millions of Zahrá Che citizens, apart from legitimate military operations. And by proxy, the abduction and deaths of my own people."

Torak snapped his head to her in alarm and abrupt silence filled the room. Kinety wasn't sure why. Catching her eye, he tried to shush her with muted facial expressions, trying to stop her.

"Anything?" asked Park.

Ding.

At her declaration, the amusement vanished from Joboba's face, but it was too late to stop now. She had no choice but to keep going, only slower. They hadn't found Torak yet. "I will also be requesting your rank and power be suspended—"

Torak began shaking his head.

"—until a full investigation on your own criminal activities," she said, willing the others to hurry, "with focus on crimes beyond civilized rules of war."

Torak rolled his eyes closed.

Joboba's veneer facade snapped, and his brown eyes went cold. Finally, the real him had arrived, the one she'd encountered before. Apparently, she'd struck a nerve.

Haha! Butthead.

"Well," he said with an icy chill, "then I'll simply add one more crime to the long list you've provided. How about murder?"

Or not.

O … kay, maybe it hadn't been a good idea to make him mad.

Kinety wanted to take a recess and back out of the room to regroup, but there would be none of that. There was no backing down now, so she pretended to focus all her attention on Joboba, despite her keen awareness of Torak standing rigid and unfound. Her distraction mission was tanking badly. She had no more accusations, yet to fail her mission would be disastrous. Now more than before, theater was everything. She gaped at Joboba in indignant outrage, then pointed to herself. "Are you *threat*ening me?" she demanded, hoping to start an argument.

Joboba and his audience laughed, loud and shrill. "Of course," he chortled, making a can-you-believe-this-shit face at the appreciative crowd.

"I am trying to have a civilized conversation with you, and you're talking nonsense," she railed.

Joboba seemed perplexed by her lack of concern but covered it with his own nonchalance. "We have long since passed the point of civilized conversation."

"Then focus!"

Joboba startled visibly again, earning another roar of laughter.

"You are *not* going to murder me."

"Why not?"

"Because! Your crime spree has to end. I've had enough of it."

"Well ... you can't go to the council if you're dead," he reasoned. "It makes sense to me."

Kinety tossed her hands in exasperation.

The audience hooted at the ridiculousness.

Only Torak failed to find amusement in the banter. Locked in his box, he moved about his space, fidgeting helplessly.

Kinety thought of another topic, and her eyes lit up. The war! "Look, the Zahrá Che just need someplace to go because their planet is dying," she argued, hoping to redirect the conversation from Torak's execution or her own murder. "Neontak has the atmosphere they need. Give them the damn planet! Charge them for it if you want, but stop this foolish war. You have the ability to find planets all over the universe," she added a spin here, "with suitable atmospheres for colonization, and you *don't* need Torak to do it. Use your resources for something good instead of acting like a tyrant. I don't understand why this is so hard," she finished.

Joboba's brows lifted.

Torak's agitation increased. "Kinety," he said softly, pleading with her to stop.

"Tell me," Joboba said, sitting forward on his elbows and crossing his arms in interest, "what is the atmospheric composition on your planet—Earth is it?"

Kinety didn't answer right away. A burn sizzled in her stomach, and she worried that she may have just made a boo-boo. "What? Wait. Why?"

Someone else answered for her, the speaker an apparent female. "78% nitrogen, 21% oxygen, 0.9% argon, 0.1% other including carbon dioxide, methane, water vapor, and neon. Prime!"

Joboba contemplated the details with a pause of interest. "I've never been to Earth," he told Kinety amiably.

Shit.

Please hurry, Deek. Please, please hurry.

Kinety glared at the alien, this time with sincerity. "Don't you dare threaten my planet," she hissed angrily.

"I mentioned before, there are plenty of charges against you," Joboba waved at Torak, "—theft of a weapon of mass destruction, et cetera—all of which count as an act of war against the Saphiridians."

"Theft?" she cried. "You're the one holding Torak hostage."

But Joboba had taken the floor. "As a representative of your race, you have revealed yourself and your soldiers to be Zahrá Che sympathizers. Therefore, I declare that all Earthlings are to be considered agents of war against the Saphiridians. You, my dear, will be detained as a prisoner of war and placed in your own neutralization chamber."

"Anything?" asked Park.

Ding.

Just then, Torak wobbled and looked around. Nobody else seemed to notice, but Kinety's pulse went through the roof. She could feel adrenaline in her eyebrows and pinky toes, and her cheeks flushed hot.

Ding. Ding.

Park's voice came back loud in her ear. *"Did he just wobble?"*

Kinety flinched at the volume. "Yes!" she blurted to Park, then glanced around to be sure nobody else heard him through her tiny radio. She met their blank stares, then remembered she'd just said 'yes.' "Er … yes," she said again, waving an indignant hand and giving the clicker two more beeps. "I expected you to say something stupid like that."

Torak pinched his temples.

That was it. She had nothing brilliant to say, so … took the opportunity to set her hands on her hips, daring him to reply with something she could counter with.

Joboba gave her a curious look, waiting to see if she was finished. It was a standoff.

"Deek! That one!" Park shouted into the radio. *"We're coming back around, Commander. Stand by to confirm."*

When Joboba realized Kinety was waiting for him to respond, he gestured. "Something stupid like what?"

Kinety, who had been listening to Park, blinked herself back into the conversation. "A neutralization chamber," she said, hoping she hadn't missed something. "Why the hell would I need a neutralization chamber?"

Torak wobbled.

Ding. Ding.

*****

Park gave Deek a sharp affirmative, then pointed at the skypod below. Arnie and Rixton were already on their feet, ready to drop. Deek eased the ship close to the capacitor, trying to get the men near enough to drop onto it, but the magnets recoiled sharply when they got too close. He quickly backed the ship away.

Arnie communicated with Deek using hand signals, easing him in carefully until the craft recaptured the magnets, stabilizing the sway. Locked in attraction, the immobile skypod stretched upward toward them, vibrating with its effort.

Arnie gave Deek a quick thumbs-up and an open palm, telling him not to move, then motioned to Rixton. "That sharp-ass spike on the top," he called over the hum of the skypod, "we've got to get the rope around that so we don't slide off."

Rixton nodded sharply.

"Don't land on it!"

"Agreed, Sir."

"Ready? One, two, three ... jump!"

*****

Joboba adopted a thoughtful expression. "I would keep you in neutralization because Torak cannot reach you there."

Kinety paused in confusion.

"I've changed my mind. I'm not going to murder you. I'll hold you hostage. You will be kept alive so long as Torak cooperates with every order and finishes his missions *exactly* as instructed."

Torak jolted at the thud, wobbled sharply, and looked around.

"What!" Kinety threw her arms wildly into the air, keeping all eyes on her. "Are you insane?" she railed, stomping sharply away from Torak and whirling dramatically to face Joboba. "You can't keep me! I am an American citizen," she announced, slicing an imperial hand through the air.

"A what?"

Apparently, that argument only worked on Earth. Kinety narrowed suspicious green eyes. "How will Torak know I'm alive if I'm locked in a neutralization chamber?"

Joboba paused to consider this, then snapped his fingers. "You're right," he agreed with enthusiasm. "I'll set up a live video feed."

"Oh."

Joboba seemed, once again, to be enjoying himself. His politician voice returned, as well. "Savage Bride, Wife of Torak," he declared with melodramatic flair, "I hereby place you under arrest for the crime of Theft of a Weapon of Mass Destruction."

Torak looked up.

Kinety slammed her hand down on a table. "*You*," she cried, regaining Torak's attention, and faced Joboba. "have lost your mind! I haven't theft-ed anything! Are you not in possession of your weapon of mass destruction?"

Joboba continued. "Your crime is an act of war and considered a direct provocation of the Saphiridian people by the people of Earth. I accept your aggressive declaration of war. Take her into custody," he barked, pointing his security into motion.

Kinety blinked at him. "Wait … what?"

*****

Arnie caught the spike. The skypod wobbled, nearly dropping them. Arnie snatched the rope and yanked, stopping the wide-eyed Rixton from sliding off. Both men froze, looking down at the ground so far beneath them that neither could see it. One slip from either, and they were both dead. Rixton moved first his eyes and then his raised thumb, signaling that he'd found traction. Very carefully, he eased back up onto the skypod.

Arnie, shaking with adrenaline, looped their rope around the spike, while Rixton rolled onto his stomach. Very carefully, Rixton eased his feet onto a small lip and tested his grip on the surface to be sure he wouldn't slide off, then signaled for Arnie to release the spike and join him.

While Arnie tightened the slack in his rope and moved down, Rixton accidentally touched the skypod with a bare patch of skin by his wrist. It sizzled. He snatched it off with a sharp hiss and cursed at the blister already forming. The skypod was a helluva lot hotter than it looked. Bracing himself carefully on the rough rounded surface, he clamped his teeth against the heat burning his elbows through his elbow pads and prepared the magnets. It would take both of them to get in.

Beside him, Arnie readied his gel, preparing to melt through the skin of the skypod. "Get ready," he warned. "Once I open this, the magnet will destabilize and start spinning. I'll need you to capture the rotation and hold it still. Do not touch the energy barrier."

Rixton gave a curt nod, signaling he was ready. Arnie drew a wide horseshoe shape with the cut at the top so the bottom would hold the

302

flap. Seconds later, he was peeling the metal skin away, exposing the flickering blue energy barrier. Rixton used a magnet to pull the skin down. Exposed now, a magnetic pulse spun into a gyroscopic spin, holding the energy in place around the outside of the ball. The intensity of the energy sent both men rolling away, gasping for air as the flap folded down by their legs.

"Don't touch that," Arnie warned, more than impressed.

Rixton mouthed a few curse words, then tightened his hand around the rope. When they'd caught their breaths, both rolled back in, brows high, and carefully peered inside.

Standing between two metal plates at the center of the capacitor was Torak, frozen still in surprise. His wide eyes flicked upward. Arnie put his finger to his lips, warning him to be very quiet, then repositioned himself above the energy barrier. Torak returned his attention to the flickering holographic image before him—the inside of the courtroom—and to Kinety, who was about to be arrested.

*****

A security guard grabbed Kinety, startling her. With a cry of surprise, she threw her hand out and fired off a blue pulse. The security guard crashed backward into a group of shrieking people, his chest caved, and rolled to the floor by their feet.

He was dead.

Kinety, who hadn't meant to kill him ... *that* badly, froze and glanced down at her hands. Oh, shit. Oh, shit, her mind screamed.

The room went silent.

Trying to play it cool, a farce at best, she cut her eyes to the second security guard, mere feet away, and spoke in a breathy voice that probably sounded intentional. "Your death will be slower," she warned, impressed by how convincing she actually sounded using Torak's line. It was a lie, though. She was still trying to learn 'collect, hold, discharge' with impressively poor results. She had no idea how to moderate the pulse.

The silence grew louder.

In disbelief, every eye locked on Kinety. "There's two of them," said a small, horrified voice from the back of the room.

Another voice was barely audible. "Her eyes have toojidium current."

Torak gaped at her and broke a smile.

Joboba recovered first and stood. Brown eyes blazing, he glared at Torak. "Duluth! Execute Torak!" he barked to the executioner.

Kinety's heart stopped. She pointed at Duluth in warning, effectively stopping him, and rounded on Joboba. "On what charge!" she demanded.

"Treason!" he shouted.

"No!" Kinety snapped. "You betrayed him. On what charge!"

Joboba leaned forward on both hands. "On the illegal creation of a weapon of mass destruction," he spat, spewing spittle. "I have seventeen bounty contracts on you. Once I kill this freak," he jabbed a point at Torak, "you won't have anyone in this universe who can protect you from me. And then, I'll take your planet! Ignite the skypod, Duluth!"

*****

Rixton tried again to capture the magnetic field, but the fluctuation was so sporadic he couldn't grab it.

"It's heating up in there, boys," Park warned, keeping the volume on their radios down while they worked. *"Something just happened."*

Rixton slid the magnets into position again and focused on the pulsating rhythm, syncing his count with it to capture the gyroscopically spinning shafts. Watching closely, he picked up a pattern for the first, counted one, two, three, and turned one magnet on with a click. He caught it.

One left.

Concentrating again, he waited, picking up the second shaft's pattern. One, two—

The skypod jolted sharply, and Rixton fell. Arnie snatched him by the shirt and slammed him backward into the skypod, nearly losing his own footing on the lip. Both looked up. Just overhead, a Saphiridian ship, unaware of the invisible Zahrá Che ship hovering just below, rumbled by collecting power. Silently, both men watched, unable to move without risking detection. Soldiers in brown uniforms were visible inside, none of whom were looking at the skypod, but there was one walking around atop the ship, presumably doing maintenance.

Arnie and Rixton watched him, praying he didn't see them.

He saw them.

Before the man could open his mouth, a silent gunshot took him out. He grabbed his chest, wincing sharply, and dropped out of sight onto the ship.

Arnie lifted his brows at Rixton. "We have to hurry," he said, getting back into position.

Rixton quickly got back to work, localizing the magnet's pattern again. Within moments, he'd caught them both. Very carefully, he slid the shafts apart, giving Arnie enough room to puncture the energy barrier. It was Arnie's turn, but he wasn't interested in the skypod any longer. With a foul curse, he watched as four Saphiridian ships moved in, priming their weapons. Overhead, Zhang aimed, but there were too many.

Rixton touched Arnie's shoulder. "Don't worry about them," he coached. "Keep going. If they're going to kill us, there's nothing we can do about it now."

Arnie, knowing Rixton was right, turned his back on the invasion. "Don't drop those," he said, preparing to penetrate the deadly blue barrier with an insulated gauge.

Rixton held the magnets in place but stole a quick look over his shoulder. "Holy shit," he whispered.

Arnie carefully pushed the tube through the barrier. "Whatever is going on behind me sounds mighty interesting. I do hope they aren't about to shoot me in the back. Enlighten me, please," he said, concentrating on his delicate task.

"Oh, no, no," Rixton said nonchalantly. "I'm seriously doubting the Saphiridians are worried about us anymore. They're completely surrounded by Zahrá Che."

Arnie didn't look up. "I find myself comforted by your news and, yet, a bit alarmed. How many Zahrá Che?"

"All of them, I think."

*****

Kinety threw a pulse at Duluth, trying to kill him, but missed and struck his table, knocking it into him and him into the wall behind it. He was pinned and wounded. Frustrated, she cursed silently at the mistake, then quickly corrected her expression and slid her eyes to Joboba. Now! her mind screamed. They needed to get him out now!

Desperate to buy her men more time, she paced in front of the seething Prime, forbidding herself to peek at Torak, whose unblinking eyes followed her. She didn't need the distraction now and certainly didn't want to bring anyone's attention to him. She tried and tried to gather more of the blue stuff, covertly, of course, but couldn't make her fingers tingle. She had to keep talking.

The only thing left in her arsenal—utter bullshit.

"Once there is direct exposure to Torakonium," she said, deciding a lecture in imaginary physics was just the thing, "it becomes permanent and cannot be turned off. Torak shared some with me. My atoms and molecules have reorganized and are now able to conduct."

Kinety looked pensively at her fingers. She had no idea what she was talking about, but it sounded good. Joboba was listening, rather intently, actually. Moving slowly, she approached the Prime's table and ran a scuffed, ever-so-delicate finger across the edge. With dramatic flair timed perfectly with her lashes, she slowed her speech. "I know how to open a portal," she lied, wishing the guys would hurry, and flicked a coy glance at the red-faced leader.

He glared back.

"If you harm my husband or come near my planet, I'll open Neontak into Saphiridia," she said with an inviting wave, "and let the Gaki dispose of the garbage on this planet," she finished, indicating the no-longer-amused audience.

Joboba paled slightly and snapped a hand up to Duluth, who was trying to stand, staying the unsatisfied execution order.

"*That* won't be necessary," said a new voice.

Everyone turned as several members of the hybrid council holographed into the courtroom. At the same time, live Federation troops entered with their weapons raised.

There was a collective gasp and a murmur of confusion.

The transparent green councilperson stepped forward in a glow. "We heard the entire exchange and are quite appalled," it said angrily. "Prime Joboba, an unedited video of Torak killing ill Zahrá Che has also come to our possession. The very one you just confessed to creating—"

"Merely propaganda," he said firmly. "It was necessary to demonstrate Torak's might. In a war as destructive as this, we cannot afford to be seen as weaklings."

"By murdering civilians!" a different transparent councilman bellowed.

Joboba fell silent.

"You have much explaining to do, Prime Joboba," he informed haughtily.

Joboba shifted his glare to Kinety, seething.

"Effective immediately," the angry councilman continued, waving angry hands, "Saphiridia's position within the Federation is hereby suspended, and a full investigation will be launched. You may not leave Saphiridia," he ordered, then addressed the other people in the courtroom. "As of this moment, the Saphiridian war with the Zahrá Che is officially ended. Any further aggression against them will be punishable as a war crime. Do I make myself clear!"

Joboba smiled. "Crystal," he snarled, then dove for the execution panel. "I'll execute him myself!"

*****

The explosion was enormous. Arnie and Rixton spun wildly around each other in a tangle of ropes as the ship moved away from the flames.

"Hurry up, Deek," Arnie grunted, "this son-of-a-bitch is heavy!"

Torak, clutching Arnie's wrist, ducked the intense heat and blinked down at the massive fireball.

He was alive.

Chapter 24

Kinety ran to the window in horror. "Park!" she cried.

"We got him," said Park with a smile in his voice.

Kinety sagged in relief.

The green council-thing faced Kinety. "Did they get him out?" it asked quietly.

Weak in the knees, Kinety nodded.

Joboba gaped at her in disbelief. "This ... was a rescue—nooo!" he screamed.

The councilwoman pointed at Joboba in anger. "Arrest him!" she ordered the Federation troops.

Joboba's eyes widened as the troops neared and he tried to back up. "This is a Saphiridian matter—"

"By declaration of the Federation," the councilwoman said clearly, "all charges against Torak and his bride are dropped."

"He's a traitor!" screamed Joboba. "As a Saphiridian citizen—"

Kinety rounded on the man. "You can take whatever citizenship Torak may have held with the Saphiridians," she hissed nastily, "and shove it up your ass." There were gasps behind her, but she didn't care. "You stay away from us. I won't warn you twice," she vowed dangerously.

Joboba, restrained now by Federation troops, writhed and twisted. "Execute her! Kill her!" he cried to his people.

Nobody moved.

Without warning, the courtroom doors blew off their hinges, and a furious Torak marched through.

Joboba screamed like a girl.

Kinety spun to face him and her knees went weak with relief. "Tooji," she whispered.

The councilwoman rushed forward, her hands spread in alarm. "Torak, we have this under control," she hurried to say.

Very calmly, Torak walked to Kinety and slid his arm around her waist. "I'm here to get my wife," he told the woman and, with a snap of his wrist, blew out the side wall. Gently, he slid his ring off her finger and replaced it onto his own.

"Torak," the councilwoman said, approaching carefully.

He gave her a sidelong look and paused.

"There's another portal, letting the Gaki into Neontak from their home planet Fareh-Nombie, isn't there."

"Yes."

"Please remove the Gaki from Neontak."

Torak narrowed his eyes at the woman. "Are you giving it to the Zahrá Che?"

"It isn't mine to give."

He huffed into something of a smile, but it lacked amusement. "As long as it belongs to the Saphiridians, I will not," he said, losing the smile.

"We can take it from them," she assured.

"How quickly?"

"It's a legal process."

Torak gave her a piercing stare. "When I see proof of that," he said carefully, "*then* I will remove the Gaki."

"I'll get on it immediately."

Torak gave the woman a tight nod, lifted Kinety's feet from the floor, and jumped out the hole in the side of the building. With a pop, they were inside his star-fighter.

*****

Holding Kinety between his knees, Torak zipped his star-fighter away from Saphiridia, leading the entire Zahrá Che fleet back into the blackness of space. When they were well away from the awful planet, he set the controls to drift and turned Kinety to face him. Wrapping her in a fierce hug, he closed his eyes and kissed the side of her head. "You are the worst coward I have ever met," he said into her hair.

"I am a coward. That was scary."

"It was me who was scared," he said with a catch in his voice. "I didn't know what you were doing."

"Making an ass of myself."

Torak set her from him. "You were brilliant. How in the world did you learn to open a portal?"

Kinety snorted. "I don't have the foggiest notion how to open a portal. I can barely use the blue stuff," she said, peering down at her hands.

"You were bluffing?"

"Every word," she giggled. "I had to distract him until the boys found where you were hidden," she whispered, brushing wild hair from his eyes. "Please, tell me you're finished with those horrible people."

Torak gripped her upturned face. "I'm finished with them and their petty wars. I want you. From now on, I go where you go," he swore.

Kinety smiled into his handsome face. "What happens when you tire of me?"

"I'll sit quietly by and watch eternity come to an end," he vowed, lowering his head to kiss her. "It'll be a magnificent show."

Kinety slid her arms around his neck, smiling, and let him have it.

When Torak raised his head, he looked out the window at the silver ship hovering just outside, then took her hand in his. "I never want to be separated from you or my friends again."

"Even Deek?" she teased, fingering his collar.

"Even Deek."

"Oh!" Kinety exclaimed, remembering she wasn't done. From her pocket, she pulled the folded piece of paper she'd gotten from her favorite Earth astrophysicist and opened it for him to see. "I need to see the emperor."

Torak straightened her between his legs and reached around to work the controls. "Deek will know where to find him."

*****

Onboard Deek's ship, Torak slapped Arnie's hand and curled their fingers into a tight grip, then did the same with Rixton. "I thought I was done," he said, giving Zhang a fist bump. "I had no idea you were coming. That was impressive. *She* was impressive," he said, giving Kinety a brilliant smile. "I cannot describe the spectacle she'd made of herself. I didn't know what to think," he admitted, looking at all of them, "but it certainly wasn't rescue. Did Deek pick you up?"

Deek joined the group with bright pink cheeks and, almost smiling, kicked at the floor.

"You know you're a hero, right?" Kinety beamed.

The alien waved the disgusting compliment away.

Kinety grabbed his big head and kissed it, earning a spaz and screech. "Deek, Zhang, and Park planned it out," she said, laughing as the little alien hurried away from her, trying to wipe his head off. "Deek explained how to cross the energy barrier, Zhang mapped out the logistics, and Park coached me on distraction."

Deek scowled at Kinety but moved right back into position beside her.

"Here." Kinety unfolded her paper and handed it to him. "I brought this for you," she told him.

Deek snatched the paper from her, still disgusted, and read it. There was a pause. As he read it again, his cross expression turned to one of disbelief. *"Is ... this ... ?"*

"Three planets with potential life-sustaining atmosphere," she said, then quickly added, "but we've never been to any of them. I have no idea what you'll find."

Deek blinked big eyes up to her. *"What is the origin of the coordinates!"* he demanded.

"Our sun is called Sol. The origin would be from there."

Deek backed up, nearly tripping over his hover-seat, and rushed to the panel to summon the emperor. Within moments, the monarch was ordering explorer ships to investigate each location.

Torak stepped up behind Deek so that Emperor Dinruk could see him. "Have your explorers bring back rocks from the planet you choose," he instructed.

The emperor inclined his head and Torak gave Deek his panel back.

Rixton put his arm around Kinety's shoulder. "You're my little hero, you know that," he said, then glared sharply at his sister. "If you put one lip on me, I'll paint the living room black."

Kinety unpuckered her lips and snuggled against him. "Now, we can go home," she sighed, watching Deek gather information on the uncharted solar system. "I'm ready for a decent meal."

As Deek researched the locations, his skinny legs bounced in excitement.

"Yeah, I miss the food," said Rixton.

Kinety gave her brother a thumbs up. "Barbecue at the Dash house?"

Arnie squeezed between them. "Is the whole team invited?"

"Damn right, we are," said Park.

Zhang stood sharply. "I can cook!"

Torak slid his arm around Kinety and eased her away from the others. "If you'll excuse us," he said to his friends, "Kinety and I have married people business to discuss in my star-fighter while you all organize the festivities. We'll be back later."

EPILOG

One year later, Torak talked Park through the docking process, guiding him toward the approved dock at Jag Mosrog space station. It wasn't docking that was so hard; it was the wake zone around the station and the spaceships moving through it that held Park's rapt attention.

"Once you pick up the pattern," Torak was saying, "it'll begin to make sense."

Park watched the other ships carefully. "I'm starting to see it. It's geometric."

"Exactly," Torak agreed, then indicated their speed. "Back it down. You have a cruiser coming in at your high three. He has the right of way …"

Behind them, Kinety's team sat around a holographic table. It glowed with neon edging, but no image stood over the flat surface. Pale blue light radiated outward, casting a soft glow across their faces as they chatted quietly together. General Nelson sat beside him, listening to the team's ridiculous conversations while they waited for Arnie to brief them on their mission.

Arnie leaned forward on his elbows, making notes on a tablet.

"Arnie, did you see Deek's flower garden?" Kinety asked with a mischievous glance at her brother. "Some of his plants are blooming. I think he is a master gardener."

Deek's cheeks went pink at the compliment. He was incredibly proud of his garden, but more than that, he loved being complimented. He was also enjoying having friends, though would absolutely die before admitting either.

"Yep. I saw them last week when we were playing badminton at Park and Zhang's house," Arnie said without looking up from his papers. "If I recall, Deek kept winning at that too."

Deek, the distinguished Zahrá Che ambassador to Earth, sat a little straighter in his seat, pleased by the distinction. *"Of course, I won. Badminton is composed of simple calculus and a slow birdie."*

The team nodded, unable to dispute such logic.

As Deek spoke, his telepathic words appeared on the team's wrist computers. He'd fashioned the handy communication device to enable conversation with all the low-IQ humans he was stuck with now that he was stationed on Earth.

Kinety's eyes sparkled. "Torak and I can see your flowers from our window. I like that we're all neighbors now."

Deek folded his arms, careful to maintain his gruff demeanor. *"That is apparent,"* he muttered. *"Stop looking at my garden."*

"We should sing karaoke at our next barbecue," said Zhang, his accent light and pleasant now. "Park, you can sing for us."

"I will in a minute. I'm trying to dock," called a distracted Park.

Rixton drummed his fingers onto the table in a percussive beat. "What are we celebrating?"

"I know!" Kinety clapped her hands together. With a bounce, she summoned a holographic image. Within seconds, a bouquet of flowers hovered above the table and slowly spun. "We should celebrate Deek's flowers! It's his first garden."

"Stay away from my flowers."

"That's it! I vote for a celebration barbecue when we get back," she said. "In honor of Deek's first garden."

"You had a celebration barbecue last week."

"That was a badminton championship celebration barbecue," said Zhang. "This one is a flower celebration barbecue."

Kinety tickled her fingers over Deek's large head. "Deek, I am formally inviting you to our flower celebration barbecue."

He bristled in annoyance and snapped his head away. Dusting her fingerprints off his head, he switched to the empty seat on her other side and plopped into it. *"I am not eating a burnt carcass,"* he informed her haughtily.

"Not a problem. We can grill your blob. Who wants to be grill master?"

"I'm grill master." Rixton thumped himself in the chest. "I'm always grill master."

"You won't be if you catch the meat on fire again," Arnie warned.

"Hey!" Rixton barked. "That was an accident."

"I am not attending your flower celebration barbecue," grumbled Deek. *"I prefer to stay home."*

Kinety popped wide eyes. "That's a great idea! We'll have the barbecue in Deek's garden," she smiled and faced the others. "It makes sense since this is a flower celebration barbecue!"

"You are not barbecuing anywhere near my garden."

"Zhang, bring the karaoke machine! Park can sing for Deek's flowers."

Deek's head angled toward Arnie. *"Why would he sing for my flowers?"*

"Oh, flowers like when you sing for them," Arnie assured.

Deek looked at Park at the control panel, then shook his head. *"My flowers won't like that."*

Kinety sighed in disappointment. "Okay, then let's have a swimming pool celebration party," she decided, summoning a new image.

Zhang touched his chin pensively. "That sounds fun," he marveled. "We can all wear matching bathing suits!"

An image of a rotund man in a tiny red swimsuit replaced the flowers.

Deek recoiled in his seat.

"I'll bet Deek will be cute in his little bathing suit," Kinety squealed in tight-fisted excitement and conjured up a corresponding image. "We'll get him a red suit ... with polka dots! It'll be a polka dot celebration barbecue!"

The alien looked horrified. *"We're having a flower celebration barbecue for my garden,"* he corrected. *"Rixton is going to grill blob, and Park is singing."*

"Okay. If you prefer a flower party at your house, we can do that," Kinety conceded, switching the image back to flowers.

"I insist," Deek fumed, folding his little arms across his chest.

General Nelson shook his head in amusement, earning an exaggerated wink from Arnie.

Finally, Arnie snapped his papers, indicating he was ready. "Let's recap what we all know. As of now, the Zahrá Che have inhabited a new planet and have recovered their position among the council at Jag Mosrog. As a courtesy for our assistance when they needed it, the Zahrá Che are introducing Earthlings to the board and will formally invite our race to join the interstellar coalition. Deek's esteemed colleague Sin Chin is waiting for us at the docking station and will escort our diplomats and their entourage to the council to address the request. General Nelson, who was kind enough to join us for our humble mission," he said with a bow, "will represent Earth leadership."

The group golf-clapped for him.

Arnie continued, indicating each person named with a point. "The security team, consisting of Torak, Rixton, and myself, will accompany General Nelson and Kinety into the space station. *Please,"* he enunciated woefully, "try not to destroy anything, do not get arrested, and do not start an interstellar war," he said, pausing to look at Kinety.

Kinety drew a halo over her head, swearing to behave.

Arnie's face implied he didn't believe her, but he went on. "Park and Zhang, you will remain with the spacecraft. Do *not* abandon your posts, and do *not* damage our spacecraft. This is the only deep space transport we have."

"We should buy another one," suggested Park.

Zhang agreed.

Arnie inclined his head at the men. "Noted. I'll mention that to the boss," he said, then leaned the other way. "Commander, we want another spaceship."

General Nelson laughed and folded his hands together.

Arnie went on. "I am very well aware that we've gone over this already, but we're going to do it again just for fun," he said firmly. "Torak has many enemies, which means Kinety is always a target. They will kill us to get to her. Position yourself accordingly. Protect yourself accordingly. There are also lingering hostilities regarding the Zahrá Che. Expect it. Ignore it. Does anyone have questions?"

There were none.

"Ladies and gentlemen," Park announced over his shoulder from the flight deck, "please place your seat-backs in the upright position, put away your tray tables, and keep your seatbelts fastened as we will be docking at the beautiful Jag Mosrog space station in approximately five minutes—"

"Or less if you keep firing that particular thruster," Torak interjected.

"—or ... Whoa! ... three minutes," Park corrected, pausing his announcement to adjust his controls. "Temperatures at our destination are a balmy 2.7 Kelvin, so it is recommended that if you do venture outside the space station you bring a jacket ... and a tank of oxygen and probably a flashing locator beacon so we can find your dumb ass. Thank you for flying the friendly ... space ... with Galaxy No-Air Lines."

Torak made an adjustment on the screen in front of Park. "Lay into the gravitational orbit. Your docking station is ahead. Line up your trajectory, and now you can hit that thruster. The bay will flash when it sees you. There it is," he coached. "Hold your speed. Select it. Wait for the tractor links to pair and ... it's got us. Begin sixty-second countdown to capture."

One minute later, a jolt and artificial gravity from the spinning space station secured them to the floor.

"Yeah!" Park shrieked in celebration, then faced his adoring passengers and enjoyed his well-earned applause.

While this was going on, a flexible tube sealed itself outside the exit door, inflated with air, and signaled an all-clear.

Torak took Kinety's hand, and the team exited.

Sin Chin stood waiting for them on the arrival platform.

After polite formalities, Deek began the introductions. *"Sin Chin, meet Earth Representative General Nelson and his Diplomatic Relations team. Torak, Rixton, and Arnie are in charge of security. Kinety is the General's interpreter. Park is our pilot, and Zhang is in charge of the spacecraft."*

Sin Chin gave a light bow at the waist. *"The pleasure is mine,"* he thought in a deep voice. *"How are your soldiers?"*

"They are doing well," Kinety answered proudly. "Surprisingly few are in therapy. Most have joined intergalactic studies, and a new military branch has emerged. Our leaders extended their gratitude again for the spaceship. I hope your news is as good."

Sin Chin inclined his bulbous head. *"Morale is high among the Zahrá Che. A new constitution is being drawn up, one that addresses past mistakes and aims to prevent future altercations,"* he said and addressed Torak specifically. *"Joboba and his cabinet are in prison for life. Saphiridia has been sanctioned and is in isolation. Trials are ongoing. In the meantime, all interstellar transport vessels have been confiscated by the coalition, and the planet is awaiting the installation of a new government."*

Torak inclined his head, pleased to hear this.

"Now," Sin Chin continued, *"if you will follow me, the council is waiting ..."*

www.dcsargent.com

www.ingramcontent.com/pod-product-compliance
Lightning Source LLC
Chambersburg PA
CBHW062035170626
46813CB00001B/346